To all the readers who have joined me on
this ride – and who know that it's not
about the destination, it's about the
journey – my love and thanks to you all

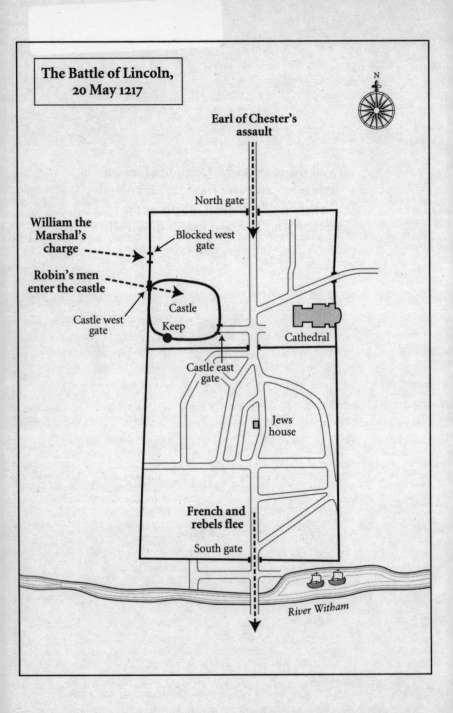

The Battle of Lincoln,
20 May 1217

Earl of Chester's
assault

North gate

William the
Marshal's
charge

Blocked west
gate

Robin's men
enter the castle

Castle west
gate

Castle
Keep

Cathedral

Castle east
gate

Jews
house

French and
rebels flee

South gate

River Witham

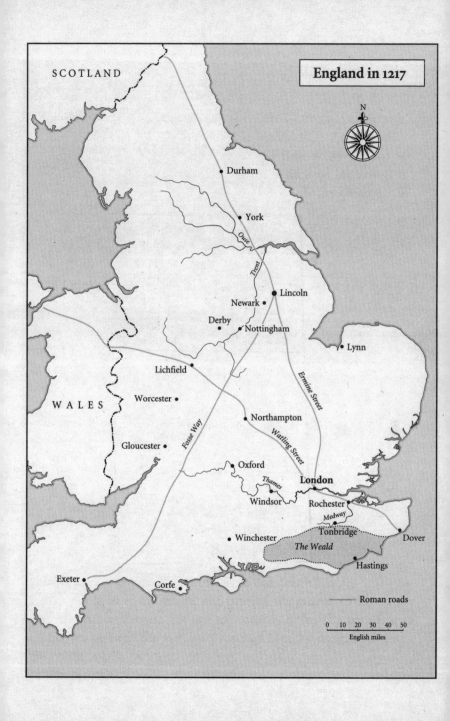

SCOTLAND

England in 1217

N

• Durham

• York

Ouse

Trent

• Lincoln

Newark • • Lincoln

Derby • • Nottingham

• Lynn

Lichfield •

WALES

Worcester •

• Northampton

Fosse Way

Watling Street

Ermine Street

Gloucester •

• Oxford

Thames

London

Windsor •

Rochester •

Medway

• Winchester

Tonbridge •

The Weald

• Dover

Exeter •

• Corfe

Hastings •

—— Roman roads

0 10 20 30 40 50
English miles

Part One

I humbly pray that whomsoever wishes to read these parchments in the years to come shall indeed be able to do so, for in parts my falling tears have caused the black ink to run and the words to mingle together on the page. I am not a lachrymose man, I believe, but this tale is filled with so much sorrow that it would make the angels weep – yet also laugh, perhaps, and maybe even rejoice in the courage, strength and resourcefulness of mortal men. The words contained herein are not my own, they have flown to me straight from the mouth of Brother Alan, one of our most venerable monks here at Newstead Priory, and it has been my task to copy them down as faithfully as I am able.

Brother Alan is too frail now to write himself. Indeed, he is very close to death and spends nearly all his days in his cell, wrapped in blankets and furs, despite the first warm breath of spring in the air. And yet his mind is still clear and his memory sharp. Some might argue that this task is beneath my dignity – I am after all the Prior of Newstead, in the county of Nottinghamshire, and lord of a community of a dozen monks and a score of lay workers and servants – but Christ taught humility and Brother Alan was the man who taught me my letters when I first came to this House of God nearly ten years ago. I have never forgotten his kindness and now that I have been elevated above my fellows, I shall endeavour to make some repayment of that debt.

Christ also taught us to hate the lie – and I must not pretend that I undertake this task solely from piety and gratitude. Brother Alan's past as a knight, as one of the most renowned fighting men of his day, and the stories he tells of battle and bloodshed, of comradeship in combat, give me a thrill of pleasure that is not entirely godly. Yet I believe I am doing God's work in recording his story, for it sheds light upon the last years of the reign of King John and the accession of our beloved Henry of Winchester, his son and, by the grace of God in this blessed year twelve hundred and forty-six, our sovereign lord and King – long may he reign over us.

This work also aims to reveal the stark truth about the crimes and contributions of another great man, one who was Brother Alan's friend and comrade for many years, about whom much has been said and sung, and most of that false, up and down the land. To expose these lies and calumnies – that is God's work, indeed; as it is to reveal the true nature of this strange man, the rebel baron who fought for an evil King, the former outlaw who used the law to bring justice to the land, the unrepentant murderer and thief, the loving father and loyal husband, the friend of the poor and champion of the oppressed. It is the Lord's will, I do earnestly believe, that the whole truth shall be known at last about the man called Robin Hood.

Chapter One

The square bulk of the keep of Rochester Castle thrust upwards into the twilight, ominous as a vast tombstone, and cast a long black shadow over the outer bailey, the cathedral beyond the walls and the sprawling smoke-wreathed town around it. From my post, at the centre of the old wooden bridge over the River Medway, the keep was almost due south and about three hundred paces distant. Shading my eyes from the glare of the westering sun off the water, I caught the silvery glint of the sentries' helmets as they patrolled the battlements, and on the dark, eastern side of the massive stone walls, the first slivers of candlelight leaking from arrow slits.

It was a forbidding fortress, one of the mightiest in England, built to guard this crossing of the river on the road from Dover to London, the most direct route an invading enemy would take to attack the largest and richest city in England. Yet the castle's dominating stone, its implacable solidity, was of great comfort to me. Battle was surely coming – a day or two, a week at most, and it would be upon us in all its blood and agony and fury, and then, when the arrows began to soar, the steel to scrape and men to scream in pain, I knew I would be more than grateful for the castle's twelve-foot-thick walls that climbed a hundred feet into the air.

The east wind was freshening, wafting a light mizzle from the cold waters of the estuary a couple of miles behind my back, and I pulled the damp green cloak tighter around my shoulders. My stomach gurgled unhappily – it must surely be almost time for supper and my relief – and I rubbed my reddened hands together and stamped my numb feet. By night's fall I should be snug in the guardhouse on the southern side of the bridge – there would be hot mutton broth and fresh bread and butter, a cup of warm spiced wine and the company of old friends. But where the hell was Sir Thomas Blood? The sun was already squatting on the western horizon.

I looked hopefully to my left towards the stout two-storey wooden box arching over the planks of the bridge on the southern bank. Was I imagining it or could I already smell the broth? A pair of thick-set men in green cloaks, long yew bows in their hands, were propped against the rail staring silently over the water, vacant as cows at a gate. I looked right, past the piles of boulders, each roughly the size of a human head, collected below the rail in little cairns of three or four rocks every ten feet, and saw a young, slim, fair-haired swordsman, similarly green-cloaked, fifty paces away at the northern end of the bridge. He leaned over the rail and lowered his head, and I saw a gobbet of spittle shoot from his mouth and disappear below. Perhaps inevitably, echoing up from underneath, came the faint roar of a complaint, its maker at first unseen from my vantage point. A slim rowing boat emerged, heading upstream, with a red-faced bald fellow mopping his pate and shaking his fist at the handsome young devil laughing above him.

'Don't do that, Miles,' I bellowed. 'It's churlish, it's unseemly . . . it's plain disgusting, for God's sake.'

The young man turned to look at me. His long, lean face seemed lit from within, like the All Souls' candle inside a hollowed-out turnip, illuminated by a mischievous almost child-like delight.

'I'm bored half to death, old man,' he shouted back. 'Bored as a boy-loving eunuch in an all-girl brothel. Surely our watch must be over by now. Besides, that baldy fellow sells bad fish. He's a cheat. Father says so. That basket of carp he sold us yesterday was mostly mud, skin and bones.'

His father, of course, was my lord, the Earl of Locksley, my old friend Robin, who on this chill October day was, no doubt, sitting in the warmth of the guardhouse toasting his boots by a brazier. But, even if Miles's father had not been my lord, I would have been loath to scold the youngster – despite him daring to call me an old man. Not only because I liked his irreverent high spirits, which cheered the hearts of our whole company, but also because he was a fine fighting man in his own right, a quicksilver fiend with a blade and utterly fearless in the storm of battle.

Apart from the angry fisherman, now pulling away at a pace, leaving a string of ripe insults in his wake, the river upstream was as placid as a pond. A few ancient craft lay hauled up on the slick banks and two old salts sat on boxes, their heads bent together, knitting their nets slowly, rhythmically, from time to time pausing to pass a leather bottle between them. I turned around, full into the cold breeze, the drizzle spitting directly in my face, and looked towards the curve of the river where it disappeared into the low pasturelands. Nothing but slow brown water and low grey fields, and a few scattered sheep casting monstrous shadows, as the sun nestled down behind me. Not an enemy in sight. Not a sniff of danger either. I could have been safe and snug at home in my manor of Westbury in Nottinghamshire rather than doing sentry duty on a mist-sprayed bridge in the flatlands of east Kent.

I heard a discreet cough. 'Sir Alan,' said a deep voice behind me and I turned to behold a short, powerfully built, dark-haired knight in full mail, helmet under one arm, smiling up at me.

'About time, Thomas,' I said. 'About bloody time. All quiet. Nothing to report. This godforsaken bridge is all yours.'

As I stepped into the guardhouse, I saw my lord seated at the long table in the centre of the room, spooning the last drops from an earthenware bowl. A battered, soot-blackened steaming cauldron had been placed in the middle of the board, next to a basket of bread, a jug of wine and a stack of crockery.

'Report?' said Robin.

'There is nobody out there,' I replied, reaching for a bowl. 'If John really is coming here, he is taking his own sweet time about it.'

'Oh, the King is coming all right,' said Robin cheerfully. 'He has to. His new men, his Flemings, will surely cross the Channel and land at Dover, and we bar the route to London. He must take Rochester, if he wishes to take London from the Army of God. And he must take London if he wishes to win this war.'

The so-called Army of God, under the command of the less-than-saintly Robert, Lord Fitzwalter, did indeed hold London. Robin and I had stormed the walls for him just over three months ago and as a result we had captured the capital and been able to force the King to set his seal on a great charter at Runnymede, a document that was supposed to guarantee the rights of free Englishmen for ever. But, despite solemnly swearing to abide by the charter, calling for peace in the land and renewing the oaths of loyalty with his barons, the King had renounced the agreement a mere handful of weeks afterwards. The Pope in Rome, at the King's behest, had damned the charter, too, as shameful and illegal and had excommunicated all the rebel barons.

We had struggled and suffered and bled for that square piece of smoothed calf skin, and wrangled day and night over the terse Latin words it contained. Yet despite Robin's insistence that by forcing the King's hand we had struck a blow for liberty that would be remembered for generations to come, I sometimes wondered

8

what all the strife and bloodshed had achieved. If it had, in fact, achieved anything at all. King John, that cowardly, murderous snake, had simply ignored the great charter and spent thousands of pounds in tax silver recruiting fresh mercenary troops from Flanders and northern France. War had broken out again almost immediately between the rebel barons and the King's new continental hirelings.

Nevertheless, our position was not hopeless. Since the sealing of the charter, many English barons who had previously been fearful of resisting the King had rallied to our cause – the Pope's mass excommunications notwithstanding. Indeed, the constable of this very castle, Reginald de Cornhill, once a staunch King's man, had opened its gates to Lord Fitzwalter and his men not two days before and declared himself a lover of liberty, before departing with unashamed haste and all his men for his lands in Surrey.

Yet we rebels held London, and Exeter in the south-west, and a scatter of small castles in the north – and now we held Rochester too. And, while Fitzwalter prepared the defences of this mighty fortress with his grizzled captain William d'Aubigny, Robin's detachment of twenty archers and a dozen men-at-arms had been given the task of holding the bridge. For the King was surely coming up from Dover. And I knew it just as well as Robin.

The door of the guardhouse crashed open, impelled by an impetuous boot. 'Do I smell yesterday's mutton broth?' said Miles, striding inside and unfastening the golden clasp to drop his wet green cloak on the dirty rushes of the floor. 'Isn't there anything a bit more substantial to eat? I could make short work of a bloody beefsteak or a dripping roast chicken – God's bones, that would suit.'

'It's broth or nothing,' said his father, with an edge in his voice. 'You know as well as I that we are on short commons, all of us, till the supply train comes through from London. We must tighten our belts till then. And do try not to whine quite so much, son.'

'Not whining. Just making polite dinner conversation.' Miles plonked himself down on the bench next to me, helped himself to a clay bowl and filled it to the brim. 'Mmmm. Mutton broth. Nice and watery. And plenty of gristle, too, I see.'

I could actually hear Robin grinding teeth. But my lord held his peace.

'What news from the castle?' I said, after a long uncomfortable pause.

'D'Aubigny has it nicely in hand, I believe,' said my lord. 'He says the fortifications are sound, the walls in good repair throughout, and he has enough men and arms to hold it for months against a determined assault – providing of course that sufficient food stores can be brought in.'

William d'Aubigny was a bear of a man, immensely strong and quick, and with a reputation for ferocity in battle. He was lord of Belvoir Castle, a fortress in Leicestershire about fifteen miles east of Nottingham. As a not-too-distant neighbour of ours, he was well known to Robin and to me.

'Fitzwalter is planning to leave us, though,' Robin said.

'What?' I said, swallowing a mouthful of hot soup too quickly. 'Why?'

'He says he's needed in London. A grand council of the barons has been called. They're to discuss recruiting aid from overseas and Fitzwalter says he must attend or who knows what foolishness will occur.'

'So our gallant commander is deserting us on the eve of battle?' said Miles. 'Scuttling back to London. Hardly inspiring behaviour in a leader.'

Robin ignored his son and concentrated on wiping clean his bowl with a crust but I felt called on to defend Lord Fitzwalter's honour. My relationship with the captain-general of the Army of God had not always been cordial but since the war began I had grown to like the man.

'He is our leader and it makes sense that he should attend this important council with all the other senior barons,' I said.

'Were you not invited to attend this vaunted gathering then, Father?' said Miles. 'How strange! Perhaps they feel that playing watchman on this ancient bridge is more your mark.'

I could have punched the lad off the bench for that insult. Indeed, I felt my right fist clench and rise from the board. But Robin beat me to it.

'The sentry on the roof has been complaining of the cold this past hour,' said Robin serenely. 'When you have finished that nourishing bowl of broth, Miles, get yourself up there and take his place. I'll be sure to send someone up to relieve you at midnight' – Robin pretended to think – 'or perhaps at dawn. We'll have to see. I'd like all the serious fighting men to get a good night's rest.'

'But, Father, I had plans to visit the town tonight. There is this girl I want to see and as I'm not on duty—'

'Well, you are on duty now,' said Robin. 'Off you go.'

'But it's not fair . . .'

'Don't whine, lad,' I said, perhaps a touch smugly. 'Obey your lord's command.'

Miles opened his mouth to argue but before he could speak the door swung towards us and we all three looked up in surprise at the dark entrance, now wholly filled by Sir Thomas Blood's short form, broad shoulders and steel-helmeted head.

'Boats, my lord,' said Sir Thomas. 'Boats on the river. Scores of them.'

From the roof of the guardhouse, we had our first glimpse of the enemy, of the feared Flemish legions of King John. At least fifty rowing boats, downstream, three hundred yards away. Each boat was showing a single pinprick of yellow light, a lantern or open fire-pot, enabling us to see them against the blackness of the water in the failing light, and every vessel was pulling hard for the centre of the bridge.

11

'Miles, get back to the castle now. Alert Lord Fitzwalter – tell him . . . tell him that the bridge is under attack by several hundred of the King's men and that we will hold as long as we can. But it cannot be for long. Tell him to come with all speed.'

'But I want to fight. If you send me away, I'll miss everything—'

'For once, Miles, just do as you are bloody well told!' My lord did not raise his voice above a murmur but there was a whip-crack in his tone that sent his younger son scurrying for the wooden stair.

'Now, Alan, let's see about discouraging these Flemish fellows, shall we?'

Chapter Two

I fear, my dear Prior, that I have begun my tale in the wrong place. My mind is not what it was, I am old and I become easily confused these days, and my tales of blood and glory stray from their proper paths. I crave your indulgence for I must tell you of what occurred some weeks before the battle at Rochester Castle, else it will make no sense to you or to anyone who might read of my deeds and those of my comrades in the years to come.

As you well know, my dear Anthony, I have spent many hours in the past few days studying the Bible, and I find much comfort there. Robin would have scoffed at my new-found piety in the face of death but it is not salvation I seek – that I leave in the hands of a merciful God – but wisdom. There is much to be found in the holy book. I am reading Ecclesiastes and that wise old man wrote, if I have managed to untangle the Latin correctly, that there is a time for everything, a season for every activity under Heaven; there is a time to be born and a time to die; a time to plant and a time to uproot; a time to kill and a time to heal . . .

I was healing that August of the year of Our Lord twelve hundred and fifteen, a little slowly but surely, from a painful wound to the waist I had taken in a short, bloody fight on the walls of London that June. England, too, it seemed, was slowly healing after the struggle between the rebellious barons and the King. After Runnymede, I had dared to hope that all would be well in the kingdom for the rest of my life. That peace would reign in the land and folk would be left to sow and reap, to live, love and raise children.

A vain hope, it must now appear, but honestly held.

It was also the time to uproot, or at least to cut the barley, rye, oats and wheat that had grown tall and bright in the fields around and about my manor of Westbury in Nottinghamshire. That summer was a blazing, golden joy, long days of sunshine with only the occasional growling of a distant thunderstorm to remind us that the Heavenly Kingdom was not, in truth, at hand. All the menfolk of Westbury – my tenants from the village, the manor servants and the few freemen, old soldiers for the most part – were in their strips of field, backs bent and sickles in hand, as they lopped the nodding heads of grain from the stalks before the women following gathered them in bundles and stacked them to dry. All the local children came behind their parents, collecting the kernels of grain that spilled from the flashing blades and tucking them safely in their pouches before the wheeling flocks of birds could settle and gorge. The little ones made a game of their labours as often as not, chasing each other and shrieking with mirth. It would be a bountiful harvest, all were agreed, and if the weather continued to favour us there would be no fear of hunger or hardship till the following spring at least.

I confess I was not labouring in the fields with the other men. I was nursing my wound by drowsing in the strong afternoon sunshine, slumped on a comfortable bench outside my hall in the courtyard of Westbury, a jug of ale at my elbow, my belly full of venison stew and a blissful contentment suffusing my frame, when I heard the trumpet sound. I jerked upright fully awake – for while

14

England might appear to be at peace, I still kept a pair of sentries day and night on the roof of the squat stone tower in the courtyard, which was the manor's highest point and its last refuge in war, and their duty it was to warn of the approach of strangers.

Standing, straightening my clothing, brushing at a patch of drool on my tunic and vaguely looking around for my sword – it was hanging on the wall in my bedchamber, I remembered – I heard the sentry call down to me from the tower.

'A woman, sir, all alone. No horse, nor baggage. Looks like a beggarly type wanting a free meal.'

My elderly steward Baldwin, who with his unmarried sister Alice ran the daily business of the manor, was by my shoulder. He lifted an eyebrow. 'Sir Alan?' he said.

'Let her in, Baldwin,' I said, still filled with a glowing benevolence for the world. 'If she needs a meal, give her a good one and whatever scraps of meat and bread we can spare for her journeying and then send her on her way.'

'As you say, sir.'

'I'm going to my solar to take a little n— That is to say, I shall retire to my chamber for a while to study my scrolls.'

I left the glare of the sunshine and pushed past Baldwin into the gloom of the hall. I gave no more thought to the beggar woman, for as I entered my solar at the far end and lay down on the big, comfortable bed, I fell into a deep and delightful sleep.

I awoke in the pinkish twilight of the long summer evening, refreshed and still brimming with contentment, and lay for a while listening to the sounds of the servants clattering plates in the hall, no doubt preparing the evening meal. I could hear the voice of my fifteen-year-old son Robert but I could not quite make out his words over the noise of the hall servants. He seemed animated, though, unusually cheerful, and I wondered who he was talking to. And then I heard *her* voice.

I sat up abruptly and an icy chill puckered the skin of my forearms. I was out the door of the solar in an instant – and there she was. Seated at the big hall table a few feet from Robert, elbows on the board, deep in conversation.

'Get away from her!' I bawled, running towards my son and the beggar woman. They both started to their feet, shocked.

'Robert, get away from that woman right now.'

'Why, Father, we were—'

'Get away. Come and stand behind me.'

My heart was racing, I could feel my face and neck hot with surging blood. I curled a protective arm around Robert. 'Did she feed you anything? Robert – did she give you anything to eat or drink?'

'Father, you are behaving in a very—'

'Answer me. Did she give you anything to eat or touch your skin?'

'Father . . .' My son looked into my face and saw that I was in deadly earnest. 'She gave me nothing. She did not touch me. We were waiting for you to wake before we ate. She will take supper with us tonight.'

'She will not,' I said. My right hand was groping wildly across my waist for my sword hilt but, of course, the blade was still hanging on the wall in the bedchamber. I looked at the woman, now smiling crookedly at me from the other side of the table.

'Sir Alan,' said Matilda Giffard in her wood-smoke-deepened voice, 'what a joy it is to set eyes on you again.'

'I cannot say the same,' I said coldly.

I looked at her. Matilda Giffard, Tilda, as she was to me . . . a woman I had once – no, twice – thought I was in love with but who had proved herself as treacherous and cunning as a starving rat.

She had once been a great beauty – a woman to stop a man's heart – but on this day, although her looks had not entirely deserted her, she cut a poor figure: she was thin as a twig and dressed in a raggedy black nun's robe, greyed by the dust of the road. Her

16

once swan-white face was decidedly grubby, she had the remains of a black eye, now faded to streaks of brown and yellow, and the lines on her brow beneath her midnight black hair and around her grey-blue eyes were cut deeper than I remembered.

'My dear, you have nothing to fear from me, I swear it,' said Tilda, smiling. Her familiar voice sent ripples running down my spine.

She stepped away from the table and came towards me. With difficulty, I managed not to take a step backwards, and pulled Robert tighter to my side.

'I do not fear you,' I said, lying once more.

'That is as it should be. I know that we had harsh words when we last met. And you cannot know how much I regret them—'

'I do not fear you,' I cut her off, 'I merely ask that you leave my hall, my home and my lands immediately.'

'I have wronged you; Robert, too. I freely admit it. But I come humbly to seek your forgiveness for my actions. I know you are a kind man—'

'You shall not have it. You schemed to kill us. You used your wiles and my own loving foolishness to snare me. You betrayed me to my enemies. At every turn you have sought my destruction. Whatever it is that you say you require, you shall not have from my hand. I shall have no more dealings with you. Now, I must ask you to leave. This instant. Or I shall fetch my men and have you thrown from the ramparts.'

To my utter astonishment, Tilda fell to her knees in front of me. She clasped her hands before her in supplication and I swear that a succession of oily tears began to course down her dirty white cheeks.

'Sir Alan, I beg you. It was so hard for me to come here. Forgive me. Dear God, I ask you in all humility. Show me mercy. Forgive me and grant me sanctuary. I have nowhere else to turn. In the name of the love you once professed, forgive me. I beg you.'

I was utterly at a loss. I had seen Tilda merry, fearful, sad and scornful, even spitting bile-bitter hatred at me. But I'd never seen her like this. So . . . broken. So stripped of dignity. Pleading for my forgiveness on her knees. My heart twisted in pity.

'Go back to Kirklees. Go back home to the Priory, woman, and do not trouble us again. You shall have food. An armed escort, if you want it. But you will not stay here.'

'I cannot,' she said. Tilda was sobbing without restraint. She buried her face in her hands and her words came out jerkily, muffled and odd sounding.

'Expelled. The mother Prioress. Anna. She and I, we . . . She threw me out. I have nowhere to go. I have no place. I am lost.'

A weeping woman on her knees is a hard thing for a man to witness, particularly if she was once his lover. But I knew Tilda of old and, while her grief did seem genuine, I could not bring myself to trust her once again. I hardened my heart and called for help.

'Baldwin,' I said to my steward, who was hovering by the table with his mouth open in shock. 'Fetch the lady a satchel of food, a flask of wine and a warm cloak, and escort her from the manor. If she will not go, get Hal and some of the men-at-arms to help you. Robert and I will be in my solar. Report to me when she is gone.'

I turned my back on the sobbing woman on her knees in the hall and, half-pushing Robert to force him along, I stalked back to my chamber.

Inside, with the door closed and my weight leaning securely against it, I felt my heart pounding as if I had run a mile in full armour.

'I do think that was rather harsh, Father,' said Robert.

I had thought I was rid of Tilda once and for all but life is never that simple. Baldwin reported that he had provided her with food and drink and a cloak and escorted her – she was meek as a lamb,

18

he said – out of the main gate. He had stayed to watch her set out on the road towards Nottingham but after only a few hundred yards she had veered off the track headed towards the river and had collapsed down under a willow tree on the bank, a huddle of misery, still within a half-mile of my gates.

'Do you wish me to send the men-at-arms to roust her?' Baldwin asked.

'No,' I said. It was dark by then and to send a troop of mounted men to move along one tearful middle-aged woman seemed excessively cruel. 'Let her sleep the night there in peace. Doubtless she will be gone in the morning.'

She wasn't, of course.

The next morning, from the roof of my tower, I could clearly see her, a black shape under the willow tree, still as a stone. It crossed my mind to order out the men-at-arms then, and have them move her on with their spear butts, but I had not the heart for it. I contented myself with issuing stern orders to all the servants that Matilda Giffard must not be allowed to set so much as a toe within my walls again.

We were very busy over the next few days with the harvest and, while I cannot pretend that Tilda disappeared from my mind completely – she hovered constantly on the fringes of my thoughts like an unpaid debt – I did manage to banish her from my daily processes. I ignored her, in truth. She stayed by the willow tree day after day, moving very seldom, at least in daylight, troubling nobody as far as I could tell and slowly, almost imperceptibly, becoming absorbed into the landscape of Westbury.

Four days after the tearful scene in the hall, Robin arrived.

Chapter Three

My lord came apparelled for war and with two score mounted men-at-arms at his back. He was in high spirits, oddly, for the news he bore was almost all bad. Over a cup of wine in my hall, he informed me that the King had reneged on the promises given at Runnymede and that we were summoned once more to war by Lord Fitzwalter and the Army of God. I confess my heart sank at the news.

'We knew it couldn't last, Alan,' said my lord. 'When has King John ever kept a promise, let alone one extracted at the point of a sword?'

He made a good argument: John was one of the most duplicitous men I have ever had the misfortune to encounter, indeed the bitter hatred felt for him by the barons of England had much to do with his untrustworthiness, but my dreams of a peaceful existence had been scattered to the winds by Robin's arrival.

'I need you, Sir Alan,' he said. 'I need your sword once more. Will you come?'

I nodded dutifully. I could not in good conscience resist a call to arms from my lord: he had made me, raising me from a penniless thief to the prosperous knight I was today. He'd given me everything. I owed him my life and my lands.

We were joined at dinner by Sir Thomas Blood, Robin's man and an old friend of mine too who had once served as my squire and had painstakingly trained my son Robert in the arts of the sword. He also was in high spirits and he proudly showed me his shield, which was freshly painted with a new blazon, the head of a buck with an arrow in its mouth. The buck and the arrow were in Robin's honour – a reference to a time in his youth when he was a famous outlaw.

Robin had granted Sir Thomas the small manor of Makeney in Derbyshire, a richly deserved reward, for Thomas had been his loyal knight for many years now. He was also a newly married man, having taken a bride, a pretty girl from Westbury, in fact, called Mary, who had recently given birth to their first child, a dark, chubby, perpetually bawling boy. Clearly they needed their own home.

'You will probably have learned this already, Alan,' said Robin, 'but Philip Marc is back, too. Despite what the charter decreed, John has returned him to the exalted post of High Sheriff of Nottinghamshire, Derbyshire and the Royal Forests.'

This was news to me. 'What happened to Eustace de Lowdham?'

'Oh, he has graciously agreed to step aside and has accepted the role of deputy sheriff. The fool says he's happy to have been relieved of the burden of high office.'

Philip Marc was my enemy. He was a French mercenary, fanatically loyal to the King, who had hounded me for taxes I did not owe and had even seized my son Robert for a while in an attempt to force me to pay. Lord de Lowdham was a weak-willed but amiable fellow who the rebel barons had induced to take the shrievalty after Runnymede. I was surprised King John had not had him permanently removed.

'It gets worse,' said Robin. 'Sheriff Marc has a remit to destroy all unlicensed stone castles in Nottinghamshire and there are more than a few landholders hereabouts who are hastily pulling down their new walls to avoid exciting his ire.'

I looked out of the open door of the hall at the squat stone tower that I had built in the courtyard two years before. My keep, my refuge in time of trouble. I had been so proud to have raised it. It made me feel like a real knight, less of a gutter-born churl who had done suspiciously well for himself and was now aping his superiors.

I tore my eyes from it and said: 'How are Marie-Anne and the boys?'

As well as Miles, Robin had another son, Hugh. They were as unalike as iron and silk. Hugh, the eldest, was a steady, sensible man, a little dull and priggish to my mind but a decent fighter and a fellow who once he had fixed his mind to something would never give up until it was accomplished. Miles was another man altogether: wild, pleasure-seeking, irresponsible – and loved by almost everybody who met him.

'They are busy,' said Robin. 'Hugh is to be constable of Kirkton while I am away – he's recruiting more men and strengthening the walls of the castle. Marie-Anne is laying in stores in case of a long siege. Though I hope it won't come to that. You are welcome to send your household there if Philip Marc becomes overly oppressive.'

I thanked him distractedly. I was still thinking about the tower and wondering, given its relative insignificance compared with some of the greater fortifications in the county, whether it might escape the sheriff's notice. 'And Miles?' I asked.

Robin said nothing for five whole heartbeats.

'I cannot understand that boy,' he said at last. 'He has no regard for discipline at all. He tells me he is wedded to the rebel cause, to the great charter of liberties, that he is afire to teach the King and all his foreign mercenaries a bloody lesson – but when it comes to training with our men, organising our forces for battle, preparing, if you like, to teach that bloody lesson, he seems to have no interest.

'He spends half the day abed. He is up half the night with the wine jug. Every week he is involved in some new scrape, usually involving too much drink and some unfortunate local girl. I tried confining him to the castle and he blithely ignored my orders and spent two days absent – God knows where. He came back, refusing to give an account of himself but with a badly cut lip and his best clothes torn and stained with blood. I took away his horse and his purse; he borrowed a mount from a farmer, robbed a travelling monk of two shillings and set out on his revels again. He is twenty years of age yet behaving like an unruly apprentice: always surly, disrespectful to Marie-Anne, downright rude to me. He is a thorn in my backside, to be honest.'

I tried not to smile at Robin's words. Miles sounded exactly how I imagined Robin to have been when he was his son's age. There was a secret about Robin's sons that was never mentioned for fear of angering the Earl of Locksley: while Miles was truly his son, in looks as well as character, Hugh was not. He was the fruit of a forced coupling between Robin's enemy, the former sheriff of Nottinghamshire Ralph Murdac, and Marie-Anne, who had briefly been his prisoner. Murdac was long dead but Hugh resembled him in many ways – the same colouring and shortness of stature, although, praise God, he did not seem to have Murdac's evil ways and had proved himself to be as true a man as any in Robin's ranks.

'You can wipe that foolish grin off your face, Alan Dale,' said Robin. 'Miles is joining us here tomorrow. And you will see how much you like his company then. At least, I left orders to that effect at Kirkton. I couldn't find the damn boy when I left. I'm taking him with us on campaign. I dare not leave him at home: he'd probably burn the castle around his mother's ears.'

'So where are we going?' I asked.

'South,' said Robin. 'To London first; we will receive further orders from Fitzwalter there.'

Dinner was served by Robert and his massive servant Boot, a dark-skinned giant from the forests of Africa who had once been the sheriff's executioner at Nottingham Castle, and we ate heartily – venison, roast goose and pigeon pie, fresh bread, cheese and preserves, for who could tell what privations the future might hold. At the table Robin introduced me to his new squire, a broad-shouldered, deep-chested, red-haired young fellow of good family in Kent named William of Cassingham, and known by all as Cass. He seemed an amiable sort, who clearly worshipped Robin. He was, for a squire, unusually armed. At his waist, on the left side, in a two-foot long, five-inch broad leather sheath, he wore a falchion, a crude, wide, single-bladed weapon that was more like a butcher's cleaver than a proper sword. At the other side of his belt was an arrow bag filled with two dozen shafts topped with goose feathers; and it was very difficult to part him from the long yew bow that he carried as if it were an extra limb.

'He's a talented lad,' said Robin quietly, as the squire took his place at the board, 'if a little savage in his habits. But strong as a bull – and brave with it.' My lord obviously had regard for the fellow and that was enough reason for me to like him. But beyond a few mumbled pleasantries, Cass said little at the feast and ate as if this were to be his last meal on earth, tearing at great chunks of meat with his teeth and barely chewing them before swallowing the lump down with vast draughts of red wine. He reminded me of the strange tales I had heard of the pagan cannibals of Africa – ferocious creatures who filed their teeth into points and craved human flesh. But, in truth, he was no wild man. He merely ate with a great determination, almost as if he were challenged, as if he were determined to vanquish all the meat and drink before him.

When they had served the dishes and poured the wine, Boot and Robert joined us at the table and listened in silence while Robin regaled us with tales of Kirkton, the misadventures of Miles and all the doings in his Yorkshire lands. After the meal, while Robin was seeing to the comforts of his men-at-arms in the barns out in the courtyard, Sir Thomas took me aside.

He seemed embarrassed but he clearly wished to speak to me alone.

'Alan,' he said, 'have you received any visitors in the past few weeks, any visitors connected with the Church?'

I told him about the appearance of Tilda and her tearful entreaties.

'Yes, I heard that she was expelled from Kirklees,' he said. 'She upset the prioress somehow and Matilda was thrown out without a penny, just in the clothes she stood up in. We all laughed about it, to be honest. A bad woman come to a bad end. But that was not what I was aiming at. Have you received any visitors from, ah, the Poor Fellow-Soldiers of Christ and the Temple of Solomon?'

I looked at him more keenly then. Thomas, unasked, had done me a great service in the summer. A Templar knight, one Brother Geoffrey, a foul deviant who had had charge of the training of young squires in the Earl of Pembroke's household, had pestered my son while he was there. I did not know the full details, Robert had never revealed them to me, and I did not like to press my enquiries, but I knew it was bad enough to warrant the knight's death at my hands. However, Thomas had dispatched the wretch on my behalf, in secret, without my knowledge, and had even gone so far as to slice off his manhood and leave it in the corpse's open mouth as a message to other men of his hideous kind.

Thomas had been very discreet; indeed, he had never directly admitted his guilt to me, merely alluding to it. He still did not seem willing to own to the crime. But I knew what he had done and I was grateful. I also knew that the Templars had vowed to

25

seek out the killer and have their revenge. The English Master of the Templars, Sir Aymeric de St Maur, had told me he would do so himself.

'I haven't seen a Templar since Runnymede,' I said. 'Why? Are you worried?'

'Not . . . worried. I do not think there is any immediate danger. But they sent someone to Kirkton, an elderly priest, St Maur's chaplain, and he spent some time with Robin asking him about the movements of his men in June. Of course, Robin told him nothing and sent him packing soon enough, but it seems they are making enquiries. And, well, they are dogged men and I do not think they will cease their investigations until they have found the guilty man . . . whoever he is.'

'If they ask, I will tell them nothing that could lead them to the killer. But I will tell them exactly what kind of filth Brother Geoffrey was and I shall also say that I would have butchered him myself had I had the chance and that I'd wager half a dozen other good men, fathers like me, might have had equal cause to end him.'

'I don't think we should go out of our way to antagonise the Templars, Alan,' said Thomas. 'I do not like the odds against us in a war with them. They have more power than any baron in the land. Far more than Robin. More even than the King, I'd venture. Certainly more silver. If it came to a battle between us – I wouldn't wager on victory for our side.'

I smiled at Thomas – I knew he had a weakness for games of chance, although he had sworn off the knucklebones to please his new bride. But he also seemed to have almost no sense of the absurdity of his words sometimes. For if it came to war with the Templars and he wagered on them winning, he would never be able to collect his winnings. A corpse claims no silver. 'We will have no need to quarrel with them, Thomas.' I said. 'And Robin would never give you up to them. For that matter, I'd wade through blood before I'd allow them to touch you. Do not fear, my friend.'

Thomas gripped my shoulder. 'Perhaps I am starting at shadows,' he said. 'Perhaps, if God is merciful, we will hear no more about this matter.'

Chapter Four

If you will allow me, my dear Anthony, I shall now continue with my tale of what befell us at Rochester that terrible autumn when King John's Flemish mercenaries attacked from the river. On the bridge, Robin divided his small force of archers, setting ten men under his master bowman Mastin, a bald, furry-bodied, foul-mouthed rogue from Cheshire, at the northern end, and taking command of ten archers himself at the southern. I took up position in the centre of the structure, with Sir Thomas Blood at my shoulder and a dozen men-at-arms around me. My lord's plan was simple. His bowmen would shoot into the oncoming boats – now less than a hundred and fifty yards away downstream – to kill as many of the enemy at a distance as possible and Thomas and I would deal with any who managed to make it through the arrow storm and on to the bridge.

'They're coming on damnably slowly,' said Thomas, fidgeting with impatience beside me. He was right: we could make out the rowers struggling at their oars, these flashing weakly in the darkness as light from the lanterns reflected off the wet blades, but they were making pitiful progress, coming on slower than a tired man might walk.

'They must fight the flow of the water before they reach us,' I said. 'The river is trying to drag them out towards the sea. I thank God for it, for it gives Robin a little more time to—'

At that moment, the Earl of Locksley's men loosed. There was a sound like a rushing wind and a cloud of shafts sped away into the darkness towards the boats. An instant later, Mastin's men on the far end of the bridge sent their volley to chase Robin's. I saw two black shapes splash from the leading boat and heard the first sharp cries of pain, and then Robin and Mastin's men found their rhythm: the creak of yew bows drawn to their fullest, a swoosh as the arrows left the string, and the cracks as steel tips struck the wood of the boats or the mail or weapons of armed men. With both groups of archers shooting every two or three heartbeats, the arrow onslaught became almost continuous, a withering rain that pelted the unfortunate attackers as they struggled against the current. But still they came on – now a hundred paces away. The awful screams and cries of the wounded echoed across the water, the smack of shafts driving home and the zip and twang of our archers filled the air as the boats splashed and surged, with deeper, angrier shouts from the sergeants encouraging their men to hold fast and row like devils if they valued their lives.

The leading boat was now directionless, filled as it was with dead and dying men, feathered many times over. It listed sideways, borne back by the current, untended oars tangling other boats behind it. Two craft rowed around, one left, one to the right, the men, backs towards us, hauling like souls possessed. They were fifty yards away now. The arrows still slashed into them, punching through mail into soft flesh beneath. I saw one man, in the right-hand boat, struck by three arrows one after the other along the line of his spine. He turned his face towards us screaming hatred, a pale flash in the darkness, before slumping forward over his oars.

The archers were no longer shooting volleys; each bowman was

29

drawing and loosing in his own time, killing and maiming with every shaft.

Still they came on.

Boats of fresh men fought their way through the tangle of wreckage in the river, shouting defiance. Other craft crept up the banks on both sides, like dark arms reaching out for us. I could make out hundreds of the bastards, see their faces, white blobs in the gloom. Some men were standing upright in their boats now, some arrow-stuck and bloodied, but with weapons brandished. A crossbowman loosed at us, the knot of a dozen English men-at-arms standing on the bridge, awaiting their assault, our shields raised, but swords still scabbarded. I heard the hiss as the deadly quarrel whipped past my ear, inches away.

'Right, lads,' I said. 'Disperse. To the stones now.'

The boats were twenty yards away. Two dozen craft, each carrying six men, four rowing but two crouched in the prow, facing us, shields up, steel bared, ready to leap.

My men, who had been bunched in the middle of the bridge, now split and ran to the small cairns that Robin had ordered piled every ten paces along its whole length. I took the cairn in the very centre of the bridge, with Sir Thomas to my right, between me and Robin. The enemy were ten yards away and I could make out fierce faces, glittering eyes, and hear the alien shouts of battle. I slipped my shield from its loops on my left arm, dropped it to the planks of the bridge and seized a boulder about the size and shape of a haunch of venison from the pile at my feet. It was almost more than I could lift, but I heaved it up to the rail and rested it on the edge.

A quick peek over. There was a boat directly under me, bumping against one of the thick wooden support pillars, a boat filled with steel and malice and red shouting mouths. A crossbow twanged. I jerked my head back and the quarrel tinged off the dome of my helmet. I hefted the stone and hurled it downwards. It struck the shoulder of a mailed man, knocking him to his knees, and then plunged straight through the bottom of the boat, tearing a hole that filled with black water.

One man was already climbing the pillar, a knife clenched sideways in his teeth. I bent and seized a smaller boulder and smashed it into his face as he appeared over the rail, crunching the knife blade into his back teeth. He fell away groaning and splashed into the darkness. And I pitched the stone down after him, breaking the out-reaching arm of another who was just beginning his climb. The boat was now almost completely full of water, sinking fast, the desperate men-at-arms scrambling against each other to avoid being dragged down to the depths in their heavy armour.

I plucked up another boulder, almost as big as the first, and hurled it on to the wreckage of the boat and its few struggling survivors.

I snatched a look along the bridge and saw a big Westbury man-at-arms called Hal, a devil with an axe in any fight, tossing a head-sized rock over the edge, shouting an insult and bending for another. But beyond him – disaster. Mastin's men were no longer loosing, as far as I could see in the torchlight flickering above the north entrance to the bridge. Three empty boats bobbed at the pillar below. A mob of half a dozen men-at-arms were on the bridge itself, surging all around Mastin and his men, bloodied swords in the air, hacking and cutting. And more black shapes, glinting with wet steel, were swarming up the side of the bridge and over the rail to join them. Robin's archers, supreme killers with a bow, were mostly no hands at all with a blade; up close the enemy would slaughter them.

And that slaughter had already begun.

I looked behind me. Robin's detachment was still shooting, some men leaning far out over the rail to aim straight down into the huddle of packed boats that were now massed below us, scores

31

of craft, hundreds of men. Robin himself leaped up and stood tall on top of the rail, balancing with the grace of a tumbler, no mean feat for a man who had seen fifty winters. He drew his bow and loosed a shaft that smacked into the eye of an older man urging his soldiers upwards just ten feet below Robin. The arrow tore through the man's skull, showering brains behind, and knocking the fellow out of the boat with a splash. Robin plucked another shaft from the bag at his waist . . .

Mastin! I scooped up my shield, pulled Fidelity from its scabbard and charged away from Robin, towards the northern end of the bridge, screaming 'Westbury! On me, on me!'

I ran along the bridge at full pelt, dimly aware that most of the rest of our men were running at my shoulder. A helm-less black-headed man hopped over the rail right into my path waving a mace and I separated him from the top of his head with one swinging hack of the blade. I saw another fellow, dripping wet, behind him, cowering at the rail looking at me with vast eyes but ignored him.

I had to get to Mastin.

With half a dozen good men at my back, I slammed into the struggling knot at the north end of the bridge, my sword crunching into a mailed back. The man I struck turned, snarling, and I punched him full in the face with my shield, knocking him aside. I stepped into the space he had vacated, Fidelity chopping down. A huge blond fellow lunged at me with a two-handed axe, trying to hook my shield and pull it down. I slipped the shield sideways, out of the grip of his axe, and lunged down at his left leg, steel point biting into his calf, half severing the lower leg, crippling him. He screamed as he fell. And I got my first glimpse of Mastin, pinned against the rail and laying about him with his bow, using it like a quarterstaff, the broken string lashing impotently through the air. There were dead and dying archers all round him, and two still living at either shoulder, fending off the attackers clumsily with their swords. I parried a sword blow from a knight and my counterstroke hacked into his mailed neck. He wobbled and I smashed my pommel into the side of his helmet. My men were all around me, cutting, hacking, slicing into the foe. We made short work of the enemy around Mastin, Hal splitting one man's face along the line of his mouth with a colossal blow from his axe, while I disembowelled a fat man-at-arms in a raggedy gambeson with a lunge to the belly and a swift twist of my blade. Then there were no more enemy on their feet before me and my men were swiftly dispatching the fallen, punching their swords down into dead and wounded alike.

Mastin looked at me with relief in his eyes, the only part of his face that was not covered in hair. But all he said was: 'Too many fucking bastards, Sir Alan. Too many.' Then, immediately: 'Look yonder,' and he nodded back down the length of the bridge. I turned and saw a mass of men swarming over the rail in the centre where I had begun the fight, a score, two score, a tide of humanity armed and angry, wild with fear and a lust for revenge on the bowmen who had galled them so from a distance, and yet more coming up from the crush of boats below. Despite the slaughter our arrows had wrought, we had hardly even slowed their attack. I could see no sign of Robin or his archers and my heart missed a beat. Surely they could not have been overrun already?

I did not have time to digest this terror: there were forty or fifty men-at-arms coming towards me, surging up the length of the bridge, swords and axes lofted. We closed up in a compact group, shields high, seven men about me, with Mastin behind, cursing steadily, filthily, and trying to restring his bow with trembling hands.

The enemy fell on us, a jostling mob hammering at us with a desperate hatred and cold hard steel. They screamed and shoved, blades licking out to clatter against helmet and mail. I took a solid blow on my shield and thrust Fidelity out in response to rip through the cheek of my attacker below his helmet rim. Out of the corner of my eye I saw one of my Westbury men, a fellow named Deakin, cut down by a pair of snarling, hacking foes. The sheer weight of enemies was pushing us back against the rail. We were surrounded; outnumbered five to one. My shield was trapped against my body. I bullocked forward, lunging repeatedly with Fidelity, short, straight strokes, and made myself a little space. But this could not last. An archer dropped to my left, choking, a crossbow quarrel through his cheek. Only five of us were standing now. Something smashed against my shoulder and I was pushed backwards; I thrust the cross-guard of my sword into a bawling mouth and felt the clean snap of teeth. I felt a knife blade probing against my ribs, grinding against me, driven by an unseen hand – and thanked God for decent mail. But we were going under. Time seemed to slow. Only three men and Mastin were still fighting. I could barely move my arms. A Fleming's roaring face was inches from my own. I tried to bite his nose. Missed. Teeth snapping on air. A blow to my helm and I almost lost my footing. I could feel the hard wooden rail digging into the small of my back. I surged up and outwards, using my armoured weight and all the strength of both of my legs, knocking a man down and lashing out with Fidelity, finding contact. The jar of bone. A scream. My mail sleeve was drenched in red. Then an enormous buffet against my shield, a hammer blow that thrust me sideways against Mastin's solid form. The shouting of the enemy was deafening. The smell of gore and sweat and opened bowels was a solid thing. My sword arm was trapped against my body. I could not move my shield. Hal, on my left, screamed and dropped to his knees, his neck pierced through with a thrown spear, the bright frothy blood bubbling from the wound. We were all dying. We were all dead men.

And then I heard the trumpets.

Lord Fitzwalter's mounted men, a full *conroi* of thirty knights poured on to the bridge, thundering in from the southern side, horses at full gallop and lances couched. The whole structure shook with the force of their charge, the very planks bouncing beneath my feet. They smashed into the enemy and cut through their mass like a plough turning earth in the furrow, King John's mercenaries leaping for the rail on either side, desperate to escape the deadly spear points of the pounding cavalry and willing to risk the river if it meant they would not be crushed to red offal beneath the churning hooves.

The trumpets sounded again.

The men in front of us were miraculously gone but Mastin, myself and the one surviving archer pressed ourselves back against the rail, all crying, 'A Locksley! A Locksley!' to identify ourselves, fearful the cavalry in the madness of their victory would cut us down too.

I saw Miles, bare-headed, his long fair hair flying out behind him, clatter past on a pure white stallion, his lance-point red and glistening. He set himself at a big fellow, wounded in the leg, who was limping away through the northern gateway, just yards from quitting the bridge. Miles's lance dipped and he plunged it into the running man's back with a cry of triumph, the force of the blow lifting the man in the air, his feet kicking ludicrously as he tried to run.

In the middle of the bridge, the knights were cutting down the last of the enemy, those too slow or too fearful to trust themselves to the river. Screams for mercy, hands waving in a vain attempt to ward off the chopping blades. Horses reared and plunged, their hooves shattering skulls and limbs and sinking into a writhing carpet of bodies. In the flickering light of the *conroi*'s torch bearers, the bridge seemed littered with dying men, the whole area drenched with blood, as if vast barrels of gore had been poured on to it. A man gashed by many swords slipped over the rail and splashed down below. The last enemy to escape.

The bridge was still ours. In the dark water below it, I could hear the slosh of oars and the panicked shouts of men, and on the fringes of the light the shapes of small boats, the rowers straining to carry themselves away as swiftly as they could.

Then I smelled it, a choking acrid taste in the back of my mouth, and the first thin tendrils of smoke leaking upwards through the cracks between the blood-soaked planks, snaking over the bodies of the dead. Now a trickle but within a dozen heartbeats a stream, then thick grey plumes appearing from both sides of the bridge. An orange glow from underneath, like walking past the mouth of a forge.

'Fire!' I shouted. 'They have fired the bridge!'

Chapter Five

Two days later, early morning in October, grey and dismal, and my lord and I were playing chess in the grand hall of the keep of Rochester Castle using one of the slim windows on the northern side to light the board.

'We won, didn't we?' I said to Robin. 'We beat them off. The cavalry destroyed at least half of them. The victory honours must go to us, surely?'

'Depends what you mean by victory,' said Robin. 'If you look out that window, you can see that they achieved exactly what they set out to do. King John charged them with destroying the bridge, cutting us off from aid from London, and it is destroyed.'

I glanced out of the narrow arch and saw that what he said was true. Where the bridge – the only practical crossing of the Medway for fifteen miles – had once stood was now a large expanse of brown water, with two charred gatehouses and the skeletons of a dozen blackened rowing boats littering both muddy banks.

'*That* was a victory for King John, I would say. But *this* one is mine,' said Robin, moving his queen and trapping my lonely king behind a wall of three pawns. 'Checkmate, I believe.'

I looked at the board dumbfounded. I hated playing this stupid, dry-as-dust game with him. Mainly because he beat me almost every time.

As Robin began to reset the pieces, I said: 'So you think we are now beyond help from London?'

'The destruction of the bridge has certainly made it harder for aid to reach us,' he said. 'But it's not impossible. If Fitzwalter is determined enough he could ford an army at a couple of places upstream. And if he could commandeer enough small boats . . .'

Lord Fitzwalter, our leader, captain-general of the Army of God, had ridden across the burning bridge with a pair of his knights almost immediately after the enemy had been cleared by his charge. He had paused only to confer with Robin, who had wisely pulled his archers off the bridge just before the cavalry charge.

'If I am going to go, I must go now,' Fitzwalter had said to my lord, just as I was striding over to Robin to congratulate him on his timely escape and our victory. Robin had looked at the flames, now licking up the bridge's support pillars, even dancing along the rail, but said nothing, his face as blank as a stone.

'I have to go, Locksley,' said Fitzwalter. 'But I will return with a sizeable relief force and as much food as you could hope for. You have my word on it. And it must be me who goes. Who else can persuade the barons in London to part with sufficient men and provisions?'

'Go then,' said Robin. 'But know, sir, that I hold you to your word.'

'Good, look for me in a couple of weeks or so. I know that you and d'Aubigny between you can keep out the King till then. I have confidence in you, my friend. I will rest easy knowing that Rochester is in safe hands.'

'Just go, man,' said Robin, turning away. And Lord Fitzwalter did, trotting his horse through the drifting smoke across the bridge with the two knights at his back.

Robin frowned, scratched his fair head and tentatively advanced a pawn, threatening my knight in the centre. The moment he lifted his fingers from the piece, I pounced. I slid the knight two squares forward and one left.

'Ha ha!' I said, trying not to sound too pleased with myself. 'I have you now!' The knight threatened both his bishop and his queen. And when he duly moved his queen out of danger and I took his bishop, he would be in check. Two moves after that and it would be mate. The second game was as good as mine.

I looked at my lord's face to see how he would take this unexpected reversal in his fortunes and was irritated to see that he was not paying either me or the board the attention it surely deserved. He was looking beyond my shoulder at one of the open doors that connected the two halves of the great hall.

Rochester was an unusual castle in this respect. It had a massive square keep, on three floors, with strong towers at each corner, but the great hall was divided into two parts by a thick stone spine wall running down the centre punctuated by two stout iron-bound oak doors and a portal opening on to a well shaft. I turned on my stool and saw that the second chamber was in turmoil, servants were running here and there, mailed knights were calling for their squires and striding through the open doors.

Cass appeared at the chess table. 'Sir, the enemy have been sighted. King John is approaching the walls,' he said.

Robin was on his feet. I got to mine more slowly. 'Come, Robin, let us finish the game,' I said. 'You have seen the King before, many times.'

'In what strength?' he said to Cass.

'I cannot truly say, sir. Many hundreds of knights. Horse, baggage, siege engines, I think. Thousands. His whole army, I believe.'

Robin was already moving across the hall.

'Wait,' I shouted. 'Just a few more moves. You can't leave now.'

He was gone. I remembered myself, felt ashamed. I beckoned a servant.

'No one is to touch this board,' I said. 'No one – on pain of death. Do you hear me? I am quite serious. Do *not* clear away this chessboard.'

The man nodded and I clapped him on the shoulder and hurried after my lord.

When I had puffed my way up to the roof of the south tower – I was no longer in the first flush of youth, to be honest, and at forty years of age, after decades of war, running up stairs was becoming something of an ordeal – I found the square space crowded with knights, men-at-arms and the castle servants. I nodded to a few of the knights that I knew – Osbert Giffard, William d'Einford and Thomas de Melutan – and forced my way through the throng to find a place beside Robin and Cass, on the eastern side, overlooking the cathedral. Far below us the curtain wall that marked the exterior of the outer bailey was also lined with men and women, all staring out over the walled town of Rochester. It seemed everyone in the castle had stopped whatever they were doing to come out and watch.

And what a sight it was: a huge cloud of dust kicked up by a column of marching men, about five or six miles away to the south-east, on the main road from Dover. Broad standards flew above the moving mass and here and there was the glitter of weak sunlight on steel spear-tips. The men who had attacked and burned the bridge were just an advance party: this was the main force, the full strength. Around the central column were horsemen, many hundreds of them, riding through the fields on either side of the road, their surcoats and the cloth trappers of their horses brilliant against the drab fields of stubble. It was an army on the march, a horde some three thousand strong, I would guess, heading straight for us.

The King had come to Rochester.

As we gazed out at the advancing column, with men-at-arms, and even some knights, on either side of us muttering fearfully at the size of the King's army, I felt a jostling ripple in the crowd about me. Pushing lesser men out of his path without the slightest compunction, a huge figure in a black velvet tunic trimmed with silver thread forced his way through to Robin's side.

William d'Aubigny, lord of Belvoir, leaned his ham-thick forearms on the battlements and stared impassively out at the advancing foe. His vast leonine head was extended to the fullest on his thick neck, as if to help him see a few inches further, and I noticed that the curls of silver-grey hair falling to the collar of his tunic matched the bullion trim of his attire perfectly. He was a man who had seen more than sixty summers yet he was as strong and as brisk in his speech as a man half his age.

He let out a long gusty breath. 'I had hoped we'd have more time, Locksley,' he said. 'At least a day or two more. But he's here now and so the dance begins.'

'We are ready, are we not?' said Robin.

'Depends how long Fitzwalter takes to get back here.'

D'Aubigny turned suddenly to face the murmuring crowd behind him, and all the talk stopped dead.

'Every man who does not have business here is to leave. Off this roof. Go on. It's not a fair-day show, it's not an Easter parade. Be about your duties now. Be off.'

The crowd began to disperse down the spiral steps to the floors below.

'Give me a moment of your time, Locksley. I want a word. You too, Sir Alan, if you are not needed elsewhere.'

Cass looked enquiringly at his lord and I saw Robin give him a quick sideways nod to indicate that he should leave.

A few moments later and we three were alone on the roof, the wind suddenly fiercer and the height of the tower more apparent.

Robin said: 'The town won't hold even a day against those numbers, sir, you know that, don't you.'

'Yes, Locksley, I know. We can't feed those extra mouths in the castle either. The townspeople must go. I need a willing knight for a hard task.'

He looked at me.

'I'm told you did very well on the bridge, Sir Alan,' he said. 'My compliments. You know how to deal with an enemy, clearly. But how are you at dealing with obstinate townsfolk – or self-righteous churchmen?'

The question confused me momentarily.

'What are you asking of him?' said my lord, with an edge in his voice.

'I know he's your man, Locksley, but I want Sir Alan to clear out the town, send the people away – unless any of the able-bodied young men choose to fight with us – get them to head south, to Boxley Abbey, while there is still time. I want a good man to lead them south and install them with the abbot. They should be safe enough there, under the protection of Holy Mother Church. Thing is, they won't want to go. They must be made to go.'

I understood then what d'Aubigny was asking.

'Would you do it?' Robin asked me.

I shrugged. 'Certainly – but do you not need me here?'

'I have nigh-on a hundred knights,' said d'Aubigny, 'one fellow more or less—' He stopped, fearing he had insulted me: 'Although, of course, we would undoubtedly miss your valour on the walls . . . In truth, there is something else I require you to do. Something important. Once you have shepherded the townspeople safely to Boxley, I want you to ride to London and wait on my lord Fitzwalter. Tell him the King is at Rochester in his full strength and we need him back here as soon as he can arrive.'

'Fitzwalter knows that already,' said Robin.

'Yes, he does. But this is a real chance for victory. If Fitzwalter's army can fall on the King while he is outside these walls, still disorganised and spread out from the march, we can sortie and crush John like a walnut between two stones. I need a trusted man who knows Fitzwalter well, who has his respect, to spur him on. I believe Sir Alan is that man.'

I looked at Robin. 'Will you do it?' he said.

What could I say but yes?

I passed through the great hall on my way to collect my mail, arms and a few necessaries, and looked longingly towards the window on the northern side. I could clearly see the chessboard, the pieces in exactly the same position as Robin and I had left them. It occurred to me that even when you know for certain you are going to win the game, fickle chance can sometimes snatch victory from your grasp.

Robin, Cass and twenty archers came with me as I passed out of the main gatehouse in the curtain wall of the outer bailey. When the huge iron-bound gate boomed shut behind us, I felt a chill of apprehension. It is no pleasant feeling to be locked out of a safe refuge with a vast army bearing down on you. Cass was to accompany me; his knowledge of the county of Kent – even though his family manor was a good twenty-five miles to the south – would prove helpful, Robin had said, as he commended his red-headed squire to my care. My lord had also agreed to help with the townspeople; he had orders from d'Aubigny to seize any food that he could from the town and bring it into the castle.

I made the proclamation from the back of my horse outside the western door of the cathedral. It was not hard to attract a crowd – word of King John's arrival had spread and the streets were thronging with anxious townspeople, chattering and calling questions out to each other. It was a dry, grey day, but with a biting wind that reminded me that winter was no more than a few weeks away. I kept it short – brutally short, you might say. I told them I would be leading all the people who would come with me to

Boxley Abbey, where they would be safe. They were to take only what they could carry. I told them the town must fall to the King's forces and their lives would be in grave danger. They would not be admitted to the castle unless they were willing and able to fight. Then I told them I would be leaving within the hour.

As I made my little speech, I could see Robin's muscular archers already going house to house, turning the occupants into the street, sometimes none too gently, and emerging with arms full of loaves of bread, sacks of grain, smoked hams, cheeses, anything edible they could find and carry away.

There was a good deal of grumbling from the crowd. One pinched-faced man in a red hood shouted that it should be my task to protect them, to defend the town against their enemies and, if I would not do that, to give him sanctuary in the castle. I told him if he wished to enter the castle he should present himself at the gate and enlist as one of Lord d'Aubigny's men-at-arms. He could then take his place among the defenders on the walls. That silenced him.

Some of the cathedral monks echoed Red-hood's plea, saying that we should protect their house of God. It was my clear duty as a Christian knight, one cried. I told him God would surely protect his own, if he saw fit, and that my duty, my lord's command, indeed, was to save as many people as I could from the malice of John's foreign mercenaries.

'King John is almost at your gates,' I said. 'Many of you will have already seen his host from the walls. These are ruthless men. Killers without pity or remorse. The simple truth is that the castle cannot shelter you all *and* hold out against the tyrant. It would be starved into submission in days. Only men who will fight shall be admitted. If you will not or cannot fight, the choice before you is stark. Come with me and live. Or stay and allow your wives to be defiled and your children to be slaughtered before your eyes. You must make that choice now.'

I spoke the truth yet I did not feel entirely comfortable with my words. I knew that it was indeed the duty of the lord of a castle to defend the townspeople – but I have been at sieges where the 'useless mouths', the non-combatant weak, old and sick, have been admitted, and it does not end well for anybody. In all, it truly was better to get these people away from the fighting. As fast as possible.

In the end it was easier than I had feared and less than an hour later, with Cass mounted at my side, I was leading a mob of about two hundred frightened men, women and children down St Margaret's Street, roughly south, along the riverbank. As we passed out of the town gate, I saw Mastin and a pair of his archers on the walls above, outlined against the pale grey sky.

'Bastards are not more than three or four miles away, Sir Alan, best hurry your fucking flock along!' he shouted.

I waved in reply.

Mastin's words were heeded by the folk of Rochester and some began to make more haste. But, as most people had ignored my instruction to bring only what they could carry, we were a snail-paced column with men pushing carts piled with goods, others staggering under huge burdens and some folk even herding pigs, cows and sheep along with them as they walked. One woman was trying to drive a gaggle of geese in front of her, using only a twelve-foot-long ash wand with a rag on the end.

By noon we had put only two miles or so between us and the town, and the column was strung out over several hundred yards. I looked over my left shoulder, to the north-east, and saw that the enemy host was but half a mile from the town walls, and was already spilling out on either side of the road and beginning to seek out places to pitch their tents. If we could see them, they could surely see us.

Cass and I rode back along the column, urging the stragglers to greater speed as we went, and keeping one eye on the King's army. At the rear I stopped to berate a very fat, middle-aged woman who was sitting on a great cloth bundle, breathing like a bellows. Her face was the colour of a ripe cherry and covered with pearls of sweat. Her dog, a mangy black-and-white beast with one eye, started barking at me and snapping at my horse's legs. I was tempted to end the cur and urge the fat besom along with my sword-tip, when Cass called out to me: 'Sir, over there, sir, we have visitors!'

I twisted in the saddle and saw to my dismay a knot of horsemen spurring towards us across the open sheep pasture. Six, no, seven men. Not knights – light armour, no pennants on their spears – but mounted men-at-arms anyway, probably scouts. I cursed. I looked beyond the head of the straggling column to a wood of beech and ash not half a mile to the south, a possible refuge of sorts.

'Orders, sir?' said Cass.

'Christ. Orders, yes.' I could not think what to do. There could be no disguising what the column truly was and, poor as the Rochester folk were, they still had goods and chattels worth plundering. Even if they had not, the King's Flemings might slaughter us just for the joy of it. Cass and I were the only fighting men among this multitude. Two against seven. Not good. Worse, we could not allow the scouts to reconnoitre us and report back to their commander. That would bring down half the King's army on our heads.

'Have to kill them all – every single man,' I muttered under my breath. I hauled out my sword and took a deep breath. 'Can't let them escape.'

'Very good, sir,' said Cass, slipping from his horse. I looked at him in amazement. Why was the squire dismounting? We had a desperate fight on our hands and he should be dragging out that ugly great falchion he always wore and charging the enemy knee to knee with me. Instead he was unhorsed, bent over and fiddling with something I could not see on the other side of his mount's head. Did he expect me to take on seven men alone?

The horsemen were two hundred paces from us now and coming on at the canter. Let them come, I thought. I'd rather fight them here, as far from the King's host as possible. Let them mingle with the column; some of the more able-bodied folk might aid me. I began to consider how on earth I could take on seven men and defeat them all. Robin would have some trick up his sleeve. If I could take the first man unawares, a dagger thrust, perhaps, then maybe the second—

A bow cord thrummed beside me. I saw the flight of the arrow. A black line in the sky. A second followed while the first was still in flight.

I looked at Cass in shock. He had strung his great yew bow and was already drawing and loosing for the third time. I jerked my head round to the knot of cantering horsemen in time to see the first shaft strike. A perfect shot, punching into the chest of the leading rider, knocking him clean out of the saddle. The second arrow transfixed the neck of the horse behind his and I heard the scream of equine pain from a hundred and fifty yards away. The third shaft drove into the face of another man-at-arms – and now all was confusion, the horses rearing, the men shouting in alarm. And still Cass was drawing and loosing. He poured his steel-tipped missiles into them, one after another after another. As one struck, another was in the air and yet another was on the cord. He loosed a dozen arrows in total and I swear he hit a man or mount with every one. I have no doubt he would have continued until they were all dead, had I not seen one of the men, unhorsed, with a bloody fletching sticking from the mail at his ribs, trying to scramble back across the pasture to return to the King's host.

I put spurs to my mount and covered the ground to the enemy in twenty heartbeats. He saw me coming, or felt the pounding of hooves through the turf. As I reached him, he dodged left and I knocked him down with a hard chop from my shield edge. Past him, I wheeled, dug in my spurs, making straight back for him – and he was up again and running, this time in his confusion towards the column of Rochester townsfolk. I closed on him easily. He looked up once as I neared, his face a white terrified blur, and I hacked down with Fidelity, splitting his helmet and the skull beneath, dropping him to the grass in a twitching heap.

I circled back to the bodies of the men skewered by Cass, scattered in a long line along their path of advance. Three of the foes were still alive, bloodied and moaning, some trying to crawl. I killed them all with swift, merciless blows. And when I was certain none had survived I trotted back to our column to find that Cass had managed to get the fat woman up off her bundle and waddling down the road after the rest.

'That was some fine shooting, youngster,' I said to him, breathing heavily after my exertions. 'You saved me a deal of hard labour.'

Cass smiled shyly. 'Thank you, sir,' he said. 'I have been practising since I was a lad. And my lord of Locksley has been kind enough to give me some personal instruction, too. He says I show promise.'

In truth the young man's archery had been nigh-on supernatural but there was no time for flowery compliments.

'I don't believe our little dust-up has yet been observed,' I said, looking over my shoulder, 'but those riderless horses will not go unnoticed for long. We must get the people into that wood yonder as soon as possible.'

'Yes, sir,' said Cass, nodding his red-golden head.

And between us, with much cursing and harrying of the sluggish Rochester folk, with cajolery well mingled with dire threats of bloody violence, we did just that.

Chapter Six

I was astounded to discover that the abbot of Boxley was a man I had known more than twenty years ago. He had undertaken a long and dangerous journey with me in Germany, and between us we had discovered the whereabouts of the captive King Richard and helped to secure his release and return to England. I had been a mere stripling then and even King Richard was now long dead, but the abbot – although become frail and very elderly, and entirely bald but for a few silver wisps of what had been his tonsure – was still hale and whole and delighted to see me, and he remembered our German adventure with startling clarity.

Abbot John welcomed us to Boxley with true Christian kindness late that October afternoon and while I washed the dust of the road off my face and hands, he set his monks to finding nourishment and accommodation for the two hundred and thirty-three Rochester townspeople.

We had had the Devil's own luck on the five-mile journey from the wood outside Rochester to Boxley – or God's mighty hand had shielded us on our pilgrimage to His House, if you prefer – for we got into the trees just in time. As the last of the stragglers entered its bosky sanctuary, I saw two dozen King's cavalry come cantering over the pasture to investigate the dead men-at-arms and their horses standing forlornly beside the bodies.

Cass stood at the edge of the wood, ready to discourage them with his bow if they came too close, but they evidently decided it was a wiser course to loot the bodies of their fallen comrades, collect up the horses and report back to their commanders, than to follow our trail into what might be an archers' trap. I thanked God for it anyway and the rest of the journey was uneventful, despite it taking several hours to travel a distance I could have covered on foot in half that time. We saw no one but a few shepherd boys with their flocks.

Nevertheless, we were now safe at Boxley, and the abbot was insisting I dine with him and tell him everything that had happened to me in the past two decades of my life.

For a man of God, an elderly and doddering one at that, living in seclusion in the tranquil Kent countryside, the abbot had a surprisingly good grasp of the events of the wider world. His table was lavish, too, which I much appreciated after several days of little but greasy mutton broth.

He told me with sadness that the abbot of Robertsbridge, his great friend and our companion on the German adventure, had died a few years ago.

'Alas, he was called far too soon,' my host said solemnly. 'He cannot have been much more than eighty-nine years of age. And yet it seems that God had more need of him than I.'

I commiserated with the abbot and then I told him a little of my exploits over the past twenty years.

'You have seen too much of battle, my young friend,' he said, when I had finished. 'Too much killing hollows out a man, leaves him empty inside, like a dry leather cup. His soul leaves his body and wanders the universe and all that can fill the bodily void is blood and yet more blood. Take care that you do not end up in that condition, my son. Take very great care. I shall pray for you and for your preservation from sin.'

I thanked him and told him that I wished for nothing more than to lay down my sword and be at peace, but my duty to my lord forbade it.

'You could renounce the world, my son – many a fighting man has done it. Why, the abbey here would welcome you as a brother should you choose to embrace the way of Christ and forsake the sword. Or you might look for a House nearer to your home. You could spend the rest of your life in the service of God and perhaps – forgive me if I presume too much – atone for some of the innocent blood you may have spilled.'

For a moment then, just a brief moment, the abbot's offer seemed the most wonderful idea. From that good man's chamber, I could hear the beautiful but haunting chanting of the monks at practice in the church across the courtyard and the skin puckered into tiny bumps on my arms. I took a sip of my friend's fine wine. A life filled with this Heavenly music; a life dedicated to God's love. Why not? So peaceful, so simple, so godly. I'd make an end to all the killing, all the horror, pain and death.

The moment passed. I had been entrusted with a vital mission by my lord and by d'Aubigny. My friends were counting on me and there was my son Robert to consider, too. I could not yet abandon my boy to face the cruelties of this world all alone.

I shook my head. 'Perhaps one day, your grace,' I said. 'Perhaps one day.'

Our talk naturally turned to the war between the barons and the King. The abbot had strong opinions but he adamantly refused to take sides in John's dispute with his rebellious noblemen. Each, he insisted, was as bad as the other.

'I am a man who serves God,' he said. 'Although I believe I am loyal to England as well. I would not help to put another man on the throne.'

'If you are worrying that Lord Fitzwalter seeks the crown, I can assure you I and many other men would prevent that from happening. All we ask is that the King respects and abides by the charter to which he has already agreed and set his seal.'

'I do not fear Fitzwalter's ambitions, prodigious though they undoubtedly are. It's the French I fear.'

'The French?' I said, surprised. 'What have they to do with England?'

'You have not heard?'

I shook my head.

'There is some talk that the rebels are seeking arms and men from the French – perhaps even a small army.'

'What of it?' I said.

'I fear that a French army might seek a suitable recompense for their aid – the throne of England, perhaps.'

I laughed out loud. The notion was absurd. 'My lord Fitzwalter proudly calls himself an English patriot. He would not offer the crown to Philip of France, even if he had it within his gift. No Englishman would – all men, rebel and royalist alike, would take up arms to repel the common enemy.'

'Can you be so sure?' the abbot said.

'I'm certain. Fitzwalter would not do it. And my lord of Locksley would never allow a French tyrant to rule here. Never. And, for that matter, neither would I.'

'Perhaps it is only idle talk, Sir Alan,' said the abbot soothingly, 'mere dairy maids' gossip. Have a little more wine and tell me about your family and your manor – you reside at Westbury, did you not say? Tell me about it.'

'Thank you but no, your grace. I must be away to bed,' I said. 'I am grateful for your hospitality, your prayers and for succouring the people of Rochester in their hour of need, but duty dictates that I ride to London at first light to speak with Lord Fitzwalter.'

*   *   *

Although the walls of London were well manned by disciplined troops, as I clattered over the bridge and rode into the filthy narrow streets of the city, I sensed an air of revelry, wild gaiety, almost outright debauchery everywhere. Many of the citizens I passed appeared to be drunk; others were sleeping in the streets, sprawled like dead men. Slatternly women, lips painted carmine, their abundant breasts spilling out of their chemises, called to me from the upper storeys of the houses, inviting me to spend time with them. Gangs of purple-faced men at the street corners roared and jostled and swilled from wine flasks and tankards. It might have been the aftermath of a great victory, as if we had already triumphed over the enemy – or the opposite, that disaster had fallen, all hope lost and the desperate folk were snatching a few moments of pleasure before perdition.

Cass had pleaded with me the night before to allow him to visit his family home not far from the south coast of Kent. He had heard from one of the Boxley monks that his father was sick, and did not know if he would live long. I allowed him to go, but I gave him instructions to join me in London as soon as he could and, if I had already left with the relief force when he arrived, to make his way back to Rochester. I was grateful to the youngster for his fine shooting in the sheep pastures – he had probably saved my life and the lives of many of the townsfolk – and felt he was more than owed a little time off duty to bring order to his family affairs.

Lord Fitzwalter was to be found in the great hall of the Tower of London. I made my way there and was announced by a herald at the vast double doors. Upon seeing my face, Fitzwalter gave me a friendly, long-armed wave from the centre of a throng of knights, priests and merchants, a dozen yards away. Then a servant quietly told me that his lordship was extremely busy at present and asked with exquisite politeness whether I would prefer to wait for what might be some little while or return the next day. I elected to wait and was shown to a bench by a window, served a cup of wine and told to possess my soul with patience.

I was not the only one waiting for a chance to speak to the great man. There was a young dark-haired fellow, evidently a man of wealth, dressed entirely from top to toe in cream-coloured velvet and silk embroidered with silver stitching. Even his shoes were pure white kidskin. The man was playing with a tiny tortoiseshell kitten in his lap, teasing it with a long white feather, tickling its pink nose and jerking the feather out of the way when the little bundle swiped at it with its miniature claws. He looked up as I sat on the bench a few feet from him, and smiled. His long, lean face was bloodless, white as a lily, and with the same soft yet dense waxy texture as the petals of the flower, as if it had never once seen the light of the sun. His eyes were pale blue, and brilliant, but lacking humour or warmth. They did, however, display a keen curiosity and intelligence. Overall, he seemed to project the impression that he was somehow less – but also more – than completely human: indeed, he had a rather ethereal, angelic quality that was most disturbing, as if his soul were superior in every way to an ordinary mortal's. The friendly smile he offered did nothing to change the blank expression in his chilly blue eyes.

'God's blessings on you, sir,' he murmured in French. This, in itself, was not that significant: many, indeed most members of the English nobility in those years spoke to each other in French. But his accent was strange. It was not the jocular, barrack-room, no-nonsense Norman French spoken by the turbulent knights of England, his silky accent and precise intonation came straight from the perfumed courts of France. Indeed, his voice carried more than a whiff of the great city of Paris itself.

'Sir Alan Dale, knight of Westbury, at your service,' I said in the same language, taking care over my pronunciation and trying, perhaps not very successfully, to echo his sophisticated Parisian style.

'Thomas, Comte du Perche, minister to His Royal Highness King Philip Augustus, at yours,' he said, then extinguished his smile and resumed playing with the kitten, driving it to a tiny frenzy with the feather tip.

So, he was an ambassador from Paris and Fitzwalter *was* either in talks with or contemplating talks with the French about military aid. Well, after what Abbot Boxley had said, it was only to be expected. And, God knew, a few score well-trained, well-armed French knights on our side would be most welcome in the struggle against the King and his legions of brutal Flemish mercenaries.

I looked at the man under my brows. He did not look like much of a fighting man. He was too slim in the shoulder and chest. And his long, pale hands were unscarred – most unusual in a man who wielded a blade with any degree of regularity. My own two fists were criss-crossed with old yellow and white cicatrices, purple lumps and bumps and even a few fresh scabs.

I was contemplating the Frenchman, discreetly assessing him, when he looked up at me suddenly. 'Did you say Dale – or D'Alle?' he asked, his eyes boring into me like beams of blue sunlight.

I was thrown momentarily and began to mumble something about the name being originally French until my father had made it an English name.

He said nothing at all for a good three heartbeats, he just stared at me, appraising me as I had him, and then to my utter surprise he gave a harsh seabird-like cry and looked down at his lap. The top of his thumb on his right hand had a long red scratch in the waxy white skin and a bead of scarlet was welling. The exasperated kitten had clearly become a little too exercised by the Comte's cruel game with the feather and had carelessly scratched its human tormentor.

'Oh, *ma petite*, so you wish to play for real?' murmured the Comte. He grasped the cat's left forepaw in both his long white hands and with a single wrench snapped the limb, breaking the delicate bones as easily as if they were those of a roasted chicken.

The kitten screamed. The lower half of the tiny leg was now bent at an extreme, grotesque angle to the rest of the limb.

'You, sir,' I said, my gut suddenly filled with a boiling rage. 'What in God's name do you think you are playing at?' I was standing, hand on hilt, and I believe I might well have drawn steel and struck the French ambassador down if a black-garbed servant had not been drawn over by the animal's pitiable cries.

'I fear I may have broken your little pussycat,' said the Comte in English, handing the yowling, struggling animal into the astonished hands of the servant. 'Be so good as to have it taken away and given physic, knocked on the head, whatever you think right . . .'

I was a hair away from assaulting this French fellow when I saw that Lord Fitzwalter was at my side. He stared at the mangled kitten, still struggling and wailing in the gently cupped hands of the servant, who now bore it away.

'My dear Comte du Perche,' said Fitzwalter. 'I regret it extremely but I fear I will not have time to indulge in the pleasure of a private conversation with you this day. If you would be so good as to return tomorrow morning, I am sure my fellow knights of the Army of God and I would be more than delighted to receive you. A thousand apologies, of course, but as you can see I am quite overwhelmed at present.'

The Comte had risen to his feet the moment he saw Fitzwalter, and his white and silver clothing seemed to flash like the sun in the dim light of the hall. He bowed low at the captain-general's words and said in French: 'Of course, my dear sir, whenever it suits you. I shall be most delighted to engage with you tomorrow morning, if that is more convenient. I can see that you already have a vast number of grave affairs to vex you.'

The Comte's words were as smooth as his accent, but I did detect a faint flush of pink on his lily-white cheeks, for there could be no mistaking Fitzwalter's rudeness in refusing to speak to the envoy. He had been made to wait for some time for an audience and then been summarily dismissed without it as if he were an insignificant churl rather than the highly bred emissary of one of the most powerful monarchs in Christendom.

'You are most gracious,' said Fitzwalter. 'Tomorrow it shall be, then.'

The Comte bowed again, nodded to me and, whistling to a pair of servants in a similar bright livery to his own, he stalked away, pushing through the crowds towards the big double doors.

'I do not like that fellow,' said Fitzwalter quietly in my ear. 'I do not like him at all. Quite apart from his disgusting casual brutality, there is something very odd, almost uncanny about him, don't you find?'

Fitzwalter's breath, so close to my cheek, reeked of wine. As I looked at the man, I saw that his square face was flushed with drink, although it was not yet noon. He looked strained and exhausted, too, with bags under each eye.

'He comes with promises of aid from King Philip?' I said.

'Empty promises most likely. And after that disgusting display with the kitten, I am inclined to send him straight back to Paris without giving him a moment of my time. But enough of him. What news of Rochester, Sir Alan?' he said. 'The castle cannot have fallen already. Why are you here? Have you deserted your post?'

I bristled at the implication. 'I have not,' I said. 'I come at the command of William d'Aubigny, with a personal message for you.'

'Very well,' said Fitzwalter, and he waved over a servant with a wine jug and sat on the bench. When we had both been served with brimming cups of red wine, had sipped and pledged each other's health, he asked me to deliver my message.

57

'King John has come to Rochester in great force – with at least two and maybe as many as three thousand men.'

'This is as we expected,' said Fitzwalter. 'Continue.'

'They will have almost certainly taken the town by now and I expect they are besetting the castle walls. With such numbers, it cannot be long before Rochester Castle falls. D'Aubigny is well prepared to withstand them but he urges you to come with all speed, with as much strength as you can muster to its relief. Time is of the essence. You must ride to the relief of Rochester as soon as you possibly can.'

'When last I looked,' said Fitzwalter, draining his goblet and setting it on the window ledge, 'I was in command of the Army of God, not d'Aubigny, nor your master Locksley. I – and I alone – will decide what we do and when.'

I was taken aback. 'I meant no disrespect, my lord, but each day will cost us dearly in the blood of good men. The sooner we can come to their relief the better.'

'Rochester is a mighty bastion,' he said. 'If d'Aubigny cannot hold for a day or two without me then I don't know why I entrusted the castle to him in the first place.'

I stared at Fitzwalter. What possible reason could there be for his delay?

He lowered his shoulders and attempted to smile charmingly.

'You must trust me, Sir Alan,' he said. 'I have matters in hand – but we cannot leave London for some days yet. There are important affairs that must be discussed here first, vital concerns that are of greater import than the fate of a single castle.'

I started to protest once more that men were most probably fighting against overwhelming numbers of enemies as we spoke, but Fitzwalter stopped me, almost rudely. 'We cannot leave London now. That is final.'

Then he smiled again. 'Take your ease, my dear Alan, have something to eat; another glass or two of wine will take the edge off your urgency. We will discuss this further tomorrow. Do you have somewhere to stay?'

I said that I would be staying with a friend of my lord's, a wealthy wine importer who had a huge house at Queen's Hythe, on the river.

'Excellent, I know the place well,' he said, slapping my shoulder. 'Now that I come to think of it, tomorrow may be a little difficult for me, but no matter – I will send for you when we are ready to ride. Have faith in me, have faith in our cause, Sir Alan, for God is on our side. It may appear that we are in difficulties at present but I promise you that we shall triumph in the end.'

In the event, I spent a full week kicking my heels in the merchant's house in Queen's Hythe – my host was absent on business in Bordeaux, I was told, but, as Robin's honoured representative, a chamber had been prepared for me and my every comfort was, if not anticipated, then swiftly fulfilled by the dozens of richly dressed servants in the house. After three days I sent a page to the Tower with a message for Fitzwalter, reminding him that with every passing day, it was likely the garrison of Rochester was being further weakened. Good men were dying while we did nothing. The return message a full day later, while filled with flowery phrases and flattery, did nothing more than to urge me to have patience.

During that time, I fretted and twitched and paced the courtyard of the house, and in the lonely evenings I made myself free of the extensive cellar of my host. The debauched spirit of London seemed to have contaminated me as well. And I began to understand it a little better. London had no King, an unnatural and enervating state of affairs. The barons of the Army of God had some temporal power but everyone knew they were not a legitimate authority – and if they were to lose this contest with the King, London would be punished for their sins. The rich merchants would be fined or imprisoned; the poor might well be subjected to the horrors of the sack of the city, if John's mercenaries were let loose:

all the rape, pillage and wanton mayhem that that catastrophe would entail. No wonder so many had been driven to debauchery. I drank deeply, too, to fill the empty hours before bedtime.

However, I did have one valuable meeting towards the end of that week, with a cousin of Robin's, a fat cleric called Henry Odo.

Henry lived in the Priory of St Mary's just across the bridge in Southwark, although he seemed to spend most of his days in London, chatting, eating and drinking with his many friends and acquaintances. He was an effusive fellow, a little quick with a compliment, but Robin relied upon him. And there was no better man if you wanted the latest gossip.

How he knew I was in the city, I never discovered, but that was part of his mystery. One afternoon as I was tending to my horse, giving it a thorough rubdown and singing to it softly, I found him at my elbow.

'Sir Alan,' he said, 'what a great joy to see you again.'

I did not know the man very well but as I was somewhat starved for company in Cass's absence, I greeted him with enthusiasm. I invited him to take supper with me.

Over the evening meal – it was a feast, in truth, for the servants seemed to take great pleasure in providing fine fare and plenty of it – Henry entertained me with scurrilous tales of the doings of the rebel barons in the Tower. The lily-pale French ambassador had whipped a servant to death over some small mistake, Henry told me, and no one knew quite whether he should be censured or the incident overlooked since it was his own man he had killed. That did not surprise me, having seen what he did to a kitten for giving him a tiny scratch. What did surprise me was the news that Fitzwalter had no fewer than three beautiful mistresses and a pretty little Moorish catamite. If that were true, I wondered how he had the time to do anything but rut. No wonder he looked so exhausted.

Henry asked after my lord and the state of the siege at Rochester;

when I had told him all I knew, which was precious little, he asked if I would be returning to my lord's side in the near future.

'I will if I can ever get Fitzwalter to stir himself,' I said grumpily.

'Perhaps you might be kind enough to give Robin a message from me,' Henry said. 'My people in York tell me a force is being raised by the King's loyal men in the north to attack and seize the castles of all the rebel barons and knights in Yorkshire, Derbyshire and Nottinghamshire. Many of them are here in London and their lands are weakly defended. Tell him that no moves have yet been made but that Kirkton Castle was on a list of targets for the King's wrath.'

My blood ran cold.

'Is Westbury on that list?'

'I could not swear to it either way. I have not seen the list. Although, I understand that you have recently built a tower, is that so?'

He really did know everything. I nodded.

'Then I think it would be safe to assume Westbury will be numbered among the other illegal fortifications. Unlicensed castellation is one of the transgressions that the King is particularly keen to stamp out.'

'I will deliver your message to Robin,' I said, 'but will you do me the same kindness and get a message to my household in Nottinghamshire?'

'Of course, Sir Alan,' said this excellent fellow, 'with the greatest of pleasure.'

'Tell my son Robert, and my steward Baldwin, to take all the wealth they can lay their hands on, all the livestock and manor people, and decamp to Robin's castle in Yorkshire. And to go as soon as they can.'

'I will send my swiftest rider in the morning,' said Henry.

I was slightly relieved by his promise. The small garrison at Westbury was much depleted, as I had taken most of the men

61

with me to Rochester, and I knew that the few who remained would not be able to hold out for very long against a determined attack by the sheriff's men. Robert would be much safer under the protection of Robin's eldest son Hugh at Kirkton and the fifty seasoned men-at-arms he had there.

I went to bed that night almost sober and determined that I would confront Lord Fitzwalter in the morning and force him to ride to the relief of my friends. The sooner I could bring relief to Rochester, the sooner I could ride back to the north and protect my son. I would threaten Fitzwalter's life if I absolutely had to. I would give him an ultimatum: ride or die. He must sally out to fight King John.

At Rochester.

Chapter Seven

There was no need for dire threats, for when I attended Lord Fitzwalter at the Tower the next morning, the first thing he said to me was: 'I have done it, Sir Alan, I have triumphed. I have persuaded the barons that we must support William d'Aubigny and the Earl of Locksley with all our strength.'

Having been running over in my mind all the things I was going to say to force him on this very course, I was much taken aback. But I smiled and congratulated Fitzwalter on his success.

'When do we leave, sir?' I said.

'Tomorrow,' he said. 'St Crispin's Day. We muster here at dawn. Seven hundred knights and mounted men-at-arms. A sizeable force, I hope you will agree.'

I did. If we had the element of surprise we could fall on King John's army while it was engaged with the siege and if it could be combined with a massive sortie from the castle, and a slice of good luck, we could indeed crush King John, as d'Aubigny had so neatly put it, like a walnut between two stones.

A force of seven hundred knights and men-at-arms takes a good deal of organising. The horses require fodder and horseshoes, and farriers to fit the shoes; the knights need their servants and baggage carts and mules loaded with piles of food and wine; there are mistresses too (and no doubt Moorish catamites) and their maids, and any number of other women – cooks, seamstresses, washer-women, whores – for the lesser fighting men. And to my frustration there seemed to be no kind of urgency. Dawn, Fitzwalter had said, but by the time the Army of God had assembled it was nearly noon and by mid-afternoon the lumbering column had reached only as far as the dull, rough scrubland of the Black Heath south-east of the city, less than a third of the distance we had to travel. Here Fitzwalter decided to call a halt for the night, to my exquisite fury. And though I begged him to make a few more miles that day, he calmly told me the column had to stay together, for the forces of William Longsword, the Earl of Salisbury, King John's loyal half-brother, were lurking somewhere to the south, and the Army of God must not straggle for safety's sake and therefore travel at the speed of the slowest ox-cart.

I was in a foul mood that night for another reason. I had received a message from Cass – his father was on the point of death and he begged to stay with him in his final days to be with him when he was gathered unto God, to bury him like a Christian, and to deal with certain affairs concerning the manor of Cassingham that Cass would inherit. If it had been another man, I might have suspected him of shirking but having seen him so confident in action I could not imagine that he was craven. So I was alone, among the crowds of the Army of God, the revelling barons and their shiny whores. I ate a solitary supper, wrapped myself in my cloak and went to sleep under a thorn tree in a short but drenching shower of rain.

We made better progress the next day, reaching the manor of Dartford and a crossing of the River Darent about three miles south of the Thames. We camped again that night and I brought myself to Fitzwalter's tent at sundown, hoping once more to spur the commander of the Army of God to greater speed. I had been away from Rochester for nearly two weeks and, for all I knew, the castle might have fallen and all my friends might be dead or captured. With the end of October in sight, winter and the close of the campaigning season was upon us. Already the road we travelled, Watling Street, built by those ancient engineers from Rome, was becoming hardly more than a boggy mire in the places where the big flat stones had been stolen, a serious obstacle for the awkward ox-carts, even the handcarts, to negotiate.

Fitzwalter's tent was crowded with knights and barons, a dozen big men in mail and bright flowing cloaks. As I pushed in among them, I saw they were all surrounding and listening intently to a mud-splattered, rake-thin man in a raggedy, much-patched cloak, who seemed to be rather skittish in such exalted company.

'. . . as far as the eye can see, my lords. I do not exaggerate. I . . . I . . . I swear it on the Virgin. The road to Dover is humming with men, a dozen companies of at least a hundred footmen each, I saw. And horsemen, too. I saw some five *conrois* of fine knights pass my hiding place in a span of half a day, foreigners by their speech.'

'And these had not yet reached Rochester?' said a bull-necked knight, who tugged nervously at his blond beard.

'The first troops were a dozen miles from the town, at the manor of Sidyingbourne, your lordship, yet they were spurring onwards in terrible haste.'

'I think we have heard enough,' said Fitzwalter. 'My thanks, Guilliam, the cooks are by the horse lines, they will find you something to eat. Here!' He tossed a small purse to the muddy wretch, who seized it in the air and slithered through the throng and out of the tent.

The man's exit unleashed a storm of conversation, almost every knight talking at once, arguing with his neighbour.

'Gentlemen, gentlemen, quiet, please,' said Fitzwalter. And when a partial hush had fallen: 'It is quite clear what we must do. It seems the King has been significantly reinforced. We have no hope against these fresh forces combined with the men he already has at Rochester. We must return to London at once.'

The hullabaloo returned with greater force, each man now shouting his opinion.

I shoved my way through to Fitzwalter's side. 'You cannot do this, sir,' I said, and felt my face flushing with anger. 'You must not do this. The men at Rochester are counting on you coming. My lord of Locksley—'

'You heard the wretched fellow, Sir Alan,' he said, irritated. 'Even if he is making more of the matter than he should, as spies will do, John has clearly been reinforced by perhaps as many as a thousand men. This is not the first report of this that I have heard. We have no chance against the King at Rochester.'

'That is not so,' I was shouting too by now. 'We have surprise on our side. If we march all night and attack tomorrow, before they know we are there, we can drive them from the walls in utter confusion and—'

Every man in the tent was staring at me. Fitzwalter's tired face was the colour of a peeled beetroot. 'You forget yourself, sir. I am commander of this army. And I say that we must retreat in the face of superior numbers.'

'I say we cannot leave the men in the castle to die!' I think I may even have clutched at the collar of Fitzwalter's mantel in my passion. 'You must find the courage to go on, sir. A swift march, a dawn attack—'

'You would do well not to question my courage, sir,' said Fitzwalter, pulling his cloak free from my grasp. 'I will hear no more of your wild talk. I command here. Not you. And I command you to quiet yourself and leave my tent this instant.'

'Sir, those men in Rochester are my friends. Yours, too.' I was trying to be reasonable, trying to find some lever that would move him. 'They are loyal men of the Army of God. And you gave your solemn word that—'

'Get him out of here,' Fitzwalter said to someone beyond my shoulder and before I knew what was happening, a powerful grip shackled my chest and my thighs. My feet left the ground and I was bundled like a bag of dirty laundry out of the tent by two huge knights.

Outside the flap, I picked myself up – a pair of guards levelled their spears at me, while the two knights who had ejected me growled a warning, hands on their hilts. A dozen biting phrases came to my lips. I wanted to haul out Fidelity and throw myself at all of them. But it would have been useless and I knew it. So I said nothing; did nothing. I stumbled away, sightless, on unsteady feet, with a black cloud of despair descending. My task had been to bring Fitzwalter and his army to the relief of Rochester Castle and the salvation of my friends. My friends who were now trapped inside with several thousand of King John's men around their walls.

I had failed.

Chapter Eight

I wept then in sorrow for myself and my friends as I wandered through the camp back to my horse. I leaned my head against its warm flank and the tears ran down my cheeks. I could not for the life of me think what to do. I could not move Fitzwalter, I could not force this army to march. I did not wish to return to London and my lonely lodgings. I had half a mind to ride for the north to be with my son Robert and guard him if the King's men attacked Westbury or Kirkton. But it would have felt like desertion. I could not just go home. I have rarely felt so directionless – but the plain truth was that my lord, Miles, Thomas, Mastin, the Westbury men, William d'Aubigny and all the good knights in Rochester were counting on me to come to their aid with a relief force, and I had failed.

I have found that sometimes, when one is mired in despair, it is better to do something, anything, rather than to do nothing. So I slowly climbed on to the back of my mount and threaded my way through the camp. Even now, at dusk, it was stirring itself to leave, with servants bustling about, knights calling their squires, all seemingly eager to return to their debauchery behind the walls of London. I walked the horse over the shallow ford across the Darent and spurred out the other side in the growing dark.

When neither I nor my beast could see, I tied the animal to an oak tree, just off the main road, and sat with my back to its rough trunk to think. It seemed the very least I could do was return to Robin and report this catastrophe; the garrison must be told that no help would be coming from London. And, to my surprise, I found a glimmer of hope in that. The usual conventions of war allowed a garrison that had no hope of relief to surrender with honour to a besieging force. Perhaps some deal could be struck; perhaps, if we renewed our homage to the King, swore to be his loyal men once more, we would be allowed to depart with our arms and return to our homes. In truth, I longed for peace, for Westbury, Robert and my own hearth. With that pleasant thought in my head, I fell asleep.

The next morning, after breaking my fast with a heel of almost-stale bread from my saddlebag and a drink from a nearby brook, I set out once again: but not for Rochester. I pointed my horse's head more to the south and began to make my way through the lush pasturelands below the Thames towards Boxley Abbey. I saw a few bands of mounted men from time to time, King's mercenaries out foraging no doubt, but managed to avoid them, dismounting behind hedges and spurring into small copses till they passed. I crossed the Medway at Aylesford and took the last miles to Boxley at a canter.

I reached the abbey that afternoon after a hard ride in the midst of a driving rainstorm, my horse and I just about as miserable and wet as we could be.

But the abbot's welcome was once again as warm as a mother's embrace. The abbey was still crowded with the townspeople from Rochester: almost every space conceivable seemed to contain a ragged family group. The church was filled to overflowing, the stables, even the rafters of the main barn had been planked over to form a high sleeping space beneath the roof. Nevertheless, the abbot was pleased to see me and fed me hot bean stew and listened with compassion to my tale of woe.

'I applaud your mission,' he said finally, 'and you shall have all the help I can give. The sooner that peace is made with the King, the sooner these poor people can go home and pick up their lives again – and I do not speak purely from self-interest, although they do eat like hogs. God's love is peace and our kingdom must not be subjected to the ravages of war if it can possibly be prevented.'

I asked him a boon then. I wished him to hold my baggage, my armour and helm, my sword and my horse, for I knew I could not take them in the task at hand. Even so, I was loath to leave Fidelity in another man's hands.

'I mean to enter the castle by stealth,' I said. 'And if I approach arrayed for war, John's men will kill me before I can deliver my message.'

'God will guide your path, my son,' the abbot said.

I spent much of the next day sleeping, and in the afternoon spoke to some of the townspeople, gleaning their intimate knowledge of the area and what they knew about the dispositions of the King's forces. In the evening, having bid farewell to the abbot, and dressed in dark hose and tunic, a long black countryman's cloak and hood, I set off on foot for Rochester.

Perhaps God really did guide my path for it was a bright and cloudless night, with a three-quarter moon that gave ample light to see the road before me. On the way, I ran over what I would say to Robin and d'Aubigny, when – if – I managed to find a way into the besieged castle. There was no joy in the message, all I could do was counsel immediate surrender. And I was dreading the prospect of admitting the failure of my mission and advancing such a dispiriting conclusion.

Not long after midnight I found myself in the same small wood that had sheltered the townspeople on our escape two weeks before. As I peered into the darkness from the edge of the trees, I could see the campfires of King John's army spread out before the walls – thousands of tiny pinpricks of orange light, like sparks from a bonfire, in a great sweep to the south of the castle and curling away eastwards. There was light too glimmering from the town itself, which I assumed meant that it was now occupied by the enemy. The spy had been correct: the forces arrayed against the castle had swollen from their original numbers. But some of the townspeople, those bold enough to venture to Rochester and steal a glimpse of the enemy host, had told me that the King's army was mainly to the south and east. North and west of the castle, where the river curved round close to the walls of the outer bailey, was largely free of enemy troops. That made sense. Any King's man between the walls and the river would be in easy range of a bowman on the walls, and with the bridge destroyed, there could be little chance of a relief force coming from that direction.

I headed due north towards the river, keeping low and watching carefully for any sign of life. Although I had left my sword and mail with Abbot Boxley, I was not completely unarmed. A long, thin blade in a black leather sheath was strapped to my left forearm. It was a misericorde, a dagger for close-quarter killing, and very lethal in the right hands; yet it was covered by the sleeve of my tunic and would not betray me as a fighting man, unless I was captured and searched. I loved that weapon – I can find no other word for it but love – it was sleekly beautiful and made entirely of oiled black steel in a cruciform shape, with a razor-like cutting edge and a needle point that could easily punch through the links of iron mail. The handle was a series of rounded cubes that fitted snugly into my right hand. It had been given to me by Lord Fitzwalter himself and while the very thought of the man, his treachery towards my comrades, the breaking of his solemn word, made my blood seethe, the touch of the cool steel against the skin of my wrist and its gentle weight on my arm gave me both the courage and strength to continue.

The river was a dark snake before me, moonlight reflecting from the gentle ripples like a thousand silver scales, and I could see no sign of life on either bank, except for several hundred yards up to my right, where a dozen camp fires glowed. Suppressing a shiver, I slid down the muddy bank and with as little noise as possible, lowered myself into the water.

God it was cold. The water soaked through my woollen clothes, weighing me down, sheathing me with its chill. I dipped my head under and smoothed the hood over my head and shoulders. I smeared a handful of foul-smelling mud across my face to darken my pale skin, then began to swim across to the far bank. I wanted to be as far from the campfires as possible.

The swimming was surprisingly easy, for the current carried me naturally down towards the sea, and I lay on my back and made only a few strokes from time to time to keep close to the northern shore. As I passed the encampments of the enemy, I turned on my front, keeping my head low, only my nose above the water line, and watched the blundering of black shapes around the tents and heard the low laughter of sleepy men-at-arms and a snatch of a peasant song in Flemish. I saw the flare of light as a man threw a billet of wood on the fire. I drifted silently and safely past. My whole body was numb with the cold; it ate into my marrow and knotted the muscles of my back. I would have given a fat purse of silver, just then, to be sitting by that blaze, passing a jug of warmed ale, gnawing on a mutton chop and joshing merrily with my comrades.

But my comrades were behind the tall shadowy walls, inside the great stone bulk of the keep that I could clearly see grey on grey in the moonlight, with, yes, little bars of jolly yellow candle-light beaming from the arrow slits. The bridge, what remained of it, was up ahead, ghostly ruins with a few stark uptilted timbers like accusing fingers pointing at the night sky. I swam a dozen swift strokes to the southern bank, fighting the tugging current that would have swept me past, and pulled myself on to a spit of muddy shingle. I lay there quiet for a dozen heartbeats, listening, watching, as my body began to shake involuntarily and my teeth clashed wildly in my head. Something splashed in the water behind me, a leaping fish or a night-hunting owl. I waited for a count of twenty, then stood fully upright.

The wall of the outer bailey was forty yards in front at the top of a steep grassy slope. I saw the shadow of a sentry pass along the walkway. I considered trying to scale that wall but it occurred to me that I would most likely get a crossbow bolt in the eye for my pains, if I were seen. And the main gatehouse, the barbican, was up ahead, over a hump of land, beyond my view. If I could attract the attention of a sergeant, someone with a scrap of wit, I could identify myself and – I hoped, I prayed to God – merely knock at the small door inset in the massive gates and be admitted. That was the plan, anyway.

I scrambled up the slight rise of the shoulder of land and looked down on to the flattish section of turf between the northern gatehouse and the ruins of the bridge. I could clearly see the barbican, one of two heavily fortified entrances to the outer bailey of the castle, and the light coming from the arrow slits above the heavy doors. I began to slither down the other side, and stopped. Something was very wrong.

On the stretch of scrubby land between the walls and the river I could see a square black shape that I swear had not been there before. And I could hear the murmur of voices. Indistinct, but English-sounding. Surely the men in the castle could not have built a barn or a stable outside the walls? That would be madness. A doorway opened inwards into the black structure and I saw a man emerge, black against the red brazier light. He turned and said something to someone behind him, a jest evidently, as the response was laughter. It was not English, however it sounded. It was Flemish. All fell into place: this was a guard hut constructed by the enemy as a shelter from arrows and bolts from the castle to allow a section of men to watch the barbican and the ruins of the bridge unmolested.

I was squatting near the foot of the shoulder of land, just ten yards from the hut, and the fellow was coming towards me, his steps blundering and uncertain in the darkness. I tucked my head between my knees, my right hand slipping into my left sleeve, and trusted to my dark hood and cloak and my stillness to hide me. The fellow was singing softly to himself. My heart was hammering against my ribs, banging out the familiar rhythm of the moments before combat. I dared not breathe. He walked right past me, not five yards away and headed to the river, his boots crunching on the shingle. There, he proceeded to fumble in his hose and then release a happy sigh and a stream of urine that tinkled merrily into the water.

Should I wait till he returned to his friends and try to slip past? No, I would have to call out to the barbican in order to be admitted, perhaps loudly enough to rouse the guard. I would certainly be heard in the hut. If I were not allowed into the castle swiftly, I would be caught between the walls and my enemies. How many men would be in the guard hut? Not many. Two, three? No more surely?

The decision was made.

I stood tall. Ten swift, quiet paces took me to a spot just behind the man's back. He was still happily pissing away and singing softly. I snaked my left hand around his head, slapped my palm over his mouth and, in the very same instant, shoved the misericorde's needle point into the hollow at the base of his skull, just above the spine. He tried to cry out but the sound was muffled by my gripping left hand. His whole body spasmed, arms and legs flailing. I ground the blade, left, right, inside the cavity of his skull and he went completely loose and then I was supporting his whole weight with only my grip on his head. I lowered him as quietly as I could to the muddy riverbank, pulled the misericorde free of his skull and wiped the mess on his tunic. I glanced quickly behind me at the hut.

The door was closed. A dead man lay at my feet. There was no other way to go but onward.

I slipped the long sword from the sheath at the dead man's waist – a good ordinary blade, not up to Fidelity's standard, but perfectly serviceable – and strode over to the hut, misericorde in my left hand, borrowed weapon in my right.

The door opened to one determined blow of my right foot – and I was inside. A blaze of light seared my night-wide eyes. But I could just make out five men: two asleep on low cots on either side of the space, three seated on stools in the centre around a brazier glowing cherry red. They were slow to react. Gaping at me like cretins, not even giving a shout of alarm before I was on them. I booted the brazier over, dumping its red coals into the lap of the man to my left, at the same time my sword licked out and punched into the belly of the right-hand man. The one in the centre jumped towards me . . . and as he came forward he received the misericorde, a round-arm blow, smack in his left eye. Two men down. I pulled both blades free. The fellow on the left was screaming, scooping burning coals from his tunic and hose with his bare hands. The stink of seared flesh filled the hut. I ended the fellow's pain by splitting his skull with the sword, a single downward chop.

I heard a roar behind me. The man on the cot had seized up a wicked-looking axe and was coming at me swinging. I ducked and swept at the back of his left knee with the borrowed sword, and left him sprawled, cursing and bloody on the floor. The fifth man on the cot on the other side of the room was only now awakening. He lifted his head from the pillow and frowned at me stupidly –

75

and died. I flipped the grip on the misericorde, stepped in and slammed it into the middle of his chest, a hammer blow that pinned him to his bed. He gurgled, coughed blood and lay still. The axe man was still moving, scrabbling across the floor to reach his long-handled weapon, shouting out with pain from his ripped leg tendons. I tugged the misericorde free of the dead man's ribs, stepped over to the axe man, pinned his out-reaching wrist with my boot, and thrust down hard into his back with the point of the sword.

Five men – all down within the space of a dozen heartbeats.

And Miles had called me an old man!

I was panting though, heart bumping manically against my ribs, and my hands were trembling wildly. I stood dripping in the middle of the hut, a red blade in each hand, looking at what I had wrought. The joy of victory coursed through my veins, as intoxicating as hot, strong wine. The belly-stabbed man, still on his stool and folded over his lethal wound, groaned. I stepped behind him and sliced through the fat artery at the side of his neck with my misericorde. The mercy strike. The blood pumped and pulsed, splattering my soaking tunic. He slid from the stool into a heap on the floor.

I was alive – as filled with bounding life as an eighteen-year-old. Five of my enemies were dead at my feet. With a sixth outside by the river. I lifted both bloody weapons high in the air and felt the spirits of a thousand dead English warriors nod and grunt their approval, their shades no doubt summoned by the smell of fresh blood. But this was no time to relish my triumph. Above the stink of gore and piss, old ale, stale farts and singed flesh, I could smell smoke. A pile of dirty linen, ignited by the spilled brazier, was smouldering in the corner of the room, red flames beginning to lick up the walls.

Time to go.

I snatched up a shield by the door as I left. And, weapons wiped and sheathed, I edged along the side of the hut, its bulk between me and the barbican. With my back pressed against the wall, I peered out at the gatehouse. The shouts and screams of the six men I had dispatched had not gone unnoticed on the castle walls. I could see many men moving on the battlements; shouted commands and torches flaring.

Already the wood at my back was growing warm.

I cautiously stepped out, away from the hut. Shield high. A bow twanged. An arrow smashed into the wall next to my ear.

'I'm a friend,' I shouted. 'A friend. Stop shooting, for God's sake.'

Silence from the bulk of the barbican.

'I'm coming forward,' I shouted again. 'Don't loose your bows.'

'Who are you?' came a voice from the darkness. A voice I recognised.

'I'm Sir Alan Dale – alone. In God's name, don't shoot.'

I took a few steps towards the walls.

'Come into the light where I can see you. Sir Alan – fuck me sideways with an overgrown marrow – it is you!'

'Maybe later, my friend,' I said, stifling a madman's cackle, 'I am a little too cold, wet and exhausted for that sort of caper.'

It was Mastin.

Chapter Nine

An hour later, warm, dry and spooning down a big bowl of hot mutton broth – it tasted heavenly after the night's exertions – I gave Robin the news from Cousin Henry about the list of targets the King planned to attack in the north, that Kirkton was likely to be besieged. I had already told him Fitzwalter would not be coming to our rescue and he had absorbed the information silently but with no great air of surprise, or so it seemed to me.

'That's Hugh's problem,' he said. 'There is nothing we can do from inside here. Kirkton is strong and there are enough men there to keep out all but a proper royal army with siege engines. You were wise to send Robert and your Westbury folk there, Alan,' he said. 'They will be quite safe, I am sure. And by the way, it is good to have you back with us, with or without the Army of God.'

There was a faint note of disdain in his voice when he mentioned the grandiose name of Fitzwalter's force, but it was his only hint of emotion.

'If we surrender to the King swiftly, there will be no danger to Kirkton or our people,' I said.

'We will put it to d'Aubigny this morning,' my lord said, 'but I do not think it likely.'

The soup was warm in my belly. My eyelids were leaden and my limbs submitted to the lassitude that comes with combat's blessed end. I fell asleep pondering Robin's words.

I reported to William d'Aubigny, lord of Rochester Castle, on the same south tower in the keep from which he had dispatched me just over two weeks before. He listened in silence, his tawny brown eyes searching my face as if to ensure that I spoke the truth. I say in silence, for he did not speak till I was finished, but my report was punctuated every so often by the ominous crack of stone on stone. And when I looked beyond him over the occupied town of Rochester, I could see that King John had not been idle in my absence.

To our right, to the west, on a patch of rising ground called Boley Hill, no fewer than five huge siege engines had been set up in a semicircle, just out of bowshot, all being served by scores of leather-clad men in dark cloth caps. The engines, known as trebuchets, were vast catapults that hurled great stones, some as heavy as three hundred pounds in weight, from a leather sling attached to a long timber arm. They were slow to load, for the arms had to be drawn back by many ropes pulled by human muscle power alone to raise the great semi-circular counterweight at the front of the engine. Then a round missile the size of a large sheep was rolled on to the leather sling spread out flat on the ground behind the machine. When all was secure, the trigger mechanism was released, the counterweight dropped and the arm sprung upwards, hauling the sling behind it, and hurling the stone up in a giant arc to shatter against the masonry of the wall of the outer bailey.

The trebuchets had obviously been active for some time, for they were all well aimed and briskly served by the engineers and their servants, and each missile crashed more or less against the same target: a square, squat tower in the wall of the outer bailey almost directly below our position. I could see cracks in the curtain wall where the missiles had struck. The pounding from the five engines was slow but relentless. It would serve its purpose.

I tore my eyes from our crumbling outer defences and tried to concentrate on what d'Aubigny was saying.

'. . . they were mostly townspeople, those who were too stubborn or too bloody stupid to go with you to Boxley. Many were sick, old and feeble, and some of our wounded went with them. I was certain that even John would not harm them, as they came out under a flag of truce. But our so-called King, that black-hearted bastard, had a platform set up before the cathedral and every man – and woman and child – that we sent out was seized and held down by his mercenaries and . . .' the burly lord swallowed, hesitating, '. . . and each one had both hands and both feet hacked clean from their living bodies.'

I stared at d'Aubigny. I felt suddenly ill, my stomach moving like the wild sea.

'Thirty-seven unarmed folk maimed in a morning. Cut up before our very eyes like so much meat at a shambles. And for what? So that this monstrous King can demonstrate to us that he is serious about punishing those who defy him.'

I could taste last night's greasy mutton soup, sour at the back of my throat.

'That would doubtless be our fate, if we were to fall into the King's hands,' said d'Aubigny. 'Even under a flag of truce.'

'You see, Alan, surrender is not an option,' said Robin.

D'Aubigny left us a few moments later, and Robin and I stared out over the town below. I could see that while a goodly number of the houses had been burned to the ground, some efforts had been made to stamp out the fire. And many dwellings, shops and warehouses remained. There were rough-looking men in mail and leather armour strolling along the high street. The cathedral's doors were wide open and a constant stream of men was heading in and out – some of them leading horses. I blinked in shock. He is using this venerable House of God as a common stables, I thought. His cavalry mounts are shitting and pissing in the space where generations have offered up their earnest prayers. Is there no end to his depravity?

'How long will the outer walls hold?' I asked Robin.

'A week, maybe two, at most,' said my lord.

A stone, perhaps lighter than the others, flew right over the outer bailey wall and crashed to pieces against the lower part of the keep. I flinched.

'But it's not the trebuchets that concern me the most. See there!' Robin pointed to a low wooden structure, a plain box about the size of a villein's cottage, on the sloping ground due south of us, behind and a little to the left of the siege engines and about three hundred yards away. It looked innocuous. I knew it was not. As I watched, a pair of burly men with long-handled shovels over their shoulders, as small as a child's toys at that distance, came out of the mouth of the box, chatting casually to each other.

'They are mining the walls?' I said. 'Already?'

'John wants this castle – and as fast as possible. Winter is coming, Alan, and though his men are snug in the town, you know what happens when an army stays in one place too long. So, yes, he's already mining under our walls.'

I did know. Disease seemed to hover about all large gatherings of men, although no man could say why. An army that stayed put for some months could lose a third of its strength to the bloody flux, slowly bleeding their lives away through their ever-running arseholes, without the besieged enemy even raising a blade to them.

'Christ,' I said, letting out a long breath. 'He has overwhelming force; we cannot surrender; and he will have battered apart or undermined our walls in a week or two. We are all dead men.'

'You should have stayed in London, Alan,' said Robin. But then he favoured me with a grim smile. 'Come on, old friend, we're

81

not dead quite yet. What do you say to a cup of wine and game of chess?'

The wine was sour and well-watered to make it go further, and I was trapped and soundly beaten on the chessboard by Robin in a shamefully short time. In truth I could not concentrate. Even in the great hall, the noise of the trebuchets battering the outer bailey was a constant irritation, alarming, jarring, a pounding pulse that counted down to our doom. Robin, damn him, was thoroughly cheerful as he destroyed me in the second game we played, too. When the bell rang for dinner and all the knights who were not on duty gathered at the long trestle table in the second part of the divided hall by the big wall-set fire, I had another unpleasant shock, for the meal we sat down to was as meagre as any I have eaten: a watery stew of carrots and onions, a few slivers of cheese, rough maslin bread that seemed to be half sawdust and more of the sour wine.

'Oh,' said Robin casually, when I mentioned it, 'we have almost run through the stores since you've been gone. They are down to the bottom of the barrels in the granary. We never had the resupply that your friend Fitzwalter promised us. We'll be eating rats and sparrows before long, and we'll be grateful to have them.'

I remembered a great siege in Normandy that Robin and I had endured more than ten years ago, and shuddered. I had been worn down to skin and bones and towards the end of that affair we had subsisted on a watery concoction of old bones, spiders, beetles, moss, uncured leather, anything we could boil up for some scrap of nourishment.

'So do you think we will starve to death first,' I asked Robin, 'or be slaughtered by the King's mercenaries when the castle is no more than a heap of smoking rubble?'

Robin actually laughed. 'That's the spirit, Alan. Keep up these merry, thigh-slapping jests and we will never have to worry about becoming downhearted.'

I opened my mouth to say something cutting – and then closed it. What was the point? We would fight; we would do our duty as men, as knights – I had no doubts about that – and then we would die. No doubts there either.

After dinner was done, I found myself standing beside Osbert Giffard, a bald, middle-aged knight I knew slightly, by the fireplace in the south-western half of the hall. He was staring into the flames with a gloomy expression on his long face, which was scarcely surprising; I doubt my own mien was a picture of joy. He grunted an offhand greeting, looked again at my face and appeared to recall something.

'Am I right in thinking that you were at Château Gaillard, Sir Alan, during the great siege . . . oh, it must be eleven years ago?'

I admitted it.

'So you know what we can expect here then.'

'Yes,' I said, 'I wish I did not. It will go hard for us.'

He nodded. 'A cousin of mine was at Château Gaillard,' he said. 'He said it was very bad. Though he managed to survive it. He's dead now, of course. Murdered by some brigands in the north, we were told.'

I said nothing for a while, but I found my hand was resting lightly on my sword hilt. I was almost certain he was referring to Sir Joscelyn Giffard, who had been with me at Château Gaillard. Tilda's father. Shortly after the siege, I had killed him in a duel, man to man. But, if Sir Osbert did not know this, I was not about to tell him that I had slain one of his kinsmen. His remarks put Tilda into my mind. I wondered if she was still sitting under the willow by the stream at Westbury, forlorn, destitute.

I said, as casually as I could, 'Sir Joscelyn had a pretty daughter, I recall. Do you know what became of her after her father died?'

He gave a snort of derision. 'Oh yes, Matilda. A slut. Quite the little whore. She was betrothed to Henry, my eldest, but she set out to seduce my second son William when he was just fourteen. She can't have been much older than my boy at the time. My wife Sarah caught them at it, going like a pair of stoats in one of the barns on the estate. Caused no end of trouble between my two boys. Sarah sent Matilda packing, straight back to her father quick as thought, you may be sure of that.'

Even though I knew it to be true, I resented hearing Tilda called a whore by this priggish old baldicoot. There was no reason to fall out with him over a woman who had sought my destruction but, nevertheless, it rankled.

'What happened to the girl when her father was gone?'

'Joscelyn always said he would put her away in a nunnery, get the Church to beat the sin out of her. She's probably singing psalms and praising Jesus in some chilly cloister about now. Who cares, anyway. She was no good, that one, and her father wasn't much better, if you ask me. Never trusted him. Good riddance to both of 'em.'

'So you would not find a place for her in your household, if she came to you now, say, in some kind of trouble?'

'God, no. Sarah would never allow it. She is a bad apple, Matilda. Let the Church keep her, do what it will with her, so long as she's kept away from my door.'

I do not know why I had continued to pursue my questions with Sir Osbert – some bizarre feeling of guilt maybe, because I had shunned Tilda when she came to me in need. In a confused way, I may have felt that I should at least try to find her somewhere to lodge, and this cousin of her father's had seemed an appropriate person to ask. But it was quite clear that even her family would have nothing to do with her. From my own experience of the woman, I concluded that they were wise. I vowed to put Tilda from my mind. Her troubles were not mine, her future not my concern, and like Sir Osbert, I should endeavour to keep her away from my family at all costs.

Over the next few days, d'Aubigny set me to work. He gave me command of a *conroi* of knights – unhorsed, of course, as there is little call for a cavalry charge inside a castle's walls – thirty-two good men, many of them younger, stronger and fitter than I, and most of much more illustrious parentage, but under my authority nonetheless. Sir Thomas and Miles were my lieutenants – although I was slightly worried about the reliability of Miles, who according to his father was growing increasingly bored by confinement within our battered walls – and I was given the whole of the southern half of the outer bailey to defend, some two hundred yards of wall in the shape of a wide V, with its square south tower at the point of the V, the main gatehouse at the eastern end and the muddy beach at the River Medway at the western. It was a goodly stretch of the defences to watch with only a handful of knights, but most of them had servants, pages, squires and common men-at-arms in their retinue so, in fact, including a handful of my Westbury men, I had near a hundred under my command.

I gave half to Sir Thomas and posted them to the western wall, and my half looked after the eastern stretch between the main gatehouse and the south tower. I emptied the tower of men by day – a controversial order that had d'Aubigny knitting his eyebrows when I reported to him in the great hall at the end of my long, exhausting first stint on duty. He was seated at the table with one of his clerks examining a parchment roll that listed the remaining stores. He saw my approach, dismissed the clerk and nodded at me pleasantly.

I told him of my plan and he frowned and said: 'Why?'

'The outer bailey's south tower is the target of the full force of the enemy artillery,' I said. 'It is not so difficult to divine that they mean to make a breach there and attack it with overwhelming force. And there is nothing we can do to stop the trebuchet battering, except perhaps to sally out and try to kill the engineers and burn the siege machines. But I am told you've forbidden any of our men to make sorties.'

'No attacks outside the walls,' said d'Aubigny. 'I'm not wasting men's lives in daredevil adventures that will likely achieve almost nothing. Even if you drove off the guards and burned the machines, the King has the resources and men to build more in a few days.'

'I understand that,' I said. 'Neither do I wish to waste men's lives. But only this morning one man was killed inside the south tower and another two were injured on the walls by flying splinters of stone. Three casualties in a couple of hours. I need those men for when the tower falls and a breach is opened.'

D'Aubigny said: 'You plan to sit idly by while they knock a hole in my walls?'

'Not idly. The trebuchet barrage ceases at dusk, when my men and I will go into the tower and with the help of the castle's carpenters and masons we will do whatever we can to shore up the damage and strengthen the walls. But that tower will fall. The only uncertainty is when. By day, my men, on either side of the tower, clear of the flying shards, will wait and watch for a breach. When that happens we will plug the gap with our bodies and hurl the enemy back. I need every man fit and ready for that hour. That is the moment of greatest peril. If we can stop them, hold them, keep them out till nightfall, the masons may be able to repair the breach overnight. They will have achieved nothing for their pains.'

'You will have to be alert and quick off the mark, when it happens. You know the King's men will be swarming into that hole the moment it is opened.'

'We will be ready,' I said.

'Good,' said d'Aubigny. 'Yes, very good, Sir Alan. I'm allocating you another ten knights to strengthen your numbers. Sir George Farnham and his Surrey men will report to you at dawn. That will be all.'

He dismissed me and looked back down at the parchment roll.

'Sir, might I ask something?'

'What is it?'

'Some of the men have been asking what our strategy is – and I do not know what to tell them.'

'You may tell them our strategy is to defeat King John here at Rochester, teach him a lesson, force him to reissue the great charter and bring peace to England.'

'With the greatest respect, sir, that is not a strategy, that is a series of rather vague war aims. How exactly are we going to achieve this?'

I thought I'd gone too far but d'Aubigny smiled.

'Very well, Sir Alan, if you prefer plain speaking, I will indulge you. Though I will leave it up to your conscience whether to tell your men. Our strategy is to hold the King here for as long as we can, to defy him and deny him this castle until Lord Fitzwalter or any of our other so-called friends grows a pair of balls and comes to our rescue. How likely is that to happen? Well, that is in God's hands. But our duty is clear. We deny John this castle until the last of us lies dead among the ruins. Or, more likely, till we can no longer stand from lack of food and are too weak to defend ourselves.' He tapped the parchment roll under his hand. 'Our strategy is to die here. And to die hard. Is that plain enough for you?'

'Yes, sir,' I said.

My own strategy of emptying the south tower by day was sound enough, but King John's response set it almost at nought. As Robin had rightly said, John wanted this castle and he wanted it now.

His men kept up a series of attacks on the southern walls, four or five every day that had my men running here and there to respond to the peril. None of the attacks was pressed hard enough to present a real danger of the enemy actually over-running the walls, yet each one had to be treated seriously. Two score or so of men-at-arms carrying ladders, or knotted ropes with iron hooks attached, would run screaming at a section of outer bailey wall under a lethal cloud of crossbow bolts from the town walls and would attempt to scale it and come at us with the most foolhardy kind of bravery. When the alarm was called, our knights would immediately rush to the section under attack, hurl boulders or sometimes boiling oil or water down on to the attackers' heads, loose a few crossbow bolts and push the scaling ladders from the walls with pitchforks. The handful of the enemy who actually reached the top of the wall would be cut down in instants by half a dozen of my young knights. It might last for a quarter of an hour, perhaps even less, but this was a furious period of blood and noise and blurring steel, of screaming men and pumping hearts, before the surviving foes below the wall would retreat, shaking their fists and hauling their wounded behind them as they ran back to the safety of the town.

Each attack like this, while a small victory for us, might cost a man or two injured or, mercifully less frequently, dead; some to crossbow quarrels from the town walls, some to wounds from the sword-storm on our walls, some just from a well-aimed javelin. And, despite the hundreds of King's men we cut apart, crushed, boiled alive or hurled to their deaths from the walls, this steady erosion of our manpower, day after day, was lethal to our cause. We had fewer than two hundred men under arms in the whole castle garrison and every man who died was irreplaceable.

John had thousands of men, mostly mercenaries who had no claim on his loyalty beyond their pay, and he had more than enough mailed bodies to waste a few hundreds against our walls. And from atop the keep, where Robin's archers had been posted, from time to time yet more companies of men were spotted coming up the road from Dover to join the King's banner.

Worse than the constant draining away of our men was the grinding fatigue we all suffered day after day. My forty knights and

88

their serving men had to be awake at all hours and ready for battle at a moment's notice, for these petty assaults took place by night as well as in the daylight hours, and every time the cry of 'To arms, to arms,' was heard echoing along battlements, we must all of us haul ourselves to our feet and run in the direction of the alarm and enter the fray once more.

I spelled the men, each day pulling one man in three from the battlements to give them a few hours of rest in the straw-filled barns inside the walls, but that made the scramble to repel an attack even more frantic from those fewer numbers still on the watch. And with each day that passed, the tired men on duty were slower to react to an alarm and slower in the mêlée, too. More men died. More men were needlessly wounded.

The King's strategy to wear us down was succeeding. All day long the five trebuchets beat again and again, crack, crack, crack, against the crumbling corners of the south tower. The relentless noise of our coming destruction wore away at our spirits, at our courage, like the missiles, chip-chip-chipping away at the stones of the tower. The knowledge that our doom approached a little closer, every day, every hour, made even the bravest knight a little more fearful, brought a little closer to his own breaking point.

But even worse than the fatigue was the hunger.

The store barrels were empty. There was no flour left to make bread. The root vegetables were almost gone. Every rat, cat and dog in the castle had long disappeared.

Hunger was our constant companion, the ache of empty bellies, the lassitude and weakness of our limbs. My mind dwelt on the many feasts I had enjoyed in my long life, of dripping roasts, pigeon pies and milk puddings, of fresh bread smothered in butter and sweet preserves, of fat cheeses, lush fruit, salty ham. I wanted to gorge till I puked, then sleep for a year and a day.

Every day at noon, the castle cooks would haul a cauldron of hot soup up to the walls, a salty slop thickened with a handful of dusty oats that contained less and less nourishment as the days went by – a scrap of onion each, perhaps, a tiny piece of turnip. And yet when we heard the noon bell and queued for it, bowl in hand, there was not a man whose mouth was not awash in anticipation.

After I had been captain of the southern walls for just over a week, they started killing the horses.

Chapter Ten

Horse meat is good. If you have never had to eat it, and I pray you are so fortunate, I may tell you it tastes very similar to beef, but gamier. There is a guilty tang, too, a sickening sweetness at the back of the throat, that comes with spooning down a bowl of something that was once a loyal companion to a man.

William d'Aubigny ordered that his own destrier, a fine black stallion worth a hundred pounds at least, the equivalent of ten years' revenue from my lands at Westbury, be killed first. That was the mark of the man – once the decision had been taken to begin slaughtering these noble beasts, he would not let another's valuable mount feed the garrison before surrendering his own to the castle butchers. It was a gesture, for we knew that all the horses would be eaten eventually, yet it was well received by the knights under his command. When we wolfed down our horse-meat soup at noon and sipped our cups of water, tinged pink with a few drops of wine, Sir George Farnham, a bluff, stout fellow, called out a toast to our gallant commander, praising his generosity and valour. It put heart into us all – just those few scraps of good red meat – and when the alarm was sounded a few hours later for an assault on the main gatehouse, I noticed a new vigour in the knights as they contained and countered the attack of the onrushing Flemings.

It did not last. For a fighting man, one bowl of soup a day, even fortified with scraps of horse meat, is not enough to keep his body strong and his courage high.

I took a rare break from the walls on the eleventh day of November. It was the feast day of St Martin – a Roman knight who renounced violence and became a peace-loving bishop. I wondered if there were a lesson for me there and thought about my conversation with Abbot Boxley – although I could not renounce my duty, nor could I celebrate the saint's life with a feast. In fact, I quit my post because I needed to see Robin about an urgent matter that I could not discuss with anyone else. I had done my tally at midnight of the men who were still fit to fight – and come up one man short. He was still missing the next morning – and I felt a chill in my soul. I left Sir George in command of my section of wall and sought out my lord in his post at the top of the southern tower of the keep.

I found him there with Mastin and a broad-chested, brown-faced man called Simeon, the archer captain's second-in-command, and a dozen bowmen on duty, gazing beyond the outer bailey walls below and over at Boley Hill, where the trebuchets were being served. As I came up through the arched doorway, Mastin was in the act of drawing a bow – and what a bow it was. Bigger than any I had seen before. The stave was more than seven feet in length and as thick as my wrist at the centre. I could see the huge muscles on Mastin's arms and shoulders bulge and writhe as he pulled this beast of a weapon back to its fullest extent. He loosed and the arrow flew up and away over the walls, over the dry moat, over a straggle of huts before the semicircle of trebuchets, and flashed down to skewer the lower leg of a man loading one of the catapults. The man's cry of pain was audible even at this distance:

a high animal yowl. Robin and Mastin – his hairy face sweating with the effort of the shot – congratulated each other excitedly.

I had never seen an arrow shot so far before – three hundred yards, maybe even a shade more – and to hit its target at the other end was not far short of miraculous.

I joined in the words of praise.

'It's no more than dumb fucking luck,' said Mastin. 'We allow ourselves six arrows a day, no more, and I've only hit two of the bastards in the past week.'

'Are we short of shafts, then?' I asked.

'Oh, we're not too badly off,' said Robin, taking the bow from Mastin. I watched as Robin selected an arrow, nocked it and attempted to haul back the cord. My lord was a strong man – no one could doubt it. But he only managed to pull the cord about halfway back, a foot and a half, perhaps, before loosing. Even that half-draw left him purple in the face and panting. The shaft sped over the wall of the outer bailey and lost itself in the scrubby no man's land on the other side of the ditch.

Robin smiled ruefully at Mastin and his second, Simeon. 'You need to build a bit more beef up here, sir,' said Simeon, slapping his own foot-thick chest.

I saw then how gaunt Robin's face and body had become after weeks without adequate food. 'That was a foolish waste of an arrow, for sure,' he said. 'And we must husband them for the assault. I think that's enough for today, Mastin. So, Alan, tell me: how goes it on the walls? Is that south tower ready to come down yet?'

Exactly at that moment, a trebuchet ball crashed into the outer bailey's south tower below, creating a vast puff of stone dust, and I swear the whole structure shook with the impact like a willow trunk in a gale.

'Can't be long,' I said. 'But I'm not here about that. Can I speak to you in private, my lord?'

Robin waved everyone away and we went to the corner of the roof out of earshot.

'It's about Miles,' I said.

'What about him?'

'He's gone.'

'What do you mean gone? Damn you, Alan – is this how you tell me my son is dead . . .' Robin's face was as pale as milk.

'Not dead, as far as I know. Gone. Disappeared. He hasn't been seen since he finished sentry duty at dusk last night.'

Robin looked at me. 'He's not among the dead and wounded – you are sure?'

'I checked – twice. I think, Robin, I think he has gone over the walls.'

I let my words sink in. Robin let out a deep breath.

'Don't mention this to anyone,' he said. 'If you are asked, say he is with me. If it became known that he deserted . . . My God, d'Aubigny would hang him for sure. And I dare not think what King John would do if he were caught.'

'I won't tell a soul, I swear it.'

A little after dusk, I was inside the outer bailey's south tower, on the middle floor with a mason and his two assistants. A huge crack ran diagonally up the wall, from the floor below to the floor above. At its widest point I could get my clenched fist inside the fissure easily.

'Yes, sir, we can fill the crack with mortar – but it won't get anywhere near dry overnight,' the mason was saying. He was a dusty little man called Jackson. 'And when they start again tomorrow, most of it will just slop straight out again. But I suppose it might make it a bit stronger, for a little while. But I would not put my trust in it.'

'Could we set fires or braziers to speed the drying?' I said.

'Might work,' he said, scratching his unshaven chin. 'But lime mortar can take weeks, even months, to dry properly – and that's in the good warmth of high summer. Still, I don't see that it could hurt to try . . .'

At that moment, Sir Thomas's head poked round the door.

'Sir Alan,' he said, 'I think you had better come and see this.'

I gave the mason his orders and followed Thomas out of the tower and along the south-western stretch of wall to a wooden hut that protected sentries from the worst of the weather. Inside, I found Miles with William d'Einford and Thomas de Melutan sitting on stools against the wall. They were devouring a whole roast chicken and a loaf of bread, tearing at the food with their bare hands.

'Where the hell have you been?' I said to the boy.

'Foraging. In the town,' he said, and gave me his cheekiest grin. 'There's plenty of food in the sack, Sir Alan, that is if you're feeling at all peckish.'

I opened the sack and saw, all jumbled together, a dozen loaves of bread, another cooked chicken, a whole ham, some small round cheeses and about a score of green apples. My mouth flooded with water; my belly mewed like a begging cat.

'Right, all this goes to d'Aubigny,' I said, swallowing thickly. 'He will distribute it as he sees fit.' I plucked a half-eaten chicken leg out of Miles's hand, tossing it into the sack.

'You will come with me, now,' I said to him, 'your father is expecting you.'

I dragged a protesting Miles across the outer bailey, into the keep and up to the roof of the south tower.

'Ah, there you are,' said Robin icily, when presented with his errant son, who was half-smirking, half-cowering as if expecting a blow.

I left them together and lugged the sack of food back down the stairs, heading for d'Aubigny's private apartments. I heard the terms 'irresponsible . . . ill-disciplined . . . disobedient . . . and God-damned reckless' floating down the spiral stair behind me, and then the words 'foraging . . . depriving the enemy of stores . . . legitimate tactic of war . . . and I was so hungry' wafting on their heels.

It occurred to me then, as I hefted that life-giving sack down the stairway, that Miles's exploit – sneaking both in and out of the castle and returning with an abundance of enemy food – was exactly the sort of madcap thing his father would have done at his age. Did Robin recognise it? Probably not. But I could not think too badly of Miles for his actions. He had been reckless but there was no denying the boldness, imagination and skill with which he had achieved his ends.

Truly, the acorn does not fall far from the tree.

I was tempted by that sack, I will admit. I was as hungry as anyone and I had a week's worth of food in my hands. Divided between the garrison it would mean less than a mouthful each. By God, I was sorely tempted. It crossed my mind that nobody would ever know if I finished off Miles's chicken leg before I handed the rest of the sack over to d'Aubigny. Perhaps it was even my due as captain of the walls? Perhaps I deserved it for all my efforts. But I resisted temptation. With difficulty. And, ultimately, I was glad I did.

I gave the heavy sack to the constable of the castle and he greeted the gift with wonder. 'I won't ask where you got this, Sir Alan, for I suspect that I would not like the answer at all. My order stands that there must be no sorties, no sallies, no excursions outside the walls by any man. But thank you,' said d'Aubigny. 'It will make a welcome change from horse-meat slop for the wounded.'

I did not trust myself to speak, I merely nodded, mourning the half-eaten chicken leg, and turned to go.

At that moment, I felt a stony thump under my boot soles, heard a sound like the tearing of a mountain and a great rumbling crash. I spun away from d'Aubigny and peered out of the window of his chamber. But all I could see was a huge cloud of yellow-grey dust where the outer bailey's south tower had once been. I rushed for the doorway.

'Sir Alan,' my commander said, as I reached the door. I turned in time to see a small round object coming at me at some speed. I grabbed it out of the air a few inches from my face. It was an apple, large, crisp, green and bursting with sweet-tart juice. I took a bite. I swear that right then it tasted more delicious than anything I had ever eaten.

'To keep your strength up,' said d'Aubigny. 'You're going to need it today.'

Back on the walls of the outer bailey, I ran along the parapet into the slowly clearing dust cloud shouting: 'To arms, to arms!' but I saw that it was hardly necessary. Sir George Farnham had the men rallied and they were converging on the breach where the tower had stood.

And not a moment too soon. Even before the fog of masonry grit cleared, I could see the enemy advancing on the breach from several directions – for the trebuchets had smashed a hole twenty paces wide in the wall of the outer bailey, and in the place of the south tower was now a saddle of rubble a mere ten foot above the surface of the outer bailey. The tumbling of the wall had created a rough natural stair of rubble astride the fortification. An active man could easily scramble from one side to the other, from the dry moat to the interior of the castle in about the time it takes for a man to say a *Pater Noster*. If he was allowed to pass without a fight, that is.

On the eastern side of the saddle, looking west along the wall, I could just make out Thomas Blood and a band of twenty or so men-at-arms, covered from head to toe in a fine powder and scrambling into the breach.

Sir Thomas and I both stepped gingerly on to the inward rubble slope at the same time, the loose stones shifting dangerously under our feet. We met in the middle, at the highest point of the breach, and looked south over the dry moat, now half-filled with broken rock, and beyond it, past an open space of mud and scrub, through a gate in the town wall and down a broad street – along which marched a company of spearmen two hundred strong in yellow-and-black surcoats. They were a mere hundred and fifty paces away and coming on at a trot. To my right, beyond the trebuchets, I could see a crowd of horsemen with nodding plumes and tall lances, mustering with many an excited cry. And crossbowmen, dozens of those evil bastards, creeping towards us from the town gate in ones and twos, carrying their huge shields.

'Everybody down,' I shouted. 'I want every man on his belly below the ridge.'

As I spoke a trebuchet ball smashed into the front slope of the breach, showering all of us with stinging chips of rock. I felt a trickle of warm blood from a nick on my chin, but ignored it. A splash of wet mortar covered my right knee – the mason had been right, despite our braziers and all-night fires, it was a long way from being set. 'Get down everyone, behind this line, on the reverse slope.'

More men were joining us, running in from across the courtyard or along the parapet behind the unbroken outer bailey walls and crouching, kneeling or lying flat below what remained of the wall. I took up a position in the centre of the line, burrowing my way into the jagged stones between Sir Thomas and Miles – who was grinning like a happy monkey – with a good sixty men, most of them knights, iron-mailed, steel-helmed, with long swords drawn, all packed in around and below me like the silver catch on a fishmonger's tray.

I heard the first whizz of crossbow bolts and the harsh crack as they caromed off the stones. 'Heads down, gentlemen,' I said. 'Heads down till I give the word; heads down till they reach the top of the breach; then up with me and start killing the bastards as quick as you can. We will show them who we are, this day; we will show them our mettle and make our names immortal. Today, men, we fight for England – we fight for liberty, for the charter and for an end to tyranny. Today . . . we fight!'

I have never had the gift for rousing speeches on the eve of combat – Robin managed it with ease and flair – but I did my best and my words were greeted by a suitably warlike growl from the knights around me and that warmed my soul.

Sir George Farnham, off to my left, shouted: 'For England, for liberty!'

We might be lying flat on our bellies like dogs, we might be only a few men, but I knew that most of my little command were supremely trained in war, men of proven strength, skill and courage, and I knew too that those who had not fought before had been preparing for this moment since they were seven years old. They were English knights. The best in the land. And this was the bloody work they were trained to do. I was not without fear, no sane man is before battle. But I knew we could hold the breach until the sky fell and we would send all these savage Flemish dogs to hell.

I twisted my neck around and squinted up, behind me, looking to the south tower of the keep, the intact elder sister of the one that had been destroyed. I waved and I saw with a wash of joy a thin, fair figure, high above, holding a bow horizontally in the air above his head, pumping it up and down in response to my waving arm.

For we were not facing this onslaught alone.

Chapter Eleven

The arrow volley struck the first ranks of the Flemish spearmen like a shower of lethal hail. I was peering over the lip of the breach and I saw almost the entire first line of mercenaries, more than a score of men, knocked apart like skittles in a tavern alley when the wooden ball strikes true. Men dropped outright or staggered backwards, spurting blood, the blow landing just as they were beginning to make their climb up the rubble slope towards us. The roaring of their war cries was muted and replaced by the desperate screams of stricken men. And while the second rank were still trying to get past the dead and dying, stepping over the prone bodies and on to the loose scree of rock and broken stone, the second volley from Robin's men high above up in the south tower of the keep swept into their ranks with devastating force.

Robin's two dozen bowmen loosed volley after volley and the slaughter they did was truly dreadful, but not every arrow found its mark and not every man was felled by the merciless barrage. A few hardy souls, a couple of dozen brave men, were struggling up the slope to meet us, some stuck with several shafts, others miraculously unwounded. They shouted threats and curses and called upon the saints to aid them, and they charged upwards, spears levelled.

'Up, men, and to your work!' I shouted, leaping to my feet. Behind me a wall of English iron and steel rose up to meet the men of Flanders, the long swords flashing like terrible lightning in the grey November air.

One fellow, fair-haired under a cheap steel cap, rushed at me, his feet slipping and sliding on the loose rock. He drove his spear hard at my chest but I turned to the left, deflected the point with my shield and hacked down with my sword into the base of his neck, cutting easily through his quilted gambeson. He fell away but another was behind him and as his spear lunged for my face I had to duck hastily. I felt the spear-tip score a furrow in my helm and my sword flicked out purely by instinct to puncture his unguarded groin. He screamed like a pig at slaughter as I felt the sword-tip grating against bone, and a great pulsing jet of gore shot from his upper thigh straight into my face. Momentarily blinded, I just had the mother wit to raise my shield before a heavy axe blow crashed against my protected forearm. Miles, at my left, barged past and I heard him shout, 'Die, you big Dutch bugger!' and deal a pair of savage blows to a vast shape in front of me, knocking the man down and away.

By the time I had wiped my eyes free of the sticky mess, the spearmen were already in full retreat and there was a tidemark of dead men at the feet of the sword-bristling English line, indeed the whole slope was carpeted with dead and wounded. Beside me Sir Thomas was wiping his bloodied blade on the hem of his cloak and looking thoughtfully out at the enemy hordes. Miles, dagger in hand, was grimly sawing through the throat of a writhing Fleming with a shaft through his belly and his left leg flayed open.

The arrows still fell on the enemy like an evil rain but only sporadically, for the Flemish spearmen were beaten and now

101

streaming back into the town or east towards the cathedral, leaving three score of their fellows in the dirt behind them.

'Down, back down again,' I shouted. 'Quickly now.' And with a good deal of happy grumbling, the knights went back to their prone positions on the reverse slope.

'Is it nap time already, Nanny?' called out Miles from behind me. 'Aw, what a shame. I'd only just begun to play.' Laughter rolled about us. But the men were back down into the cover of the rocks – just in time, for some of the enemy crossbowmen had crept closer and were now no more than forty paces away. With the breach clear of their own men they began to span their bows and loose their quarrels at our line in a fair imitation of Robin's murderous arrow barrage.

The iron-tipped bolts cracked and sparked against the stones or whistled overhead. I dared a peek over the top and did not like what I saw at all. Through the open town gate I could see another formation of men being herded into position. Red-and-blue surcoats adorned these spearmen and they were in twice the numbers of the first assault; worse, I could see a swollen *conroi* of knights, fifty men at least, gathering to our right behind the trebuchet lines, dismounting from their destriers and handing the reins to their squires. They would assault us on foot and, by the looks of them, they were easily a match for our English line. I glanced at the sky – the short day was nearly done, but could we hold till nightfall? I was less sure now. We were about to be menaced by some four hundred spearmen and fifty dismounted knights. Even with Robin's protective arrows it was poor odds.

Just then I heard a deep voice calling my name: it was d'Aubigny himself, with a pair of squires, below the breach on the ground of the outer bailey. Then he was making his way very carefully up the reverse slope, placing his feet between the limbs of the lying men, and giving each fellow he passed a quiet word of praise. He came to my side and knelt behind the line of rubble, just his big, grey, curly head poking over the top, and Thomas and I made room for him, squirming uncomfortably aside on the hard stones.

'They are coming again, sir,' I said, pointing at the enemy, now in a tight formation behind the town gate, a dense column of red and blue, spear points gleaming atop the forest of shafts above their heads.

D'Aubigny opened his mouth to speak and at that moment a crossbow quarrel flashed between us, inches from the constable's ruddy face, and clattered noisily against the stone of the keep twenty yards behind us. We both ignored it.

'We have most of the men and stores inside the keep, now, Sir Alan,' he said.

I nodded, not quite sure what to say.

'Hold them here, if you can, as long as you can. But when the breach falls, and it will do, mark my words, don't leave it too late to get yourself and your men inside with the rest of us. I need you alive – I need all of you alive.' He said the last slightly louder so that all the knights around us might hear.

'My lord of Locksley will give you ample cover when it's time to go.' And he jerked his head up towards my lord atop the south tower. 'God be with you!'

'Yes, sir,' I said.

D'Aubigny began to make his way carefully back down the slope. I watched him reach the level courtyard safely and begin to stride back towards the bastion. But after two strides, he turned and shouted up: 'You hear me, Alan Dale, don't leave it too late. We can fight them off from the keep much better than from here.'

They came on again in the same way, a massed charge by the spearmen, protected by crossbowmen at their flanks. And in just the same way, Robin decimated their ranks. But this time, hard on the heels of the spearmen, came the dismounted knights –

well-born but impoverished men from Hainault and Holland, Bruges and Brabant. Yet I still believe we could have held them, were it not for one appalling, unheard-of tactic that King John employed, a tactic I had never in my life imagined might be used by any commander who called himself a Christian.

We slaughtered the spearmen who survived the arrow storm and scrambled to the top of the breach. We chopped them down without mercy, the well-armoured English knights hacking apart peasants in their old leather armour and padded cloth coats with only a few weeks' marching drill under their belts. They died by the score. Miles on my left was a demon with a dancing blade, slicing, hacking, chopping and pounding the enemy down, insulting them as they fell to his sword; Sir Thomas killed with a quiet and deadly efficiency, a minimum of motion, a quick cut and a short lunge and another man fell, ripped and howling, at his feet. I did my share of killing too but all I can recall of that battle is the sheer hard labour, the effort to kill and kill again, hacking down man after man, only for another to spring up in his place. They all blurred into one, one immortal red-and-blue-clad foe, who no matter how often I hacked him apart always returned as a screaming, red-dripping spectre to challenge me again.

The enemy knights below the breach were urging the spearmen onward and upward to their deaths with the points of their swords, and in a short lull in the fighting in front of me, I saw a knight strike down a fellow in a red-and-blue surcoat who had thrown away his spear and tried to run. However, it was not this disregard for the lives of John's men that defeated us, but another brutality far worse.

The trebuchet ball smashed into the centre of the line of struggling men, red-and-blue spearmen and grey-clad English knights. It left half a dozen Flemings smeared across the rubble and cut Sir George Farnham into two pieces. There was a tiny pause – a miraculous break in the fray as every knight and spearman stopped his blow mid-strike – and each recognised what had just happened. King John had loosed his artillery on the breach despite it being filled with his own men. It was evidently worth the cost to the King to slaughter his own folk if it meant the chance of killing some of ours.

The second trebuchet ball landed short, splashing into the packed ranks of Flemings attempting to scale the breach and spattering red soup across the whole battle area. A dozen of their men were crushed by that strike alone.

A third trebuchet missile squelched through a file of their spearmen and ripped off the head and arm of an English man-at-arms on the far left of our line.

It was time to go. I prayed it was not too late.

'Back, back,' I shouted. 'To the keep!'

With Miles and Sir Thomas warding my back, I started hauling men out of the line, shouting in their ears that they must retreat. But it is no easy feat to persuade an English knight whirling high with the frenzy of battle to disengage and flee. Some men stared at me in amazement, unable to understand the order; others cursed me, shoved me off and waded back into the fight, bloody swords singing.

Another devastating trebuchet strike turned the tables. The Flemish spearmen were melting back, ignoring the cries of their knights to fight on, appalled that their own side should seek to cut them down so cruelly. And so I was able to get a few of the more blood-crazed Englishmen to begin to stumble back down the slope. The slow retreat became a rout, with men pouring down the rocky incline and running full tilt towards the fore-building, a massive stone box that guarded the main entrance to the keep. We had not far to go, a matter of fifty paces or so, and I was running with the best of them. But I did manage to snatch one last glimpse at the top of the breach, now lined with red-and-blue battle-stunned spearmen staring at our sudden flight with equal joy and utter surprise. Arrows from high on the keep were thwocking into them, slaying by the dozen, but they scarcely seemed to notice.

Then the trebuchet struck a final blow and the line of spearmen exploded into spinning limbs and bloody scraps.

After I had counted my men into the keep and slammed the iron-bound door shut behind the last, I was astounded to know that I had lost only nine men in that desperate fight, and of the seventy-two I had led to safety only two dozen were wounded and but one of those seriously. Good mail pays for itself, the better armourers are wont to tell you, and they are right.

Yet Miles was not among the men I brought back. I asked if anyone had seen him fall, but not a man could remember seeing Robin's son after I gave the order to withdraw. I wondered if he had been slain as we all rushed headlong back to the keep but, in truth, we had not been hotly pursued. The spearmen and the Flemish knights had taken possession of the breach, when the trebuchet had finally ceased the bloody execution of their comrades, and had for the most part stopped there, awaiting more of their men to scramble up the rubble and join them. We had hardly been molested at all in the pell mell sprint to the keep.

So where was Miles?

I made the climb to the top of the south tower with a heavy heart: what could I say to Robin? That I had mislaid his younger son in the scramble to save my own life? As I came through the arch and into the fresh breeze on the darkling roof of the tower, Robin turned to me from the battlements and the first thing he said was:

'He's not dead, Alan.'

I hesitated, wondering if this was a question or a statement, and my lord said, 'The bloody young fool. I saw him run the wrong way. When the rest of you came down, he went the other way, along the walls to the west. I couldn't track him; we were busy hammering their assault with all we had. When I looked again he was gone. I don't know what can have got into his thick head. That stupid, ill-disciplined child!'

Despite Robin's angry words, I could see he was racked with worry.

'I think I do,' I said. 'He knows a discreet way in and out of the castle – somewhere over there' – I waved vaguely to the west towards the river. 'It's the same way he got out to forage for food two days ago. He has evidently decided he prefers to take his chance dodging Flemings in the darkness and maybe swimming the Medway than locked up tight in the keep with us.'

Robin looked slightly relieved. 'Yes, he's a resourceful boy. That's true. Maybe he hasn't foolishly thrown his life away. Thank you, Alan. You managed to creep into the castle; so maybe, with a bit of luck, he can creep out.'

Robin beckoned me over to the battlement. Below us the outer bailey was swarming with enemy troops, surging in and out of the buildings around the edge of that great space, looking for plunder. They carried flaming pine torches to ward off the gathering dusk and already the stables – emptied of horses, of course – were beginning to smoulder and smoke. As the greyness settled heavily across the land, the first sparks of light sprang up in the encampments all around and inside the town. We were surrounded by our enemies, shut up tight in a vast stone box, with no hope of victory, rescue or surrender.

Maybe Miles had taken the sensible course, after all.

I looked at Robin and saw to my surprise that he had his head laid flat on the top of the crenellation, his ear pressed to the stone.

'Listen to that,' he said, tapping the masonry at his cheek with a finger.

I laid my head on the next crenellation along, wondering what he wished me to hear. And then it came, very faint, a short metallic sound – *tink-tink-tink* – like someone rapping a knife blade on a boulder a great distance away.

'Miners,' said Robin. 'By the sound of it, very nearly under our walls.'

Chapter Twelve

I slept for two days straight after the fall of the outer bailey and dreamed of giant rats with fire-glowing eyes gnawing at my feet until I had nothing left to stand on and tumbled into a dark spinning abyss. Hunger will do that to you, give you strange and terrifying dreams. And it was the hollowness of my belly and the corresponding lightness of my head that obsessed me over the next few days and nights.

We had plenty of fighting men to stand guard duty inside the keep – still more than a hundred and fifty under arms, and a smaller number of serving men and women, grooms, cooks and so on – and we all took turns to watch from the four towers and numerous arrow slits of the keep as the King's Flemings looted and burned the outer bailey and made merry in the town to celebrate their victory over us at the breach. Indeed, so many folk were inside the keep that it was uncomfortably crowded – and, although all the horses had been slaughtered, we were down to starvation rations: one bowl of vaguely meat-flavoured slop a day per man, no bread, no wine or ale. Robin's archers hunted mice in the dungeons of the keep with pine torches and bows, loosing at skittering shadows in the corners, and those elusive creatures too were soon gone. D'Aubigny ordered the richer knights to surrender any stores of food they still had, which rendered a few chunks of dried pork sausage, a jar or two of preserves and a couple of cheeses. But with more than two hundred people to feed, these lasted less than a day.

We tightened our belts and looked forward to the next noonday bowl of slop with a terrible, aching yearning.

King John made no infantry assaults on the keep itself. He seemed to be concentrating all his efforts on the mine. And the trebuchets, of course. These had been swiftly repositioned the day after the breach fell, and these terrible engines now began to rain missiles on the lower part of the south tower and the western wall of the keep. The intensity of the barrage had lessened, however, for only three loosed their stone balls at us. I believe the other two may have become damaged or been judged unequal to the increased range. But three trebuchets bombarding us was bad enough and a dozen times an hour a missile would smash itself to pieces against our walls. Between strikes, the sound of the digging could be clearly heard, even without pressing an ear to the stonework, and we estimated that at least a hundred yards of tunnel had been dug from under the breach and that scores of foes were burrowing away beneath our feet. A horrible, eldritch sensation.

Some of the knights suggested countermining, but d'Aubigny vetoed this and he was probably right to do so, for while we might come at our enemies this way, and kill them all, the extra digging would also further weaken the foundations of the castle and could hasten their collapse.

I was not entirely idle. Some days to take my mind off my famishment I would join Robin and Mastin on the roof of the south tower and help them spot targets for Mastin's giant bow. The Flemings had withdrawn back to the town, but with a bit of luck, we could still occasionally kill or wound an incautious man labouring near the trebuchet lines to the south-west.

I had spotted a likely fellow, who had wandered a little too close to us for his safety, gathering horse fodder with a sickle in front of the foremost trebuchet as if he had not a care in the world, and I was just pointing him out to Mastin, when Robin said, 'Hold, look yonder!'

He pointed down towards the building that housed the mouth of the mine. I could see dozens of men running fast out of the entrance and accompanying them the first tendrils of grey smoke. The flow of men petered out but the smoke did not, thickening to become a solid stream of black, dotted with dancing orange fireflies.

'They have fired the mine,' said Robin. 'Everybody off the tower. Now! Go, Alan. Warn the men below. Everyone back into the heart of the keep.'

I flew down the stairs, a cold hard lump in my belly. In my mind's eye I could clearly see what was happening a hundred feet below my boots. A tunnel would have been hacked through mud and rock below the surface of the earth, groping forward until it reached the castle's foundations, where the masonry would be carefully levered out and a cavity created under the external walls. This huge hole would have been reinforced with rows and rows of stout wooden beams, planks and joists, just enough to support the walls above while the miners finished their dangerous work. Now the mine was ready, piles of brushwood and many barrels of pig fat would have been carried down the tunnel and stacked in the empty space at the end. At the command to fire the mine, the brushwood would have been set alight and every sane man down there would have run for his life back down the tunnel and into the safety of the open air. The brushwood would ignite the barrels of pig fat which would burn with such an intensity that the wood supporting the castle would be swiftly consumed in the

111

inferno. Then the wall would collapse under its own weight. That was what we were facing now.

On the floor below, a dozen archers were lounging in a circle with Sir Thomas Blood. They were throwing dice.

I burst into the room. Sir Thomas leaped to his feet. 'It is not what it looks like, Sir Alan,' he said. 'We were not playing for real money, just a few pennies! I swear it.'

I had no time to scold him.

'Everyone out. Get back into the great hall or anywhere away from this tower and the southern walls. They have fired the mine.'

I saw the colour drain from Thomas's face as the import of my words sank in.

'On your feet, lads, right now,' said the knight. 'Come on, quickly—'

And with a colossal rumbling growl, the bottom fell out of my world.

A sensation of falling. And crashing into something unyielding. A massive blow to my right shoulder, punching me down, and lighter ones to my helmeted head. Couldn't breathe, couldn't see, the world was filled with choking dust – and the screams of men. My right arm was pinned across my body, my left leg was bent at the knee and tucked up behind me. Uncomfortable, but not broken, I thought. My shoulder was agony though, a pulsing burning pain that stopped my breath in my throat. My right foot was resting on something hard, supporting my weight. I groped with my left hand and felt stone and gritty dust and the splintered end of a beam. Someone was sobbing a yard from me to my right, his breathing wet, laboured. He was calling for his mother.

'Thomas?' I called, my voice sounding hollow and unreal.

'Help me, in God's name, help me.' It wasn't Thomas but I recognised the voice of an archer. I tried to move but apart from my left arm, which seemed to have some space around it, I was stuck.

112

'Help will come soon,' I said. 'Hold fast, man, the Earl will come to our aid.'

'I'm bleeding,' he said. 'I'm bleeding bad.' His voice tailed off into a feeble keening of ultimate pain. I well knew that sound.

Then I heard another that I had come to know – and dread. The flat crack of stone on stone. A trebuchet strike, a missile the size of a full-grown pig, smashing itself to pieces against the broken tower. And then another. And a third.

The world around me twisted, dropped again, reconfigured itself. My body was squeezed, wrenched unbearably; I heard the bone in my left leg snap like a piece of kindling; something clonked against the back of my helmet – everything went dark.

'Alan, Alan, look at me,' said a voice.

I opened my eyes and saw a long, thin, hollow face with strange silvery eyes just inches from mine, staring at me. I knew that face. I knew it – but the name that belonged to it would not come.

'Here, drink this,' said the face. It held out a wooden bowl filled with cold well water. I sipped, coughed and tried to sit up.

The face put a strong hand on my chest, pushing me back down.

'Your leg is broken,' he said. 'Your shoulder was dislocated, but I think Mastin got it safely back in its socket. You've taken several bad knocks to the head. So don't even think about getting up for a while.'

I looked around me. I was in the north-eastern half of the great hall, lying on a pile of straw by the wall. My whole body was covered in a yellow-grey dust, except for my left leg, which had been washed and bound tight with clean white bandages between two pieces of a broken bow shaft. The pain began then, a great wave rolling up my leg and surging into my body.

'You are Robert Odo, Earl of Locksley,' I said wonderingly to the face. It smiled, a soothing balm against the wash of red pain.

'Yes, I know that. And you, Alan Dale, are damned lucky to be alive.'

'I've always been lucky,' I said, and slid back into blackness.

When next I awoke, Sir Thomas was sitting beside my pile of straw. I had no difficulty in recognising him, praise God, although the left half of his face was bruised to the colour of a ripe plum. He was cleaning his dirt-crusted fingernails with a dagger and I watched him until he noticed I was awake.

'Ah, Alan,' he said. 'Want some water?'

I nodded, and he reached behind and handed me the wooden bowl.

'We've plenty of water,' he said. 'I suppose we must count that as a blessing.'

I saw that the hall was filled, packed tight would be a better term, with men in mail wearing swords at their waists. It seemed almost the entire garrison was inside this small chamber. All the men of the castle, or so it felt.

'Is there a conference?' I said. 'A war council?'

'What? No. This is it. This is all we hold now.'

I was still confused, and conscious of the fact, but this made no sense at all.

'Tell me,' I said.

Thomas let out a breath and took a long pull on the bowl.

'We got you out, Robin and me and a few of the archers. But we lost two Westbury men – Hob and Swein – down there somewhere in the rubble. The enemy came at us at once, of course, scrambling like goats up the broken masonry. Hundreds of them coming up through the dust. We couldn't hold them, although d'Aubigny and Robin battled like lions, and the young knights fought them tooth and nail. The commander ordered us to fall back into the hall but they were right on our heels. They were in the wall-walk, in the hall itself. We just managed to get the doors shut, bolted and barred. And we have blocked off the other floors with rubble and timbers. We are keeping them out – but only just. And now here we are. Shut up like

114

rats in a root cellar. Half the castle ours, half theirs – and no way out.'

'When did this happen?'

'It's been two days since the south tower collapsed. And the fighting has been almost continuous. The men are near the end of their strength.'

I saw then that Thomas was grey and drawn, except where the bruise purpled the skin of his face. I wondered when he had last slept. Or eaten.

'And food?'

He laughed, an unpleasant creaking sound. 'There is none. But we still have access to the well, at least.'

He passed me the bowl and I stared into the clear liquid, seeing my own dusty gaunt face looking back at me from its surface.

I drank, wiped a sleeve across my lips and returned the bowl.

'What is to be done?'

Thomas shrugged and glanced at the oak door that connected the two parts of the hall. I followed his eyes. It was strange to think that a score of yards away, in the other side of this very chamber were hundreds of our enemies who wanted nothing more than to chop us into offal. There could be no escape.

'Robin will think of something,' Thomas said. 'You should rest yourself, Alan, you won't be fighting or even walking any time soon.'

My friend got up and walked to the other side of the room, where a group of knights were huddled in a circle, gesticulating, arguing, but in low voices. Osbert Giffard's bald head was red with anger. Thomas de Melutan looked to be on the verge of tears. I saw d'Aubigny straighten up and walk away from the other men, making for the chapel. A dozen other wounded lay against the walls of the hall, some attended by their friends, others alone. The chamber smelled of blood and sweat, stale air and desperate men. There was no sign of Robin.

I sank back on the pile of straw, and in spite of the turmoil of sorrow and rage in my heart, my eyelids were heavy and once more I slept.

I awoke screaming. My leg was vibrating with pain.

'Be careful with him, you handless buggers, or I will cut your eyes out.' Robin's voice. I was on a blanket being carried by two deep-chested archers, who looked suitably shame-faced for having knocked my broken leg against the wall. I was being hauled like a side of beef down the main staircase of the castle entrance. The rain was falling into my face. Icy needles. We were outside, daylight, mid-morning I guessed. It was very cold.

'What? Why are we here?'

'Be quiet, Alan,' said Robin. 'Just lie still.'

A group of red-and-blue-surcoated spearmen were lounging at the bottom of the stone stairs, next to a two-wheeled cart. They were laughing, drinking ale, drunk.

'Get a move on, you English pigs,' said the nearest. 'Or I shall tickle you along with my pig-sticker.' He guffawed and shook his spear to ram home his hilarious jest. The two archers dropped their eyes and hurried down the last few steps.

Robin ignored the taunting man but his pale face turned even whiter. I saw with a sense of shock that the scabbard at his waist was empty. He was unarmed.

'This way,' he said quietly to my archer-porters, gesturing across the outer bailey towards the remains of the main gate, now a charred hole in the curtain wall.

'Why are we outside?' I said to Robin.

'We are the King's prisoners,' said my lord.

'What? Are you mad? He'll cut our hands and feet off.'

'Maybe not. He has given his word that we will be treated mercifully. That was the condition of our surrender. The King will show mercy. D'Aubigny made the arrangement with him through his priest. I helped him to persuade the other knights.'

116

'And you trust the King's word?'

'Not now, Alan, please, just – not now. All right?' There was enough iron in Robin's voice to quiet me. But I was scared, by God, I was plain terrified just then at the prospect of life as a limbless beggar. I knew what the King's word was worth.

Out of the castle gates we went, down the hill and across the road to the cathedral and once in that hallowed space down the aisle and into one of the side chapels with Sir Thomas, Mastin and a dozen of the Sherwood archers; all of our men who remained alive, I guessed. None of my half-dozen Westbury men had survived the final battle, it seemed, and I felt a shaft of guilt that was far worse than the pain in my leg. More good men gone.

The cathedral was filthy. Horse dung, mud and hay littered the stone floor of the nave, although someone had swept our side chapel clean. The central space in the nave was filled with hundreds of Flemish knights and men-at-arms, puffing out their chests, smirking like new fathers, lounging about armed to the teeth with spear, sword and crossbow – not that they needed weapons to display their superiority. I had noticed that each of the side bays was filled with the woebegone faces of knights from the castle and their men, sitting on the floor, downcast, humbled, hungry, thin as bean-poles after six weeks of short rations. Beaten.

I could hear a man in the next bay along moaning with pain. Occasionally his moans swelled into bouts of screaming. I could hear his comrades trying to quiet him.

Two Flemish sergeants came past our bay, with a pair of civilians – bakers by the looks of their floury linen aprons. They carried a large basket between them and carelessly threw four small brown loaves into our chapel, caught by Mastin and two of his bowmen. One of the bakers unslung a leather bag of ale from his back and dropped it unceremoniously on the floor.

We shared out the bread, no more than a handful for each man, and passed round the ale. It was the first food I had had in days and while it was only dark, coarse maslin, made with wheat and rye, and apparently the sweepings of the bakery floor, it tasted fine. The ale was days old but it washed the rough bread down well enough.

Robin came to sit beside me after he had finished his meal.

'How's the leg?' he asked.

I shrugged, and regretted it. My neck and back were badly bruised and my shoulder was aching almost as much as the snapped shin bone.

'I have a feeling it doesn't much matter,' I said, the pain making me irritable. 'As I expect to lose it soon.'

Robin looked at me steadily. 'You would rather be dead?'

I said nothing. He had made his point.

The wounded man in the next bay began screaming again – wild, untrammelled noises that echoed around the cathedral; followed by sharp, regular cries like a beast caught in a spring trap. A desperate sound that grated horribly on the nerves.

'One of d'Aubigny's men-at-arms. Stomach wound,' said Robin.

'Poor bastard,' I said.

'I don't know why his comrades do not end his pain. He's a dead man anyway with that kind of wound. Deep puncture to the lower belly. It's always the same. It will turn bad and, after five or six days of the most appalling agony, he will surely die. Better to end it now.'

'I wonder where Miles is,' I said to change the subject.

'London, with luck,' said Robin.

'If I know him, he's sitting in some cosy tavern by the docks, drunk as a bishop, with a pretty wench on each knee, both vying for his kisses.'

Robin smiled. 'Like enough.'

'I hope Robert is safe,' I said.

'He will be. Hugh will hold out at Kirkton. He's too stubborn to give in. And even if he were to be forced out somehow, he could find shelter with our friends in Sherwood. Besides, the King is here and while he is gracing us with his presence he cannot be making war on our folk in the north.'

I prayed it was true. If I was to die, at least I could hope my son would be safe.

The man next door screamed once more, a haunting wolf-like howl that seemed to last for an eternity. Then, suddenly, it was muffled, then stopped as if by a wad of cloth or thick blanket held tightly over his mouth.

'I can't complain,' said Robin. 'I have had a good life, I think. We have had some adventures, you and I, Alan. If the King plays us false, and these truly are our last hours, at least I have two strong sons to live on after me. And you have Robert, to carry your name. That is all that matters, really. That is what I have fought for these past ten years, for Marie-Anne, for my sons, for their future in this land. That is what the charter is all about – for me, anyway. That they might live in a country free from the tyranny of evil kings.'

I looked at Robin then. I had never seen him so close to despair.

'You think this is it, that this is the end?' I said.

'What do you think?'

'I always remember what Little John once said before that terrible battle at Bouvines. He said, "Live, Alan, live like a man until you die!"'

'As he did.'

'Yes. As he did.'

'I miss him,' said Robin. 'Although I should not like to see him in the mire we're in now. He was right, too. We're not dead yet, old friend, so let us live. And I think . . . I think I would like to sing if this is indeed to be our last day on earth.'

Robin raised his voice. 'Who here knows "The Thrush and the Honey-Bee"? Come on, surely you all remember it?'

And my lord began to sing. He had a fine voice and it echoed most pleasingly off the walls. That is how we spent the rest of that long, long day: sitting on the cold floor of that side chapel in Rochester Cathedral singing the old songs of England, with me pitching in as best I might over the pain of my leg and the archers joining in the choruses with a surprising and even sometimes tuneful vigour.

We never heard another peep from the stomach-wounded man in the next bay. Praise God.

At sunrise, we were fed again and a barber-surgeon came round asking if any man required his attention. He was a grubby fellow, his clothes stained with blood and slime, and he reeked of ale and armpits. He had a string of dirty yellow molars hanging around his neck, a sign of his other trade as a tooth-puller.

I declined his attentions: Mastin, who had doctored many a wounded man in his time, had set my leg well and I did not want this wretch pawing at his handiwork.

Shortly before noon, they came to bind us. It came as no surprise. For all morning we had heard the work of hammers and saws, and the whisper came round that a wide platform was being built in front of the cathedral. I said nothing but I could not forget d'Aubigny's tale of the men, women and children whose hands and feet had been lopped on another such platform at the beginning of the siege.

When our hands were all bound with rough ropes, we were herded into the nave, more than a hundred men. I hopped along, my roped arms looped over Thomas's shoulder and using his tough frame as a crutch. I saw d'Aubigny a dozen yards away and it was evident that he had been beaten for he limped and his face was a mass of cuts and contusions. He would not meet my eye. Before the sacred altar was a knot of noblemen in bright, clean clothes, silks and satins, velvet and furs – the King's courtiers – jewellery glittering at their necks and their fingers were thick with gold rings. And lolling in the archbishop's chair in the middle of them, shorter than the other men, but even more splendidly dressed, was the King himself. He was joking with a tall, grey-bearded man-at-arms, the only unbound person of rank there who looked like he might have actually fought in the battle that had humbled the castle, a man whom I recognised as the renowned French knight Savary de Mauléon, Viscount of Thouars.

He had been a loyal vassal of Arthur, Duke of Brittany, who was captured with Mauléon at the battle of Mirebeau – a victory for King John that was almost entirely Robin's doing. John had taken Mauléon prisoner and thrown him into the dungeon at Corfe Castle, his fearsome stronghold by the sea in Dorset. But, for some reason, John had decided to pardon the man – and had accepted his homage – and now he was one of the King's greatest commanders. I had not known that Mauléon was opposing us at the siege – but I supposed it made little difference now.

The King was in high spirits, his blue eyes glinting like wet glass. He was a goodly age then – at forty-nine, just a year younger than Robin – and his once-russet hair was thinning and grey, his face pouchy and lined. Despite these signs of age, he seemed animated by a much younger spirit as if through some devilry his younger carefree self was still inhabiting his ageing body.

'Ah-ha, d'Aubigny,' he said, catching sight of our bruised commander. 'There you are! You look like you've been in the wars! Oh, ha-ha-ha!'

His voice sounded like the croaking of an evil frog yet the dazzling courtiers around the King exploded with mirth, clapping each other on the shoulder, pretending to weep for the exquisite joy of the royal jest – all except Mauléon, who gazed up at the cathedral's high arched ceiling as if seeking strength from the Almighty.

To this deeply stupid remark d'Aubigny merely gave a gruff 'Sire' and a nod of the head.

'And there's the Earl of Locksley – the infamous outlaw, as was.

The notorious Robin Hood that the villeins all sing of in the taverns. Well, no more an outlaw, no more a rebel, we have tamed you! And is that your man Sir Alan Dale? It is, by God's bones, the man who tried to cut my head off with a hidden little knife at St Paul's! Well, it's his head on the block now. Ha-ha-ha!'

And so on. The King went on to name and mock a dozen other knights, making asinine jests at the expense of each one in turn. It seemed hardly a man there had not sparked the King's ire at one time or another – and John had not forgotten a single slight, the smallest insult, nor the most inconsequential debt.

After a while even the King seemed to grow bored of his childish game. He croaked, 'Quiet!' at the giggling courtiers and frowned at the crowd of bound and bloodied rebels standing before him.

'You all defied me,' he said sternly, when the sycophantic laughter had petered out. 'You all swore to be my loyal men and then you raised the bloody flag of rebellion and challenged me in one of my own castles!' He sounded incredulous at this accusation, as if no fighting man had ever taken up arms against a king before.

'Time and again, I have shown forbearance in the face of your outrageous contumacy, I have shown compassion, I have shown infinite kindness . . .'

I very soon became bored with this mummery – there could be no good end to the King's speech, none at all – and I began to look about me. The walls of the cathedral were lined with knights and men-at-arms. I wondered briefly if I could slip my bonds and seize a weapon. It was no use. I couldn't walk a step unaided on my broken leg.

The King was still speaking: '. . . I promised you mercy and you shall indeed receive mercy at my hands.'

He paused and every man in the cathedral held his breath and waited for the judgement.

'Every man-at-arms of common stock, every villainous archer, every ignoble servant of a noble knight, every peasant spearman, even the very meanest churl . . . shall be released immediately.' The King was smiling like a cream-fed cat, play-acting the munificent monarch.

'They shall be set free this hour, henceforth to serve whomsoever they shall choose.'

I was utterly surprised, to be honest. This was indeed mercy. Generosity, even. It was the very last thing I had expected from John. The Flemish men-at-arms were moving into the crowd, picking out the common soldiers and herding them towards the rear of the cathedral. I saw Mastin being dragged away by two spearmen and heard him say, 'Get your dirty paws off me, you goat-fuckers!' before being silenced with a buffet to the face.

Robin called out: 'Get our men back to Kirkton, Mastin, tell Hugh of our fate. Tell Marie-Anne that—'

But Mastin was being hustled down the aisle and was almost out of earshot. A muffled cry of 'Don't you worry, sir, I'll fucking tell 'em,' came back towards us.

When all the men of common stock, as the King put it, had been cleared from the cathedral, only the knights and noblemen remained. They were a shuffling, murmuring crowd, craning their necks towards John expectantly, with new hope shining in their eyes.

The King called for silence.

'The rest of you, you men who claim noble blood, who glory in your valour, your titles and your ancient names, all you who hold lands in my realm . . .'

The whole cathedral was as silent as an empty tomb. I shifted my weight on Thomas's shoulder. My leg was burning as if it had been dipped into the flames of Hell.

'You men,' the King croaked, 'shall be taken from this House of God, out into the good light of day, and there you shall be hanged by the neck until you are dead like the rebellious scum you are. It shall be a lesson to all who dare oppose me.'

The cathedral erupted into uproar, every man shouting, some wrestling with their bound hands, others calling unto God, and I realised I was yelling out to the King: 'You swore we would receive mercy, you traitorous bastard, that was the condition of our surrender. Mercy, you said, you black-hearted devil—'

'Quiet!' bellowed the King. 'I will have quiet. Be still there, you scum.'

Some Flemish knights around the walls were drawing swords. Others were beating the nearest prisoners into silence. Eventually some order was restored.

'I did indeed promise you mercy. And you have received it. You've been mercifully fed, your wounds mercifully tended to, your men-at-arms' lives have been mercifully spared. Now you will receive the mercy of a swift death. Take them away!'

Part Two

Joyous news! The King has come to Newstead Priory. His Royal Highness Henry of Winchester graciously agreed to pay our humble priory a short visit. We knew for some days that Henry was in residence at his palace at Clipstone, not eight miles north of us, an hour's ride. He had been taking his ease there after the trials of his ill-starred campaign in Poitou, feasting his friends and hunting the fat red deer of Sherwood. However, we received a message only yesterday from Lord Westbury – the only grandson of Brother Alan, and one of the King's closest advisers – informing us that the King would pay a private visit to our small House of God and that he wished to speak with Brother Alan on a matter of some import.

I praise God that we have been so honoured: the King is a pious man and has made munificent gifts of silver and lands to other Houses. Perhaps, perhaps . . . but it would not be right to pray for His Highness to show his royal generosity to us. We must be grateful that he has taken notice of this small and remote community, and allowed the light of his countenance to shine upon us. Nevertheless, the whole priory has been a storm of excited activity – we are far too poor to offer dinner to our good King and all his multitude of lords and servants – it would beggar us to give every man a morsel, but there must be something to offer and the monks have been all in a frenzy, baking sweet pastries, unwrapping cheeses and bringing up the best barrels of wine so that if the King himself expressed hunger or thirst we would be able to assuage it swiftly. It would not do to shame ourselves and our House before royalty!

I told Brother Alan that he must prepare himself for the visit and rise, wash and dress himself, so that he could be presented in a respectable manner in the chapter house. The visit seems to have put heart into the old man. When I came for him last night, he nodded and began to struggle out of his blankets. 'Been a while,' he muttered as I wrapped him in a thick woollen robe and led him towards the wash house. Then he said something rather strange: 'I hope the blessed boy doesn't expect me to sing again.'

I do not know what Brother Alan meant by that but then sometimes his mind wanders and he believes himself to be in another time and place. I thank God for it, otherwise I would not have the pleasure of hearing and recording his tales of his younger self. And while his mind might sometimes be foggy in this present moment, his clarity of the past is remarkable.

We all turned out in the courtyard – the monks, the servants, almost every man of Newstead – to welcome the King this morning. And while I was awed to be in the presence of royalty for the first time, I was also silently counting heads to see if we would have enough food and wine for everyone in his retinue. Twenty-seven. A manageable number, praise God.

The King himself was a man of medium height, but thick-chested and with powerful arms. He wore a surcoat of red and gold, and a simple coronet made of a thick band of gold set with rubies. His face was open and pleasant, and seemed to shine with happiness and good humour, save for his left eye, which appeared to droop a little lower than the right, giving him a sleepy expression. We greeted him with a prayer for his health and then four of the monks sang an anthem, composed for the occasion, which lauded his nobility, his piety and the justice that he brought the land. The King seemed much moved by it and when it was over I thought I saw the glint of genuine tears in his eyes.

Old Brother Roger stepped forward with a platter of honey cakes, almond tarts and candied fruits – he had spent the whole of the night in the kitchens and his face this day was green with exhaustion. Nevertheless, he proudly held out the tray holding his delicate works and in a tiny, whispering voice invited the King to taste one.

'Not just now,' said the King, slapping his gloved hands together and looking around the faces of the assembled monks. 'We have a fine dinner being prepared for us at Clipstone and I would like to speak to Sir Alan Dale – Brother Alan, that is – without delay. We must be away within the hour.'

'He is waiting in the chapter house, Sire,' said Lord Westbury, indicating the way with an outstretched arm. 'He is infirm, alas, and cannot stand for very long.'

I saw Brother Roger's face fall – the fruits of his long night's labour scorned. And, to my amazement, the King noticed it too. He stopped mid-stride and turned back to the elderly monk and his heavily laden tray.

'On second thought, I think perhaps I will try just one,' said the King. 'They do look most extraordinarily tempting.' He reached out and seized a honey cake, taking a large bite. As the King made muffled noises to express his delight at the cake, he was ushered through the courtyard towards the chapter house. I heard a beaming Brother Roger whisper, 'Most extraordinarily tempting' to himself over and over again.

Inside the chapter house, Lord Westbury had his grandfather by the elbow and was helping him to kneel in the presence of the King. Henry affably waved him to stand, indeed to sit on the stone bench that ran all around the four sides of the room. When Brother Alan was seated, the King plumped down beside him, with Lord Westbury on Brother Alan's other flank, and asked after his health.

'I am as well as can be expected, Sire, at my age,' said Brother Alan, smiling at his King. 'At more than three score years and ten, I have no complaints and I am well looked after here – although it is but a poor House.' I swear on my soul the ancient monk caught my eye and actually winked at me. 'Yes, a very poor House of God and sadly without a great and generous lord to support it.'

'Yes, indeed,' said Henry drily. He knew when he was being softened up for a request for funds.

'Well, you are no doubt wondering why I have come to see you. And I hope I will not take up too much of your time, but Lord Westbury here tells me you are the man who can tell me about this Robin Hood character – he remembers the stories you told him when he was a child. I have encountered songs and tales about this fellow all across England – and at my courts of law no less than five impudent felons have claimed to be the man himself – two in Leicestershire, one in Yorkshire, one in Derbyshire, even one in Kent. My question to you, good brother, is this: who is this Robin Hood fellow and why does every common wife murderer and horse thief from Dover to Durham claim with such pride to be him?'

Brother Alan made an odd grunting noise and his body rocked back and forward on the bench. I wondered if he were having some sort of fit, if the exertions of this happy day had proved too much. Then I realised that he was laughing.

'You find this amusing?' said the King in a voice that seemed to suggest that a man who laughed at him would very soon regret it.

'No, Sire, not . . . amusing,' wheezed Brother Alan. 'But it is passing strange, as I hope you will admit. Because, Sire, you have already met him – the true Robin Hood. You met the man himself long ago, thirty years ago – when you were but a slip of a boy.'

Chapter Thirteen

The mercy of a quick death? King John's verdict *was* a mercy, in a way. I would not have my feet and hands hacked off and be forced to spend the rest of my days as a beggar man, whining for scraps of bread from passers-by, frightening children with the ugliness of my deformity, unable even to wipe the filth from my own body.

I looked at Robin. He was staring mutely at the King. His eyes were the colour of wet slate. And even I who knew him well was shocked by the cool intensity of hatred in his stare. That man is marked for death, I thought. Robin will surely kill him. Then I realised how absurd that notion was. However hard he glared at the King, Robin could not destroy him. In a few moments, my lord and I would be kicking our last at the end of a rope. We could only hope that our sons would take our revenge for us.

Oblivious to Robin, the King was smirking like a child who has been promised a sweetmeat, delighted by his own duplicity. Then I saw that Savary de Mauléon, that grizzled Poitevin lord, was moving towards him, pushing through the bright silks of the courtiers, his face grim as a Nottinghamshire midwinter.

'Sire,' he said quietly in French. 'You cannot do this. You cannot hang all these knights out of hand, rebels though they undoubtedly are.'

'Why the hell not?' said the King in the same language.

'I should speak to you now of decency, of fairness and the Church-blessed code of Christian chivalry, but I will not waste my breath,' said the grey-bearded baron.

The King scowled at him. For a moment I thought he would order him struck down, hanged with the rest of us. Then John smiled. 'My trusty Mauléon – what a fellow you are for plain speaking. But that is why I keep you at my side. Flatterers are a penny a dozen.' He flicked a careless hand at the throng of gaudily dressed courtiers around him. They tittered obligingly. 'Tell me, then, my blunt but loyal liege man, tell me why I may not hang these dogs.'

'Sire, I mean no disrespect. I vowed to serve you and I must serve you to the best of my abilities. And I counsel you, for the good of your own cause, not to murder these men. We have won this battle, yes. But this war is not over. I do not think it will be over very soon. There are many barons such as these who have not yet come to your side.'

'I'll hang them too,' croaked the King.

'Sire, if you do, Fitzwalter and his rebel friends will surely hang any of our men who find themselves in his hands. It will become a war without quarter given to any knight on either side. Will the barons who are wavering flock to your standard if they know that to be taken in battle means certain death? I think not. In this game of chivalry that we play, a move that may prove fatal is to be avoided at all costs. If you hang these men, few barons will join you. Maybe none. How then shall we find the numbers to crush this foul rebellion?'

'But I *want* to hang them. I want to hang them all.' The King's tone had turned querulous – a child again, now denied his promised sweetmeat. I felt a flicker of hope in my heart. We had a champion with the ear of the King.

'Sire, if you hang these men, you will lose this war – it is as simple as that. If you show royal mercy, if you show the gracious mercy that you once showed to me, men who have previously been in opposition to you will come, beg your forgiveness, renew their fealty in the sure knowledge that you will show a similar mercy to them. Think again, my King, I beg you.'

He was a good man Savary de Mauléon, and a wise soul. He had not appealed to John's good nature – he knew the King did not possess one. He couched his argument in terms of victory or defeat for John's cause. And the argument was won.

'Oh, you spoil all my little pleasures, Mauléon, but I know you are a true fellow with our best interests at heart. And I would have more men like you at my side.' The King turned to the crowd of condemned knights – almost all of whom had been able to follow the conversation.

'You deserve to hang, every one of you. But my heart has been softened by my noble Poitevin friend here. I have decided to reprieve you. Yet none of you shall be allowed to trouble me again. You will remain in my dungeons until such a time as I see fit, where you may contemplate the folly of your evil deeds against your King.'

He beckoned over a captain of his guard. 'Take half of these scum to Corfe; half are to come with me north to Nottingham. Now get them all out of my sight.'

Nottingham, I thought. Let us be taken to Nottingham. For even chained in the dark, fetid depths of that royal stronghold, I would be close to Robert and Westbury and many old friends. And who knew? Perhaps something might be managed in the way of an escape or a sly bribe to be let free. My heart was lighter than it had been for days. O God, I prayed earnestly, of your infinite mercy, let them take us to Nottingham.

133

God was deaf that day. They sent Robin, Sir Thomas and myself to Corfe Castle. First south-west to Tonbridge, which had recently surrendered to the King, then, skirting around south and keeping a healthy distance from rebel-held London, to Windsor. Finally, by slow stages to Silbury, Salisbury and Milton Abbas, and at last Corfe Castle. Those who were able to walked; I was afforded the luxury of a jouncing donkey-cart and it seemed that every rut and bump on the road in that two-hundred-mile journey sent a shrill scream up the whole length of my leg. It was the beginning of December when we set out and I seem to recall that the rain fell every single day. Although I do not remember much more about that hellish journey.

They fed us foully, I believe, just enough old bread, ale and plain oat pottage to allow the captives to march – a straggling line of wet and raggedy men, hacking, coughing, staggering, splashing through the mud, prodded ever onwards by the spears of the Flemish mercenaries, a far cry from the proud knights who had held Rochester in defiance of the might of the King. I spent most of the journey asleep or in some pain-filled fevered place outside my head. But Robin and Thomas marched alongside the cart every step of the way – that I do recall – and made sure I received my full share when the meagre rations were doled out.

I remember my first glimpse of Corfe Castle. We had been force-marched from Milton Abbas, continuing without a halt until long after nightfall in an attempt to reach the castle before the gates were shut for the night. But due to the deteriorating health of the captives – one knight died on his feet that day, just dropping lifeless to the ground as we marched – we did not reach Corfe in time and we collapsed in a small shabby manor about two miles north-west of the royal fortress. We were roughly awoken before dawn and forced to our feet, or in my case roughly slung back into my donkey cart, and were back on the road when the first grey streaks were lightening the east.

It was a cold and misty morning in mid-December and as we came over the brow of a hill I saw Corfe. The castle was built in a gap between two long shoulders of down land that ran roughly east-west, on a smaller hill all of its own. As the sun rose over the eastern hills, turning the heavens a wonderful reddish pink, I saw that the land between the two downs was filled with a pure dense white mist that made the keep of Corfe and its high towers and walls appear as if they were built on an island surrounded by a sea of cloud. The battlements were adorned with flags, now unfurling in a breeze that still held a tang from the sea a couple of miles to the south. It looked a magical place; a romantic palace fit for Guinevere, Lancelot, Arthur and his knights, a noble setting for deeds of arms and tales of illicit love.

In truth, that day I saw little of the romance of the castle. But I may reliably inform you that the dungeons of Corfe were no better than an anteroom to Hell. A damp and stinking rectangular stone box a dozen yards beneath the soaring keep. Twelve men had died on the long march from Rochester, from exhaustion and the effects of their wounds, and of the score or so of men who lived to hear the iron-bound oak door slam shut on their freedom, many might well have wished the King had given them the mercy of a swift death. D'Aubigny was a shadow of his former self. He had taken the defeat at Rochester as a personal failure, a negation of his prowess as a man of arms, and while at least we had not all been hanged out of hand, he was a broken man, silent and prone to bouts of sudden anger and violence.

On our first day at Corfe, at dusk, when we were bedding down for the night on the cold floor, a young knight from Cheshire asked one of his companions, in a spirit of genuine enquiry, I believe, if he thought we could have done anything differently to win that siege. D'Aubigny hurled himself at the man and smashed him across the face with a brawny forearm, and once the man was down proceeded to batter away at him with his fists until a group of knights summoned the will to pull him off. Few spoke to our erstwhile commander after that, or even went near him, and, as he chose not to speak to anyone either, he became an isolated figure. He sat alone in a corner of that foul stone box and brooded day after day, stirring only at dawn and dusk to jostle with the other men with spoon and bowl to get his share of food before slinking back to his corner to glower at us over his bowl and champ at his ration of swill.

Robin, Thomas and I naturally formed our own group on a patch of floor by the high, thickly barred window that was our only source of light. We ate communally, guarded our scant possessions and watched out for each other's wellbeing – for prison can cruelly change even the noblest of men. When food is scarce, as I knew well, a fine upstanding knight can turn into a beast of prey, willing to kill his companion over a scrap of gristle.

The food was bad, yes, but also monotonous, vegetable pottage made with leeks, or sometimes just thin onion soup and coarse bread, a little watered ale, just enough to keep our immortal souls within the cage of our bodies. But this grim situation did not last for long. Praise God.

The chief turnkey was a tall, austere figure called Winkyn who inhabited a cubbyhole just outside the gaol door. On the second day after our incarceration, I saw him and one of the other gaolers, who looked almost identical to the chief, whispering together and pointing at our group beneath the window. Winkyn came striding across the floor, a heavy blackthorn cudgel in his fist, casually booting men out of his path. He stopped before Robin and glared down at him. 'You, prisoner,' he said. 'Yes, you. What is your name?'

Robin, who had been carefully ignoring him up to this point, rose lithely to his feet. He turned his cool grey eyes on the man and said: 'I am Robert, Earl of Locksley – when you address me, if you are a man with any claim to courtesy at all, you will call me "my lord".'

I cringed inside. And prepared myself to fight, as best I could with my broken leg. This was not a sensible way to talk to a man with a thick club who held us in his power.

'They tell me you are also called Robin Hood? Is that true . . . my lord?' said Winkyn.

'I have been called that,' admitted Robin.

The turnkey's face bloomed with happiness. 'Robin Hood! Bless my soul. Robin Hood. In my own gaol. I never imagined such a thing. My boys will be so proud. Robin Hood! We know all the stories, of course. All of them. How you defeated the three-headed giant in Scotland! How you cut off the head of the Sheriff of Nottinghamshire and served it to his widow for dinner! Robin Hood, well, well, well. It's an honour to have you here, my lord.'

'The honour is all mine,' said Robin.

Winkyn walked to the door, happily muttering, 'Robin Hood, Robin Hood, the actual, real-life, honest-to-goodness Robin Hood,' to himself.

The next day Robin was invited to enjoy a cup of fine wine in Winkyn's cubbyhole. Vinegary stuff, Robin told me later, but well worth stomaching. Within a week, my lord had come to some sort of arrangement with the awestruck gaoler. He'd persuaded Winkyn to smuggle a message to Kirkton informing them of our whereabouts and received one back telling us that Miles had made it safely home and my son Robert and my household were ensconced there, and that all, for the moment, was well.

All was not well in the rest of the country. Buoyed by his success at Rochester, King John had left his half-brother, William Longsword, the Earl of Salisbury, to keep the rebels penned in London and hold the south, while he embarked on a great *chevauchée* north and east from his new base at St Albans.

This was a terrorising tactic, to be brutally honest, often employed in France and in other foreign lands to weaken a lord by pillaging and destroying his villages and towns. This time King John set his wild Flemish mercenaries loose on his own kingdom and his own people. Those savage warriors burned, raped and plundered their way northwards through the heartlands of England, hitting hardest at the estates owned by the rebel barons, but not always discriminating – it was said afterwards that in those dark days not a man, woman, child or cleric in England was safe. The Flemings used torture a great deal, Robin told us in a flat unemotional voice, applying hot irons or the knife to force folk to reveal where they had hidden valuables. Hearing of their advance, the denizens of York had paid a thousand pounds to one of the Flemish captains to avoid their city being sacked. So far, however, Kirkton had been overlooked by the marauders, for which I thanked God. Yet Robin was confident that Hugh could hold out against them if they did come – and had the funds for a bribe to leave them in peace, if necessary.

Hugh was a good man and a dutiful son and had even managed to send a little money to his father, through the good offices of Winkyn, with which we bought a few luxuries: a flagon of wine from time to time, a piece of cured ham and a wedge of cheese, or some dried sausages, hard-boiled eggs, decent bread.

We began to eat better.

'It is my money and my meat,' Robin said to a shame-faced William d'Einford who came over begging for scraps one day. Robin's attitude had always been that he had an absolute duty to his *familia*, to his kin and the people who served him, but absolutely none to anyone outside that charmed circle. Yet I saw him slip the hungry knight a slice of cheese later that day when he thought neither Thomas nor I was watching.

The pains in my broken leg grew much worse and then slowly better as I recovered from the journey to Corfe and the bone began to knit itself. Robin unwrapped the bandages and repositioned the splints on the first day in the dungeon, and within a month I was able, just, to hobble to the bucket in the far corner where we held our noses and emptied our bowels.

With the discomfort of my leg and the worst hunger pangs assuaged, the main curse of imprisonment was boredom. Robin and I scratched out a chessboard on the stone floor of the cell and using pieces made from chips of rock and pieces of old bone, we played for hours each day. I managed to beat him from time to time, which pleased me inordinately.

When not playing chess or silently contemplating our sorrows, we talked, openly, honestly, with almost no barriers of shame or pride or privacy. I remember Robin admitting quietly one freezing January evening, as we sat in the gloom of that stinking cell, that since they had been wed, he had never once been unfaithful to Marie-Anne. I was astounded. He, just as I, had been away from home on campaign sometimes for months and even years at a stretch, and in all that time he had never once tumbled a pretty serving girl or kissed a lord's lovely daughter, or even rutted with one of the tough, squat professional trulls that followed every marching column.

'Never,' said Robin, 'and I will tell you why. I see my fidelity to Marie-Anne as a badge of my honour. I have no doubt she would forgive me if I were to go behind a hedge with some strumpet out of dire necessity. But I choose not to because, if I did, that would make me a liar, an oath-breaker. My honour, not Marie-Anne's, would be sullied by that meaningless tupping and in all honesty I love my honour more than I wish to honour my lust.'

'But you do feel it – lust, I mean?' I said to him. In the dim light of the cell I could not be certain, but I would have sworn my lord was blushing.

'Of course, all men do.'

'And?'

'Well, I have been tempted certainly. And perhaps one day I will forfeit my honour and embrace temptation . . . if I met someone dark and lissom and lively when all the stars were aligned correctly. But I hope that will never happen. Anyway, Alan, enough of that . . . shall we have another game?'

'It's too dark to see the pieces,' I said. 'And this is much more interesting. Have you ever come close – to, ah, giving in to temptation?'

'Close, yes, several times. There was a woman in Spain, the daughter of a great Saracen lord, fiery and dark-eyed, but . . . I've never yet given in. I love Marie-Anne, Alan, it's that simple. I love her and no other. I always have. So . . . if we can't play chess, shall we sing something?'

We sang. We sang a great deal in those long dull days. We sang all the songs I had ever written, some thirty compositions, we sang all the old English folk tunes that Robin loved so much, indeed we sang almost every tune, *canso*, ditty, lament, psalm and dirty poem we had ever heard. Robin and I made a tuneful intertwining of different melodies between us and even Thomas, once he had overcome his usual shyness, joined in on the choruses with a deep rolling boom that sounded as if it should have come from a man four times his size.

In the biting cold of February, when a layer of crisp snow lay like a mantel over the hills of Dorset, and at dawn the cell sparkled with frost, Robin arranged to have thick furs and wide blankets delivered from Kirkton. A brazier with a decent amount of fuel was brought in and, at last, praise God, we were warm. My leg was mending well by then and I could walk without too much pain. Thomas, Robin and I began to exercise our limbs, my two friends working out a punishing daily routine, and me bending and stretching as much as my leg allowed. Slowly, slowly, I grew stronger. Robin spent a great deal of time working on the muscles of his arms and chest, and with the better food we were consuming, I began to notice a marked difference in his physique. I asked him why he was doing this and he brushed aside my question, merely muttering something about trying to put on a little beef. One day, I asked him discreetly if he thought Winkyn could be induced to smuggle weapons in to us, a knife or sword apiece, and whether we might try to make an escape. But my lord said no. In fact he'd already sounded out the gaoler about this and, despite the man's evident regard for Robin, had been rebuffed, with Winkyn primly claiming it would be a foul slur on his professional competence if any man were to escape.

Robin told me to be patient, he was working on a ruse of his own to get us out of Corfe, he said. If I would bide my time and put my trust in him, I would surely find myself a free man in due course. He did arrange a small parcel to be brought in for me, a gift, he said. Winkyn carried it over in person; it was wrapped in a clean piece of linen sheet and the turnkey presented it as if it were a holy relic. I unwrapped it with a rising sense of anticipation.

It was an old vielle and a horsehair bow.

I was delighted. It was not a fine instrument; the varnish had peeled from the wood of the sound box in long yellow strips and the pegs were clumsily carved and loose. Certainly it was not nearly as beautiful as the vielle I had at home in Westbury but, once it was tuned, the sounds it made were perfectly true, even rather charming in a rustic way. Our singing that night took on a deeper, richer dimension. Indeed that cold February night in the depths of Corfe, although you will say I flatter myself, we made a very fine sound, which no doubt echoed through the whole castle. Let them hear us, I thought. Let our captors know that while they may hold our bodies, our spirits cannot be caged.

The other prisoners gathered around to listen and Robin even conjured a small barrel of red wine, a whole boiled ham and several loaves of good white bread with which to aid our merrymaking. We piled the braziers high with cordwood and served out wine and bread and ham to all. It was not quite a feast but, for once, the dozen surviving knights in that cell went to sleep warm, with music in their ears and a belly full of meat. The gaolers – half a dozen sons of Winkyn who all seemed to be taller, thinner versions of their father – came into the cell and at the end of the night, the turnkey hugged me to his skinny breast and praised me to the moon and back. That night shone like a beacon in the grey sea of tedium that made up most of our time in Corfe.

And it was a night that bore rich fruit.

Two days later, Robin came back from another cosy conference with Winkyn in his cubbyhole and said, 'We have been summoned.'

I looked at him blankly.

'The Prince commands us to attend him and we are to amuse his royal ears, and those of his noble mother, with our music.'

Chapter Fourteen

Henry of Winchester, the eldest living legitimate son of King John and Queen Isabella of Angoulême, was a small chubby boy of about eight years, dressed in a purple velvet tunic with a thick sable collar, black silk hose and fine purple kidskin shoes. He had a pleasingly round face, a healthy boyish glow to his cheeks and one eye, the left, over which the lid seemed to droop as if he were always tired. I had never set eyes on him before, yet his greeting to Robin, myself and Thomas was as warm and enthusiastic that afternoon as if we were old and trusted playmates. In contrast, his mother Isabella, could not have been less welcoming. Seated beside him on a pair of thrones at the end of the great hall of Corfe, the Queen was a stiff icy figure in a tall square gilded headdress secured under her chin by a band of cloth.

'You will stand over there and play your instruments quietly,' she ordered in French, flicking a hand to the side of the room furthest from the roaring fireplace. 'You will be still – no capering about, no hooting, snorting or making lewd gestures. You will take care not to distract us from our conversations.'

'Nonsense, Mother, I want to hear them. I invited them to play for my pleasure not to stand silently in a dusty corner. Over here, gentlemen, over here by me, if you please.'

The Prince turned back to his mother: 'Winkyn says they are quite marvellous. Come closer, good sirs, do not stand on ceremony. Do you need a table? Stools? Some water for your throats? Or perhaps some wine. Hey, Matteus, bring these fellows some of that new Bordeaux, hot, sweet and spiced. And be quick about it.'

'Winkyn says . . .' the Queen sniffed.

That morning we had begged a bucket of hot water from Winkyn and a razor and soap, and while the gaoler looked on unhappily, his hand on the cudgel stuffed into his belt, we took turns to shave each other with that keen blade and to make as best a job of our ablutions as we were able from the bucket and one thin, grey linen towel. The cell door stood open while we three made our toilet, splashing and joking at the novelty of it all, and we saw no sign of Winkyn's lanky sons – it occurred to me that it was now quite within the power of my strength to overcome the gaoler, cut his throat with the razor and make an escape through the castle, scrambling down an outer wall, stealing horses and riding north for freedom.

'Don't get any silly ideas, Alan,' murmured Robin, who had clearly been looking directly into my mind, as he so often did. 'Let us see where this royal summons takes us. Don't do anything hasty, I beg you.'

'What are you two muttering about?' said Winkyn, taking a tighter grip on his club and eyeing the long open razor in my right hand. 'I want more shaving of chins and less wagging of them.'

In the great hall four hours later, with a cup of spiced wine warming my belly and loosening my throat cords, I was glad I had not sliced up the old fellow and made a dash for freedom (he had, after all, dealt fairly with us, even been kind). With an expectant Prince before me and a vielle and bow in my hands, this was a most pleasant change to our circumstances. I felt almost like my old self.

I introduced Sir Thomas and named Robin and his title, and we all bowed low before the Queen and the Prince, and then I tucked the vielle into my elbow, raised the horsehair bow and began to play.

I began with an old favourite, 'My Joy Summons Me', which I had written with King Richard many years ago, and it seemed I had made the correct choice. Prince Harry clapped his hands with delight, lightly bouncing up and down on his throne-like chair and beaming at me like the sun in midsummer. We continued with some of the old French lays, stirring but simple works about ancient heroes dying nobly surrounded by a ring of their slain foes. Then we moved on to the love songs, *cansos* about young knights who loved their lord's ladies and yet could never have them. We ended the recital with a couple of amusing ditties about animals and their ludicrous adventures. And I had the young Prince actually crying with laughter over 'The Lusty Fox and the Lady Rabbit'.

It seemed a good note to end on. But when we stopped and made our bows, Prince Harry cried, 'More, more, give us some more, for pity's sake!'

I pleaded a sore throat after so much singing, and Henry ordered more wine, a jug of ale, too, some sweetmeats and an almond cake to sustain us.

While we waited for the food and drink, he questioned us about our homes and families and the battles in which we had fought, and when the servants appeared and we were filling our bellies with his cake and wine, he turned to the Queen and said, 'You see, Mother, these men are not murderous devils, not at all; they are good fellows who have only had the misfortune to fall prisoner in battle.'

'They are traitors and rebels,' snapped Isabella. 'If your father could see you mollycoddling them like this, he would order you beaten black and blue.'

'Father is in the north,' said Henry a little sulkily, 'beating King Alexander's Scots black and blue, I have no doubt. But come, Mother, if they have been rebels against their rightful King in the past, I am sure they are heartily sorry for it now.'

'That is quite true,' said Robin sadly. 'We have been shown the error of our ways these past few weeks. Now, we seek only to make amends for our sins.'

Isabella glared at him. 'You will open your mouth only to make your vulgar music for my son,' she said. To my surprise, Robin bowed meekly and said nothing.

We played and sang for another hour before the Prince allowed us to return to the dungeon beneath his feet, where we took our well-earned rest. But two days later, we were summoned again and invited to repeat the performance, this time in the Prince's private apartments and without the Queen's baleful presence.

Over the next few weeks, as the county of Dorset slowly shook off its winter slumber, our lot improved considerably. Prince Harry began to send gifts of food and wine, fresh clothes too, and once, to me, a small jewelled golden clasp to grip a fine crimson, double-thick woollen cloak. Robin was allowed to receive visitors – at first a trickle, then a flowing river, of mud-spattered men came to the castle to confer with my lord.

In March, I began to give the Prince private lessons in the rudiments of music, with the tacit agreement of his mother, and I visited his apartments every morning after I had broken my fast in the dungeon on the Prince's fine white bread and hot, spiced red wine. He proved an apt and enthusiastic pupil, with no small measure of talent, although he did not much like to be told when he had made a mistake and when I corrected his fingering on the vielle he would sometimes glower at me in a way that reminded me a little too much of his vindictive father. At first a trio of fierce-looking Flemish men-at-arms hovered in the doorway, watching silently as I took the Prince through his exercises and repeated various basic tunes in different styles, but Harry sent them away after a week, saying they put him off his bowing, and we were left alone.

'Do you swear that you will do me no harm, Sir Alan?' he said on the first day that he was left in my sole charge. I might have snapped his slender neck then as easily as a twig but I readily agreed and gave him my solemn word – and with no wish to deceive on my part. I found the lad a charming pupil and although from time to time that famous Angevin temper would flare, he soon recovered his manners and would apologise handsomely for any cross word or slight. He reminded me painfully of Robert – although he was younger and did not have my son's dazzling acuity of mind, he had the same puzzled goodness that seemed to shine like the rays from a lantern. I had an abiding sense of the essential decency of his soul – and, in truth, I wouldn't have hurt him for all the riches in the world.

By then, I had put aside any notions of escape, for our imprisonment was no longer in the slightest way irksome – indeed, it was almost pleasant. We were well fed and well treated – and even the other imprisoned knights who were not part of our music-making had benefited from our camaraderie with Prince Harry.

William d'Einford almost wept for joy on the day I gave him part of a roasted haunch of venison – a royal gift – and a dozen freshly baked manchet loaves. I saw Lord d'Aubigny smile for the first time in months when Robin made him a present of a new suit of clothes, which he had also obtained from Prince Harry. And this was a man sorely in need of cheer. Our former commander's castle at Belvoir in Leicestershire had surrendered to the King's forces: John had threatened to have d'Aubigny starved to death if his castle did not capitulate and d'Aubigny's men had wisely handed over the keys the very next day. The broken old man had retreated even more into his angry gloom at the news of the loss of his home and lands; but Robin's gift of a blue woollen tunic, cloak and hose helped d'Aubigny forget his troubles for a short while. Most gratifyingly of all, on the Prince's orders, Robin, Thomas and I had been lifted out of the squalor of that dank dungeon and allocated a small blue-painted chamber in the east tower. We had one large four-poster bed with a feather mattress between us, and a large down quilt, eight blankets, four linen sheets and two pairs of pillows for our comfort.

One day Winkyn came to see us in our new quarters, whistling at their splendour. 'There's some high and mighty fellow in the courtyard calling himself Seymour who says he wishes for an audience with you, my lord,' said our former gaoler.

Winkyn had grown much more respectful since we had been moved out of the dungeon and into our fine new lodgings. Robin pulled on a clean tunic and ran a comb through his hair. In the slanting sunlight from the arched window, I noticed for the first time that his hair was now mostly a silky grey and his face, I also observed, was no longer that of a young man – it was still lean and striking, of course, but the smile and frown lines were deeply etched into his pale skin.

'I'd better see what this fellow wants, Alan,' he said, before departing with Winkyn.

Thomas, who had been watching the courtyard through the open window, said, 'Seymour, my arse. Winkyn is an ignorant fool. That is Aymeric de St Maur, Master of the English Templars, down there. What on earth could *he* want with Robin, I wonder?'

I wondered the same thing. Aymeric de St Maur had a complicated history with Robin – and with me. Years ago, he had tried my lord for heresy and sought to have him burned at the stake; more recently, we had been at odds over a sacred relic, the true Cup of Christ, the Holy Grail no less, that Robin had denied the Templars through trickery. To make amends for that deception

148

and to make peace with the powerful Order, Robin had promised Aymeric de St Maur that he would grant the Templars any favour they cared to ask. Just one – but whatever it was, whether the murder of a kinsman or a command to dance naked on the Sabbath in St Paul's Cathedral, he would obey. I wondered if that was the reason for the Templar's visit – I could not conceive of any other business the Master might have with Robin. And if the Templar had come to demand his boon, what could that favour be?

When Robin returned to the chamber, some hours later, his face was as tightly closed as a tapped mussel.

'What did that Templar want?' Thomas asked at once. I sensed a note of, if not fear, then certainly unusual nervousness in his voice.

'Oh, he was delivering some news,' Robin said casually. 'He tells me the Scots have been pushed back again beyond the border, Berwick has been burned and there has been more fighting at Durham, Scarborough and York. Hardly a castle in the north stands against the King now. And he told me something else, too. A strong force of French knights has joined the rebels in London. They are an advance party, two hundred and forty vassals of Prince Louis of France, along with a hundred and forty crossbowmen, a goodly quantity of stores, weapons and other war materiel. Fitzwalter, it seems, has invited the eldest son of Philip Augustus to take the throne of England. And this generous offer has been gratefully accepted.'

'Jesus Christ!' I was shocked to my soul, but I saw Thomas frown at my impiety. Despite what Abbot Boxley had suggested some months ago, and the presence of that pale, cat-torturing envoy in the Tower of London, I would never in a thousand years have believed that Fitzwalter would offer the crown to a Frenchman.

'He can't do it!' I said. 'He can't hand the country over to the enemy. None of us will stand for it.'

'It is done, Alan. It cannot be undone. Fitzwalter and the other rebels are desperate. Prince Louis is a powerful force to unleash on their behalf. It's a clever stroke, too, I would say. It may well be the winning move in this war.'

'Don't tell me you support this?' I said angrily.

'How can you ask that?' said my lord, sounding deeply stung. 'We have fought the French, you and I, all of our lives, in Flanders, in Normandy . . . Too many of our friends have fallen to Philip's men for me to see him as anything other than an enemy. But I can see why Fitzwalter did it. And, purely as a move in this game, I can admire it.'

I grunted boorishly. To be honest, I could hardly encompass the fact that Fitzwalter – the man who claimed to act only in the interests of his country – could be so base. He had sold his country to the French to win his own war against King John.

'There is more,' Robin said. 'They expect Louis to land here with an army at Easter or earlier, St Maur said. In just a few weeks' time. It will be a full-scale invasion. King John is riding south again to confront them. He will be here with us at Corfe within the week.'

It occurred to me later that Robin had been lying – or at least not telling the whole truth. I knew him well, I knew all his moods and ways, and he was certainly not completely candid. A man as powerful as Aymeric de St Maur would not ride all the way from London to a castle tucked away in Dorset just to give us news that we would discover for ourselves within the week. But I was too appalled by the news of the French invasion to ponder any motives for my lord's secretiveness.

I got no more out of the Earl of Locksley that day, nor on the following days, about the true reason for the visit of Aymeric de St Maur. Life at Corfe went on. Thomas and Robin loafed in our chamber and were occasionally allowed to exercise at arms in the castle courtyard. I continued my tutelage of Prince Harry. The rest of the prisoners languished in the dungeons, although now better fed and clothed, thanks to the Prince's generosity. However, I found increasingly that my mind was no longer gripped by the task at hand. The prospect of another Conquest – of French knights rampaging through our land, slaying, stealing, burning at will – stalked my mind by day and gave me nightmares in the crowded four-poster bed at night. The French would violate England as if she were a naked virgin. Although from what I had heard of the depredations of John's mercenaries in the north, perhaps this was already happening. Of more concern to my restive mind was this: when the King came to Corfe, would our new freedoms be respected? Or would we be slung back into the dungeon to subsist on leek pottage and hard bread?

I feared I knew the answer.

The King arrived in a burst of April sunshine, with a hundred knights in his retinue and an old friend of mine at his side: William the Marshal, Earl of Pembroke.

The Marshal greeted me with a bear hug and a friendly insult in the great hall, where I had been working quietly on a small composition I was hoping to share with Prince Harry that afternoon.

'Sir Alan Dale, as I live and breathe,' said the Marshal, striding across the open space and enfolding me in his strong arms and squeezing painfully. 'You've been fighting on the wrong side again, you bone-headed baboon. And my God you've become old; you look like my grandfather!'

This was rich, coming as it did from a spindle-shanked veteran pushing seventy, who had scarcely a hair on his wrinkled, sun-browned head. And I told him so.

'Although it seems your imprisonment has not been all that vexatious,' the Marshal continued blithely, nodding at the jug of red and plate of candied figs on the table at my side. 'They are not starving you to death this time, I see.'

I took his hint and offered him refreshment, and we chatted

like the old friends we were rather than the adversaries on opposite sides of the battlefield that we had so recently been. He asked after Robert, who had briefly been one of his squires, and who he had kindly taken the time to instruct in swordsmanship at Westbury. I asked him, in turn, if it were true that the French were coming.

He sighed. 'Yes, it is true. Fitzwalter has gone too far this time, even for a scoundrel like him. He's opened Pandora's jar and every good Englishman will pay the price – perhaps for many generations to come.'

I was not sure who Pandora was but I said nothing.

'At least your rebel lord has come to his senses,' he said, grinning at me. 'That is something. All cannot be lost when Sir Alan Dale and the Earl of Locksley stand shoulder to shoulder beside you on the ramparts.'

I must have looked as baffled as I felt, for the Marshal frowned. 'Did you not know?' he said. 'Surely Robin told you? He will do homage to the King for his lands this afternoon. He will renew his fealty and accept the King's pardon for his many crimes and misdemeanours. You and I, my friend, will be seeing off these French dogs together. The Earl of Locksley is to be the King's man once more!'

Chapter Fifteen

The mixture of emotions in my heart can scarcely be described. Robin was to renew his fealty to King John: that duplicitous, treacherous, cowardly shit-weasel was to be our sovereign lord once more. The man who had taken our surrender, then ignored his promise of mercy and casually ordered us hanged. The man we had fought against and given up our blood to defeat, who was the living embodiment of all that was wrong, cruel and evil in England. The man whose mercenaries were even now defiling the land and slaughtering our own folk in the north. We were going to swear that we would serve him and be his good and true men. I could not believe it. I would not do it, whatever Robin said. However persuasive he was. I would never serve that vile man while I drew breath.

'I didn't make the decision idly, Alan, surely you know that,' said Robin. 'It's not a casual whim. I know John as well as you do. But think of the alternatives.'

'I won't do it,' I said. 'I will not swear to serve him.'

'Just hear me out,' said my lord. We were in our chamber in the east tower of Corfe, an hour after noon, and the crumbs of a rather splendid dinner were scattered on the table before us. Thomas was still chewing on a thick slice of apple pie emblazoned with a dollop of yellow Dorset cream. Below us in the great hall the King was feasting his knights.

'Fitzwalter has invited Prince Louis in,' Robin said. 'You know what that means – a French king sitting on the throne of England; French lords in all the high positions in the land, a huge French army right here, ready and willing to stamp out any opposition to Louis's rule. All English landholders will eventually be squeezed out, they have to be; Louis must reward the French knights who support him with lands in England, indeed he has already promised to do so. He cannot make land; he must take it from Englishmen and give it to his followers. It truly will be the Conquest all over again. Do you want that?'

I stayed mulishly silent.

'Believe me, Alan, I do not trust John any more than you do. But we follow him or we join the French. And after all these years of struggle against them, all the good men who died, that I could not easily stomach. Little John was killed by the French; old Claes, too, and your squire Kit. Remember? And consider this: if the French were to win, how long do you think I would survive as Earl of Locksley? The French will begin to remove the English lords the moment Louis is the supreme power in the land. I wouldn't last a year. A Frenchman will rule my lands from Kirkton. I'd be executed or exiled, my sons disinherited. And as my loyal vassal, you would lose Westbury. Do you want that?'

'Why do we have to pick a side? They are both as bad as each other.'

'Think it through, Alan. If we are not players on this chessboard, we lose whoever ultimately wins the game. If I were to refuse to give my fealty to King John, we would be kept here at Corfe for years, perhaps until we died, and not in these snug apartments, back in that bloody dungeon. Or if I were to swear fealty, accept my freedom, then turn my coat and return to the rebels, neither side would trust me again. I'd surely lose all, whichever side wins. This is the least worst option, believe me.'

His logic was faultless.

'What say you, Thomas?' Robin said.

'I say you are my lord and I serve whomever you serve,' said the knight, in a strange dead tone. 'Your King is my King, your enemies are mine.' Thomas paused, then said, 'As I hope mine are yours.'

'Of course they are, Thomas,' said Robin jovially. 'Of course they are.' He looked at me. 'The King is not asking for you to swear fealty, Alan, he asks only for mine. All you have to do is remain loyal to me. Like good Sir Thomas here. Can you do that?'

All I could manage was a surly grunt of assent.

I kept my mouth shut later that afternoon as I watched the Earl of Locksley kneel before John in the great hall of Corfe, place his hands between the King's and vow before a God that neither believed in henceforth to be his man.

The King said little too, except for the ritual words, but as Robin got to his feet, he said, loudly enough for all to hear: 'You may think this is absolution for your crimes, Locksley; it is not. I know you and your tricks, and if you play me false I shall have no compunction at all about hanging you and all your men from the nearest oak tree. My soft-hearted friend Savary de Mauléon will not baulk me again. You have not yet earned my forgiveness, but if you labour tirelessly in my service, if you fight hard, if you help me defeat these rebellious dogs and this ridiculous French usurper, then I may reconsider.'

'I have sworn to be faithful to you and your line for ever,' said my lord coolly. 'You shall not find me wanting in my service.'

The next day, I collected my few possessions and bade a tearful farewell to Prince Harry and most of the prisoners, including William d'Aubigny, who had staunchly refused to renew their fealty to the King. Then Thomas, Robin and I rode from Corfe Castle as free men. With a fresh April wind in my face and a bitter, hollow feeling beneath my ribs, I pointed my horse's head north, to Nottinghamshire, to Westbury.

The King had reluctantly granted us a few weeks of liberty. Restored to his grudging grace and favour, Robin had sent riders to Kirkton to spread the tidings of his new allegiance – which we hoped would alleviate the danger of an attack on his lands from the Sheriff of Yorkshire – and we planned to gather men, arms and supplies and rejoin our sovereign lord at a muster of arms at Tonbridge at the beginning of May. We were King's men once more. And the battle for England was about to begin.

We took our time on the roads northwards, a full week. I had not ridden a horse for six months and the muscles in my newly mended leg protested at this strange activity. We also enjoyed the feeling of freedom that the journey gave us. Three well-armed, well-mounted men had little to fear from brigands, and we stopped frequently along the way to eat and drink and rest, mainly at houses of God: Sherborne Abbey the first night, then Bath cathedral, followed by Gloucester, Worcester, Lichfield and Derby.

On the road, Sir Thomas Blood was unusually quiet, even for a taciturn man such as he, hardly speaking sometimes for hours, even whole days at a time. He brooded and scowled, looking as grim as the lands we passed through, for the scars of war were apparent wherever we looked – every mile or so we came across a burned-out barn or an abandoned village, blackened and silent. Unmilked cows roared their discomfort in the fields. The trees at the side of the road were quite often adorned with the naked dangling corpses of hanged men. This was the work of the Flemings, bringing the King's brutal justice to the land. This was the work of John, now our sovereign lord.

On the last night of our journey, in Darley Abbey, when Robin had claimed the abbot's finest hospitality as a loyal lieutenant of the King, I grew tired of Thomas's taciturnity and asked my friend quite sharply if anything were amiss. He would not speak at first but when pressed, and told he was acting like a spoiled child, he took me to a quiet corner of the refectory where we could talk undisturbed.

'You have served Robin longer than I, Alan,' he said. We were sitting at a broad oak table, two large untouched mugs of strong local ale before us. 'You think he's a man of his word? A man of honour?'

I protested that of course he was.

'Yes, you would say that. He can do no wrong in your eyes. For you he walks on water.'

Thomas reached for his mug, put it to his lips and, in a series of huge gulps, swallowed the entire contents, a good pint. I tilted my head, looking at him closely. So what, I thought, sometimes a man needs a drink. But I knew it was more than that. Thomas appeared coldly furious – with me and with our lord. Like a black and heavy thunder-cloud about to crack out a bolt of lightning.

'What is the matter, Thomas? Tell me – what is making you behave this way?'

'I have just seen the Earl of Locksley abandon his cause, a righteous cause to my eyes, and swear meekly to serve a monstrous King . . . and for why? For no better reason than expediency. He took the oath of fealty to John so that he might keep his lands, and for that reason only. I ask myself, what is his code? Where is his honour? Is there anything he would not do to further his own interests? Is there anything, or anyone, he would not sacrifice to keep his title as Earl of Locksley and the lands that come with it? And, on contemplation, I answer my own question. No.'

I sat back, slightly shocked by Thomas's words. But I had to think hard before I answered for there was a good deal of truth in his bitterness. Yet it was also true that Robin's honour was invested in his wife, his family and the folk who served him. He had done terrible things in his time, for money, for mischief and for revenge, cruel things, evil things, but he had always cleaved to this principle; he had never harmed anyone who was loyal to him, indeed he had often put his own life in grave danger to save them from harm. Surely Thomas must recognise this.

'What is troubling you, my friend? Tell me – I swear I shall not speak of it, if that is your wish, to any man, even Robin.'

Thomas reached over and grasped my mug of ale without a by your leave. Once again he drank it down in a series of long swallows and replaced the empty cup on the oak with a thump. The drink seemed to loosen his tongue.

'It's that bloody Templar,' he said finally. 'Aymeric de St Maur, the high and mighty lord of the English Temple, perhaps the most powerful man in the land after the King, who rides all the way to Corfe Castle in the rain, if you believe Robin, just to give us some tattle-tale about the state of the war. Robin lied to us, Alan, about the words he had with the Templar. He lied. I know that. I think you do, too.'

It was my turn to shrug.

'Robin lies. Yes, but what man does not? He keeps his secrets close. He always has. He cannot help it.'

Thomas said nothing.

I said: 'So what do you think they really talked about?'

'I think they talked about me. About Brother Geoffrey, the beast who defiled your boy. I believe the favour the Templar asked of Robin was that he deliver me up to their justice. I believe he means to betray me.'

Westbury was filled with people when I arrived the next morning. The manor had the air of market day, with folk bustling here and there, servants carrying piles of crockery and bedding, men-at-arms bearing stacks of weapons about the courtyard, and stray geese and sheep bleating and honking and tripping up the unwary. Baldwin was at the door of the hall berating a serving girl over the shards of a smashed bowl, his finger wagging like a puppy dog's tail. I stopped my horse at the open gates of the compound, sat a while and took it in.

I had finally convinced Thomas the evening before that Robin could not truly mean to betray him, that Robin simply would never do such a thing – but it took some doing. I stressed again and again that Robin's personal code would not allow him to give up one of his closest men to torture and death at the hands of the Templars, whatever boon he had promised them, and then I pointed out that Thomas could do little about it anyway, even if his fears did come to pass. What could he do? Run away and become a masterless man living wild in the forests? No longer a knight, hardly better than a vagabond. What would happen to his manor of Makeney? His wife and baby? Thomas accepted my arguments and my repeated promise that I would not speak to Robin about this matter and that I would never allow harm to come to him as a result of his actions on behalf of my son's honour.

The next morning he and Robin had ridden on northwards towards Kirkton and I had headed east, to find this scene of pleasing muddle in my courtyard. I was relishing the thought of a few days at my own hearth, when, like a basin of freezing water being dashed into my face, I saw that something was seriously amiss. It took a moment to understand what it was.

The tower was gone. In its place in the corner of the courtyard there was now no more than a shoulder-high pile of blackened rubble. As I stared at it, I felt a sense of loss, almost grief, that took me aback me with its strength and intensity. The tower had been a symbol of legitimacy, my claim to a true membership at last of the knightly class, and now, like so many of my other hopes and dreams for the future, it lay in ruins.

Baldwin came bustling up to my horse, beaming with joy. 'Sir

Alan, welcome home. I cannot tell you how glad I am to see you here at last.'

'My tower,' I said, my happiness at the homecoming draining away. 'What in the name of God has happened to my keep?'

'I am so sorry, sir,' said Baldwin. 'It seems that a large company of men-at-arms came from Nottingham, Sheriff Marc's men, and using mules and ropes, pry-bars and picks, fire and water, they tore it down. We were all at Kirkton at the time – this place was quite undefended. We had received your orders to abandon Westbury and make for Yorkshire. I hope we were not wrong to do so, sir. And while we were away these sheriff's men came here and did this. And we are not the only ones – unlicensed castration, I think they called it, something like that, and folk have had their walls, their storehouses, even their entire homes pulled down all across Nottinghamshire. I am sorry for it, sir. I feel I have failed you again.'

'My tower is gone,' I said stupidly, dismounting and blindly giving the horse's reins into Baldwin's hands.

'Come into the hall, sir, and have a cup of wine. We only returned from Yorkshire yesterday and all is at sixes and sevens, but I believe we can find a cup of wine. Come into the hall and sit awhile, sir, I beg you.'

Another unpleasant shock awaited me there.

As I walked through the entrance, I glimpsed a figure of a woman – tall, slim, in a plain grey shift dress, with dark hair gathered under a white cap – carrying a wide bowl piled high with brown onions across the western side of the hall and out the little door that led to the kitchen block.

It was Matilda Giffard.

Once again I was shocked speechless. I had forbidden that woman my hall. I had given strict orders that she was not to be admitted. And the last time I had seen her she was a penniless outcast, camping by the river under a willow tree, forlorn and friendless

160

on the very edge of humanity. What on earth was she doing carrying food around my home as if she were a trusted servant or family member, instead of an avowed enemy of me and my son?

My son. He was sitting at the long table in the centre of the hall, reading a parchment scroll and eating an apple. He got to his feet when he saw me, called out 'Father!' joyfully, and came over to greet me. But even Robert was scarcely recognisable: he had shot up over the past six months and was tall now, as tall as me, but as thin as a wand and with a long hank of blond hair hanging over his left eye. My God, I thought, he is nearly a man – how old was he now? Still fifteen? Close on sixteen years, that was for sure.

I hugged my son and he led me to the table where Baldwin was fussing with earthenware cups and a jug of wine. I sat and accepted a drink: a cool white liquor that tasted of lemons and wild flowers. Robert was chattering away, telling me of his doings at Kirkton, how Hugh had allowed him to lead a company of mounted men-at-arms in their exercises – he was almost a captain of men, wasn't that splendid? Then he was telling me about the tower and what a shame, but that we had got off lightly, considering; they might have burned the whole place to the ground. Terrible things had been happening all over the north while I was away. But perhaps, now that I was returned to royal favour, we might ask for permission to rebuild it, perhaps even make it taller. And what did I think about converting the palisade around the courtyard into a stone wall?

'Was that Matilda Giffard?' I said, interrupting Robert's chattering. 'I could almost swear I just saw that bitch leaving the hall. Surely I am mistaken.'

'Ah, yes, Tilda. She lives here; she is a useful member of the household. And I would ask you not to use that vile barrack-room term about her in my presence.'

I could only stare at my son.

'You left me in charge of the manor while you were away, Father. And, as temporary lord of Westbury, I made that decision. She is one of us now.'

Robert's eyes were burning bright with defiance. But I saw no fear in them.

'I left very clear instructions—' I began.

'Sir, if I might explain.' Baldwin was standing beside me wringing his hands and hopping gently from one foot to the other as if he needed to relieve himself.

I glared at him. 'Explain then,' I said.

'It was shortly after you left,' the old man said, 'and the young master was taken ill. A fever and a bad one, he was delirious for several days—'

'What? Why was I not told?'

'Clearly it wasn't fatal,' said Robert, trying for a smile.

'We did not know how to get a message to you,' said Baldwin. 'I was at my wits' end when Mistress Giffard came to the gates and claimed she could cure the boy. You had said she was not to be admitted, but I feared the boy would die. He was so pale and weak. When the fever struck he was raving like a madman, seeing demons and devils. I did not know what to do. She swore by the Virgin that she would not harm him, but only heal and, and . . .'

'She cured me, Father. She brewed herbs and made me drink the concoction. Disgusting it was too. She stayed with me day and night, nursed me until the fever broke. She wiped the night sweats from my skin and cleared away my filth when I soiled myself. She saved my life. I know she did. I felt myself going towards God, towards a great and powerful light, and she brought me back to earth. The very least I could do, when I was fully recovered, was to offer her a place as a maidservant in our household.'

'She is our enemy, Robert, surely you can understand this.' I was close to boiling over but just managed to keep my temper. 'She sought to harm you.'

162

'If she wished me harm, she could easily have killed me when I was in the grip of the fever. I drank up whatever she gave me; if she's an enemy, why am I alive?'

I had no answer to that. 'She should leave here at once,' I said.

'I offered her shelter, Father. She had no one else. I gave her my word that she should have a place here with us for as long as she wishes. You would not make me break my word, surely you would not do that, Father?'

'I don't trust her,' I said, my resolve weakening.

'But I do,' said Robert. 'And you will be gone again, very soon, back to the war, and I will be the master of Westbury once more. If you send her away, I will only invite her to return. I made a promise to her, Father. I mean to keep it. After all, I owe her my life.'

'You better make sure she stays out of my way while I am here. Keep her out of my sight, you hear me. And I will not eat or drink anything, anything at all that she has touched – let us be absolutely clear about that!'

Both Robert and Baldwin were beaming at me now.

And there it was. I was no longer master in my own house. I was living with a woman who had once been and who perhaps still was a dangerous foe, and I had not the strength of will to expel her from my home.

163

Chapter Sixteen

Two days later I left for Kirkton. I was not exactly driven out of Westbury by Tilda's presence – indeed I did not set eyes on her again after that glimpse in the hall on the first day – but I could not help but feel uneasy about her occupying the same space as me and every morsel of food I had eaten, even after seeing Baldwin and Robert eating from the same dish, had tasted like dry ashes in my mouth.

Before I left, I went to see Boot, Robert's huge dark-skinned servant, whom I had charged with my son's protection in my absence. I found him in the cattle sheds, overseeing the difficult birth of a calf. He was cradling the head of the mother cow in his thick arms when I arrived and singing sweetly and quietly in her wide twitching ear. Before too long, leaning against a beam at the back of the shed, I was privileged to watch the miracle of life. A healthy newborn calf emerged from her rear end in a great slippery rush of blood and fluid. Boot took a handful of straw and began to clean the filth from the little beast but he was soon butted out the way as the mother staggered to her feet to lick her newborn clean.

I had a present for Boot, a man who loved music as much as I did. It was the vielle that Robin had procured for me in Corfe Castle. I had been teaching Boot to play over the course of the past year, when I could spare the time, sharing my instrument for the practice sessions. Now he would have his own. He was delighted. He plucked a few notes and praised its tone.

We admired it together for a few moments and spoke about some tunes we might try to play with two vielles and two voices.

Before I took my leave, I took him to task about Matilda Giffard.

'I am very disappointed with you, Boot,' I said sternly. 'How could you let that woman into Westbury – you know as well as I do that she is no good.'

'I thought so at first, sir,' said the giant. He had a surprisingly high-pitched voice, the result of a sad operation performed by Moorish slavers, who had removed his testicles as a child. 'When Baldwin took her into the house, I stopped her and spoke to her privately. I told her that if Robert died – whether it was by her hand or not – that I would tear her living head from her body. I believe it gave her some encouragement to do her utmost to heal him.'

When I first met him, Boot had been the executioner at Nottingham Castle and his method had been to snap the necks of the condemned prisoners with his bare hands, like so many chickens. I had no doubt Tilda had been 'encouraged' to do her best for Robert by the threat.

'But I do not believe she means to harm him,' Boot continued. 'I think she is exactly what she seems, a poor woman who has nowhere else to go in the world and who merely seeks a roof over her head and a little company.'

'You are to keep a very close watch on her, my friend,' I said. 'Very close. If she even looks as if she is a threat to Robert or anyone at all – you know what to do.'

Boot sighed. 'I know, sir,' he said. 'I know very well what I must do.'

165

Remarkably, when I arrived at Kirkton later that afternoon, my lord's wife, the ever-beautiful Marie-Anne, echoed Boot's appraisal of Tilda's situation. I sat by the hearth with her and sipped on a mug of ale, while she sat spindle in hand, turning a vast mound of sheep's wool into fine thread.

'She had every reason to hate you, Alan,' she said. 'You killed her father; you killed her lover Benedict. And, indirectly, she was expelled from the Priory because of you. But I watched her carefully over several months when she was with us at Kirkton and I think she is a changed woman, contrite, humble, meek and just what she seems: a poor lost soul with no kin who will own her, and no home.'

'What I don't understand is why she wants to make my home hers,' I said. 'There are plenty of other comfortable homes in England that she could blight – why infest mine?'

'You really can't imagine why she would want to be in your household?' said Marie-Anne with a womanly smile.

'No, I cannot.'

'You were once lovers, were you not?'

I stared at the woman, astonished. 'You cannot be suggesting that she still has, uh, tender feelings for me?'

'Is that so strange?'

I saw that Marie-Anne was perilously close to laughter. I didn't like it at all.

'It is different for women, Alan. We cannot just love where and when we like, we do not just spray our seed like men and skip merrily away along the road. For a few ecstatic moments you and Tilda were physically joined together, you were a part of her body, her being. There are few women who can forget that loving union, however brief and no matter what happens afterwards.'

'This is utter nonsense,' I said. 'She tried to kill me.'

'What's nonsense?' asked Robin, coming into the hall.

'Your moon-crazed wife suspects that Tilda is in love with me and that is why she has moved into my hall at Westbury.'

'Absolute nonsense, I entirely agree with Alan. How absurd! Nobody could possibly love someone as pig-ugly as you, or as thoroughly dim-witted, mule-stubborn and utterly lacking in the proper gentlemanly graces. Nonsense indeed!'

I glared at Robin. Between his silly jests and Marie-Anne's suppressed hilarity – she was making tiny hiccupping noises of mirth even now – I was beginning to regret paying them this visit.

'Come now, Alan,' said my lord, 'she doesn't have to be madly in love with you to enjoy a dry place to sleep at night, food in her belly, some companionship. She knows that you are her last chance in this life and that if she steps out of line, just once, it will be the end of her. I said something of that nature to her myself. She knows not to try to harm either you or Robert – on pain of death. Forgiveness, isn't that what the Church preaches? Why don't you show her a little Christian forgiveness. I really don't think you have anything to fear.'

I spent the next few days helping Robin to organise his forces for battle. Hugh had recruited two score men-at-arms from the farms and villages around the Locksley Valley that he was training up as cavalry, and he had found a couple of dozen archers from somewhere – Sherwood probably, and men who had lived outside the law – to add to the dozen or so of men who had come back from Rochester with Mastin. In total, Robin commanded nearly a hundred and fifty fighting men, but despite his renewed allegiance to King John he was not about to strip Kirkton and take all of them away to war. When we joined the King at the muster in Tonbridge, he would take with him only thirty mounted archers under Mastin and a dozen cavalrymen, with myself, Sir Thomas and Miles to stiffen their ranks. The rest would be held in reserve at Kirkton, under Hugh's command, in case the King or his sheriffs decided to try to make life difficult for Robin in Yorkshire.

That was my lord's plan. Miles, of course, had other ideas. The young man had returned to Kirkton not long after the fall of Rochester, choosing, correctly as it turned out, to take the risk of scaling the wall and swimming the Medway to escape the final and, as he saw it, inevitable catastrophe. He had walked all the way to London, where he gave news of the disaster at Rochester to Lord Fitzwalter and, by his account, was treated as something of a hero by the rebels in the capital. They fêted him and filled him with wine and kept him in debauched splendour for a couple of weeks before sending him back to Kirkton with their praises ringing in his young ears. All this back-stroking had made Miles more devoted to the rebel cause than ever before – and he was not shy about telling the world what he thought of his father's recent renewal of allegiance to the King.

'It is a gross betrayal of all that we have fought for these past few years,' said Miles at the dinner table on the second night I was there. His sapphire eyes glittered with mischief. 'It is tantamount to treachery,' he went on loudly.

Robin, sitting across the table from him smiling faintly, looking as serene as a saint – as he often did when under pressure – chose to ignore the taunts and insults. But his eldest son Hugh did not.

'Oh do shut up, Miles,' he said. 'We all know how you feel, you've told us often enough. Why don't you give that flapping tongue of yours a rest.'

'Let us not quarrel over the dinner table,' said Marie-Anne.

'Tell me, Alan, how do things stand at Westbury?' said Robin.

'Good idea! Let us ask our guest's opinion. What do you think, Sir Alan, about the Earl of Locksley's shameful behaviour? Would you say it was a move that was justified because it preserved our lord's precious skin, not to mention his lands and titles? Or would you rather call it the action of a cowardly turncoat?'

I saw then that Miles was very drunk. But I also knew that

Robin would not stomach his insults for much longer. There would be blood spilled before long.

Hugh got up from his place at the far end of the table. He came and stood behind Miles's stool, put a hard hand on his brother's shoulder and spoke quietly into his ear. He spoke too low for most of the diners to catch, but I heard him.

'If you cannot speak civilly at this table, then leave it,' whispered Hugh, with unmistakable menace in his voice. 'You will not speak to Father like that again in my presence. He will not raise his hand to you; he loves you too much. But I have absolutely no problem in bringing you to heel. This is your only warning.'

'Oh, things are not too bad at Westbury,' I said brightly to Robin. 'Apart from the business of Tilda, everything is in good order. Baldwin, for all his many faults, is an excellent organiser and his sister Alice has everything in hand among the servants. She made the most wonderful milk pudding the other day—'

Miles's voice cut through my prattle. 'It seems my opinions and even my presence are not welcome here,' he said, getting heavily to his feet. 'So I will bid you all good night and farewell.' And, swaying a little, he walked from the table towards the far end of the hall, where he made his bed.

The next morning Miles was gone. He had taken arms, armour and a horse from the stables and departed before the sun was up.

He took Sir Thomas Blood with him.

'It is my fault,' said Robin when the disappearances were noticed. 'I have always been far too indulgent of him. You heard him last night, Alan, he as good as called me a coward to my face – and I did nothing. It is weakness, sheer feebleness of will. I have spoiled my own child, ruined him with a surfeit of kindness.'

'He's a wilful fellow, there's no doubt of that,' I said. 'But he is also grown now and every youngster has to challenge his father, stand up to him at some point, in order to believe himself a man. Where d'you think he has gone?'

169

'Oh London, I suppose, back to his rebel friends and the delights of debauchery without consequence. What I don't understand is why Sir Thomas went with him. He has always been the very model of loyalty to me. I cannot see why he would absent himself like this. Unless he felt he had to protect Miles on the journey south.'

I felt uncomfortable. I had promised Thomas that I would not speak of it to Robin but I was sure his departure was a result of the threat he perceived from the Templars. Evidently I had not convinced him that Robin would not betray him. I desperately wanted to speak of this to Robin but was bound to painful silence.

We busied ourselves with training the new men over the next few days. But Robin grew increasingly concerned over Thomas's absence.

'I do not greatly mind if he has taken a few days' leave from my service on some errand – though it would have been only right, and courteous for that matter, to ask my permission,' he said to me at the end of a long, exhausting day trying to teach the new cavalry to wheel in formation and mostly failing. 'But I need him back with us now. I had thought to knight Miles and present myself to the King next week with three fully armed knights in my retinue: now I shall arrive at the muster with only one. Do you think he is playing the dice again? At York or Nottingham or somewhere? I know he has a penchant for it.'

I could say nothing to aid Robin's speculation. And in the end, inevitably, his worry turned to anger. He sent a message to Makeney, to Thomas's wife Mary, saying that he expected Sir Thomas Blood to present himself at Kirkton for duty within three days or he might consider himself dismissed from the Earl of Locksley's service, in which case, he and all his adherents should vacate the Derbyshire manor forthwith.

It was past the time for us to leave for Tonbridge Castle in Kent to rejoin the King. So I returned to Westbury, to make my own preparations, a few days before Robin and his raw troops were to make their departure. Of course, the first person I saw when I walked into the hall that evening was Tilda. She was sitting on a bench by the far wall, with a candle beside her and a needle and thread in her hands, mending a pair of old hose that must have belonged to Robert.

She did not see me, intent as she was on her work, and as I walked towards her I was struck by how much her looks had improved. Good food, regular bathing and a roof over her head had done wonders for her. She was no longer the starving, battered beggar woman who had come to my hall seeking forgiveness. Her unbound hair was as glossy as a raven's wing in the candlelight and it fell forward in a graceful sable curtain over her creamy cheek; her pink tongue was poking from the side of her mouth as she made the tiny stitches in the seam of the fabric and it made her look as if she were about twelve years old.

Baldwin came rushing over as I advanced on Tilda, as close as an old man ever comes to running, intercepting me before I could reach the woman – I think he suspected that I would try to harm her – and he said loudly, too loudly, 'Ah, Sir Alan, welcome home! I have a letter for you, which arrived while you were at Kirkton.'

He thrust a parchment scroll into my hands. As I looked at it, I could see from the corner of my eye my steward making frantic gestures at Tilda, silently trying to shoo her away, out of my sight. Without looking up, I said, 'Leave her be, Baldwin. I would not disturb a woman at her work.' I turned my back on the pair of them and went over to the firelight by the hearth to read the letter.

It was from Paris.

My dearest cousin,

Greetings! I write to you with sad news and a warning. My father, your uncle Thibault, the Seigneur d'Alle, has finally been called to God. He had been ill for some months with a pain in his belly that the finest doctors in Paris were powerless to cure. As the sickness spread, his sufferings grew worse, yet he bore his pain like a man until the very end when the battle was lost. Now his mortal body is at rest in the churchyard of St Opportune, next to our house in the Rue St-Denis, and I trust his soul is with Our Lord Jesus Christ and the angels. My father asked after you, towards the end, and made me vow that I would always be friends and allies, my duty and honour permitting, with the distinguished English branch of our family – a promise I was pleased to make. So I send you my friendship along with this sad news.

There is something more that I must impart. As you will doubtless know, Prince Louis, the son of our good King Philip, has set his heart upon the English crown and will be making his way across the Channel with a mighty army in the days and weeks to come. I have stepped into my father's shoes with regards to his position at court and his proximity to the King, and I believe that it does not hurt my honour to tell you that, on my advice, King Philip has refused publicly to support his son Louis's English adventure. The King will not be attempting to invade your island himself in support of his son's claims to the throne. This, I think you will agree, is excellent news for any loyal Englishman, such as yourself. However, there are deep stratagems in play here and Philip would certainly not weep bitter tears if his son were to be successful in his endeavours. To see a single King ruling over both England and France would be the culmination of all his many successes against the English over the past twenty years. That is the situation: the King will not support Louis in public, nor give him any additional troops, but he would be greatly pleased if he were to succeed.

Finally, I must give you a warning. I do not know if you

will be engaging Louis's forces in battle – for I have heard you are among the party that opposes King John and backs the Prince – but there is a man I must counsel you to beware of, whether you find yourself pitted against him on the battle-field or even on the same side. He is deadly to friend and foe alike: his name is Thomas, Comte du Perche, and he is now the right-hand man, the sword and hammer, of Prince Louis.

Although outwardly he resembles a gentleman, this man has the soul of a wild beast. They call him the 'White Count' or sometimes 'The Tanner' – not because of any lack of nobility in his antecedents, hardly so, but because it is his pleasure to strip the skin from his living enemies, to have it tanned and to use this human leather to furnish himself with garments. There are many other sins and obscenities that he is guilty of, too many and too foul for me to list here, but all I can say is have nothing to do with this ghoul and pray that you do not cross his path, and further that you never, never fall into his power.

But enough of this sadness and evil. My mother Adele sends you a warm kiss and an invitation for you and Robert to visit us in Paris or in our castle in Alle whenever you should wish to come; and I give you a brotherly embrace and a prayer that God shall keep you safe in all the struggles that lie before you.

I remain, your affectionate cousin,
Roland, Seigneur d'Alle

I blinked back a tear or two at the news that the Seigneur was dead. He had been a fine man. But I knew my cousin Roland would fill his place as the new lord of Alle with strength and grace. His warning about the White Count set me thinking: that oddly dressed Frenchman, the bastard all in white that I had met in the Tower last year, had he not been named Thomas, Comte du Perche? I was fairly sure he had. And I could easily believe that a fellow who snapped a kitten's leg because it scratched him had the soul of a beast. I could easily believe that he flayed his enemies, too. Very well, I would try to stay out of his way. On the other hand, if I did encounter him, since he was now, as a follower of Prince Louis, my sworn enemy, I might just slaughter him on the spot.

Yet all thoughts of dead uncles and vicious French noblemen were pushed from my mind over the next few days, for I was busy with my own preparations. And on the last golden day of April, I left Westbury in Robert's care and rode south again to war.

Chapter Seventeen

The King's muster at Tonbridge was less than impressive. The castle that guards the north bank of the River Medway there – about twenty miles upstream from Rochester – was a decent-sized moated fortress, with a yellow stone gatehouse and tower overlooking the bridge, an old round Norman keep atop a motte, and a high curtain wall. But the royal army gathered in response to the King's command were too few to strike much fear into the enemy's heart. Scarcely five hundred knights answered the King's call, for news of the imminent arrival of the French had forced many barons to reconsider their allegiances and despite the King's successful *chevauchée* and the havoc he had wreaked in the north, the rebels were still full of spirit.

Indeed, in some respects the poor showing at Tonbridge was a result of the King's success in ejecting the rebellious barons from their fortified manors and castles. Many of the men with small or weak fortifications had done the same as I had at Westbury and had removed themselves and their goods and livestock from the path of the King's ravaging mercenaries and found a stronger refuge. Some of the northernmost barons had simply retreated to

Scotland, where they had been made welcome by the young King Alexander. As Robert had pointed out, I was lucky Westbury had been overlooked and that I had only suffered the loss of my tower, for many abandoned fortifications had been either utterly destroyed (slighted, as military men called it) or left intact but garrisoned by the King's men and held against their rightful owners. This was the cause of the depletion of the King's army – for even though only a handful of knights, mercenaries or trusted men-at-arms had been left in each manor or castle that the King had captured, so many places had been taken that his forces were spread thinly across the land.

I wondered if Miles was right to side with Lord Fitzwalter against the King. He was not the only son to take a different side to his father: even staunch William the Marshal, King John's most trusted Englishman, had his son John in the enemy camp. Then I wondered what Miles and Thomas were doing just then in London. Drinking and chasing wenches, if I knew Miles; and Thomas was probably throwing the knucklebones. But was he winning – or losing?

There had been no reply to Robin's ultimatum to the manor of Makeney – the messenger reported the holding abandoned, the hearth ashes cold, the hall empty. Clearly Thomas had decided to make a clean break with Robin. But it grieved me deeply that my old friend was no longer with us. I had known him, raggedy Welsh boy, squire and knight, and trusted him, for more than twenty years. I missed him and knew that I'd miss him even more when the trumpets sounded for battle.

There was one piece of good news. Robin's squire William of Cassingham was at the Tonbridge muster and had brought with him two dozen veteran bowmen from his family lands in the south of the county. These were tough men from the Weald, many of them former poachers by the gnarled look of them, and all well versed with the bow and in moving silently and swiftly through the thick forests of their native lands. Oddly, Cass appeared entirely indifferent to our change of allegiance: when I asked how he felt about serving the King, he merely shrugged and said something similar to Thomas's comment that Robin's enemies were his enemies. 'Truth be told, sir,' he went on, 'I will like killing Frenchmen every bit as much as I liked killing Flemings. They're all dirty foreigners to me.'

Cass's father had indeed died, as the squire had predicted in his letter to me, and the young fellow was now master of a sprawling holding, much of it almost impenetrable woodland, a dozen miles north of Hastings. He was a landed man of equal consequence to me now and in command of a formidable company of bowmen, yet it was a mark of his breeding that he continued to treat me with a pleasing deference as his superior. I did at least have the distinction of having been knighted by King Richard, as well as being the Earl of Locksley's second-in-command.

The addition of Cass's forces to Robin's men made our lord one of the more powerful barons in the King's retinue and should have given him a good deal more weight among the council, the handful of senior knights and lords that the King was supposed to confide in. In truth though, the King trusted no one but his Flemish captains – those whose loyalty was commanded by royal silver.

Savary de Mauléon had been badly wounded in a skirmish with the London rebels in April and was recovering at Waltham Abbey. William the Marshal was on the Welsh marches striving to contain the inhabitants of that wild region who, like the Scots, had naturally sided with the rebels against the crown. So the King should have been leaning on Robin, taking his counsel from the Earl of Locksley, now that he was once again within the fold, but John continued to treat my lord with a contemptuous indifference. Robin responded with a coolness of his own, combined with a determined punctiliousness about obeying orders. He reported to the King every morning just after first light and asked for that day's royal commands. His duties mostly involved sending out parties to forage across Kent and Sussex for grain and livestock. In fact, he was asked to do very little by the King and I knew Robin was making work for his men to prevent them from being idle – scouting south into the woods of the Weald, discovering its pathways, passages and rare clearings; he was also occasionally sending a few men to the outskirts of London, twenty miles north, to keep an eye on rebel movements. He wanted his troops busy and familiar with the terrain of this southern land. And yet there was no sense of urgency. We were all marking time until the King should reveal his will. I took it upon myself during these days to pay a swift visit to Boxley Abbey and retrieve my arms and armour from my friend the abbot. On my return to Robin, the comforting weight of Fidelity at my side did much for my spirits.

The last time I had been at Tonbridge, I was a wretched prisoner of war with a broken leg, wheeled into a leaky barn in the castle courtyard on a donkey cart under guard with the rest of the men from Rochester. It gave me great pleasure to be a free man able to wander the outer bailey at my leisure, sword at my side, and to explore the sprawling walled town beyond and the lush green countryside around. My leg was completely healed and gave me no more than a twinge at the end of a day's walking.

Robin had found us quarters not far outside the town and to the north and east in a customs house named Hadlow Stair, beside the Medway. It was a large, three-storied hall with a red-tiled roof and timbers a foot or more thick, built on a slight rise of land above the marshy river valley, looking south across the forested hills and valleys of the Weald of Kent. There was a wharf below the house, a platform of stout planks a few feet above the river, and the cargo boats that plied up and down to Rochester and even to the German Sea beyond were expected to stop and pay river taxes to the bailiff who resided in the hall. When Tonbridge Castle fell to the King, the bailiff, a vassal of Gilbert de Clare, the lord of Tonbridge, had decamped with his master, leaving this comfortable hall vacant. On their arrival in Tonbridge, Cass's bowmen had quickly discovered it, reported to their lord, and Robin had declared it perfect for his needs.

I met the Earl of Locksley there on the sixth day after we had been summoned to Tonbridge, the day I returned from Boxley, and asked what news he had of the war.

'John has summoned large ships from the leading ports on the south and east coast, filled them with Flemings and they are blockading Calais, where Prince Louis has mustered his troops. The King boasted to the council this morning that he will hold the French invaders there until they turn into greybeards, that they will never find the strength to break out. We loyal men of the royal council all agreed it was a brilliant plan.'

I made a non-committal sound in the back of my throat. It still infuriated me that Robin had to dance attendance on John and worse that he seemed to have turned into a yea-saying lickspittle like all the rest. But I vowed to keep a tight curb on my anger.

'Prince Louis has hired a pirate from the Channel Islands, a ruffian called Eustace the Monk, to be his admiral – an unsavoury fellow if rumours are true, utterly ruthless, a man who has switched sides as often as—'

'As often as we have?'

Robin gave me a steely glare. 'Don't start, Alan. I'm not in the mood.'

I mumbled an apology and after a few moments Robin continued. 'This Eustace's task is to lead the French across the Channel from Calais when the time is right.'

'So when are they coming?'

'Louis cannot come out of port with John's ships waiting for him. A sea battle is a chancy thing and even if Louis were to triumph, the blockading force is strong enough to maul him badly. He might lose half his fighting strength before he set foot on English soil.'

179

'Is there much danger of an invasion, then?'

'Not while the royal navy is in place, no. But the King can't decide what to do. I have told him we should be tackling London. Storming it with all our strength – now. We could be at its gates the day after tomorrow, if only he would move. It could be ours within the week; the walls are long and only lightly held. I've told him that with the city in our hands, we could end the rebellion; kill it stone dead. London is the greatest rebel stronghold in England and if we were to hold the city it would be all over for Fitzwalter and his men. The north is subdued; without London they are finished. There would be no point Louis coming at all. There would be no one to receive him, no one to offer him the crown.'

Robin's frustration was clear to behold.

'But the King won't listen. He doesn't trust me, Alan. He doesn't trust anyone. He even fears the navy will betray him; that they will go over to Louis if offered enough silver. He talks about going to Sandwich with all his forces to make ready to confront the invasion. To fight them on the beaches; to hurl them back off the cliffs. He's a fool. And he's going to lose the war with his foolishness.'

I could have pointed out that this was hardly a surprise. We both knew John of old and he had never been, to my recollection, anything other than a disaster as a commander. But I kept my mouth shut. There was no point in starting a quarrel.

We sat quietly, companionably, for a good half an hour, looking beyond the river over the rolling waves of woodland that rose up to a ridge on the skyline three or four miles to the south. It looked like a vast green and black wall, stretching east-west before us and forbidding us entrance to the fastness of the Weald. Guarding its secrets. For some reason, I felt a shiver of fear ripple down my spine at the sight of that ancient wilderness. Yet there was nothing to fear from a forest, surely?

I heard the bells of a nearby church begin to ring out for Vespers and the urgent clatter of servants in the house at our back. The sun had sunk, leaving no more than a few wisps of golden cloud on the western horizon, and to the south-west the cheery lights of the castle were beginning to twinkle from the window-slits. I caught the rich scent of beef and onion stew on the air and my thoughts turned towards a hearty supper, a jug of ale and a warm pallet by the hearth. Then Robin spoke.

'It's not so different to Sherwood, is it? It's an outlaw's natural playground.'

'Hmm?'

'The Weald, I mean. It's untamed woodland, virgin forest, some of it. Perfect for ambushes. Plenty of places to hide. Very few people. I'd warrant you could still find wild bears in there, if you looked hard enough.'

I looked out again at the sea of dark green to the south. It was more hilly, I thought, more daunting. There was definitely something menacing about it.

'I'd choose Sherwood over this wasteland any day,' I said.

'Well, yes, so would I,' said Robin. 'It's home ground for us. We know it as well as the stones of our hearths. But the point I was making is that a man who wanted to hide from the law, for example, or who wanted to avoid meeting anyone at all, would not find it hard to conceal himself in the Weald. As long as he knew it well.'

I couldn't see the point he was making. We weren't outlaws any longer, thank God, and I prayed we never would be again.

My stomach gurgled; my mouth was awash from the smell of the beef stew. I got up from the table and muttered about finding something to eat.

'All right, Alan, go and eat – eat to your heart's content – but first would you find Cass and send him out here to see me? Thank you.'

The King finally made up his mind. The day after the next, which was around the middle of May, we quit Tonbridge, heading east for the port of Sandwich. A few hundred more men had answered John's call during the week that we had sat idle in the town and we were now some seven hundred knights and their squires, pages, men-at-arms and servants – most of them mounted – when we took the road in a long muddled cavalcade of bawling men, whinnying beasts, ox-carts, covered wagons, flapping standards and jostling folk.

We had just left Maidstone on the second day of the march, when it pleased God to reveal the extent of his fury at mankind. It came in the form of a mighty wind, driving in from the southeast, with gusts so strong a man had to lean his weight right forward to take a step in the face of the onrushing air. Heavy banks of black and purple cloud rode the winds, rolling in from the coast and lashing the column with a deluge that would have sunk the ark. White spikes of lightning split the sky, stabbing the earth from Heaven. The column disintegrated, with dripping men rushing from the road to find shelter where they could, hauling horses with them by the reins.

Robin, Cass and I found ourselves with the majority of our men in a small wood fifty yards from the road, drenched to the bone, while the gale whipped the branches of the trees above our heads with a manic rage and stinging pellets of water pounded our faces. I sat at the base of an oak with my sodden cloak bunched around my shoulders and my shield held over my head. Robin sat to my left, with Cass pressed into his far side, the squire holding a shield above them both.

I thought longingly of the warm hall at Hadlow Stair and my straw pallet by the hearth. It was not even noon and yet the sky was as dark as dusk. The constant noise was appalling: the shrieking of the wind, the clattering of the branches, the endless hiss of the rain. I could barely make out the words when Robin leaned over and said in a half-shout, 'If you think this is bad, imagine what it must be like at sea.'

He gave me a significant look.

I frowned at him. Then I grasped his meaning: the blockade. John's navy was supposed to be keeping the French invasion fleet penned at Calais – but how would it fare in this tempest? Not well.

We stayed huddled in the wood for all of that day and the night that followed, while the wind pounded us unceasingly and the rain turned the peaty earth beneath our feet into a quagmire. It was bitterly cold, too, and we shivered and chattered in our damp attire with no hope of a fire and only the warm flanks of our companions to cheer us. Robin broke out a small barrel of strong ale and a bag of dried strips of beef from the stores so at least we were able to put a little heart into our bedraggled company as we waited for the sun to rise and the wrath of God to abate.

Not long before dawn, as I was dozing with my head jammed uncomfortably between the tree and Robin's mailed shoulder, the noise of the storm faded, the rain receded to the random patter of drops falling from leaves to the woodland floor, and men began to stand and stretch, blink and look about them in the gloaming as if they had never seen the world before.

'Would you like a fire, sir?' said William of Cassingham to his lord. 'I could heat up some of the wine.'

'God, yes,' said Robin. 'Can you truly make one?'

'Oh sir, there is always some dry stuff to be found, even after a blow like that, if you know where to look.'

And that honest fellow was as good as his word, disappearing for a spell and returning with an armful of almost-dry wood. After a few moments with steel and flint, he had a blaze going and a score of grinning bowmen standing around and warming their hands above the flames.

'The King's fine navy will be scattered halfway across the oceans,'

I said to Robin quietly, as I handed him a hot earthenware cup of gently steaming red wine.

'Or sunk,' he replied.

'So now there's nothing to prevent Prince Louis crossing the Channel and invading England.'

'Well,' said my lord, 'not exactly nothing. I think *we* might have a go at preventing him.'

Chapter Eighteen

Two days later I stood with Robin on the long sand and shingle beach a mile east of the port of Sandwich looking out at the sea. Six or seven miles to the north-east, we could see a mass of big ships, their sails bellied by the offshore breeze, heading to some destination north of Ramsgate. The largest, with two high square castles front and rear, displayed a long blue-and-gold banner from its main mast: the colours of Louis of France. There were smaller sailing boats among the bigger craft, darting between them and doubtless delivering messages between the Prince and his vassals.

'It's not much of an invasion fleet,' I said. 'I count only seven big ships, troop transporters that is, and even they can hold only fifty men and their horses in each. Not many men-at-arms to try to seize a kingdom.'

'There will be more coming, many more,' said Robin. 'I am amazed so many stayed together during the crossing. But you make a very good point, Alan. They cannot land much more than four hundred men today. If we strike hard we can crush them before they even get their boots dry. Come on, we must speak to the King.'

King John was to be found a quarter of a mile further south on the beach, just outside a huge gold-and-scarlet-striped tent that had been pitched on the shore. As Robin and I approached, I saw that he was surrounded by the usual dozen or so beautifully dressed courtiers in silk and velvet and half a dozen grizzled mercenary captains in mail and leather. The courtiers were chattering like sparrows, drinking wine and marvelling at the sight of the small French fleet, now no more than half a mile from the shore. A dark-faced rather plump Italian churchman in scarlet, who I had heard called Monsignor Guala, seemed to be in the very act of excommunicating the enemy in the ships as they came on, declaiming sonorously in deep rolling Latin phrases. The mercenaries were silent, lean-faced men who ignored the chanting churchman and looked intently at the King, hands on hilts, awaiting his orders.

'You see them, Locksley, you see the French dogs,' called out the King as Robin shouldered his way through the throng.

'I see them, Sire,' said Robin.

'They have the temerity, the audacity to challenge me in my own kingdom. I am God's anointed ruler of this land and He will not stand by while His will is flouted. God will smash them – isn't that right, Guala? He will rend them asunder, He will smite them and destroy them for ever . . .'

'Sire, we could do a little of that smiting ourselves,' said Robin. 'They are only a few at present and if we were to ride north beyond Ramsgate, we could catch them in the act of disembarking on the beach and hurl them back into the sea. We're a match for them at this moment. Indeed—'

'No, no, no, Locksley – you are too hasty. We cannot engage them here; I have not my full strength with me. I must summon Salisbury and his men, he is loyal at least, and bring the Marshal back from Wales. I will withdraw to the east and gather my full might and at the right time I shall smash them into a thousand pieces.'

'Sire, with the greatest respect, the time is now. They are few and they are weak, their ships scattered, their horses sick from the motion of the sea, and I swear we are easily a match for them. We must strike now.'

The King looked at Robin. His eyes narrowed and seemed to gleam yellow with suspicion. 'And what possible reason could you have to insist that I attack them now, hmm? What makes you so determined to move me from my chosen course? Have you had commerce with Louis, perhaps? Do you seek to lure me to my doom?'

'Sire,' said Robin, and while there was no change to his tone (indeed, he sounded perfectly sincere and humble), I could tell he was on the edge of a scalding rage, 'Sire, I have no desire to mislead you. I only tell you in all truthfulness that now is the moment to strike. I seek only to defeat these Frenchmen, as you do. We can break them as they land on the beach yonder,' and my lord flung out an arm to the north-east. 'We have a unique opportunity to beat Prince Louis – today – and win this war – today. Sire! I beg you, heed me. I seek only to confound your enemies.'

The King gave Robin a twisted smile. 'Since you seem so aflame to fight the French, I shall grant your wish. I shall retire to Dover and gather my loyal forces to me and you shall have the honour of opposing the French here.'

'Sire, I have only three score men-at-arms. I cannot singlehand-edly confront the whole French army—'

'Is that not what you were just urging me to do?' said the King, and he chuckled unpleasantly. 'I will hear none of your wriggling excuses, Locksley. You claim you are keen to fight the French. Well, there are the French – run along and fight them. And meanwhile I shall take the more prudent course. To Dover!'

The King began croaking for his steward and the royal servants, ordering them to strike camp. I looked at Robin standing alone in a bubble of lonely space on the crowded shore and saw once again that frankly murderous look in his slate-grey eyes.

We rode half a dozen miles north, Robin, Cass and I and a mixed force of sixty-seven cavalrymen and mounted archers. On a bluff overlooking a quiet bay on the Isle of Thanet, we watched as the army of Prince Louis of France disembarked on to the soil of England. We could, I suppose, have crept much closer, loosed a few shafts at them and killed a handful of Frenchmen as they landed, but further out to sea, beyond the first wave of ships containing Louis's entourage, hundreds more had appeared, vessels packed with men sailing hard for the shore. We few could never have stood against them. But King John and his whole force might well have made mincemeat of them, killing them in detail, a score at a time as they jumped from their ships and waded through the waves to the beach. Robin had spoken the honest truth. King John could have won the war that very day, if only he had had the courage to face his enemies.

We watched in bitter silence as craft after craft crunched on to the shingle in the shallows and the enemy disgorged. Unopposed, they poured ashore – knights, men-at-arms, crossbowmen, servants, priests, camp followers, splashing through the shallow water, some kissing the sand of the beach in their joy at being on *terra firma*, others stopping to pray and give thanks for a safe crossing, yet others comically brandishing swords and challenging the wheeling English seagulls to fight. After an hour or two of watching from a distance, shaking with a mixture of cold from the biting wind and our own impotent rage, we turned our mounts and rode away.

We headed south and west, riding hard with few breaks for food and rest. As Robin posted me at the tail of our small column, I was not privy to the conversations – long discussions – that my lord entered into with Cass at the head of our handful of troops. We rode all day through woodland and stopped at night-fall – but only to rub down our horses, give them a drink and the oat-bag, and snatch a mouthful of dried beef and a gulp of ale ourselves, before resaddling our mounts and continuing for another four hours in the darkness. I could see nothing ahead but the backs of the men in front, and little around me but the wall of black trees on either side and a sprinkle of stars above. We turned off roads and on to narrower paths and our pace slowed, the branches now brushing at our sides, but still we did not stop. Shy of midnight, with a half-moon overhead, and me nodding in the saddle, we came to a very long palisade in the middle of a huge clearing and, following it round, to a high wooden barbican over a wide gateway of oak planks. We passed through into a courtyard with many darkened buildings around the perimeter and a large hall, lit as bright as day by candles and firelight and torches next to the wide-open door. Even in the half-darkness I could see it was a grand place – much bigger than Westbury – with two storeys on the wide hall, a straw-thatched roof, and two wings jutting forward from the main building like a pair of embracing arms.

'Welcome to Cassingham,' said Robin's squire as he held my bridle and I climbed stiffly from my horse's back. 'I am truly honoured to have you as my guest.'

I discovered what Robin and Cass had been discussing during the long ride the next morning – after a welcome night of death-like sleep – as we broke our fasts with Mastin, Robin's captain of archers, and our host William, the new lord of the manor of Cassingham. We were brought yoghurt and honey, spelt bread, yellow butter and bramble preserves by a beautiful fair-haired serving girl named Sarah, and I ate heartily and washed the food down with several cups of excellent nutty brown ale.

I was feeling perfectly contented when Robin, too, pushed his plate away, brushed the crumbs from his lips and said, 'Well, gentlemen, we had best get to business.'

'We are heading homeward, I presume,' I said, picking at a

189

bramble pip stuck in my back teeth with a splinter prised from the vast oak table.

'Not a bit of it, Alan. Heading homeward? With a French army just landed on English soil? I'm surprised at you!' said Robin, pretending to be shocked. His rage from the previous day had passed and he was in a jovial mood.

'So, if we are not going home,' I said, 'what exactly are we going to do?'

'His Royal Highness has given us clear orders. King John has personally charged me and my men with fighting the French, resisting the invasion of the sacred soil of England, and that, my dear old friend, is what we shall do.'

Robin was grinning like a happy monkey. His odd grey eyes were alight with a silver flame of sheer glee.

I sat up straight on my stool. 'By your expression, I take it we are not going to be throwing our handful of men into full-pitched battle with the entire French army. So would you mind very much telling me, how are we going to resist them?'

'We are going to tap their life-blood, we are going to drain their sustenance, we are going to gnaw at the sinews of war, nibble through its delicate tendons – we are going to take from the enemy that shiny-bright and jingling commodity that sustains every fighting man from a duke to a dung-collector, we are going—'

'You are going to steal all their money,' I said. 'You are going to rob the French army blind!'

'After all these years, Alan, I think you are finally beginning to understand my methods,' said Robin, grinning. Although I didn't much like his teasing tone, I could do nothing but smile in return.

We refrained from outright thievery for a whole month after the arrival of the French forces at the Isle of Thanet, indeed we spent most of that time in recruiting and training men. A good bowman cannot be made overnight, of course. To gain full mastery of that instrument of war takes a lifetime, starting at the age of seven and training daily, and the physiques of bowmen are quite distinctive, being thick in the chest and particularly brawny in the upper arm and shoulder. But Mastin and Cass between them managed to recruits scores of experienced men from the lands around the manor of Cassingham, and from manors as far as fifty miles away, who were already well versed with a bow; and those volunteers who were not were given into my care to be trained with sword and spear. We would need plenty of ordinary men-at-arms, too, for the scale of the enterprise that Robin was planning.

By mid-June we had about a hundred and eighty skilled bowmen and a similar number of untrained men-at-arms. The promise of licensed larceny, the chance to steal from rich men and never pay the price demanded by the law, was a lure as good as a pot of bramble jam to a wasp. In short, the bold men of the Weald swarmed in. So while Robin busied himself sending out scouts and collecting information about the French movements, and Mastin, his lieutenant Simeon and Cass put the archers through their paces at the butts we set up in the fields around the manor, I took the untrained men under my wing.

After issuing them with weapons made from the surrounding trees – two items each, one a stick with a tied crosspiece to make the shape of a sword, the other a ten-foot pole sharpened at the tip like a spear – I set them to their labours.

In truth, you cannot make a swordsman overnight either, but after a month I had most of them able to make the three basic lateral blows to neck, waist and knees from both left and right, and to block those same blows from an opponent. They knew how to move their feet in the elementary combinations, how to lunge at the body with a spear, how to parry the lunge, sweep at the feet with a spear butt – and how to scream.

Yes, scream. Nothing puts an enemy off his stroke like a sudden hellish scream from a foeman. And I had scores of young men

191

from the seven hundreds of the Weald screaming like devils as they attacked with their childish wooden swords and long sharpened sticks. They were only moderately fearsome, in truth, but practising the war scream put heart into these simple men – even as it terrified the wildlife for miles around.

Not that we lacked for food. Mastin, when not training the archers, sent out teams of hunters and they came back day after day laden with carcasses: roebuck, red deer, fallow deer, rabbits and hares, even wild boar. He told me – and I passed this glad news on to Robin – that he had actually seen a black bear lumbering through the forest but he had foregone killing it because his father once told him that killing bears was most unlucky. I believed him and Robin was delighted. But the Weald, though in many places as densely forested as Sherwood, also had cleared areas, farmland and villages. We bought sheep and oxen from the manors around Cassingham as far west as Horsham and north up to the high ridge before Sevenoaks, and cheeses and ale and good white bread, and honey and fruit – and how did we pay for it all? Well, I shall tell you.

Robin came to find me one June morning while I was exercising my charges in the courtyard of Cassingham, setting wooden swordsmen against spearmen, tapping men on the shoulder and telling them when they were dead.

'We need to put some proper steel in these lads' hands,' he said. 'And soon.'

We set out on horseback at dawn the next morning heading south-east. We were a column of only thirty: ten first-rank archers under Mastin, ten under Cass, each man with a full arrow bag of twenty-four shafts, and ten cavalrymen under my command, no long lances but each man armed with a real sword, mace or axe, and shield. Robin rode beside me humming to himself as happily as a man setting out on a saints' day jaunt in the countryside.

When asked where we were going, he was vague and muttered

something about Winchelsea, which I gathered the French were using as one of their supply ports. I had a fairly good idea what Robin had in mind – I had been riding at his side like this for more than twenty years – and so, if he wanted to be mysterious, I was content to allow him that small pleasure. Instead, I asked him what tidings if any he had of the rest of England and the doings of the King and Prince Louis.

'It's not going well, Alan, I can tell you that,' said my lord rather too cheerfully. 'John is getting his foolish arse kicked westwards almost daily. Last I heard he was back in Corfe Castle doing his best to avoid Louis and his advancing men. The French main forces have got as far as Winchester, I hear; indeed Louis is winning hands down and is facing almost no opposition. Since he landed, the barons of England have flocked to his banner. The earls of Arundel, Warren and Aumale have gone over – even the Earl of Salisbury, the King's half-brother, has bent the knee to the French Prince. You remember William Longsword?'

I did. He had commanded us at the disastrous battle of Bouvines two years before. I had liked the man, even admired him for his open-handedness, and was astonished he would turn traitor to his own kin.

'So is no one but us still fighting for England?' I said, dismayed at Robin's news.

'The West Country remains loyal to the King,' said Robin. 'Some folk in the north, too. And here in the south, Dover is holding out for him yet. And Windsor Castle is still held by royalist mercenaries – they won't crack that. But Louis was received rapturously in London, I heard – Fitzwalter and all the rest acclaimed him King of the English; the mayor of London did homage for the city and they feasted him, petted him and treated him as if he were the Messiah returning to earth for a second visit.'

I bridled a bit at Robin's blasphemy. Partly to punish him for it, I said, 'Talking of London rebels, any news of young Miles – and Sir Thomas Blood?'

Robin frowned and I thought he would not reply. But then he said crossly, 'Cousin Henry did manage to smuggle a letter out to me, since you ask. Miles and Thomas have been riding through Essex, Suffolk and Norfolk with Fitzwalter and his men, raiding, ravaging and burning the King's manors, the usual sort of thing – but they are both well. Unharmed and in good spirits. Or at least they were a week ago.'

We rode on in silence for a while and then Robin said, unexpectedly, 'The war is not lost, you know, Alan. Not by a long country mile. Louis has the momentum, he is conquering all before him, and I know it looks bad, but I'd say he is about to get something of a shock. And we're the ones to give it to him. This land will not be ruled by Frenchmen, not again – not while I breathe and have my strength. Take heart, Alan. The pendulum will swing the other way. It always does.'

A mile or so later, my lord called the column to a halt.

I knew roughly where we were, having taken the time in the past month to scout a wide area around William of Cassingham's manor, even as far down as Hastings and the sea. We were, I calculated, about half a mile west of the hamlet of Peasmarch on the broad track that led from Winchelsea to the main road between Hastings and London. We were on flat land, not yet in the coastal marshes, in thick forest, on a road tangled on both sides with ancient greenery that made it hard to penetrate. It was lonely countryside and it might have been specially designed by God for an ambush – and I recalled then Robin's comparison of this Weald to Sherwood.

He posted three archers up the road to the west and three to the east, leading the remaining fourteen bowmen in a long loose group out of sight behind the wall of foliage, about twenty yards back from the track. My ten cavalrymen were more difficult to hide and we took up our station well behind Robin's men, dismounted and holding our horses' bridles, ready to block their noses with our hands if they started to whinny. Each man had a strip of bright green cloth tied around his upper right arm over his mail coat, if he had one – in the confusion of war it sometimes pays to be easily identified, lest an overexcited bowmen spit you by accident. We were fifty yards back from the road and it would take us time to mount up, force our horses through the thick undergrowth and make an attack, but Robin had decreed it more important for us to be unseen than to get into action swiftly.

'When we start shooting, make your way to the road as fast as you can and ride down anyone on it who is still alive. I don't want any of them to escape this affair. No one. Bring all the bodies and mounts back here. Clear?'

William of Cassingham passed out food and well-watered ale and we dispersed and took our allotted places cloaked by the silent forest.

An hour passed, and then another. It was hot even in the deep shade of the woods and I felt a trickle of sweat slide down my thigh under my mail chausses. This was not my first ambush, nor my tenth – I had done this sort of thing with Robin more times than I could count and yet on that day the hours were frozen, locked solid, the day seemed to stand still. I felt an itch on the back of my neck where my iron-link coif was bunched, and fought the urge to scratch it. The more I ignored it, the worse it became. In my head I said a prayer to St Michael, the warrior archangel. *O holy one, guard me in the coming fray and keep my courage high and my name renowned among my fellow men.* A man beside me, one of Cassingham's few trained riders and a likeable, dull-witted rogue, began to fiddle with the strap on his reins, tightening it and loosening it over and over. I put out a hand to still him and he gave me an apologetic grin.

Another hour crept by. My knees and upper thighs were stiff

from standing still, my feet ached, Fidelity hung heavily at my side, and I thought seriously about giving the order for the men to lie down, take their ease. What was the point of standing here in the forest, hour after hour? And then I heard it: the singing of a Kentish farming man, just a thread of an old tune caught on the breeze and wafted to where I stood by some freak of the air currents. Then the creaking of the wheels of an ox-cart.

I looked around at my men; all had heard it except for one, an ageing man-at-arms from Kirkton called Joseph, who seemed to have fallen asleep standing on his own two feet. I gestured angrily and he was shaken awake by his neighbour but with a palm over the old fellow's mouth to prevent him crying out.

I could see nothing through the wood but a glimpse of the broad back of a Cassingham archer ahead. The man was slowly standing up. The sound of the wheels and the singing grew louder. Then came the crack of a whip and the low booing of an ox stirred to quicken its gait. I heard a man laugh, a high shrill sound, like a fellow only feigning amusement. And another man laugh, deeper, more confident.

Then it began.

First came the creak of old wood from fifteen yew bows, a whooshing sound of flight, the wet thuds of steel-tipped shafts sinking into flesh and the first horrible shrieks of pain. I was in the saddle in an instant, urging my men on to their mounts and fighting through the tangle of low-growing ferns, grasping gorse bushes and tree branches. A man behind cried out as a whippy ash branch I'd pushed past slashed him full face, but I ignored it. The arrows were whistling forward, again and again – I heard cries aplenty, shouts, roars too, coming from ahead. Then I was through, on to the road, the sunlight dazzling, a scene of bloody chaos before my eyes.

There had been about twenty French men-at-arms with the two wagons, a weak *conroi*, but the arrows had done their work and a mere half-dozen saddles still held occupants. Riderless horses, panicking and some stuck with shafts, were milling everywhere, a few lashing out with hind hooves in pain, a pair of them galloping madly down the road. Blood-spattered human bodies feathered with shafts had tumbled to the road-bed, some still feebly moving. Other men had collapsed on the two high-sided wagons and lay bleeding on the wax-covered sheets that covered the loads, punched out of their saddles by the power of the yew bows. And arrows still hissed and flashed in the air.

I came out of the tree line at the canter, shouting 'Westbury!' with all my might – I had Fidelity in my right hand, left holding up my red boar shield, reins looped over the pommel, and controlling the horse with my thighs alone.

A man, a knight, I believe, was shouting to his men in French to rally and charge the archers in the trees. I aimed my horse directly at him and the French knight lashed out with his sword and our blades clanged together as we met. I stopped his strike dead but my hilt-grasping fist continued onward to smash into his jaw beneath his helmet. I felt the blow shudder up my arm, his head rocked back and then I was past. I wheeled tightly and cut back-handed at his neck; the steel crunched home and he flopped in the saddle. My men were out of the woods and all around me now, cutting down the last remaining French. I saw sleepy old Joseph take a clean axe blow to his back from a frenzied fellow in a red surcoat and flat-topped tubular helmet. The arrows had more or less stopped by now. The axeman was on a black gelding and as I approached Joseph's slumped form, he turned his horse and spurred at me screaming his hatred and hacked at my leg with his weapon. I took the blow plumb on my shield and lunged past with Fidelity, ramming the steel as hard as I could at his oncoming body, punching the blade through mail and deep into his belly.

Then it was done.

Robin and the rest of the archers were emerging from the trees,

197

faces alight with victory. All our enemies were down or dead in the saddle. Back down the road towards Winchelsea, the archers had stopped and were calming the two runaway horses, and were even now bringing them back up the track towards us.

William Cassingham had set aside his bow and, as he strode towards the wagons grinning like a demon, I noticed the broad-bladed falchion grasped in his right hand. Robin was by my stirrup, looking happily up at me.

'Just like the old days,' he said. 'I feel like a twenty-year-old again.' And he leaped lithely up on to the side of the first wagon. After hauling a blood-smeared corpse out of the way and letting it tumble to the road, he tugged at the waxed cloth.

I saw movement out of the corner of my eye, the unmistakable flash of a blade. I whipped round and saw it was only Cass. He was hacking savagely at the neck of a dead man with his falchion, the corpse's head gripped firmly in his left hand by its long brown hair, the rest of the body trailing on the road. It took three short blows to free the head and then he had his bloody trophy.

'Robin,' I said, gesturing at the blood-smeared lord of Cassingham. 'Seriously? You're going to allow him to do this revolting sort of thing? We are not savages . . .'

'Come now, Alan. Don't be so prim,' said my lord. 'Don't make something out of this. There is purpose to the lad's butchery. Wait. You'll see.'

I screwed up my face in disgust but held my tongue. These men were enemies, invaders of my country, after all, and they were dead. I did not wish to fall out with my companions over the handling of a few French corpses.

Robin took my mind off this grisly matter in a time-honoured fashion by showing me our booty. In the first wagon, in neatly tied sheaves of a dozen, well slathered in goose grease, were spears, swords and daggers, newly forged and of the highest quality. Enough weapons for fifty men, and there was more: chests containing full suits of mail, sheaves of arrows and a dozen oiled crossbows with hundreds of iron-tipped oak bolts to match them.

The contents of the second wagon truly took my breath away. At first glance it seemed not as full as the first, but when the waxed cloth covering had been stripped back I saw it was filled with dozens of small oblong oak chests, iron-bound, padlocked shut and almost too heavy for one man to lift.

At Robin's urging, Cass took his falchion to one at random. It took all of the young man's strength and no little time to chop through the seasoned oak, but once the chest had been breached we all crowded around to see the mound of bright silver coins glinting beautifully on the soft green grass – glinting beautifully by a small congealing puddle of crimson blood.

Chapter Nineteen

I didn't like the taking of heads. It seemed to me barbaric, unchristian, cruel and altogether wrong. But I understood why Robin had ordered Cass to undertake that bloody task. The lad appeared to lack entirely the sense of horror an ordinary man feels at the sight of blood and death. I also understood, eventually, why it needed to be done. My lord had always used fear as a weapon of war: long ago in Yorkshire he had once had me murder and decapitate a man-at-arms and replace his head with that of a horse in order to sow fear into the hearts of our enemies. That memory still makes me shudder. But it was undoubtedly effective. The outrages committed by Cass and his men on the road to Winchelsea had a similar result. The wagons and the surviving horses were spirited back to Cassingham as swiftly as possible and some efforts were made to erase the signs of the battle. But in the deep pools of blood, Cass and his men planted a short, well-sharpened stake and mounted a severed head garlanded with leaves, flowers and moss. It was as if some gruesome man-headed plant had suddenly sprouted where the poor fellow had died.

The bodies of the men we killed were stripped of their arms

and armour and sunk in the local marshes with heavy stones bound to their chests, with luck never to be seen again. We did not allow the wounded to live to tell the true tale of the fight.

The rumours began almost at once of a great bloodthirsty demon loose in the countryside who ate up Frenchmen and their worldly possessions and left only their heads, which, apparently because they were so full of the French language, he found too difficult to stomach. Other tales told of an English ogre who lived below the earth and rose up to pull Frenchmen into his underground lair, leaving their heads behind as a warning. These rustic fantasies delighted Robin, who did all he could to encourage them. He even urged Cass to hang half-decomposed polls, similarly decorated, from the trees around the manor and on the tracks leading to it to frighten away any curious strangers who might come this way.

None of this behaviour surprised me. I knew that parts of Robin's soul were very dark indeed. Yet what he did with the chests of silver – that did surprise me.

Robin had always been an open-handed lord, almost recklessly generous to his followers, but to folk outside the circle of his *familia* it was a different story. He quite often treated them as no more than prey. As long as I had known him, his ambition had been to amass as much wealth as possible, by means fair or foul, and to guard it jealously like a dragon from the old tales. He justified this by telling me this wealth protected his family, and as it was his paramount duty to protect his wife and sons, it was also his duty to accumulate wealth. I had never been comfortable with this side of Robin's nature and we had frequently fallen out over his blatant worship of Mammon.

In the summer of the year of Our Lord twelve hundred and sixteen all that changed. It began with the purchase of foodstuffs for the manor. Men were flocking to join us, sometimes several dozen a week. We swiftly ran through the provisions that Cass's steward had hoarded against the lean times of winter and, to feed the swollen numbers of men training at our camp, we had to buy grain and meat and ale and wine from all across the counties of Kent and Sussex. Robin was overly generous to the farmers who brought these foods to him, paying sometimes as much as twice the market price.

'I want these men happy to supply us,' Robin said when I caught him slipping a honey-seller a couple of extra shillings and attempted to tease him about it. 'I want them to sell to us and not to Prince Louis's victuallers nor the rebels in London. I also want them to keep their mouths shut about exactly where we are.'

I was relieved to see that my lord did add a level of good old-fashioned menace to his dealings with the local peasants. He had Mastin and a couple of the bigger archers seize one fellow – who had made a sly joke about selling his oats to the French for a better price – and threaten to feed him his own testicles if he so much as spoke to a Frenchman again. And though the fellow was suitably cowed and swore that he would never have dealings with the enemy, it had all been no more than a jest, your honour – that day I missed my old friend Little John even more than usual.

Robin's solution to the problem of keeping our training camp at the manor of Cassingham undiscovered by the French was to bribe every man, woman and child in the Weald to keep our secret. If the sheriff's tax demands had been too harsh, Robin would make good the difference in bright silver. If your milk cow died of sickness, here was the kindly old Earl of Locksley with the coin to replace the animal. A poor man bound to make a pilgrimage but without the funds for the road? Robin would oblige him with a fat travelling purse. When the local churches needed money to help the sick of the parish, there was my lord with a generous contribution.

They loved him for it. He was greeted everywhere he went with a smile. Working men doffed their caps and called out his name.

Young maids brought him bunches of wildflowers; ale wives brewed him special vats of their finest ale. And Robin loved to be loved. In those weeks, dispensing largesse with both fists, he was cheerier than I had ever known him. He joked with the Wealden men, flirted with the ladies, dandled their newborn babies on his knee and proclaimed them all – even the squashed-faced, puke-dripping bawlers – beautiful.

No one went away from an encounter with Robin empty-handed.

I found it absolutely infuriating. Every time he doled out another handful of our precious silver, I ground my teeth and thought about the many times when we'd had nothing, not a penny to bless ourselves with. He was broadcasting coin about like seed corn scattered upon a field: throwing it away, as far as I could see. But somehow I could not find the words to remonstrate effectively with him.

Every few days the men under his command, sometimes led by him, sometimes by Cass or one of his captains, or by me or Mastin, would sally out. Based on information that was happily passed to him by the local people, we would ambush a convoy of pay for the French troops or a line of food wagons, or just cut up a foraging party and perform the now familiar grisly rites with the beheaded Frenchmen. We ranged from Sevenoaks to Sandwich, from Worthing to Wrotham. We slaughtered the French and we stole their money and, almost as importantly, their arms and armour. And each time we killed the French, Cass and his men made their gruesome tableaux with the severed heads. The money came in by the barrel. Every week, no matter how much Robin gave away to the poor, our coffers at Cassingham were replenished. The young lord of the manor seemed to have no interest in money at all and was content to have Robin providing his largesse to all and sundry. I pulled my hair but could not reproach Robin. For he had given me a small barrel of coin and told me solemnly that I should preserve it for Robert's future.

I had been paid off too.

'Don't think of it as money,' said my lord, to my intense irritation, when I finally summoned up the power to suggest he need not give an entire chest of new silver pennies to the monks at Canterbury, who had asked him to help contribute to a special jewelled crucifix for the cathedral's lady chapel. 'Think of it as the silver armour that keeps us all safe from harm.'

And for a few glorious weeks that summer, it did.

Of course, the idyll came to an end – and with shocking brutality. One afternoon in early July, I was training the men – now all fully armed with sword, spear, helm and shield, thanks to Robin and Cass's endeavours, some even sporting iron-link mail hauberks that hung to their knees – when Robin and a score of his men-at-arms rode into the courtyard of Cassingham with a donkey cart in their midst. I could tell something was wrong: Robin had a fixed carefree smile on his lean face but his eyes were as small and hard as granite pebbles.

I dismissed the troop of spearmen, releasing them to wash off the sweat in the bathhouse, and went over to Robin. The men were gathered around the cart looking inside with expressions of disgust, horror and fear. As I forced my way through the crowd, I caught a waft of putrid odour that almost made me cough up my dinner. Inside the cart were two reddish-brown bodies, clearly dead and having been in that state for some days, for maggots writhed and glistened in the eye sockets. Keeping a hand over my mouth and nose, I examined the corpses: they were two of Cass's new recruits, bowmen I thought, from up near Penshurst, although it was difficult to be certain. I fancied at first that they had been coated in blood, dipped in it, for the amount of gore could not possibly have come from their wounds alone. Then I realised that every inch of skin had been peeled from their bodies, slowly, carefully, perhaps over several hours, days even. I could not begin to imagine the expanse of pain that they had endured before they died.

I blundered away from the cart and nearly crashed into Robin, who was standing beside me. 'You Frank, and you Stephen, get these men decently buried, will you?' he was saying. 'Get them in the ground as quick as you like and find a priest to say the right words over them. But most importantly get them buried quickly, you understand?'

I felt a wash of nausea surge up from my belly into the back of my throat and I very nearly splashed it all over my old friend. But he put a hand on my shoulder and looked into my watering eyes with concern.

'You know what this is?' I said, when I could speak again. 'You know what this foul act represents?'

Robin nodded. But I put it into words anyway: 'It is revenge. For the beheadings, for the ambushes. Somebody is coming after us and he is very serious about taking his revenge on us, on all of us.'

'I know, Alan,' said Robin tiredly. 'But I think it is worse than that: those two men would have talked. They would have done anything to stop the pain. Anything. They will have told whoever it is, the revenge-seeker, that we are here.'

I had the full story from Robin over a jug of ale, when my stomach could finally accept nourishment. The two men had been with us for no more than ten days and had slipped off one night to pay a visit to their sweethearts in the village of Hever. It seems they opened their mouths too wide in an inn there. They had been seized by the French and taken to Rochester Castle – now in the hands of Prince Louis's men – and when the foul stripping work was done, and they had told everything they knew, they had been dumped on the road near Ashford and discovered by one of Cass's patrols that morning.

'The French know we are here, Alan,' said Robin. 'It can be only a matter of time before they come for us with all their forces. It is time for the second phase.'

205

'Dispersal,' I said. 'Which is a way of saying: every man for himself; *sauve qui peut*, as our foes would put it.'

'Don't be so gloomy, Alan. It's not like that. And it's not as if we expected to go undetected here for ever, is it? Cass and I have it all worked out. As you know very well – you've sat in on enough of our council gatherings.'

Our conversation was interrupted then by shouts from the palisade. 'Alarm! Alarm! They're coming! Knights are coming,' a man on the walkway was shouting wildly and the courtyard of Cassingham became a kicked ant-hill, with men and women rushing everywhere, yelling in fear and anger, pushing other folk out of the way, snatching up weapons. Sheer bloody pandemonium.

It seemed the French had come to Cassingham.

Chapter Twenty

Knights did come to Cassingham that hot July afternoon. But they were not French. They were a quartet of Norman knights, some of the very few lords of the duchy who had remained in the service of King John after the fall of his continental possessions. Robin and Cass gave them wine in the hall, while I arranged for their horses to be cared for, then I joined them for the council of war.

Robin had not completely cut his ties with the King after the humiliating episode at Sandwich in May; he had, in fact, been sending John reports from time to time of his activities and his actions against the French. My lord was concerned lest the King should believe we had switched sides and rejoined the rebels; if the King thought us traitors, it could be lethal for Marie-Anne and Hugh at Kirkton – and for Robert.

As it happened, I knew one of the Norman knights who paid us a visit that afternoon: he was Hubert de Burgh, a proud hawk-like man who had been castellan of Falaise Castle before Normandy was lost. I had served under him there and while he could be rather stiff-necked and touchy about his honour, he was a good man at heart. He had remained unwaveringly loyal to King John – despite the reservations he must have had – through disaster, defeat and civil war. I could not but feel a grudging respect for his constancy.

De Burgh was now the constable of Dover Castle, which, with Windsor, was one of the last major fortresses holding out against the French in the south-east. It soon became clear he intended to hold it for the King to the last man. It was in this cause that he and his three knights had made the perilous journey to Cassingham through French-held territory to seek us out.

'The King is pleased with you, Locksley,' said de Burgh. 'He likes what you have been doing in these parts. And you, too, Cassingham. He boasts that no man-at-arms of Prince Louis's is safe anywhere on the roads of Kent.'

Cass was red-faced with pride, beaming at Hubert de Burgh as if he were a favourite uncle. 'We do try to do our duty, sir,' the squire mumbled.

'Well, you are doing that and more, William,' said de Burgh. 'The King even has a nickname for you: he calls you Willikin of the Weald. He asks why there are not more like you fighting the good fight in the other counties.'

Robin gave a snort of derision. I could tell what he was thinking: we were only behaving here as we had for years in Nottinghamshire, Yorkshire and Derbyshire, only then we had been outside the law.

'It is on the King's instructions that I come to you today,' de Burgh continued. 'As I'm sure you know, Dover has been beset by Louis's men these past few weeks. We have been attacked repeatedly and until now have been able to hold them off, even to inflict significant damage. But our scouts tell us a new commander has been appointed, a fellow recently arrived from France, and he has vowed to take Dover and' – here Hubert de Burgh paused significantly to make sure we were paying attention – 'to eradicate all resistance to Prince Louis's reign in southern England. This

Comte du Perche, as he is titled, is a rather odd fellow by all accounts. He has particularly boasted that he will sniff out any brigands and outlaws in the Weald and strip the living skin from their flesh to make an example of them.'

Thomas, Comte du Perche, the White Count, the Tanner, that pasty-faced cat-torturing bastard from the Tower. He had done that terrible thing to the two captured bowmen from Penshurst. And he was coming for us. Well, let him. I'd gladly face him with Fidelity in hand and briskly send him to Hell where he belonged.

'The Comte du Perche has since tightened his grip around Dover,' de Burgh was saying. 'The siege is being pursued in earnest and his men are encamped around our walls. Yet they have neglected, thus far, to dig their own protective walls around the camp. This is why I come to you now. The King commands you – of course, I merely ask you, of your kindness – to attack the French in their lines around Dover. My men and I will guide you and accompany you in the assault, and I have left instructions in the castle for a powerful sortie to be made when our attack goes in. Between us, with your brave men attacking from the woods and my own folk coming over the walls, we can crush the enemy like . . . like . . .'

'Like a walnut between two stones?' I said helpfully.

'Exactly,' said Hubert de Burgh.

'If the King commands it, we must certainly obey,' said Cass fervently.

I saw Robin looking at him sideways. 'Yes,' he said slowly. 'Yes . . . well, this does seem like a good opportunity to bloody this new fellow's nose. The Comte du Perche, you say. And he is threatening to cut the skin from all our bones. Yes, we'll do it. I'd be more than happy to teach this particular Frenchman a lesson.'

We spent an hour or two discussing the attack on Dover, and then Robin insisted we make plans to break up the training camp and disperse the men not coming with us to the coast. Hubert de Burgh had suggested that the attack on the Dover camp be a hit-and-run affair, undertaken by cavalry alone, with archers in support, of course. We had more than four hundred men under arms at that time but most were farming men and few were trained to fight on horseback.

We decided to take with us sixty trained cavalry and sixty of the best archers, which left just shy of three hundred fighting men of various levels of skill at arms at Cassingham. The young lord of the manor divided them in to ten groups of about thirty men – *conrois*, he jokingly called them, although they were men on foot armed with a motley collection of swords, spears, clubs and bows, rather than an elite squad of highly trained cavalry. Each of the ten groups was to be sent to a different part of the Weald and commanded by a man familiar with that part, and their task was simple: to kill any Frenchman they could lay their hands on. The manor of Cassingham would be returned to its condition as a sleepy backwater, with just a handful of men-at-arms, but it would act as a clearing house for news. The ten '*conrois*' would report to the manor on a weekly basis and could be alerted to any threats in their areas, or summoned to form a small army if required, at Cass's command.

Much to the young man's chagrin, Robin insisted he not accompany the assault on the lines of Dover.

'I want to kill Frenchmen,' he said almost petulantly.

'We cannot risk losing you,' Robin said. 'If this attack fails and we all fall, who would carry on the fight against the French? England needs you, William!'

Cass reluctantly agreed and he and Robin summoned the men to give them their orders. I went off to find Mastin, who was to command the sixty archers, and found him in the graveyard of the little church of Cassingham in a small forest clearing half a mile from the walls of the manor. The big bald fellow was on his knees, beside the mounded earth of the freshly dug graves of the two Penshurst bowmen, praying hard, with tears glistening on his heavily bearded cheeks.

I got down on my knees in the dirt beside him and joined him in prayer, asking God to receive their eternal souls in Heaven and to grant me the strength to take my vengeance on the White Count, who was the author of their final agonies.

'They was a pair of useless buggers,' said Mastin. 'Couldn't shoot a bow for shit. Never would bend their elbows properly. They talked a deal too much as well. Cheeky to me. I told them they were born to hang. And they were. But they didn't deserve to die like that, inch by bloody inch. Peeled like a fucking apple.'

He sniffed, cuffed at his dripping nose and got to his feet.

I stood too and put my hand on his shoulder. 'We're going to have a chance to pay the French back for what they did,' I said.

The burly archer nodded at the pair of graves. 'Won't bring them back, though, will it?'

Before we left, after breakfast at dawn the next morning, Robin took me aside. He seemed embarrassed and he was holding a linen-wrapped parcel.

'I've been waiting for the right moment to give this to you,' he said. 'And this moment is not it, I'm afraid. But I'm giving it to you anyway. So . . .'

I looked in puzzlement at the long bundle in his hand. He made no move to give it to me. 'I got Savary de Mauléon to find this for you,' he said. 'I wrote to him about it when we were leaving Corfe. Apparently, it was among the piles of loot taken after Rochester fell and Savary had to buy it off a Flemish knight who had claimed it. Cost him a pretty penny, he says. Anyway, here you are. Think of it as a saint's day gift or a reward for long service, or a token of friendship or whatever you like . . .'

I took the bundle in my hand and unwrapped it eagerly. To my exquisite joy, inside was a lace-up leather bracer with long black

211

steel scabbard attached holding a slim steel cruciform blade. It was my misericorde. Tears formed under my eyelids as I felt the weight of it in my hands.

It seemed to whisper to me as I slipped it out of its sheath in all its black gleaming beauty. I looked up at Robin, groping for the words to thank him and tell him how much this slim weapon meant to me – and coming up empty.

'Don't go all womanish on me, Alan,' said my lord. 'I'm giving this to you for a very good reason.'

I nodded without understanding.

'Be very clear on this: you do not under any circumstances want to be captured by this Comte du Perche; and I do not wish to fall into his hands either. So I charge you with this grave duty. Are you listening? I charge you, Sir Alan Dale, with administering my death. If I fall and you cannot get me away alive. I want you to use this blade on me. At the end of the game, I would rather die at your hand than any other. I will not be slowly torn apart, my living skin stripped piece by piece for a French fop's amusement. Swear this to me. Give me your solemn word.'

So I swore that I would take my friend's life if it was necessary, with the very gift he had just bestowed on me. I also privately swore that I'd take my own, if all else failed. I had no wish to be torn apart piece by piece either.

The French occupied Dover and the busy port, which was to the west of the great castle built by King Henry a generation past, a hundred feet below it and in its deep shadow. To the east and north of the castle, in a great sweeping curve that straddled the road heading to Sandwich, their thousand-odd fighting men were encamped. They lived in grubby white canvas tents, fine pavilions, turf-roofed wooden huts, or just huddled in cloaks in shallow scrapes in the ground under the double-sized crossbowmen's shields known as pavises. It was not a tidy ground: campfires, portable ovens, stacks of spears, piles of leather gear, saddles, tack and bales of hay and so on were placed wherever their owners wished in a joyous abandonment of good discipline. This encircling French army had made no headway at all against the massive walls, ditches and lines of fortification that protected one of the greatest fortresses in England. Yet they had little to fear from the local English knights. King John was hundreds of miles away, lying low in the West Country as Prince Louis's men captured town after town and accepted the surrender of castle after castle. Apart from a few hundred men now cowering inside Dover Castle, and the lawless thieves skulking in the dank forests of the Weald, the whole of the south-east of England belonged to Prince Louis and his victorious French invaders. They had nothing to fear here.

Or so they thought.

We blew no trumpets. We uttered no war cries. But just before dawn on the twentieth day of July in the year of Our Lord twelve hundred and sixteen, sixty-six iron-mailed English horsemen came out of the tree line half a mile east of Dover Castle with absolutely no warning and tore into the French encampment like a mailed fist punching through a rotten pumpkin.

Hubert de Burgh led the charge. During the night the Norman lord had steered us unerringly around the enemy lines, crossing both the Canterbury road to the west and the one to Sandwich to the east of the castle, so that by the small hours we were positioned in a wood above the famous white cliffs. With his three knights, de Burgh made up the narrow front rank, the spear point, of our column. They were armed with twelve-foot steel-tipped lances, as well as sword and mace. Three horse-lengths behind them, also wielding lances, came Robin and myself and a dozen of our best cavalry – mostly men Robin had trained himself at Kirkton. Behind our rank came the rest of our force: more than two score riders, well mailed and helmed and eager for the fray, armed with swords, shields, long axes and burning pine-tar torches.

213

They were mostly new recruits, farmers from the Wealden lands whom I had tried to form into an effective fighting unit in less than two months. In truth, I had not made them particularly skilful, but I was proud of them. They might not stand a chance against a *conroi* of fully trained French knights but now they could all ride and wield their weapons from the back of a horse with some degree of competence and, more importantly, without injuring either themselves or their horses – harder to do than you might think – and they had no lack of one of the most important qualities of a warrior: raw courage.

We took the sleeping French camp almost entirely by surprise, the only sound the pounding thuds of our horses' hooves. In the grey light before true dawn, the tents and shacks of the enemy seemed like monstrous black shapes and the dull glow of the scattered campfires like the eyes of huge wild beasts hidden by the darkness. I saw Hubert de Burgh, galloping half a dozen yards ahead of me, draw first blood. He burst out of the night like a dream-demon and plunged his lance into the belly of a man standing outside his pavilion on the edge of the encampment, yawning and stretching his arms to the lightening sky. The fellow screamed, curled around the lance as it punctured his half-naked body, and de Burgh hurled the shaft away, swiftly drawing his sword as he thundered past.

The quiet spell was broken by the man's appalling death shrieks and we began to sing out our own war cries – I was pleased to hear the men giving the screams they had practised so long with wild enthusiasm. I guided my galloping horse between two tents and found myself facing a man with a long dagger in his hand, staring stupidly up as I thundered down upon him. He shouted: À *l'armes!* À *l'armes. Les Anglais* . . .' Yelling 'Westbury!', I thrust the lance hard into his chest, smashing through his ribs, knocking him off his feet, silencing him for good.

I hauled out Fidelity and began chopping at a line of guy-ropes holding up a tent to my right. Robin had been clear in his instructions: our objective was to cause fear and mayhem – to kill and maim as many as we could, of course, but to sow confusion as much as anything. It would safeguard us, he said, for in the chaos of battle who knows who is an enemy and who a friend? And that would help us to withdraw from the field in due course. We were just three score men, he said, attacking more than a thousand. We could not hope to win a proper battle. But we could cause them serious harm and shatter their sense of safety and confidence.

I could smell smoke now and burning canvas. Here and there I saw dark horsemen flitting between the tents, blazing torches in hand, leaving a trail of red fire behind them. The new recruits had been told to set alight anything that would burn and as I rode into an open area before a circle of gold-and-black-striped pavilions, I saw that the whole eastern edge of the camp was now merrily aflame. A French squire, crouched with laced hands, was hoisting his man into the saddle, and the knight, armoured in helm and coif but without his mail hauberk or leggings, saw me and began hallooing to summon his compatriots.

I rode straight at him but before my horse had taken more than three strides, the knight kicked back his heels and, leaving his astounded squire with fingers still interlaced, cantered his horse around the back of his gaudy pavilion to escape me.

The coward.

Now two men-at-arms on foot were rushing at me from my shield side. The squire – who had more courage than his master – snatched up the knight's sword and ran at me from the right. Enemies on both sides, I spurred straight forward, forcing my horse to charge into the side of the pavilion, which thank God sagged and then collapsed under its high stepping forefeet.

The squire seemed outraged at the destruction of his master's property and slashed at my horse's rump with his blade. I flicked Fidelity backwards, caught the blow and at the same time took one of the men-at-arms' sword hack on the front on my shield. I urged the horse forward, trampling through thick folds of black-and-gold canvas as the tent billowed and sank before me. A tricky overhand blow, across my line, cracked the helmet of one of the men-at-arms to my left, dropping him like a sack of meal, but the squire behind was readying for another double-handed swipe at my horse's rump, so I swivelled in the saddle to slice at his face. I missed by inches but he jumped back, tripped over a guy-rope and fell hard on his behind. I urged the horse on again and we were free and clear of the trampled tent and in space. I spurred onwards, away from the wreckage. We had to keep moving, Robin had said.

I caught a glimpse of Hubert de Burgh, nearer the centre of the camp, laying about a crowd of footmen on both sides of him with a long sword, doing terrible destruction, clots of blood and matter flying with every stroke. I rode down a spearman and neatly lopped the wrist off a swordsman who ran at me swinging from my right. A riderless horse ran across my path, followed incongruously by three bleating sheep. A scarlet, pure silk pavilion took fire twenty yards from my horse's nose and was burned to nothing but wisps before I got within spitting distance. Then Robin was shouting from my left: 'Push on to the road, Alan. That way! Follow me! Don't stop for anything!'

The whole camp was wide awake now and men were emerging from their tents, armed, alert and as ready for battle as any man can be who has been asleep a handful of moments earlier. I ran Fidelity's steel through the side of a naked fat man's stomach just as he stepped blinking out of his pointed ash-pole shelter, and ripped the blade free, spilling his blue-white guts around his ankles. He fell to his knees, soundless with shock and then, keening, desperately began trying to scoop his innards back into his ripped belly.

By sheer chance, a few instants later I lifted my left arm to

216

check my horse with the reins and caught an unseen crossbow bolt in the top of my shield – it would have pierced my cheek, had I not. I charged the man who had loosed it and he fled. Following him at the canter around an abandoned trebuchet, I caught him against its side and hacked through his face, slicing off the jaw in a spray of red while he desperately tried to fend me off with his unloaded bow.

I pushed onwards, north-west mostly, as best I could, heading towards the Canterbury road, as Robin had commanded. Men ran at me, I cut them down. Others ran from me and, mostly, I left them alone. The encampment was filled with noise. The shouts, the war cries, screams of pain from men and beasts. Laughter sometimes. Howls of rage. The crackle of flames. The shrill clash of steel and thud of wood on iron. Once I heard the sound of a man singing, a filthy French ballad, I think. My sword was dripping. And sweat oozed from under my helmet into my eyes, stingingly salty. A mounted knight shouted a challenge and came at me. I blocked his strike with Fidelity, swung back at him as he passed, but missed and was dangerously unbalanced as a spearman charged in and lunged at my face with his pole arm. I just got my head out of the line of attack and as my horse stepped forward towards him, I hacked down, cutting deeply into his shoulder. He screamed and fell.

It was much lighter now and I could see men running everywhere. Occasionally though, through gaps between the tents, I saw my comrades fighting, men whose faces I knew well, chopping into their foes, trampling tents, firing wooden structures, hooting with joy. These Wealden men were simple folk, suddenly unleashed from the shackles of family, community, law – from their humanity even. They were free to kill – and die – like wild animals. I saw two of them walking their horses over a Frenchman, stabbing down again and again with their swords. Then they were surrounded by a mob, a score at least, of angry Frenchmen on foot: knights, men-at-arms, servants, too, I think. Too far away for me to help them. Their beasts were hamstrung and both were pulled down into a scrum of flashing knives, screaming faces, spraying gore.

I spurred onwards into an open space. And there I found my anger. A square platform had been set up in the centre of the circle and a long cross bar set above it. I saw the forms of two men hanging by their arms from ropes tied to the cross beam. Both were naked. One was covered in blood and, though it was barely dawn, the flies were already crawling over his red, glistening body. Only one arm and part of his left side remained untouched, the skin horribly white. Beside him, at about knee height, a box-like frame had been set up, like the contraptions washerwomen use to dry laundry on the march. But the thick strips of material stretched over the bars of the frame were not wool or linen. They were his peeled skin.

I felt my stomach squeeze and hot bile shot up my throat. With my anger, the world became sharper, more real. The noise of the embattled camp became louder. This was why I fought. To end this sort of barbarity. To stand against a man who thought that he could do this to anyone – friend or foe.

The second man hanging by his arms was completely untouched but had clearly been driven mad with fear as he watched the torture of his friend. He was babbling, 'Christ our Saviour, Christ our Saviour – a saviour with a blood red shield,' as I sliced through the ropes holding him to the beam. He collapsed in a heap on the platform and began praying and calling on God Almighty and all the saints.

'Run, you fool,' I said. 'Run while you can.'

I cut down his companion, the flayed man, but by the way he landed in a boneless heap, I knew his soul had already departed from his body. Thank God.

Horns sounded to my left and behind me. I looked and saw the big gates of a powerful stone barbican at the northern end of

218

Dover Castle swinging open. Wider, wider, the doors gaped. Now cavalry was coming out at the trot in a neat column of twos in perfect formation. A sortie. The trumpets sounded again and these men – a heavy *conroi* of at least forty knights, all comrades of Hubert de Burgh and probably some of the best men the castle had to offer – burst into a gallop and hurtled towards the French encampment. They smashed into a knot of a dozen French men-at-arms who were either trying feebly to oppose them or just too slow to run, scattering them and leaving at least four bodies lying on the ground.

The cavalry roared into the heart of the camp. I heard them shouting 'England! For England!' and 'God save the King!' as they took their swords to the foe. Their timing was flawless: the impetus of our attack from the east was dying, almost extinguished; our Wealden men were scattered, many dead or wounded, and the rest were trying desperately to extricate themselves from the fight, escape the overwhelming number of their enemies and make for the Canterbury road. Still the French were not yet organised; indeed many newly awakened men had no idea what was happening and I had seen some of the more faint-hearted scrambling into the saddle, panicked, and riding away hard north-east.

The battle raged in the middle of the camp. I saw Hubert de Burgh greet his comrades with a cheer, join up with a dozen of them and charge a perfectly formed wall of mounted French knights as if they were at a tournament.

Then I saw him. The White Count. The man who had flayed the two men from Penshurst and the two I had just cut down from their gibbet; the man my cousin Roland had warned me about. He was bare-headed, mounted on a huge black stallion and clad in a long silvery-white woollen cloak over his mail that reflected the first rays of the rising sun like a mirror. And he was entirely in command of the situation. He was gathering mounted men around him, many in various states of undress, yet all armed with lance and sword. He had a dozen about him now, then a score, and he was moving to tackle the English knights who had made the bold sortie from the castle.

It crossed my mind that I would be doing a great service to mankind if I spurred at the White Count and took his head off this instant – and I might well have attempted it, despite the crowd of knights around him, solely because of the rage washing through my belly from encountering the flayed man and his crazed companion.

Whatever I might think about the White Count, he was a soldier and his knights were equally of the first rank. They were fifty yards distant now and heading away from me. But they had formed a line at the canter, at the canter by God, twenty men on charging horses, and they swept into the surging mêlée in the centre of the camp.

I was tempted to follow them but I recalled Robin's orders. Besides, I had my own problems. A pair of crossbowmen, fifty yards downhill on the northern edge of the encampment, had picked me as their target. The first loosed and the quarrel glanced off my shield and snagged harmlessly in the bunched mail around my neck. He then ducked behind an upright pavise to reload while his mate popped out with a spanned bow ready to take another shot at me. I was moving by then, galloping down the slope away from the tents, closing the distance and fast, but the second man was not intimidated. He waited until I was ten yards from him, put his crossbow to his shoulder almost slowly and loosed. The bolt cracked a corner of my shield, snapping off a triangular piece the size of an apple, and smashed painfully into my right shoulder. My whole right arm went numb. I couldn't raise Fidelity, let alone strike with it. The man cast away his bow and dived out of my path. I let the horse do the work my arm could not, charging straight into the pavise that sheltered the first man, who was now reloading, knocking the big shield flat with momentum alone and clattering over it and the screaming man underneath. I did not stop to engage the second sprawling bowman but carried straight on, my itching back anticipating a bolt, making as fast as I could for the Canterbury road now some two hundred yards ahead of me due west.

I could do no more. It was time to run. My right shoulder was shrieking in agony. As I galloped my overexcited horse west, desperately trying to control it with one hand, I looked behind and saw that somehow Hubert de Burgh had won free of the mêlée in the centre and he and a handful of English knights were going hell for leather back towards the barbican and the safety of the castle. The French camp was a trampled muddy mess, alight in more than a dozen places, smoke drifting in fleecy layers, and with dead and wounded scattered all over the bloodied turf. Other horsemen were, like me, heading for the road and I recognised many of their tight-screwed faces as they urged their horses to take them to safety. I looked behind my comrades and saw, with the sun rising behind him, the White Count. He was trying to rally his scattered knights for a pursuit of the fleeing Wealden recruits. We had stormed through the camp like a whirlwind, killed or wounded scores of men and destroyed many of their possessions – but in no sense had we defeated them. We had stung them, that was all, perhaps dented their confidence, but their numbers still massively overmatched ours. Angry and bloodied, wide awake, fully armed and ready for battle, led by their dazzling-white nobleman, the French were coming after us to take their revenge.

I reined in for a few moments when my horse's hooves hit the Canterbury road, turning in the saddle for a proper look. The White Count had mustered nearly two hundred men on the brow of the hill a few hundred yards above, the various horsemen all mixed together, knights, mounted squires and men-at-arms, milling around, eager to charge but not sure in which direction. The Count was haranguing them, holding them together with the force of his voice, riding up and down their front in his shining white cloak, his right hand held high in the air as he declaimed like a Roman emperor of old.

I heard Robin's voice shouting behind me. 'Alan, Alan, come on – don't dally there like a simpleton. We are all over here, man!'

I turned and trotted my horse the fifty yards up the road to where Robin and Mastin and a dozen horsemen were waiting by a narrow bridlepath that led away from the main road into the fastness of woodland.

'Most of us have already got away,' Robin was saying. Then he stopped and reached forward and plucked out a crossbow bolt hanging from a rent in my mail, the last, close-range shot that had smashed into my shoulder.

'Are you fit? Can you still fight?' he said, looking into my face.

'I can't raise my arm. It's the joint. The same one I injured at Rochester. I think, I think it has come out of the damn socket again.'

'Let me see that fucking thing,' said Mastin, moving his horse close to mine. He grasped my shoulder in one hand and my elbow in the other and he seemed to be twisting them against each other. I had to bite my lip to stop myself crying aloud like a girl.

'Yes, it's popped out all right. But I'll have you right as fucking rain, Sir Alan, just give me one shake of a lamb's little bum,' said the bowman.

'Alan,' Robin said urgently, 'look down the road yonder, will you? Tell me what you see down there.'

I turned my head to where Robin was pointing. 'That black-haired fellow in the pretty white cloak is the Comte du Perche. He has his men across the road, they are properly formed now and I think they are almost ready to— *aaaarggggghhhh!*'

Pain like a sheet of white lightning exploded in my shoulder joint. It blossomed like a gigantic rose but then faded within

222

moments into a bearable background hum. I glared at Mastin who had now released me from his grip and whose grinning bearded face was inches from mine. I lifted my right hand to my left sleeve and touched the hilt of the misericorde. That bloody man was going to get the full length of its slim blade through his throat if he didn't stop smirking at me.

'There we go,' said the hairy archer smugly. 'Right as fucking rain!'

'All better?' said Robin.

'All better? That cretin has just mangled my shoulder with his filthy great paws!' I realised I was shouting in Robin's face, spraying him with spittle.

'What I actually meant by "all better",' said my lord, cool as a trout at the bottom of a frozen lake, 'is can you use your sword now? Because I suspect it really would be quite an advantage if you could.'

I lifted my right arm. It hurt like sin but I could move it. I could hear the clatter of hooves on the flint surface of the road and looked back towards the camp. The White Count's men were surging forwards in a disciplined column, no more than a hundred and fifty yards away.

'Right, everybody off the road and into the trees,' said Robin. 'Mastin, my dear fellow, if you wouldn't mind doing the honours?'

At Mastin's brisk hand signal, sixty of the finest archers in England stood up from the tangled undergrowth on the western side of the Canterbury road and calmly, methodically, without the slightest fuss, demonstrated their appalling killing power to the oncoming cavalry.

Chapter Twenty-one

For the sake of brevity, I shall say only that we slaughtered the
French attackers on the Canterbury road. After a short and bloody
encounter, in which at least four dozen of their men were flicked
out of the saddle by the shafts of our superb Wealden archers, and
in which not a single horseman got closer than fifty yards to our
positions, the White Count was wise enough to withdraw his men
out of bowshot and regroup. We were wise enough to withdraw
completely, heading west along the bridlepath into the woods and
away – the sixty archers and our surviving cavalry, some forty-five
men, many of them wounded – before the White Count could
muster his own crossbowmen and send them in on foot down the
road against us.

I was very happy that I did not have to test my sword arm that
morning after Mastin's brutal ministrations. I had been grouped
to the side with Robin and a dozen other experienced horsemen
while the archers plied their trade, ready to counterattack if the
White Count's men looked like endangering our line of bowmen.
My shoulder did feel a little better and might even have been

serviceable in a crisis, but I doubt I would have given of my best in the mêlée.

I was even happier to be back at Cassingham late that night, and to slide off my horse and not long afterwards into a tub of hot water in the bathhouse.

The manor, now largely empty of troops, except for the returning heroes of the Dover expedition, felt odd and a little alien. The continuous jolly hubbub of the past two months was gone; the sea of cheerful champing faces at mealtimes was no more; the bustle of men in the courtyard was absent. The double-winged hall felt too big, the hearth fire too large for the handful of stern-faced men gathered around it, sipping mugs of warmed ale. Cassingham's very air, its ambience, had changed. The battle at Dover had demonstrated, not least to us as well as the French, that we were a force to be reckoned with in the south of England. Ambushing convoys of food and killing a handful of foes at a time was all very well, but it was a frivolous game compared with an all-out attack on the enemy's encampment. We'd shown our mettle. Few Frenchmen outside Dover, or anywhere else in southern England, would sleep well henceforth.

Cass, although disappointed not to have taken part, was delighted by the success of the attack. And a success it was, for while we had not lifted the siege of Dover, and we had probably lost more than a score of men including de Burgh's knights, we had achieved our aim of disrupting the enemy and causing havoc in his lines: and we reckoned we had killed or wounded more than two hundred men-at-arms, although such tallies after a battle are always a little inflated. However, when Cass suggested a return match, another slap at the enemy outside Dover, Robin firmly said no.

'We were lucky,' he said. 'They had not bothered to set proper sentries, nor had they built the usual outer earth walls to protect them from attack. We caught them napping. But you can be certain the White Count will not allow that to happen again.'

After a long discussion at the depleted dinner table that night, Robin persuaded Cass that the manor had to be abandoned. The young lord was extremely reluctant to leave his ancestral home, but Robin's logic won through. The manor must surely be compromised by now and it was only safe to assume the French would be seeking revenge.

Cass did manage to wring two concessions from the Earl of Locksley: first that the hall should continue to be occupied but only by the servants – local men and women whom, it was felt, would be able to flee into the woods to hide if Cassingham were attacked; and second that the manor should be monitored. Other bands of archers were operating in the Weald, under Cass's command, and the squire had told them to leave messages at Cassingham if they needed help. And so Mastin volunteered to come by the place at least once a week.

As Robin had planned, the rest of us would scatter to all parts of the Weald and operate as roving bands to harass the French. It was a good plan. While I was loath to leave the comforts of Cassingham and return, at my advancing age, to sleeping on hard ground in inhospitable woods, I knew it was the right thing to do in the circumstances.

Robin and I and twenty-eight men from Kirkton rode out the next morning, heading north towards Tonbridge. The castle itself was, of course, occupied by a new French lord, a vassal of Prince Louis's, but Robin and I felt we knew the area a little – better than the wilder parts of the Weald anyway – and we believed we could cause a good deal of trouble to the garrison when it tried to move men, goods or war materiel along the roads or up and down the Medway. We would strike, kill as many as we could, plunder the wagon trains or boats and then retreat back into the fastness to the south before the men of Tonbridge knew what had hit them. We chose that location for another reason, too. Robin wished, if possible, to be close to London – not only because Miles and Sir Thomas Blood were there and he hoped to effect a reconciliation, but also because he was in regular communication with his cousin Henry, who kept him informed about happenings in the outside world.

For more than a month, most of the time in gloriously warm summer sunshine, we waylaid wagons carrying goods to Rochester in the east and Winchester in the west; our technique was very similar to the first ambush that Robin and Cass had laid just outside Winchelsea. Robin and his archers lay in wait, shot the wagon guards full of arrows, then I rode out with the cavalry or men on foot and finished off any who had survived the arrow storm. As a system it worked very well. The Tonbridge garrison soon realised that a band was operating in their vicinity and responded by doubling, then quadrupling the guard on each wagon convoy – but that proved fruitless. We reconnoitred very carefully before an attack, and if our scouts looked half a mile down the road and spied half a hundred men-at-arms guarding a single ox-wagon piled with goods, we simply melted back into the woods and allowed the wagon to pass without molestation.

The French tried subterfuge next. For example, there might be much talk in and around the ale-houses of Tonbridge of a fat wagon train – loaded with gold and silver, precious jewels, furs, exotic spices and the like – that would be leaving on such and such a day and going to such and such a place. And yet, these well-paid gossips would say wonderingly, this train of miraculous riches would be only lightly guarded for the men-at-arms were all needed elsewhere. Of course, if this tempting plum were to be attacked, the ambushers would find that instead of holding all the riches of Solomon, the wagons carried a dozen tough French crossbowmen crouching under a canvas sheet with their weapons ready and murder in their hearts.

These crude tricks never troubled us. Not once. Robin was an old hand at this 'frivolous game' and he could smell a sheriff's trap a mile away. He had been robbing folk from ambush in Sherwood since he was a stripling.

Yet things did not always go our way: we attempted to seize a well-laden barge on the River Medway that was heading up to Rochester with a load of wine for the castle there. But when we attacked from the south bank of the river, the bargemen merely poled their craft away to the north side and took cover from our arrows behind the stout wooden walls of their boat as they drifted swiftly away downstream. We were left standing flat-footed on the bank, feeling like fools. That was the first and last time we tried to tackle the river craft.

One day, hearing of a haul of expensive spices from the Saracen lands that had been landed at Newhaven and was coming up to London by road in a convoy, we lay in ambush at a spot near the village of Crowborough. It was the perfect site for an attack: the main road turned suddenly and passed between steep banks on either side, and our archers had plenty of foliage and undergrowth in which to take cover. We heard the approach of the wagons clearly and just as Robin was about to give the signal to loose, a storm of arrows burst from the woods slightly further down and on the other side of the road. We joined in the barrage, of course, and when all the guards were dead, each stuck like a hedgehog with arrows from both sides, we cautiously emerged to find ourselves face to face with another of Cass's 'conrois', led by a big ugly bowman called Ralph.

We laughed and shared the loot – Ralph was an admirer of Robin's – and once we were all safely away from the site of the robbery we pooled our food and drink and, making good use of the captured spices to flavour our ale, made merry into the night under the stars.

Robin was as happy as an apprentice on a holy day. He was

reliving his youthful adventures, leaping out from cover, slaughtering his enemies and disappearing back into the forest laden with booty. He also kept up his new practice in those weeks of giving money away like a drink-addled sailor in port and this ensured that he received a steady stream of information from the local inhabitants and that he was not once betrayed.

The hammer blow fell when we were returning to our temporary camp near Goudhurst with a wagon full of grain sacks taken from a poorly guarded French convoy. I heard the pounding of hooves behind and, fearing attack, Robin had everyone off the road and into the scrubby woodland beside in a trice, weapons drawn, ready to flee or fight. A single rider on a sweat-splattered dun horse came tearing round a bend in the road and Robin stepped into its path, stopping it with an upheld palm. It was a strapping young man named Frank, one of Ralph's men whom we had met a week or so before at the comical double ambush at Crowborough. There was nothing amusing about this meeting. The man slid exhausted from his horse and Robin had to support his considerable weight to stop him crashing to the ground.

'My lord,' he panted, his young face beetroot with exertion. 'Thank God I have found you. It's Cassingham. They came there. They came in force and did . . . terrible things. Sir, we must go. Master William is there already. It is too, too horrible, I can't—' He began coughing violently.

We got little more out of the fellow that morning. Cassingham had been attacked by the French, that was clear. The servants had scattered to the woods, some had been injured. Worst of all, Mastin, who by sheer bad luck had been visiting the manor when the attack went in, had been captured along with five of his bowmen. I witnessed the youthful levity wiped from my lord's face like chalk on a child's writing slate cleaned with a damp cloth. In an instant, he looked all of his fifty-one years.

Robin and I left the man to our comrades – bidding them to

return to our barn in Goudhurst with the laden grain wagon and wait there for orders. We wasted not another instant. We were in the saddle and galloping south, driving our horses mercilessly. My own mind whirled in a tornado of fear for what awaited at our journey's end.

We found the lord of the manor of Cassingham sitting cross-legged on the packed earth floor of what remained of his hall. All around him were piles of ash and blackened timber. The framework of the eastern wing, two walls at least, was still standing, although it was so pitted by fire that a hard kick would send it tumbling. Here and there a few twisted iron objects poked above the charred debris, and the shape of the long oak hall table could still be made out under a heap of cinders. Even the palisade that surrounded the courtyard had been incinerated, as had almost all of the outbuildings. The hall itself had burned for two days, we later learned, and the blaze had only been extinguished by the first rains of autumn, which fell like a torrent on the very day we rode south. It was mid-September. The summer, that special time of sunshine and simple pleasures, was over.

Cass had his unsheathed falchion across his knees and his head was bent over it, his long red hair falling forward. When I called to him and stepped closer, he looked up and I saw his face was grimed nearly black with ash and he'd been weeping. I crouched down beside him, putting a hand on his shoulder.

'Do not upset yourself, lad,' I said. 'It is a great blow when one's home is destroyed, and all the possessions in it, all the memories of family and friends are consumed, but we can always rebuild. We have the money – God knows we have the timber – and there are plenty of willing hands. My own home in Westbury has been burned to the ground before and I understand the pain you're feeling . . .'

'It's not just my home – you are right, we can always rebuild the hall. It's . . . it's that,' and he jerked his head at the far side

230

of the courtyard. I saw that Robin was kneeling beside a scatter of bodies on the ground.

'The French strung them up by the neck over the gateway, all five of them, after they had done . . . what they did to them. I don't think they were all dead. One of them had got a hand free and was trying to save his neck from the rope. The fire killed them. That or the pain. I cut them down . . . but afterwards . . . but I couldn't. I just couldn't do . . . It was all my fault. Their deaths must be laid at my door.' He made a horrible croaking noise and I realised he was half-laughing in a lunatic way. 'Their bodies *are* at my door – ha-ha-ha – there by my burned-out door.' I gave his shoulder a hard squeeze, partly to stop the awful noise he was making.

'It is not your fault, Cass. Never say that. We know who is to blame and it is not you. Remember that.'

I squeezed his shoulder again and got to my feet. I did not want to look at the bodies. I had seen enough horror in my time to know that I wished to see no more of it. But I walked over to Robin and those awful prone forms anyway – you might call it a debt I owed to the dead men.

I was aware of other folk moving around the courtyard, Cassingham servants, the pretty blonde girl, Sarah, who had served us food, and a few of Cass's men-at-arms, eyes big with shock and grief, beginning to clear up, carrying blackened timbers away, sweeping the ash into huge piles. The lord of the manor too had got to his feet now and was starting to direct operations with a few quiet commands. Robin was standing silently beside the bodies, his eyes the colour of cold iron. I forced myself to look down at them.

These were not men, I thought, these five reddish-brown man-sized things, skinless, hairless, melted into shapelessness by fire. These crusted horrors may once have contained the essence of my comrades, but no longer. This was cooked meat, dried blood, bone and gristle – no more.

I looked away and saw that Robin was in conversation with Simeon, Mastin's second-in-command. The archer was white as a sheet, trembling and holding out a long thin object wrapped in a grubby linen sleeve, offering it to Robin.

My lord turned to me. 'Simeon says they flayed, hanged and burned the others here,' he said. 'He watched it all from hiding in the woods. But they took Mastin with them. It seems they are heading back towards Dover.'

A shiver of pure horror swept down my back, raising every tiny hair on my body in protest. I realised what lay in store for my friend.

'I'm going after them,' said Robin.

'I'm coming with you,' said Cass.

'Enough chatter,' I said. 'Let's go.'

Chapter Twenty-two

The three of us set off a half-hour later in pursuit of the White Count's men. Cass had suggested we go in force – a hundred archers and a hundred men-at-arms – but Robin said it would take time to muster the men and that we could never hope to match the French strength in numbers. We were better using stealth, he said, than marching through Kent with a small army that could be seen and heard from miles away.

'He hopes to draw us into the open,' said Robin. 'I can see no other point in keeping Mastin alive – except as bait. He wants us to mass our forces and come at him with all our strength so he can crush us once and for all. The White Count wants us to fight his kind of war – ranks of mailed knights charging at each other across the fields of glory. We need to fight our kind: the war of sudden ambush, strike and run, the war of a thousand tiny cuts. The war of the weak against the mighty.'

We went as fast as we could but did not take the direct route to Dover. Robin insisted the enemy would likely be laying ambushes on the road, hoping to trap us as we followed. So Cass led us by secret paths and ways in a loop north and east as far as the outskirts of Canterbury, and then further east so that we came into Dover from the direction of Walmer Castle, a little further up the coast.

We travelled as fast as we could urge our horses – we changed them at a friendly manor just outside Canterbury, owned by a cousin of Cass's, and pushed on all through the night – but it was dawn once again when we found ourselves hidden from sight in the woods above the white cliffs to the east of Dover Castle.

I shinned up a tall elm, a few yards back from the tree line, to get a better view. The castle itself was largely the same, a little more battered, a little more worn down, but still holding out bravely against the French. The three golden lions of England flew yet above the keep. No, it was the French encampment outside Hubert de Burgh's fortress that had changed out of all recognition. A six-foot-high earth wall with an accompanying outer ditch had been thrown up all around the French lines and watch towers stood every hundred yards along its length. The enemy had evidently learned a lesson from our surprise attack in July and in the two months that had passed they had been busy.

I also realised that Robin had been right about taking the precautions he had, for the camp was evidently on high alert. I saw several patrols of crossbowmen, twenty strong, passing along the inside of the earth walls. And in the centre of the camp, at least two full *conrois* of cavalry were mustered and mounted, ready to face any attack. There could be no surprising them.

In the middle of the encampment some three hundred yards away, I saw something that sank my heart into my boots. On the platform with the cross bar in the centre of a cleared circle, a knot of men had gathered around a struggling figure. As I looked on, ropes were slung over the beam and the men dissolved to leave the prisoner, stripped naked and secured by his arms and legs, stretched out in an X shape. Even from this distance, I recognised the burly hair-covered body of Mastin. Beside him sat a small box-shaped contraption made of rungs and struts, and I realised with a heave of my stomach that it was the skin-drying rack.

I climbed down the tree to confer with my friends.

'We could wait till nightfall,' said Cass, 'create some sort of diversion, then sneak over the wall when they are distracted, creep up to the gibbet and cut Mastin free.' There could be no doubting Cass's courage but Robin killed the idea dead.

'They are expecting us,' he said. 'From what Alan says they have mounted guards, crossbow patrols – men standing by just so that they catch us in the act of trying to rescue our friend. Even if we got to him undiscovered and cut him free – what then? We wouldn't have a hope of getting the four of us out of there alive. We would all be hanging from that bloody gibbet this time tomorrow.'

Cass looked crestfallen. Robin said gently, 'In other circumstances it might have been a splendid idea but—'

A long, yowling scream interrupted him, a noise that stole the breath from all our lungs. Cass reacted first, leaping for the lowest branch of the elm and climbing the tree like a monkey.

Robin and I looked at each other. 'We don't have time to wait for nightfall,' I said.

'You know what we must do, don't you?' he said. I swallowed, appalled. For I knew exactly.

Another scream ripped apart the morning air. Cutting through the sounds of a camp of a thousand men just waking up. Indeed the scream seemed to mute all the other hubbub with its terrifying power.

Cass jumped down to the grass beside Robin and me. He was as pale as whey. 'They've started,' he said. 'Two men in butcher's aprons are . . .' he looked for a moment as if he couldn't get out the words '. . . cutting at him.'

'I don't think we can save him,' said Robin. 'I wish we could but I cannot see how we can get inside the camp and get out again without all of us being—'

Another horrible, bubbling scream. Cass jumped half an inch in the air.

'All we can do is give him a swift death.'

We looked at each other. There was no other solution.

'If we are all agreed, the sooner we do it the better,' I said.

'But how?' said Cass. 'It is a good three hundred yards, maybe three hundred and ten. On my best day ever I could not shoot two hundred and fifty yards and be sure of hitting my mark. And we don't even have a line of sight from here,' he said, gesturing at the high earth wall thirty yards in front of us.

Robin stepped back into the trees and returned with a long linen-wrapped package. He pulled off the covering to reveal Mastin's own thick-waisted, pitch black, seven-foot yew bow.

'We know it has the range,' he said.

'There is a certain grim poetry to this,' Cass said. 'Live by the sword – or in this case the bow.' We each managed a taut smile, before another hellish shriek of pain wiped our faces clean of amusement.

'Can you shoot it? Have you ever actually hit anything with that monstrous thing?' I said to Robin.

'It's a bow, Alan. I've been shooting bows, all kinds of bows, since I was a lad.'

'But it is a blind shot, my lord. From more than three hundred yards.'

'What choice do we have? Tell me.'

It seemed impossible, even for Robin. And yet, looking at my lord's steel-grey eyes, I wanted to believe he could do it.

'You know you have only one shot,' I said. 'One shot, remember – they'll see the direction of the arrow – then they will be on us like a pack of wolves on a newborn lamb.'

'I know that, Alan,' said my lord. 'Now get up that tree and give me the angle. You are directing this. You are my eyes. Cass, you give me a hand to get a bow cord on this beast.'

In the branches of the elm, I looked over the camp. The business of the new day was continuing: folk were poking campfires into life, some were washing faces and hands in buckets of water. Others were standing around drinking from flasks of ale. I could smell frying bacon, wafting on the breeze. And in the midst of all this, a man was being stripped of the skin that covered his flesh. Mastin's whole upper body was now sheeted in blood and – by God – a tall figure in pure white clothing was standing beside him whispering in his ear.

'The White Count is there,' I said excitedly. 'Kill him. Kill that bastard.'

Cass and my lord were looking up at me, the vast bow strung and in Robin's hands. Cass stood beside him with a quiver of arrows.

'One shot, Alan,' Robin said. 'Is he stationary?'

'No, no, the French bastard is circling around Mastin, taunting him, no doubt. Oh God, now he is closing in. Is that a knife in his hand? Jesu—'

Another howl of anguish ripped across the air between us.

'Just give me the line, Alan. Quickly now.'

I pointed. Sticking my arm straight out towards the gibbet. Below me Cass dragged a long line in the earth at the base of the tree with his falchion.

'Is that right?' said Robin.

I looked down at the line and up again at the far-off gibbet. 'A little to the right,' I said.

'There's a slight breeze from the west,' Cass said. 'I was compensating.'

'Very well then,' I said.

Robin plucked an arrow from Cass's quiver. He nocked it to the string, raised the bow and with a vast heave of his chest and shoulder muscles began to haul back the cord. Back and back it went. I could see his whole arm vibrating with the strain. Back came the cord. Back until it was nearly at the level of my lord's ear. His face was the colour of a ripe plum and the muscles of his arms were standing out like a nest of writhing snakes.

He loosed. The arrow flew into the wide blue sky, sweeping up and up, then arcing down towards the gibbet. It slammed into the platform three yards wide and a yard short of Mastin's dangling, bloodied form, causing a French man-at-arms to leap sideways with the shock of its appearance.

'You missed!' I shouted, beginning to clamber down the tree. 'For God's sake, why couldn't you—'

'Stay where you are,' said Robin. 'Stay up there. You are my eyes.'

Robin snatched another arrow from Cass's hand. He nocked it.

'Three yards to the left, one short,' I said.

Robin said nothing, concentrating on pulling back that impossible cord.

Three hundred yards away, the gibbet was now emptied of men, save one hanging limply from his arms. Trumpets were sounding all over the camp, men were rushing to horses. I watched a man point with awful accuracy directly at me – I thought for a moment I had been seen, but I knew the trees were thick enough to shield me. He was merely pointing unerringly at where the arrow had come from.

Robin loosed. The shaft soared high and long and plunged down to stick quivering in the platform again. This time a bare yard to Mastin's right.

'A miss,' I said. 'Fraction too far right. A yard. Robin we have to go. We really have to go now. They are coming for us.'

A *conroi* of horsemen was trotting towards the gate in the wall nearest to us. Behind them was a marching block of a hundred crossbowmen in yellow-and-black surcoats. Spearmen were being marshalled to the right of the camp. We were about to be swamped by the enemy.

We were about to join Mastin on the gibbet.

'Give me another shaft, Cass,' Robin said below me. His voice was thick and low. 'And get the horses up here, right now.'

'Robin – we have no time,' I said.

My lord ignored me. Once more he wrestled back the cord on that huge weapon. I saw his eyeballs bulging with the effort, standing forward in his purple face. I snatched a glance at the gate. Horsemen were pouring out of it, heading for us – twenty, thirty heavily armed men, mailed knights looking to kill us, and they were not fifty yards away. A trumpet sounded again.

Robin loosed.

The arrow rose, fell and hit Mastin in the centre of his chest, plunging up to the goose feathers in his bloody torso. One last scream echoed across the space between us, a lower, softer cry. A farewell.

I leaped down to the ground, landing heavily. Robin pulled me to my feet. 'Alan?' he said. 'Alan – tell me.'

I nodded. Cass was a yard away with the horses. 'He's dead,' I said. 'Mastin is gone. That last arrow flew true. Now, can we please get out of here?'

We buried the other five archers that same afternoon in the grave-yard beside the church at Cassingham and the village priest said the prayers over their bodies. We had narrowly avoided the enemy horsemen and had half-killed our mounts getting back to the manor – but we were safe now. We said the words for Mastin in the churchyard too, although God knew where or even if the French would bury him. When the sun went down on that terrible day, we built a huge fire a mile or so away from the manor. We drank everything we could lay our hands on – ale, wine, cider, mead – we drank it all and sang songs and told stories about

239

Mastin and the men who had died. Cass drank with us, and every man and woman of Cassingham, regardless of rank, imbibed until they could no longer stand. The night is dim in my memory, naturally, but I do remember most clearly a conversation I had before I became senseless from the ale.

I was sitting by the roaring fire, a flagon between my knees, and Robin was beside me with an open cask of red. Many of the Cassingham folk lay sprawled on the ground, snoring like pigs. I could not sleep, I could not get the image out of my head of Mastin's half-peeled body hanging there by his arms.

'Everybody is dead,' I said, looking owlishly at Robin, my vision blurred by drink and tears. 'Will Scarlet is dead, Owain is dead, King Richard is dead – God rest him; my lovely Goody is dead, Hanno is dead, Tuck is dead, Kit is dead, even Little John is dead. . . and now Mastin. All gone. All no more than rotting flesh.'

'It's me and you now, Alan,' said my lord, taking a sip of his wine. The Earl of Locksley did not usually drink to excess but that evening his face was flushed and his eyes glittered in the firelight. 'We are the last men standing.'

'And the way he died – and the others. I can't imagine the agony. I could not stand it . . . I know I could not. We had no choice but to do what we did.'

'We had no choice,' said Robin. 'Were it me there on the gibbet – or you – we would want the same, yes?'

'I want to kill him – I want to slice his head from his shoulders. Watch the light die in his eyes. Piss on his body.'

'The White Count?' said my lord.

'He cannot be allowed to live. It is our duty to kill him.'

Cass came staggering out of the woods into the circle of light. I saw him adjusting his under-belt and the ties of his hose, having difficulty due to the amount of drink he had taken on board, and behind him at the edge of the firelight I glimpsed the slim figure of Sarah, smiling to herself and picking leaf-litter out of her long blonde hair as she sat next to the manor's passed-out steward.

'What are you two talking about?' Cass said, plonking himself between us and reaching for Robin's wine cup.

'Revenge,' said Robin. 'On the White Count.'

'I'm for it,' said Cass. 'I want to kill some Frenchmen. A lot of Frenchmen. I want to kill until I can't raise my arm any longer. I want to kill him most of all. Let us gather all the men we can – recruit some more if necessary – and go after him. Better: let's go back to Dover when things have quieted down, sneak into his tent and cut his lily-white throat. Or better yet, kidnap the bastard and bring him back here. He can see how he likes having his skin sliced off.'

Robin said nothing.

'What do you think?' I asked him. 'Could we do it?'

He shrugged. 'As much fun as that sounds, there is an old saying,' he said. '"When a man sets out on the path of revenge, he should first dig two graves."'

Cass looked downcast. I felt the ale swimming through my veins. 'You used to be very keen on revenge, as I recall, my lord. Now I see you've changed your tune.'

'Maybe I've seen the error of my ways,' he shrugged. 'I can no longer see the gain in it. We kill some of theirs, they kill some of ours and so it goes on. Dig two graves.'

'Mastin was our friend!' I said, raw anger stirring in my belly. 'We owe it to him.'

'Mastin is dead.' Robin's voice was hard and flat. 'We killed him this very morning.' I could tell my lord was nearly as angry as I. 'Mastin does not care one way or another – he is just happy to be dead and not still lingering on in indescribable pain. You told me what he thought of revenge after the Penshurst men were mutilated: "Won't bring them back". Was that not what he said?'

I had told him that – and forgotten it.

'Look into your heart, Alan. Look for the truth. You seek revenge to make yourself feel whole again – it's not for Mastin, it's for you. You feel bad because we killed one of our own. But revenge won't bring him back. And I will not lead men into danger and most likely get more of them killed – or, God forbid, captured – just so you can feel better about having the blood of a comrade on your hands.'

He took his wine cup out of Cass's hand and swallowed the last few drops.

'But you two can do whatever you like,' he said. 'I am leaving anyway. I've been summoned by the King and I must ride north in the morning.'

'What?' I said. This was the first I'd heard of it. 'You can't leave now – after what has passed. You can't leave!'

'Too tired to argue with you, Alan. We are both drunk. We'll talk tomorrow.'

And he rolled over and went to sleep.

Chapter Twenty-three

I went with him, of course, leaving at dawn, leather-tongued, guts churning, my whole head coming apart like a badly made helmet, and not just as far as Goudhurst to collect our men, the spare horses and the loot we had gathered. We rode all that ghastly day and the next. And it took me until we were near Windsor on the second day to get any sense out of him.

'The King is finally moving against the French,' Robin said tersely, when we stopped in a small patch of woodland near Chertsey, a few miles south of Windsor, to camp for the night. 'He summoned me a week hence but I was . . . I was enjoying myself, damn it. I was having fun. I did not want to leave the Weald and go back to being a lickspittle courtier, a nodder who is ignored or insulted at the King's will. Well, since Mastin, the pleasure is all gone. And I cannot ignore the King's summons for ever and remain in his good graces. So that is what we are doing. We are going to hold the King's hand while he dredges up the courage to confront the invaders.'

'I feel bad about leaving Cass alone to carry on the fight in Kent,' I said.

'He's hardly alone – he has four hundred men at his command, including some of my best archers,' Robin said. 'He knows how to wage this kind of war as well as you and I do – and he knows the ground a good deal better than both of us. Cass will be fine. He will run the French ragged, you'll see. And he'll be more cautious, too, after what has happened. There is your revenge, Alan – there won't be a Frenchman south of the Thames who won't have nightmares about what the fabled Willikin of the Weald and his men might do to them. More importantly, they will tie down large numbers of enemy troops just guarding the supply routes to London. While Cass torments them here, the French will be considerably weakened when we face them with the King's army.'

'You think the King will really fight?' I asked.

Robin was quiet for a long time. He pretended to be busy feeding his horse a handful of oats, and then stroking its nose, and I was on the point of asking the question a second time when he said, 'I think John truly would like to be a good King – he would be so happy to be seen as another Lionheart. But he never will be – the tyrant is too strong in him. He wants to rule unopposed: he wants to be a strong King more than a good King. By choosing power over virtue, he achieves neither. He has no true strength because he believes every man will betray him and so makes sure he betrays them first. Which means no man trusts him and every man looks only to his own advantage. This, in turn, fulfils the King's deeply held belief that none of his sworn men is truly trustworthy. The glue that holds a kingdom together – by which I mean the sacred oaths that a King takes from his barons – is dissolved. He believes power comes only from money, from having the silver to pay his fighting men. I used to think the same once. I was wrong – power and strength come from men's loyalty. My strength has come from the fidelity that you have given me, Alan. The forged-iron loyalty I have been fortunate enough to receive from you, from Little John, from Tuck, from Mastin, from all of

244

you. I know you thought me foolish to give away so much of the money we took this summer – although you were kind enough not to call me a fool. But what you don't understand is that the money means nothing. We have enough wealth, you and I, in our lands, in our sons. A few pennies more means – what? Better wine with dinner? A more expensive destrier?'

I said nothing. I was touched that he thought my loyalty iron-forged. And I did not want to spoil the mood by quibbling over a few pennies, although the coffers of Westbury were woefully light. I was glad I had remained silent, for Robin rarely spoke at such length about his innermost thoughts. And he had not yet finished.

'I spent that money lavishly on those Wealden folk – and you know what I got in return? Loyalty. They did not betray us, although they easily could have. Money freely given, without the smack of charity or the guise of payment for services rendered, warms everybody's heart. Money given to the deserving doesn't make you poorer; it makes you richer. Jesus Christ knew that – it is one of his teachings that I am happy to embrace. King John doesn't understand it. He pays money to his Flemings and demands fidelity. And they give it, but only up to the exact penny he has paid them. His barons – some of them – would give him good service if he allowed them to. But he puts his trust in cash money, in paid duty, and scorns the loyalty of honest men. That will be his downfall. If you take away John's money, he is nothing, he would have nothing left. If you take away his money, he is in effect dead. If you took away mine, I would still be me and I would still have you. You said to me on the first day we met that you would be loyal to me until death. You have been. And that, my dear Alan, is worth more to me than all the coin in this world.'

I was feeling a little embarrassed by Robin's words; my face had flushed as red as a holly berry. We did not normally speak of our bond. I think it was only to stop this unseemly flow of affection from my lord that I said, 'You still haven't answered the question. Will John fight the French?'

Robin laughed. 'If he doesn't he will lose his crown. So I would say that he must. Or, at least, that he must get some poor misguided fools to fight the French for him. And I would wager that we can guess who those poor misguided fools will be. Us. But a better question is – can he win? And that I cannot answer.'

The next day, as we rode north towards Windsor, we received news. A rider from London, one of cousin Henry's couriers, managed to find us. The news was good. The siege of Windsor had been lifted. King John had come west with a strong force of knights but like a coward had avoided a pitched battle outside Windsor. Instead he had circled north and headed off into Essex, burning all the lands in his path and slaying any suspected of having sided with the rebels. I recalled that Miles and Thomas had ravaged the lands north of London earlier in the year and wondered what the peasants of Essex, whose lands had been twice pillaged in a year, would say to Robin's dismissal of the value of cold hard cash.

I said the King had behaved in a characteristically spineless fashion; but Robin pointed out that his action in avoiding battle and moving north had achieved his objective – liberating Windsor – without the grave risk of a pitched battle, as the French forces surrounding the royal castle had abandoned their long, fruitless siege. They were at this moment riding north in the King's charred wake, hoping to provoke a confrontation and perhaps defeat John in battle, capture him and end this war at a stroke.

Henry's man also gave us news of Dover: the siege fighting had intensified since our cavalry raid in the summer. Prince Louis himself had paid a visit in late July to urge on the French besiegers to greater efforts; and King Alexander of Scotland had marched from his homeland to Dover – almost entirely unmolested by King John's troops. Eustace de Vesci, Alexander's brother-in-law and one of the senior rebel leaders, had been killed by a stray crossbow bolt at a skirmish at Barnard's Castle in County Durham. But, by and large, the young King of the Scots had made it all the way to the south coast of England as if he were making a pleasant jaunt for a swim at the beach. And once Alexander got to Dover, he had paid homage to Prince Louis as one King to another. A most significant act, Robin assured me.

I said, rather wittily I thought, that you might say that England now held two Kings – or three if you counted Alexander. Ha-ha!

'It might be a little unwise to say that aloud – or at least it will be unwise in a day or two, when we have reached our destination,' said Robin. I took his point.

It took us a week to find King John. We rode cautiously – Robin and myself and nearly thirty men-at-arms and mounted archers – through the wastelands of central England. It was only on that journey that it truly came home to me just what a long civil war meant to the ordinary folk of England. As we passed through Harrow and St Albans, Woburn and Northampton, I was brutally reminded what a *chevauchée* did to the face of the land. Whole districts were black and smoking. Ripe standing crops, half a year's sustenance for a village, had been ruthlessly put to the torch. Homes, storehouses, byres and barns, even churches ablaze. Men, women – children too – dead and rotting by the side of the roads. It was not the first time I had seen such devastation – and I had played a full and shameful part in similar destructive expeditions. But the burned-out villages and scorched fields, the army of poor and destitute who swarmed at every roadside cross and in every churchyard, were very hard on my conscience in the middle of England at harvest time. Without their crops, the poor would surely starve to death before Christmas. Robin, of course, had a shiny penny for each man, woman and child who asked for alms – taken from the fast-dwindling store of coin that we had liberated from the French. But that would only last them a day or so.

When I gently chided him for his pointless generosity, he simply said I should trust him. Then he grinned and said that doubtless Our Lord would provide. It was an oddly religious thing for the Earl of Locksley to say: he'd always been against the Church and its teachings and I assumed he was mocking me for my faith.

On the twenty-first day of September, the feast day of St Matthew the Apostle, Robin and his band of men, raggedy from living rough for so long, sore from the long journey up from Kent, but still straight as spears in the saddle, rode into the courtyard of Rockingham Castle in Northamptonshire. It was a crisp, windy day, with the first sniff of winter in the air. But I felt a sense of homecoming: Rockingham was only two days' ride from Nottingham. This was very nearly our part of the world. As I passed under the arch of the stone gatehouse and looked up towards the keep, I saw the three lions of England, gold on red, fluttering proudly above the crenellations in the stiff breeze and, while I hated the man whose presence the royal banner proclaimed, the sight of it gladdened my heart.

My spirits soared higher a moment later. For the first person I saw when I looked around the courtyard was a tall slim young man stripped to his chemise and hose, with a sword in his hand. He was sparring with a huge dark-skinned fellow armed only with a cudgel, and it took me a moment to recognise my son Robert and his bodyguard Boot.

Then my heart sank into my boots. A woman, lithe, light of step, with long raven hair gathered under a white cap, came hurrying out of the hall at the side of the courtyard. She had a thick blue woollen tunic over her arm and was calling to my son: 'Robert, oh Robert, you will catch your death out here, you thoughtless boy. Now, stop your silly play-fighting and put on your warm tunic, put it on this instant, for me. Please, Robert, for me – put on this tunic for your Tilda.'

248

Part Three

'I remember him,' said the King triumphantly. 'But was his name not something else? Lexington, Locksmith – no, Locksley. Yes, he was calling himself the Earl of Locksley.'

'The Earl of Locksley and Robin Hood are one and the same man,' said Brother Alan. He had spent the past half-hour describing to the King the events at Corfe Castle when Henry was an eight-year-old boy.

'I remember you and the music we made together. You were a fine teacher. And I remember him, too – he was a dashing fellow even in his rags, charming, I recall. Mother didn't like him but he soon talked her round. Persuaded her to allow you to move up from the dungeon to the blue room in the east tower. So that was the famous Robin Hood!'

The King beamed at the assembled company – Lord Westbury, myself and Brother Alan, and a gaggle of awestruck monks, all sitting on the hard stone benches around the sides of the chapter house.

'Well, I feel better about hanging the other ones now – damn imposters,' said the King. 'Tell me, Brother Alan, what became of the Earl of Locksley – the genuine Robin Hood – I take it he is no longer with us.'

251

'I have been recounting this tale to Prior Anthony here, telling him what became of Robin Hood after we joined your father's army at Rockingham Castle in the autumn of the year of Our Lord twelve hundred and sixteen. He has been making a record of the events for posterity.'

'Indeed?' said the King. 'Well, let us have it, then. I do love a good tale.'

'Sire,' said Brother Alan, 'I must warn you. There may be things that are difficult for you to hear, concerning your royal father.'

'I doubt there's anything about Father that I don't already know. He was an absolute shit of a man, by all accounts – awful father, terrible King. There, I said it. Now I doubt there's anything you could say about the man that would genuinely shock me.'

'You might be surprised,' said Brother Alan.

'I believe I have made my wishes perfectly clear,' said the King, his voice taking on an altogether more regal tone.

'Now, have that old fellow with the tray bring us some more of his cakes and a cup of wine – oh, and somebody had better send word to Clipstone that we'll be a little late for dinner. And you, Brother Alan, may now tell me this intriguing tale of Robin Hood.'

'As you wish, Sire,' said Brother Alan.

Chapter Twenty-four

I should have gone over and embraced my heir, my own beloved flesh and blood, but for some strange reason I did not. Perhaps it was because I did not want to have to engage with Tilda, to decide how I felt about her acting like a mother to my boy, perhaps in some way I was afraid of her. But, for whatever reason, I acted shamefully and ignored both Tilda and Robert and strode over to join my lord at the entrance to the keep. I saw Boot looking at me in astonishment – but I ignored him too as I bounded up the steps to the keep.

Robin and I were ushered into the great hall by a trio of black-clad servants, announced by a sonorous herald.

The large hall was half-full of men: royal servants and men of the Church mostly, but a few of the peacock courtiers who always accompanied the King were with him and the usual contingent of wolf-grim mercenary captains glowered around John himself as he warmed his hands at a huge fireplace set into the wall. I saw Savary de Mauléon, the man who had saved us at Rochester, leaning against a pillar, half in the shadows and watching the proceedings with a wry smile.

King John glanced over at us as we were announced. I knew better than to expect praise and thanks from him. Nonetheless, some gratitude was certainly Robin's due, for he and Cass had caused enormous damage to the French invaders in the south at a time when almost no one else was resisting them. A gracious monarch would have at least acknowledged that contribution to the war. But John was no gracious monarch.

'Locksley – here at last. Where have you been? I expected you weeks ago.'

'Sire, we had some difficulties with the forces of the enemy,' Robin lied. 'Difficulties that required us to take a more circuitous route to your side.'

'Well, you are here now, I suppose. In future, when I summon you, you are to come to me as quickly as possible. No lollygagging. No dilly-dallying. There is no excuse for this shameful tardiness.'

'Indeed, Sire,' said Robin, 'I shall strive to be supremely punctual in future.'

It never ceased to amaze me how Robin – a brave, proud warrior, jealous of his honour, even haughty in other circumstances – could transform himself into this smooth-talking, easy-mannered courtier at the drop of a silk kerchief, with his oleaginous 'Indeed, Sires' and his genuine-seeming smiles. He would be laughing at the King's feeble jokes next. I knew I could never do it.

'A man who is constantly late,' the King was saying, looking into the fire and rubbing his hands, 'is in danger of being made permanently late!'

The courtiers exploded in a gale of titters. The mercenary captains frowned.

I caught Robin wincing for just an instant before he recovered himself: 'Ah, Sire, how very droll. You mean late as in the late Lord de Vesci, God rest his soul.'

'May he burn in a traitor's Hell,' said the King. 'He brought the Scots into our realm. When we catch up with those heathen savages, we'll send them all to join him.'

'Is that your plan, Sire?' said Robin. 'To confront the Scots army as it marches home?'

'Maybe, maybe . . .' The King had taken on a ludicrously cunning look. 'Maybe I'll march east instead and take on the English rebels – your old friends, Locksley. I hear Fitzwalter and his rebel scum are raising Cain in East Anglia. We'll just have to see.'

I thought Robin would push the King for some sort of idea about his plans but he merely contented himself with another smooth 'Indeed, Sire'.

There was a short silence. The fire crackled and spat. I shifted on my feet. My right shoulder was paining me after the long ride. And I was hungry.

Savary de Mauléon stepped forward towards the fire. 'We were just discussing Lincoln, when you arrived, my lord,' he said to Robin. 'Perhaps you would care to let us know your thoughts on the matter.'

'I think Lincoln is crucial,' said Robin.

'How so?' said de Mauléon.

'Lincoln is the high-water mark,' my lord said. 'So whether it stands or falls is vital to our success in this war.'

He was met with blank looks.

Robin said slowly, as if speaking to imbeciles: 'Lincoln is besieged by the French, yes? They have the town and the lands around it but the castle is still being held against them by that extraordinary woman – what's her name?'

'Nicola de la Haye – a noble lady, both courageous and beautiful,' growled Mauléon. 'Have a care that you do not say anything against her good name.'

'I'm sure she's a paragon,' said Robin. 'She must be strong-willed to hold out so long against her enemies. How long has it been – six months? A year?'

Nobody replied.

'The thing is that this is as far north as the French have been able to get. There are a few rebel holdouts north of there but they will wither if they receive no aid. Eustace de Vesci is dead and his castle and lands in Northumberland are now held by a child. The Scots – forget about the Scots, they just want to get home before winter sets in. My advice would be to let them go. The real enemy is Prince Louis and his men have got as far as Lincoln. If Lincoln falls, they will carry on northwards, link up with what's left of the northern rebels and perhaps the Scots, too, and we will have lost. If Lincoln continues to resist or, better still, if we can ride to its relief and that of this brave lady Nicola de la Haye, we will have won. Lincoln will have been the high-water mark; after that the French tide is going out. The pendulum swings our way. Louis's territory in England shrinks and his grip on our land slips a little more each day. That is why I say Lincoln is crucial. And to me it is obvious that we must ride to its rescue.'

'So it is Lincoln today, is it, Locksley?' said the King. 'Last year you were urging me to hurl myself at London.'

Robin shrugged.

'Prince Louis has made Gilbert de Gant, who is besieging the castle, the Earl of Lincoln,' said Mauléon, with a sideways glance at Robin. And was that a wink?

'That cur! How dare he think to bestow titles in my realm,' shouted John. He had gone from jovial contempt to full-blown anger in an instant. His face was as red as a sunset; he seemed to be chewing on his own teeth. 'I will gut him like a fish. I will rip out his liver. I will smash his head between two millstones . . .' Then the King seemed to master himself. He looked around at the courtiers and mercenaries. He was breathing deeply.

'Oh, get out all of you. I would be alone. Get out, go!'

We shuffled out of the hall, many of us crowding in the doorway, leaving the King glaring at the fire, his fists bunched by his sides with rage. As we left, I found Savary de Mauléon at my shoulder.

'You did very well in the south,' the Poitevin said, speaking close to my ear, 'and the King knows it. Tell Locksley the King is grateful to him for his service.'

'But is he?'

'He's like a bad-tempered child sometimes, but he is still King. And he needs men like Locksley, even if he doesn't know it. If you won't tell Locksley the King said it, say that I thank him on the King's behalf for his service in the south.'

'I will,' I said. 'And thank you for this. I lifted up my left arm and tapped the hilt of the misericorde that was strapped beneath the wide sleeve of my chemise.

'Wield it wisely,' said Mauléon. Then he was gone.

Robert, Boot and Matilda Giffard were not the only people who had unexpectedly joined the King's army at Rockingham Castle that autumn. The next day Robin's eldest son Hugh arrived with fifty men from Kirkton. The Locksley troops were allocated a barn in the courtyard and they filled it to overflowing with their horses, war gear and baggage; Robert, Boot, Tilda and two men-at-arms from Westbury called Nicholas and Simon, who had accompanied them, were in a stable next to it. I claimed a stall in the stable and ordered Boot to rake out the horse droppings and fill it with clean straw.

I apologised to Robert for failing to greet him when I arrived, but he waved away my apologies. 'You were waiting on the King, Father,' he said, 'and I do understand that I must take second place to our sovereign. It is good to see you again.'

We discussed the affairs of Westbury for a few moments – all was well, I learned: the harvest had been gathered in without interference from either of the warring sides, and my steward Baldwin and his sister Alice had the place well in hand – and I

257

told Robert about the kind of war we had been waging in the south with William of Cassingham.

'Oh, yes, the famous Willikin of the Weald – the man who hates a Frenchman more than he hates the Devil. Who cuts the heads from all his enemies. We have heard tell of his bold exploits. They sing of them in the ale-houses.'

'And what of the bold exploits of Robin Hood and Sir Alan Dale?' I said, finding myself mildly irritated.

'Ah . . . they are not sung so much,' said my son and heir. 'The Robin Hood tales are a bit old and stale now. What the people like are new, fresh heroes. Young men.'

'Hmmf,' I said. Then I came to the question that had been dogging my thoughts since my arrival.

'Son, it is a joy to see your face and a pleasure to have you at my side but – how come you to be at Rockingham, with Boot and, ah, everybody else?'

'Did you not know? Why – Uncle Robin summoned us. He said you would have need of us. Do you not need us?'

'Ah, yes, of course, I need you. Absolutely. Thank you for coming.'

'What is it, Father, exactly, that you need us for?' asked my clever son.

'It is not so much what I need – as your needs that I am thinking of,' I said, racking my brains. 'You are sixteen now, I believe. A man, full-grown. You need to be with the army, to be around fighting men, because it is time for you to see the face of battle for the first time.' I looked solemnly into his eyes. 'I am taking you to war, my son.'

'Oh thank you, Father, thank you. I never thought the day would come when you would think me worthy . . .' I had a horrible premonition that my son was about to burst into tears. Not the sort of behaviour to be displayed around fighting men if he wanted to be accepted. Instead, he did something far worse.

'I must find Tilda and tell her about this!' he said and he ran out of the stable.

I was in something of a rage that evening when I finally tracked down Robin in the tiny room he had been allocated in one of the castle's towers. It was more a monk's cell than a chamber fit for an earl, but Robin made no comment about it and I was too full of outrage to care. I was also feeling decidedly unwell. The long wet ride, the nights of sleeping rough, had taken their toll. My body ached and my head felt as if it were stuffed with wool.

'What the Devil do you mean by bringing my son and that bloody woman to this place without a word to me? I care not if you order me around the country like some mere lackey – that is your right as my lord. But I do not understand why you feel you must meddle in my family affairs. It is egregious, it is manipulative, it is discourteous, it is . . . . just plain wrong!' I ran out of words then.

'Finished?' said Robin, coolly from his bed. He was half-dressed and holding a letter in his hands, looking at me with mild amusement.

'Yes,' I said. I took several deep breaths. 'But why did you do it, Robin? I do not want that woman around me.'

'All right,' said Robin, 'I accept that I should have told you about it before now. I apologise. But I need Tilda here and I'm sorry if it makes you uneasy but this is far more important than your temporary discomfiture.'

'Why do you need her?'

'I could lie to you. But I don't want to do that. I also do not want to tell you why. So I must ask you to trust me and put up with Tilda's presence as best you can. She is not an evil woman, I promise you. Marie-Anne rather admires her. I certainly do not believe she is a threat to you or Robert.'

'That's it? Your answer is, I'm not telling you, just shut up and trust me.'

Robin stood up, his face as hard as stone. 'Sometimes, Alan, you presume too much. We are friends, yes, but I am also your lord. These are my orders: you will suffer this woman's presence; you will cease from whining like a whipped schoolboy; furthermore you will desist from bursting into my chamber and shouting at me as if I were a tenant late with the rent. That is all. You are dismissed.'

In reply, I sneezed. And sneezed again, involuntarily spraying slime all over myself. Robin stepped across, scowling, and handed me a clean linen kerchief at arm's length. Then I went away as ordered, grumbling and muttering complaints under my breath like a grandfather.

I stomped across the courtyard of Rockingham Castle towards the stables, damning the whole of Christendom, and particularly the parts of it connected to me by ties of duty or blood, and thinking that I wanted nothing more than to down a hot meal and a cup of wine and curl up in my cloak on the straw in my stall till morning.

But when I got to the stable and poked my head inside, the scene there made me change my mind. Robert and Boot and the two Westbury men-at-arms Nicholas and Simon were seated in a half-circle while Tilda, on her knees before them, tended a small fire in the centre. A blackened pot hung from a hook over it and I could see something bubbling inside. A delicious smell filled the air.

'Father, you're back. Just in time for supper,' said Robert. 'It is ox-tail stew with carrots and onions.'

'And there is fresh bread – and wine, too,' said Boot in his oddly pitched voice.

Tilda looked up at me, towering over her in the doorway of the stable, and gave a smile of such sweetness that I was tempted just to fold myself down beside her by the fire and accept a warm bowl of soup from her hands. Instead, I sneezed mightily once again and, as I was mopping my face with Robin's kerchief, mumbled something about not being hungry and stumbled past my companions to my stall. Plucking a heavy cloak from a peg, I stripped off my tunic, boots and hose, rolled myself in it, fell into the pile of straw and went instantly to sleep.

I came struggling up from the depths of slumber and awoke knowing something was wrong. Somebody was in the stall with me; there was just enough light to see a dark figure crouching over me. I moved entirely on instinct. My left arm swept up, grasped a shoulder and heaved the form across my body, pinning it to the straw beside me with my torso. My right hand already had the misericorde unsheathed, the tip now resting below the cheekbone of a pale face, ready to plunge the blade through the eye socket into the brain.

'Who are you?'

I felt a warm, soft body squirming under my restraining arm, my chest pressed hard to it – and found I was looking into the white face and huge blue-grey eyes of Tilda.

'Good God, you are quick,' she said.

I kept the dagger where it was.

'What do you want? What are you doing in here?'

'So strong, too,' she said. I could feel her trying to move under me; I pressed down to hold her still. I was aware of her breasts against my chest. She was wearing only a thin linen chemise, clearly about to go to bed. Our faces were inches apart. Her breath smelled of honey. I felt a surge of blood to my loins – God, how long had it been since I'd had a woman under me?

I rolled off her, sheathed the misericorde and sat up.

'What are you doing here, woman?'

Tilda sat up. Her raven hair was loose, glossy, and in the dim light – a candle or rushlight was burning in the main part of the stable – I could see several pieces of loose hay caught in the black tresses. Her eyes were laughing now and she was breathing hard from our brief tussle.

261

'I am still a woman of God, you know, Sir Alan. A bride of Christ. I may have fallen from grace at the Priory but I have not entirely forsaken my vows of chastity.'

'What do you want with me?' I said. 'I could easily have killed you.'

My head was swimming. I desperately wanted to lie back down but I could not tear my eyes from her face.

She broke our gaze and looked to the ground by the entrance of the stall. I turned to see what she was looking at. It was a large clay beaker with steam rising from the surface of a dark liquid.

'I brought you a hot drink – hyssop, horehound and white poppy, some dried ginger root as well, and honey for sweetness.'

I sneezed then and scrubbed at my sore nose with the sleeve of my chemise.

'So that's it, is it? Poison?'

'It's for your cold, for your . . .' She suddenly looked very sad.

'Very likely,' I said. 'You think I would drink any of your witches' brews!'

Tilda moved away to the entrance and picked up the cup. She saluted me with it, held my eyes with hers and took a large sip. I saw her swallow the mouthful down.

'It's good for you, Alan. Drink it up – and be well.'

Then she walked out of the stall.

I stared at the cup for a long, long time. It seemed to be challenging me. Am I a fool? I thought. Am I once again making a fool of myself over this damn woman?

I picked up the cup, sniffed it. It held the smell of high summer, of meadow flowers, bees and warm sunshine. It smelled of happiness.

'Are you afraid?' the voice in my head asked. I knew that I was. So I put the warm cup to my lips and drank the whole measure in one swallow.

262

Chapter Twenty-five

I slept like a dead man and awoke mid-morning, thick-headed but very much alive. Whatever Tilda had put in the drink, it was a powerful cure for while I snuffled and sneezed that day and the next, I could feel my cold waning.

I washed my face and hands and combed my hair. I shared a beaker of ale and a slice of buttered bread with Robert and half-listened to his news of some disturbance in the baggage lines during the night. But I paid scant attention to his chatter, then, for my mind was on other things. I ruffled my son's hair in farewell and went in search of Robin.

I had an apology to make.

I found my lord in the great hall of Rockingham in the midst of a storm of royal displeasure.

'I want the wagon guards hanged for their negligence, every man jack of them,' the King was saying as I slid in to the hall. 'Hang them all – at once.'

'Oh for God's sake,' said Savary de Mauléon, not quite under his breath.

'You have something to say to me, Mauléon?' said the King.

'Sire, I do. We do not have enough men to start hanging every poor fellow who is bested in a skirmish. The guards resisted the marauders as best they could and then retreated in order to save their own lives. There were hundreds of Scotsmen, the captain tells me, and it was dark and they were masked like fiends and howling like the savages they are. The guards came straight here for reinforcements, and my men were able to drive the enemy away before they could make off with more than a wagon or two and some of the packhorses, a few sacks of grain.'

'They failed in their duty to their King,' John said. 'They must be punished.'

'Sire, perhaps we could discuss the order of march to Lincoln,' said Robin.

'We'll discuss your grand plans for Lincoln, Locksley, when we have settled this matter.'

'Hang a few guards if you wish to, Sire,' said Robin cheerfully. 'But consider what that will do to the morale of the rest of the army. Will that make it more likely or less likely that undecided men will come to your banner?'

The King glared at my lord. Robin had made the exact same argument to John that Savary de Mauléon had made after Rochester. The argument that had saved his – and my – life. I saw Mauléon, behind the King's back, grinning openly at Robin.

'Well, what do you suggest that we do, Locksley? You who think you have all the answers. Tell me. And this had better be good.'

'I think you should appoint a Master of the Royal Baggage. Someone senior, a man of high rank, and make it his sworn duty to defend the wagons, the stores and the royal treasury with his own men. He would be responsible for their safety and answerable only to you. If he fails in his duty, you could hang him, if you like.'

John looked at Robin. There was a sly gleam in his eye.

'Someone senior, you say. A nobleman of high rank?' The King

264

chuckled. 'Very well – I hereby appoint you, Robert of Locksley, Master of the Royal Baggage. You and your men will defend our wagon train to the last man. And it will be your life that is forfeit if so much as a silver thimble is stolen while you hold that position. What say you to that!'

Robin appeared aghast. 'Sire, ah, Sire . . .' he stuttered. 'You do me too much honour. But surely another man—'

'I may indeed be doing you too much honour but you will accept this task and you will protect my goods and chattels with utmost care and diligence – or it truly will be your head in the noose, mark my words.'

'As you command, Sire,' said Robin, bowing low.

'Now, to the monks of Crowland Abbey – they have defied me long enough. I want their lands ravaged, I want their villages, mills, storehouses and barns burned to the ground. I want the wealth of that fat lump, Abbot Henry de Longchamp, in my coffers and him on his knees before me begging for my mercy.

'Sire, it is a much-revered House of God,' said Robin. 'The monks of Crowland are well known for their care of the sick and generosity to the poor and needy—'

'I don't want to hear another word out of you today, Locksley – Mauléon, this is your task. Get your men to Crowland and bring me their wealth. Immediately, today.'

Savary de Mauléon opened his mouth to speak.

'No,' shouted the King. 'I don't want to hear it. You have your orders. Go! Get you to Crowland, sir.'

The Poitevin lord's face was a picture of frustrated fury. But he uttered not a word, merely bowed to the King and stalked out of the hall.

'Shall we discuss the order of march to Lincoln, Sire,' said Robin quietly when Mauléon had gone.

'Oh, you organise it, Locksley. I am too fatigued to wrangle with you any more. I'm sure you have it all planned out anyway. We ride tomorrow at dawn. Just do not forget your new honour, eh? I meant what I said about your head in a noose. You will guard that baggage train with your life. Understand? You may leave me now.'

I caught up with my lord in the antechamber and begged his pardon for my rudeness the day before.

'It is no matter, Alan. Put it behind us. We have a great deal to do today.'

He seemed disproportionally cheerful. As we walked into the courtyard, I noticed my lord was humming. He did not appear the least put out that he had just been given an extra duty that might see him hanging by the neck from a gibbet before too long. Then I remembered my conversation with Robert that morning. And everything became crystal clear.

'I gather then that the Scots have raided our baggage train,' I said.

'So it would seem,' said Robin.

'And yet the latest reports say that Alexander's army is some hundred miles north of us now. I wonder how they managed that feat.'

'Yes, it is something of a mystery.'

'And do I understand that these mysterious marauders were masked? So that not one of them could be recognised – as a Scottish knight, I mean.'

'Alan,' Robin growled. 'Have a care what you say next!' It was a warning.

'I make no further comment on the matter, my lord. Except to say that sometimes, just sometimes, it is a very great pleasure to serve you.'

It took us three days to march on Lincoln. And while I was prepared for a hard fight at the end of our journey, it was with a sneaking relief that I learned of Gilbert de Gant's abandonment of the siege. The newly made Earl of Lincoln had fled north on the news of the King's approach. Robin and I rode with the baggage train, twelve heavily laden wagons and fifty or so packhorses holding the King's belongings, his clothes and jewels, the silver plate for his table, his private dismantled chapel, the chests of coin from which he paid his mercenaries, the tax rolls of the clerks of the exchequer, carpets, bedding, shoes, spare armour, sacks of wheat, barley and oats, barrels of salted meat, flitches of bacon, stacks of round yellow cheeses, boxes of fruit, chests of spices – and fifty tuns of good red wine. Robin's eighty men rode on either side of the train in two lines, Robert and Hugh each commanding a file of men. Tilda sat high on a cart full of tapestries and bedding, wrapped in a great travelling cloak, back straight, chin high, as haughty as a queen. Boot's huge form strode along beside her vehicle, a thick oak cudgel over his massive shoulder, as if he were her personal bodyguard and not my son's – for Robert was not the only member of my household who seemed to have fallen under her spell. She ignored me and I avoided meeting her eye. I was somewhat embarrassed by our night-time encounter. I had behaved boorishly, it seemed to me, when she had tried to do me a kindness. Yet I could not quite bring myself to thank her for the cup of healing herbs that had alleviated my cold.

The King and the bulk of the army – still mostly composed of mercenary Flemings, although the numbers of English knights in the King's train had increased considerably since the muster at Tonbridge – rode far ahead of the slow-moving ox-drawn wagons, and so we struggled through the mire created by several thousand men and horses that marched before us.

On the second day, after noon, we heard the thunder of horses coming from the east – a score of mailed knights riding in, and fast. Robin had me gather a strong force of his men-at-arms and we wheeled to face them in no time at all, ready to drive off any marauders – my lord was taking his new duties as Master of the

Royal Baggage seriously, I noted – but it was a false alarm. It was merely Savary de Mauléon and his mud-spattered men returning from Crowland Abbey.

Mauléon reined in, halted his men, greeted Robin cheerfully and nodded at me.

'I see the big man has you doing all the donkey work, Locksley,' said the Poitevin, waving a hand at the lumbering column of wagons. 'About time you did more than tease him in the council chamber.'

Robin smiled serenely. 'So you're back from burning a kindly old churchman out of his House of God, slaughtering the monks, raping the nuns – good work, Mauléon. A fitting commission for a man of your quality.'

Mauléon scowled. 'I couldn't do it, if you must know, Locksley.'

'Truly?'

'Yes, I went to see the abbot and told him what I had been ordered to do. We came to an accommodation.'

'You disobeyed our lord King!' said Robin, pretending to be shocked.

'Abbot Longchamp gave over to me five chests of silver in exchange for the promise that I would leave his lands in peace. That should keep John happy.'

'A solution after my own heart,' said Robin. 'Blackmail rather than bloodshed – I thoroughly approve, Savary. I just hope our beloved King feels the same way.'

'You'll help me persuade him?'

'Of course.'

Mauléon raised a hand in farewell and he and his men galloped up the road to join the main column.

Lincoln was a beautiful and pleasingly laid-out town – I knew it slightly, of course, it being close to Nottingham, but I had never before spent more than a day or two there. It was built on the junction of two mighty roads – Fosse Way, which led hundreds of miles south-west to Exeter, and Ermine Street, the main artery south to London – on the high north bank of the River Witham. In truth, Lincoln was two towns: an upper town, which held the castle and the cathedral and the houses of the richer denizens, the famous Lincoln wool merchants, and a lower town, walled off from the upper and containing workshops, storehouses, a plethora of taverns, houses of ill-repute and the poorer sections of the community. The grandest building in the lower town was the Jews' House, a large stone building brightly painted in red and gold to demonstrate their loyalty to the crown and nestled just south of the dividing wall. In shape, Lincoln was an oblong, or two squares one on top of the other – the upper and lower towns – and walled all the way around in stone.

We approached from the south and drove the wagon convoy across the grand bridge over the river into the lower part of town. To our right was a wide area of water, a port with a few small ships that traded as far as France and the Low Countries, and this was the method by which the French had supplied their troops besieging the castle. As I crossed the bridge, I noted the port was unusually empty – the French craft had all set sail for safer harbours as soon as they heard of the King's imminent arrival. Once across the water, we carried on driving our wagons almost due north up the steep rise of the main street that led to the walled upper town, where the cathedral, on the right, and the castle, on the left, straddled the road: the twin bastions of God and the King, overlooking the common stew of grubby humanity below.

There was little sign of de Gant's occupation forces until we approached the castle walls. Here were scorch marks on the walls and empty spaces where some meaner dwellings and workshops had been pulled down to create space for crossbowmen to loose their weapons against the fortress without hindrance and men-at-arms to muster for an assault. The castle towered over this cleared space and, looking up at its sheer stone walls, I could see why Gilbert de Gant had made no headway. Once we had reached the summit – it was no easy task to get the stubborn oxen and the wagons up the steep hill, I may tell you – we turned and entered the castle through the East Gate. Inside the walls, in the wide, almost-square bailey, we secured the wagons in a series of huge barns by the northern ramparts.

Then Robin and I went in search of the King.

We found him, as expected, with his lords, knights and mercenary captains, and the usual bright crowd of sycophantic hangers-on, in the great thatched hall in the middle of the bailey sitting down to a feast. Robin and I hastily washed the smell of ox from our hands and took our places as latecomers on the lesser tables. As I ate hungrily – it had been a hard morning – I noticed Robin looking at the faces on the high table next to the King.

'See there, Alan,' said my lord. 'The young fellow next to Savary de Mauléon? In the blue tunic? Do you know who that is?'

I didn't – and didn't much care. I was excavating the delicious dish of pigeon pie that was set before me.

'That is John Marshal, the Earl of Pembroke's brother's son.'

'William the Marshal's nephew?' I said. 'I thought he was with the rebels.'

'Evidently no longer,' said Robin. 'And there is the Earl of Salisbury, King John's half-brother, also now welcomed back into the fold. There, too, is the Earl of York, next to Nicola de la Haye – the fine-looking old biddy. Do you know what this means?'

I could guess, but I allowed Robin his moment. I helped myself to another huge scoop of the pie.

'It means, my greedy friend, the tide has turned. Three major players have come back over to the King's side. I heard there were factions in the ranks of Prince Louis's men – English knights quarrelling with French over the division of the land after the

270

conquest – but I had not realised so many had changed allegiance. Our enemies are divided and our hand is strengthened.'

'It would be nice if Miles and Thomas had a change of heart,' I said, wiping the gravy from my chin with a napkin. 'But I suppose it is too much to ask – at least in Thomas's case.' I had spoken without thinking and Robin turned on me abruptly.

'You know why Thomas left?' he said. 'Tell me, Alan, why did he go?'

I blushed to the roots of my hair. 'I . . . I cannot. I swore I would not tell.'

Robin's eyes glinted silver. 'It is to do with me, is it not? Thomas thought I would harm him somehow or his family. What did he think I'd do?'

I got to my feet; I could not face Robin's inquisition and keep my word to Thomas. 'I must go,' I said, putting down my napkin and finishing my cup of wine.

'Alan – I understand that you wish to keep your honour. And you love Thomas, I know that, as do I. But think on this: by not telling me what Thomas feared, you may be endangering him. Think about what is best for him – being my friend or my enemy. One day soon we may have to face him in battle, have you considered that?'

And Miles, too, I thought, but did not say it aloud.

'He might die under my sword – or yours – if he remains with the rebels,' continued my lord. 'If the King can bring these men back to his banner, I swear I can do so as well.'

I could face no more of Robin's assault and, mumbling an apology and claiming that I had urgent duty elsewhere, I left the great hall and stumbled blindly out into the bright light of the castle courtyard, my heart in turmoil.

The world seemed to be spinning around me: what Robin had said was true. My silence was keeping Thomas, and maybe Miles, too, at odds with Robin, in the enemy camp, and that could not be for the good. Yet I had given my word. It was all horribly wrong. Here I was, serving a King I despised, supporting a cause I did not believe in and putting myself in opposition to Miles and Thomas. The tide was turning, Robin had said, the King was growing in power. I would gladly help him drive the French from England but what about my friends? How would they fare if King John was made secure again on the throne of England? How would England fare?

I could not resolve the division of my loyalties over my vow to Thomas. But there was one snarled affair, nagging like a bad back tooth, that I certainly could remedy. The world stopped spinning. I marched over to the barns where the royal baggage was housed and found Robert, now in command of a score of men-at-arms, who had been given the task of guarding the wagons.

'Where is Tilda?' I said. 'I need to speak with her.'

My son looked at me speculatively. 'She's with the washerwomen, over by the vats. On the far side of the courtyard, yonder, by the well.'

I turned and headed in the direction he had pointed. As I walked away, I heard him clearly say, 'About time, too.'

Chapter Twenty-six

I found Tilda, as Robert had promised, with the washerwomen, in a makeshift enclosure walled by flapping linen sheets hung on lines to dry. She was red-cheeked and sweaty, a black tendril of hair plastered damply to her cheek, a huge bundle of linen in her arms. A dozen women were all around her, swapping news and jests, and dumping great masses of dirty laundry into huge copper vats bubbling over small fires and stirring them with long ash poles. Steam billowed and rippled above the vats. The air inside that castle of white cloth was as muggy as on a summer day before a thunderstorm, and I felt the same sense of impending violent release. All the chatter had stopped when I pushed aside a dripping sheet and entered the washerwomen's steamy lair. And when I found myself face to face with the woman I wished to speak to, I too was struck dumb.

Tilda curtseyed awkwardly, the bundle of linen making her clumsy. 'Sir Alan,' she said, 'did you require something? Do you need something to be washed?'

The silence and stillness of the women, all their eyes on me, was paralysing.

'Ah, Tilda,' I said jovially, 'there you are.'

'Yes, Alan, here I am.'

A small powerful-looking woman with the sad eyes and jowls of a bulldog came forward and wordlessly took the bundle of washing from Tilda's arms.

'Yes, so, Tilda,' I said. 'Ah . . .'

Jesu, I was a man past the ripe age of forty and I could not find the words to speak to a woman I had known for many years, who had once been my lover, for God's sake, and was now a member of my household. My head was entirely empty.

'Ahem, it was just, you see . . . I just wondered, if you have the time, whether you might be kind enough to wash two of my spare chemises. They are a little soiled, I am sorry to say. Hard travelling, you know . . .'

Tilda gestured to the bundle of linen now in the bulldog's arms. 'I have them already, sir,' she said.

'Ah well, that's good. Good. Very good. Thank you.' I turned to go, took two paces. Stopped. Be a man, Alan, be a bloody man, said my inner voice.

I turned back. 'And I wished to say thank you for the hot posset you made for my cold. It is much better now, thanks to your kindness.'

'It was my pleasure, sir,' she said.

'Right, well, that's good. Carry on.'

Sweeping back a flap of damp linen, I began to stride away.

A voice behind stopped me in my tracks.

'Sir Alan,' said Tilda. 'Wait!'

I turned once more and looked at her. Outside of the enclosure she looked smaller, more frail, an almost doll-like figure in the expanse of the castle bailey.

'What is it?'

'I know it must have been hard for you to come and thank me publicly after all that has passed between us. I honour you for it.

274

And I too owe you thanks for taking me in to your household when I had nowhere else to go. You've been more kind than I deserve.'

I said gruffly: 'It is Robert you must thank.'

'You could have expelled me after Robert took me in – and you did not. You have given me another chance at life. I am truly grateful, Alan.'

A surge of warm affection for this woman took me completely by surprise – and I was seized by an urge to enfold her in my arms. Mercifully, I very swiftly came to my senses. This was Tilda. I must not forget that. She had always been an expert at manipulating my feelings. I had to resist these impulses or disaster would surely follow.

'Well, Baldwin and Robert tell me you have made yourself useful at Westbury . . . so we are all glad to have you and I think we need say no more about the matter.'

And I turned and walked away.

We did not stay long in Lincoln. King John sent a force north under Savary de Mauléon to harry the retreating Gilbert de Gant and the rest of the royal army turned south again. The rebels were burning and ravaging East Anglia and Robin had persuaded the King to come to the port of Lynn to resupply the army from that rich town and to threaten the rebels with a full-pitched battle. We travelled at the rear of the column once more, with Robin's men zealously guarding the baggage train. After two days, we reached Peterborough and turned east into the fenlands. On this flat, marshy ground the road was raised in many places by cut logs covered in reeds and earth, which allowed the horses to pass safely through the mire. But it was still hard going for the heavy wagons. A dozen times during that third day we had to halt the train and dismount to hoist out a wagon's wheels that had become stuck in the black mud. The oxen hated it – complaining in dull, mournful booms as they stood up to their hocks in sludge. The men and I soon became slathered and even Robin, not too proud to put his shoulder to a wheel, began to look less like an earl and more like a wretched peasant of the meanest kind. Boot's great strength was invaluable here. He would lumber down the column to where the wagon was stuck, duck down under it and seize the front axle and, with a writhe of his vast shoulders, help pluck a heavily laden treasure cart out of the morass, hauling it and the oxen back up to higher ground.

During one of these dispiriting operations, as I was taking a break from the labour, stretching my back muscles and arms, I noticed a dark smudge boiling upwards on the northern horizon.

I called to Robin and pointed out the bank of smoke a few miles away.

'Can that be the rebels?' I asked. 'Should we warn the King?'

'It's not them,' said Robin grimly. 'That's Crowland Abbey over yonder.'

'I thought they had paid the King handsomely for his protection.'

'John did not deem it enough. He abused Mauléon roundly in council last night for his "womanishness" – even accused him of disloyalty – and he sent in the Flemings this morning to torch the place and squeeze the abbot for more of his silver.'

There was nothing more to say. We freed the wagon and continued onwards across the dreary flatlands. Once again I was filled with turmoil. We served a bloody tyrant – it was not so much that he had robbed the Church, which was bad enough, but that he'd gone back on his word. It seemed to me no crime was beyond him – and any decent, right-thinking man should oppose him with all his strength. Instead, we were aiding and abetting him in his bloody tyranny.

Even after arriving safely at Lynn and having gratefully sluiced that infernal mud from our bodies, I was still outraged by the

King's actions. And the lavish feast – stuffed peacocks, boar's heads and a vast lamprey pie – that the wealthy burghers of the port had arranged for John and his knights the next day could not shake my foul temper. I ate little and quietly left the great hall before the sweetmeats and nuts were brought out. I was in an odd mood, hankering to be alone, and made my way in the golden autumn afternoon sunlight down to the taverns by the waterfront, where I ordered a flagon of wine and sat looking out at the crowded mass of shipping on the shining River Ouse, the source of Lynn's great riches.

I had barely taken a sip when I saw a familiar figure walking along the cobbles of the quay. Tilda. Before I could consider the implications, I had hailed her loudly and she was coming over to my table, smiling and asking how I did. She was wearing a black cloak and hood, and over one arm she carried a wickerwork basket, which I saw was filled with little packets of powder, pots of ointment and bunches of dried herbs.

I suddenly wished that I had not seen her or that I had pretended not to see her. I was sitting in the shade of a large canvas awning in semi-darkness and she might well have passed by without noticing me. I could not think of a thing to say to her and stared into her basket for inspiration.

'What are you doing at the quayside at this time of day, Tilda?' I asked. It came out wrong. It sounded as if I, as her master, were accusing her of neglecting her duties.

She took a sharp intake of breath. 'Beg pardon, sir. Robert said it would be all right if I took a little time for myself – I have been visiting the apothecary yonder. He has the best items being so close to all the shipping. The foreign merchants bring him medicinal spices from the Orient, curious roots, dried powdered insects, all sorts . . .'

'Is somebody ill?' I asked, looking up into her eyes for the first time. Her face was very pale.

'Not yet,' she said, looking away quickly, refusing to meet my gaze.

I took a sip of my wine; she stood awkwardly before me waiting to be dismissed. The silence stretched out before us. This was all wrong: she was better born than I, the daughter of a lord, despite her reduced circumstances. I should not be treating her like an errant servant girl, sitting at my ease while she stood. I collected my manners.

'Please,' I said, 'sit a while and have some wine.'

'I should be getting along,' she said.

'Have some wine; it will be good for you.'

She put down her basket and sat on the bench next to me and I refilled my cup and set it before her. She took a frugal sip. Once again the silence oppressed us both.

'Do you miss the Priory?' I said.

She looked at me sharply, trying to gauge what pitfalls my question might contain.

'I only meant, are you content in your new life – away from a life in the service of God?'

To my surprise, she laughed. 'It is far more interesting out in the world than ever it was at the Priory – you have no idea, Alan, how exquisitely dull my life was there.'

'Really?' I said. 'I have been thinking more and more that I would like to embrace a life of holy contemplation.'

She laughed again – a pretty sound that made my own heart lighter; I felt my hunched shoulders relax. Tilda took another sip of my wine.

'You would die of boredom, Alan – trust me – you are used to a life of action, a whirlwind existence of dash and danger. You'd go mad in a cloister inside a month.'

She began to tell me, haltingly at first and then with increasing confidence, of her time at Kirklees Priory, and how she had hated it – the daily round of work and prayer, work and prayer, the

278

thousands of hours on her knees in the cold chapel asking God's forgiveness, the endless grubbing away in the earth of the herb garden.

'It grinds away the soul, Alan. It is a waste of life for a woman – or a man – with any spirit.'

I listened, fascinated, and refilled her wine cup. Then she said something that made me sit up.

'Besides, all the other nuns hated me.'

'Why – for God's sake?'

She actually blushed then. I waved to the tavern keeper, signalling for more wine.

'Do you not know? I thought it was gossiped about in all the taverns in Yorkshire.'

I must have looked blank, for she laughed once more – this time with a note of bitterness.

'Tell me. Why did all the other nuns hate you?'

'They were jealous,' she said.

I frowned. 'Jealous – why?'

'Surely you know what takes place in a closed community – when every member is a woman. Or a man, for that matter.'

I was beginning to grasp what she meant. 'You had a love affair?' I asked, feeling out of my depth.

'Dear, sweet unworldly Alan Dale – yes, I had an affair. Anna, the Prioress; she was my lover.'

It was my turn to blush.

'So, is it truly women that you desire?'

'No, well, yes, sometimes. Love comes to us all most unexpectedly. I was so unhappy when I first came there, I was imprisoned, trapped, my father was dead . . .'

I had the grace then to look at my boots. I was the man who had killed him and Robin had arranged for her to be locked away safely at Kirklees after the siege of Château Gaillard. He was a generous patron of the Priory and they could not refuse him.

'Anna was kind to me. She nurtured me. I was so full of hate back then,' she said, looking sideways at me. 'It was making me sick, boiling inside me like molten iron. When Anna first showed me kindness it was a relief. It felt like the sun was shining for the first time in an age.'

Tilda stared at the table. A cawing seagull swooped down in front of us and seized a scrap of discarded bread before flapping away.

'It feels good to tell you all this, Alan. To make a clean breast of it. I wanted to hurt you – to hurt you through Robert. But I am a different woman now – and Anna helped me become different. I shall always be grateful to her for that, despite what happened later. I found love. She gave me her love. It was a healing balm for my sorrows.'

I had never really considered how my actions had affected Tilda. I had thought of her only in terms of the threat she posed to my son and me. But something was troubling me. 'Yet at Kirklees, and before at Château Gaillard, I understood that it was Sir Benedict Malet who was your lover. Was he not?'

'I never truly loved him,' she said. 'But at Château Gaillard he too was kind to me during the siege – when I was so terribly hungry. You remember what it was like, Alan? He gave me scraps of food, enticed me into the back of his storeroom, and I was weak. I am not proud of myself, Alan, but it was the only coin I had. It has always seemed to me that the world makes too much of the common-place act of love. We are all born with the urge to seek pleasure – God gave it to us – and it seemed silly to me that a few kisses, a few fumbling, grunting moments should mean so much to a man and so little to me and yet be the cause of so much condemnation. But you caught him, Alan, you exposed him. You were so terribly self-righteous, so full of contempt – so *fiercely* in the right.'

I had never seen myself as self-righteous. But I well remembered my anger when I discovered that she and Benedict had been stealing food from the rest of the besieged garrison. At that moment the tavern keeper came over with a fresh flask of wine and another cup. Tilda and I both remained silent while he mopped the table, cleared the empty flagon and poured out the drinks.

'Later, while I was at Kirklees, Benedict came to me – he told me he loved me and promised that together we would bring you down. And I still wanted that – God save me, but I dreamed of that, Alan. I was stifled in Kirklees – Anna was jealous of any time I spent with others. She was jealous of everyone who even looked at me. She had made me sub-prioress, to the rage of the more senior nuns, and seemed to think that meant she owned me. At least when I was with Benedict, I could breathe. When I met you that time at St Paul's and you practically told me outright you meant to kill the King, I told Benedict that night and he got word to John.'

She put a hand on mine on the table. 'I am sorry, Alan. I know you suffered as a result of my betrayal. And all I can say is I will never seek to harm you again.'

I slid my hand out from under hers. Her touch was causing strange unwelcome emotions to stir in my breast. I had to resist them. I had to be strong. I tried to make a careless jest, to ease the thick air between us.

'Two lovers, eh!' I said. 'Prioress Anna and Benedict Malet – it doesn't sound dull at all in the cloistered world.'

'Two lovers in ten years – does that seem excessive? Perhaps for a woman. But for a man? I am sure you must have had dozens since your wife passed away.'

'No,' I said quietly, 'there has only been you.'

Tilda did not seem to hear me. She was getting to her feet, collecting up her basket of medicines, arranging her shawl.

'I must be away, Alan, I have things to do,' she said. 'As pleasant as this is, I cannot sit about all day drinking wine with you. I shall never get anything done.'

I looked up at her. As she turned from the table to go, I caught her arm. 'It is none of my business, Tilda, but may I ask you one more question – is there someone now, is there someone in your life who makes your heart beat faster?'

Tilda dropped her eyes. 'There is,' she said. 'There is someone just like that.'

'Then I am heartily glad for you,' I said, releasing her arm.

I awoke the next morning, muscles aching from the unusual labours on the road and with a thumping head. After Tilda left, I'd remained at the tavern and drunk another three flagons of wine while I chewed over all that she had said. She was in love with someone, that much was clear. Good for her. I meant what I had said: I was heartily glad for her. She deserved some happiness after all she had suffered. We all deserve happiness. If her emotions were engaged with someone else, there was less chance of me falling under her spell again. All in all, it was good news, excellent news, definitely something to be celebrated, I told myself.

It was long past dawn – mid-morning, in fact – and I splashed cold water on my face in our quarters in Lynn Castle and went downstairs in search of something to eat.

The kitchens were a-bustle – a score of folk were busy preparing the day's royal dinner. In the series of big stone rooms, cooks were bawling out instructions, their assistants were chopping herbs, slicing vegetables, grinding mortars and pestles; other lackeys were stirring huge bubbling pots and the spits by the big open fires were already turning the animal carcasses, the lads working the handles drenched in sweat. Red-faced men and women were rushing about everywhere and there was an air of controlled panic, as if they were preparing for a battle rather than a banquet.

I surveyed the scene from the doorway, hoping to catch the eye of a kindly passing maid so that I might beg a slice of bread and a cup of ale to break my fast, when I was astonished to see Robin and Tilda over by a work bench in the far corner of the main room. They were very close together, leaning over the board to examine something, heads almost touching, oblivious to the mayhem all around. I did not mean to surprise them but when I found myself a yard behind Robin's back and gave a discreet cough to announce my presence, they both jerked apart and turned to stare at me. Their eyes were filled with shock and – I can find no other word for it – guilt.

'What do you want, Alan?' said Robin coldly.

I was taken aback by his tone. 'I want breakfast,' I said. 'What are you two doing here?'

'It is none of your concern,' said my lord. 'And I would be obliged if you would leave us in peace and go about your business. I'm sure you can find someone here who will feed you, if that is what you wish.'

I was too surprised to argue and started backing away. Indeed, surprised is the wrong word. I was shocked. I felt as if I had intruded on an intimate moment between the two of them, as intimate as the act of love itself. By God, was Robin Tilda's lover? That was absurd. No, it could not be. Robin had told me himself that he had never played false with Marie-Anne and that he never would. But what if he had fallen in love? Tilda was beguiling enough. Beautiful, even. And she had told me just the day before that she had someone in her life. Could it really be Robin? It was Robin who had insisted Tilda accompany Robert when he joined the army. He had deliberately brought her here. It all fell into place. Robin was obviously the one who made her heart beat faster!

Once I had overcome the shock, my next emotion was rage. I took myself for a long walk in the town, down to the wharf again to watch the merchant ships unloading their wares, but such was my state that I barely noticed my surroundings. I found myself stomping past the tavern where I had shared wine with Tilda the day before. What right had Robin to make love to a woman in my household? She was under my protection. And she had been my lover. It was a betrayal of the worst kind, I decided. There is a code among men. A sacred code. You do not sleep with your friend's former lovers, no matter how beguiling they might be.

I knew there was no point getting into a lather about this matter. I would go back and see Robin to clear the air. I would confront my lord. Ask him to his face.

But when I returned to the castle I could not find him in any of his usual haunts and, in the end, after half an hour of fruitless searching and with my head still aching from last night's wine, I took myself to my pallet and slept away the rest of the day.

Robin's eldest son Hugh awakened me at dusk.

'Why are you abed, Sir Alan?' said Hugh, frowning. 'Are you sick too?'

I told him I was not; indeed my cold was much better.

'All the senior knights are summoned to council in the great hall,' he said. 'The Earl asked me to find you and tell you to hurry.'

Chapter Twenty-seven

I was in the great hall of Lynn Castle, with two dozen other knights, English lords and half a dozen mercenary captains, as the bells of the cathedral church were ringing out for Vespers. I found Robin conferring with Savary de Mauléon. He broke off his conversation with the Poitevin lord when he saw me, came over and put his arm around my shoulders.

'After this council session, I want to speak with you. I need you to do something very important for me.'

'That is good for I urgently need to speak to you, too,' I said. 'I must ask you on your honour—'

'Later, Alan,' he said. 'After this.' Before I could reply I heard Savary de Mauléon calling for order in the crowded room and silence, if you please.

'My lords,' Mauléon said over the rumble of chatter. 'I have grave tidings that require your full attention.'

His words achieved almost complete silence.

'The King is not well today and he cannot attend this council of his lords, and so, at his request, I am to deliver the news myself.'

'What's the matter with him?' came a hearty voice from the far side of the hall.

'He is indisposed. A matter of a delicate stomach. I am sure it is merely a case of overindulgence at the feast yesterday. No doubt he will be well again very soon.'

'It's the squits,' a man muttered to his neighbour. 'I'm not surprised after watching him wade into that lamprey pie yesterday. Seen pigs with more restraint.'

'Gentlemen, please,' said Mauléon. 'The fact is that the King requires rest, that is all. I have worse news from the south. Hubert de Burgh has taken the decision to arrange a truce with the French at Dover. As many of you will know, his men have been holding out for three months now, suffering all the onslaughts of the enemy and, together with our courageous irregular forces in the area' – Mauléon gave Robin a nod of recognition – 'waging war against his lines of communication and shipping with France. However, de Burgh's men are at the point of exhaustion. He will continue to hold the castle but he will not attempt to molest the French in any other way – and in return the French will cease their mining operations against his walls and desist from their bombardment of his defences.'

Mauléon paused to let this sink in. I wondered how long the truce would last and whether Cass would be able to persuade his Wealden '*conrois*' to keep from gleefully robbing the rich French supply wagons even for a week.

'Prince Louis, we have been informed, has received reinforcements from France and, with a contingent of rebel knights from London under Lord Fitzwalter, he is coming north with the intention of bringing us to battle.'

The hall broke out in a storm of voices. I heard men shouting that Hubert de Burgh was a traitor for failing to keep the enemy occupied in the south. Others were even saying we must seek a truce of our own with the French. I did not condemn de Burgh.

I knew what three months of siege was like – the starvation, the battle fatigue, the daily sapping of manpower – and I applauded him for this neat solution. We still held Dover and that, as far as I could see, was the important point.

'Gentlemen, pray give me silence,' Mauléon was shouting over the tumult.

When a relative quiet was restored, the Poitevin lord said, 'They outnumber us two to one. Accordingly, we shall be quitting Lynn the day after tomorrow – or at least the bulk of the army will leave. I shall remain here to fortify the city and deny it to the enemy. The majority of you will join the King on a march north to Newark Castle, where we shall defy the enemy from the safety of that fortress and summon our forces from the rest of England to join us. I will give you your individual orders immediately after this. But for most, I urge you to look to your men and prepare to march.'

There was a surge towards the Poitevin, men loudly demanding to be told their orders, to see the King privately, to have the situation more thoroughly explained . . . and I saw Robin shouldering his way through the press to me.

'How ill is the King?' I said to him when he had reached my side.

My lord gave me a sharp look. 'He's ailing nicely, thank you, and making a great fuss about it – can't get off the privy, if you must know. Tilda's tending him.'

'About Tilda,' I said. 'I know it is probably none of my concern—'

'I don't have time to argue about Tilda again,' said Robin. 'I need you to do something for me that is far more important. And I need you to give me your word that you will do it and ask no questions. Also, that you will be discreet and tell not a single soul what you are doing. Can you do that?'

I was stung – but he was my lord. I nodded sulkily.

'I want you to swear on your honour that you will do this and remain as silent as the grave about it afterwards.'

'I know how to keep a secret,' I said crossly, thinking of my vow to Thomas. Then, at his insistence, I swore.

And he told me exactly what he wanted me to do.

The mood in the army as we left Lynn two days later was wholly different to that on our arrival there. Now we were retreating in the face of a looming threat, and even with our swelled ranks of newly rejoined knights, we felt like a beaten force. It was the second week of October by then and God gave us a foretaste of what winter had in store. The heavens opened and grey rain lanced down on us from the moment we rode out of the gates until the middle of the afternoon, when we made camp in the hamlet of Walpole, eight miles to the west. The King had made a bold show of riding his horse on the march, rather than taking a horse-drawn covered litter – Tilda had apparently fortified him that morning with a mighty draught of juice of the poppy that she had purchased in Lynn, which apart from its pain-killing properties also seized up a man's bowels and turned them to hard clay. The rain made the condition of the fenland roads even worse and it was clear the baggage train would not able to travel at the same speed as the rest of the army. We arrived at Walpole a good three hours after the rest of King John's force, by which time every single house, barn, hut and hovel had been commandeered by the more powerful lords. Most of the rest of the army were sleeping in their cloaks on the damp and boggy ground.

'It won't do Locksley,' croaked the King. 'It you can't manage to keep pace, what earthly use are you as Master of the Royal Baggage?'

Robin and I were in a modest hall, inside the compound of the tiny manor of Walpole, trying to warm ourselves beside a small fire in the hearth and at the same time pretend we were listening attentively to the King's tirade.

'I will tell you where we are heading in the morning and it will

288

be your duty to keep up and ensure my possessions are with me whenever I require them.'

An old black-clad priest, who until now had been piously mumbling a long Latin prayer behind the King's chair, leaned forward and whispered in the King's ear, casting a spiteful look at Robin.

'Yes, exactly,' said the King. 'Father Dominic points out that we required the portable chapel this afternoon so that a mass could be said and prayers offered up for my health. But where was my chapel? It was with you, Locksley, stuck in the mud miles away! You are holding us back, man. You're a disgrace to your new office.'

The King looked very pale and he seemed to have lost a good deal of weight even in the short time that he had been ill. While Robin and I dripped and gently steamed, he ranted about total obedience and gross negligence of duty. He threatened dire punishments for my lord if such tardiness occurred again.

I watched Tilda, who was at the far end of the hall mixing a potion from a pot of boiling water and several leather pouches of dried herbs. She too looked pale and intimidated by the royal presence, and yet to my eye she appeared quite lovely, even in her plain grey robe with her hair gathered under a simple coif. Robin was a fortunate man, I thought with a fresh stab of anger – or was it jealousy? As I watched, I noticed her hands seemed to tremble slightly as she stirred the mixture into a beaker.

'I have a solution to this problem, Sire. If you will hear me,' said Robin. 'I have found a local man who says he can lead the wagons by a safe passage through the marshes tomorrow – low tide is at noon, he says – and though there is a slight risk of becoming mired he swears he can show us the dry paths if we go at that hour. It would take less time for us to cross the Wash directly and in the meantime you could proceed via the well-trodden, more southerly route, which would be much easier on your royal person. The baggage train could meet the rest of the army at, say, Sleaford in two days' time before we proceed to Newark. That is if you can possibly do without your portable chapel for a day or so.' Robin gave the priest a brilliant smile.

Tilda was handing the King the steaming cup. He took a small sip and spat out a mouthful of dark-brown liquid. 'Too hot, you stupid bitch; much too hot, and too bitter. More honey, more water and be quick about it.'

I saw Tilda wince and hastily take the cup back from the royal hand. I was flooded with a wave of black hatred for this man. A pair of hulking Flemish crossbowmen flanked the royal seat and a dozen guards stood around the room watching our audience, but I was still mightily tempted to unsheathe Fidelity and hack the bastard's head from his shoulders, consequences be damned.

'Yes, yes, Sleaford it is, then, in two days' time,' the King was saying. 'But I will have your head if you are late. Mark me, Locksley. Your head is mine if you are late.'

We were not late in meeting the King and the rest of the army at Sleaford two days later – it was much worse than that. We arrived at the rendezvous on the fourteenth day of October, bedraggled, exhausted and slathered in mud, accompanied by only nine of the twelve wagons in the royal train.

Sleaford was a market town with a small castle and a square enclosure surrounded by deep moats on all sides. It belonged to the Bishop of Lincoln and the function of the castle seemed to be mainly to protect the huge tithe barn that housed the vast quantities of grain collected from the peasants in the bishop's See. After our arrival with the depleted wagon train, Robin first went to see the senior captain of the King's guard, a hairy Flemish thug named Wulfram, and after a quiet conversation with this man, Robin, Hugh, Wulfram and I paid a call on the King.

John was abed in the bishop's chamber in the stone keep, his face blotched and slack, his eyes large and feverish. The flesh seemed to have melted from his body, leaving him skeletally thin. The air reeked of faeces and old sweat. His illness had clearly grown worse in the two days since our meeting at Walpole; I had heard that he had been unable to ride during the journey and instead had been carried the distance in a covered wagon, halting every half-mile to allow him to ease his gushing bowels.

'I fear I must give you grave news, Sire,' said Robin, his face a mask of sorrow. 'But we have lost the royal treasury to the quicksands of the Wash. It is gone. Swallowed up by the mud. I know this will grieve you even more severely, but I must tell you we have also lost the portable chapel. Fortunately, we managed to salvage the bedding, tapestries and most of the food.'

The King moaned. He tried to raise his head but failed; his eyes flickered and fixed themselves on Robin's face.

'The treasury . . .' he quavered, his voice like that of a petulant child. 'What do you mean, Locksley? You cannot have lost it. We must have that money to pay the men.'

'We were deceived, Sire,' said my lord. 'The scoundrel who was our guide led us falsely and before we knew what had occurred, three of the wagons were plunged into the bog and, in the time it would take to say an Our Father, they were gone. Disappeared from view beneath the watery surface of the mire. We were too occupied with saving the rest of the train to salvage them. Alas!'

The King was stirred into action, straining, struggling until his head was raised a few inches from the bed. Tilda came silently forward and slipped a pillow beneath his faded locks, supporting his head, which now appeared inhumanly large on his long, skinny white neck.

'There was a hundred thousand marks in those wagons, Locksley – at least that much in jewels, plate and coin. You cannot possibly have lost it all.'

'I know, Sire, that you are a man who believes in swift punishment, so it may ease your distress to know that I hanged the rascally guide from the first tree we could find.'

The King let out an inchoate bellow of pain, a harsh rattling sound that seemed to tear at the cords in his throat. 'It is you who will hang for this – guards, guards! I want the Earl of Locksley in chains. Now! He is a thief and a liar. Guards!'

Two of the Flemish men-at-arms stepped forward. I took a grip on Fidelity's hilt. But Wulfram stopped the men dead with an upheld palm. The two men looked perplexed but stepped back against the walls of the bedchamber at their captain's command.

The King slumped back on the sheets. He whispered: 'You have killed me, Locksley, I am a dead man this day and it is all your doing – all of it. And after everything I've done for you, all my kindness, you ungrateful, cold-hearted bastard.'

'Indeed, Sire,' said Robin.

Chapter Twenty-eight

We left the King's army that very hour. Robin, Hugh, Tilda and myself rode out of Sleaford with our remaining men – Robert and Boot had already departed from the column. They had, in fact, not come with us across the treacherous mudflats of the Wash with the rascally local guide. In truth, there had never been a rascally guide outside of my lord's imagination. My son and his bodyguard, accompanied by a score of our men-at-arms, had simply taken the three wagons, heavily loaded with silver, jewels, regalia (and, at Robin's whim, the portable chapel), and headed at their greatest speed west towards Nottingham. We had paid Wulfram his agreed price, which was a single chest of silver that he said he would share with his men. I never discovered if he did so, for I never saw the man again. He and many of the mercenaries – knowing that King John was on his deathbed and now, thanks to Robin, almost as penniless as a church-porch beggar, and that Prince Louis, Lord Fitzwalter and the rebel army were fast approaching – quietly slipped away in the next few days, many taking John's possessions, weapons, tapestries, wine, furniture – anything of value – as payment for their military services.

King John, we later heard, managed to make it as far as Newark Castle in the next two days where, surrounded by monks and tended by the Abbot of Croxton, he made his last confession, dictated a will and departed this life. After his death, his body was left deserted, even by his closest servants; it was stripped of the clothes he had worn, his rings, and everything of value in the chamber was removed by the fleeing remnants of his court. The corpse of the King of England lay in a cold chamber of Newark Castle for two days, untended, unclothed, unmourned.

And may he burn for eternity in Hell.

It took us three days to reach Westbury, for the wagons we stole from King John had been the heaviest in the train and even clear of the marshy flatlands of East Anglia, it was hard-going on the roads. But all our muddy labours were made light by the joy in our hearts: Robin had sworn that every one of us would share in the treasure and when each man-at-arms had been given his share, and Robin had appropriated his own largest slice of the haul, I knew I would still be rich beyond my most excessive dreams for the rest of my life. Robert's future and the future of his children was secure. Best of all, the King – the bloody tyrant who had oppressed England for the past seventeen years, who had squeezed her lords, imprisoned her knights and despoiled her lands with fire, rape and murder – was dead at last.

On the march to Westbury, I marvelled at Robin's sense of timing. He had positioned himself as Master of the Royal Baggage just at the time when the King had accumulated all his wealth from the treasuries of his castles for the war effort and, in doing so, he had robbed the King of all his vast riches days before his death, thus ensuring there would be no royal revenge for his crime. There would be no army at the gates of Kirkton to crush him and his family. It was, I believed, a perfect coup, one that dwarfed his other exploits many times over.

We celebrated his achievement at Westbury. The wine flowed

like water. Baldwin and Alice ransacked the larders for the finest foods that my manor could provide, and we all ate like gluttons and drank until our veins ran red only with the juice of the grape.

After one such repast, when I was bursting with stewed venison, roasted hare, pork sausages and good Bordeaux wine, I staggered off to my solar at the end of the hall meaning to take a short afternoon nap while the rest of my guests continued with their jollity. I found Tilda in my chamber folding a stack of clean white chemises in the clothes chest at the foot of my bed. I was slightly embarrassed to see her in my private room and considered withdrawing to allow her to continue her duties in peace, when I saw that she was weeping.

I was astonished. I had not paid much attention to her over the past few days, being busy first with the theft of the three wagons, then with bringing them safely to Westbury and finally with housing and feeding the swollen numbers of men lodged in my home.

'Tilda, what is it? What's happened?' I asked, closing the door behind me.

She turned her white and pink face towards me and I felt a lurch in my heart: even so disarrayed she was truly beautiful; her grey-blue eyes seemed to sparkle with her tears and her bottom lip was quivering.

'It is nothing that should concern you, Alan.'

'Tell me, my dear, I cannot bear to see you distressed on such a happy day.'

'I cannot say,' she said, and a fresh burst of weeping shook her slight frame.

'You can tell me, Tilda, whatever it might be, I will not judge you.'

I put my hand on her shoulder and I could feel the fragile bones beneath the thin material of her gown.

'Tilda,' I said, my throat thick with emotion.

'I have committed a sin, a mortal sin,' she said, her voice no more than a whisper. 'And I know I shall be made to pay for it by God. Robin – he made me . . .'

'Shhh,' I said. 'Shhh, my dear, I know, I know what you have done.'

Somehow she was in the circle of my arms, her huge eyes looking up at me. Then we were kissing. I felt a roaring in my ears, like the sound of a colossal sea storm breaking over my head. Her small body was pressed hard against mine, her arms curling around my back. We tore the clothes from each other, ripping the fabric, stumbling half-naked to fall heavily on to the bed. She pulled me down on top of her and made a noise somewhere between a wail and a sob, her fingernails digging in, drawing blood against my back. I kissed her cheeks, her tightly closed eyes, her hair. As I bucked and writhed, she curled her legs behind my back, urging me onwards with loud, animal cries. I thrust brutally as if I would crush her – yet she pushed her body into me. I bellowed like a dying bull into the soft curve of her neck and thrust and thrust until I felt the pressure build inside my loins, and then with one last glorious surge against her hips I erupted deep inside.

Afterwards, spent, we lay in each other's arms, the sweat cooling on our sprawled limbs. I kissed her tenderly and gazed into her eyes. All the hatred, suspicion and fear, all the betrayals of the past, all the pain and hurt, was washed away in that first cleansing flood of love.

'Father,' came a voice at the door of the solar. 'Are you all right in there?'

'Go away, Robert!' I growled.

'It's just that I heard some odd noises – are you sure you are quite well?'

'Go away, son, and leave me in peace. I have never been better in my life.'

We did not speak, Tilda and I, we just lay in each other's arms

296

for an hour – or two? Three? Who can say? – and savoured the union of our souls. We made love again, more gently than the first time, exploring each other's bodies with lips and fingers and tongues. We kissed and held each other and then, with Tilda's head resting in the crook of my arm, I fell asleep.

I awoke to see her at the foot of the bed dressing herself in one of my chemises. The first pink of dawn showed at the solar window. She saw me watching her and came over to the bed in the ridiculously large, flapping garment and kissed me tenderly, stroking my hair back from my face.

'I must go now, my love,' she said. 'People will be wondering where I am.'

'Don't go,' I said. 'Please.'

'I must.'

I felt a pang of cold hard anguish. 'Is it Robin?' I said. 'Are you concerned about what he will say? Do not worry, I will speak to him today. He is a married man, after all, he cannot have you and Marie-Anne both. He'll see reason, I'm sure.'

'He will see reason – what on earth do you mean? What? Can you seriously believe that Robin is my lover? How can you think that? I would never . . .'

'But you told me, last night, the mortal sin – you said you had committed . . .'

Tilda stared at me. 'Surely you know. You must know. I killed the King. That is the mortal sin that will damn me. I poisoned our sovereign lord, God's anointed ruler on Earth, pretending to heal with Christ's love and . . . I killed him deliberately, slowly, painfully – and at Robin's secret orders. He . . . he made me do it . . .'

I sat up in bed. A piece of the puzzle clanked into place.

'Wait,' I said. 'You say Robin ordered you to kill the King? With poison?'

'Yes, I thought you must know. You are his closest companion,

297

his oldest friend. How could you believe that I slept with him. I *hate* him. He brought about my ruin.'

This was all going too fast for me.

'Robin brought about your ruin?'

Tilda sat down on the bed. She took my big rough hand in her tiny one.

'I love your child-like innocence above all of your other sweet qualities, Alan, but, my darling, you are being particularly slow this morning. Robin, or one of his agents, told Anna, Prioress of Kirklees, my lover, that I had been found in the bed of Benedict Malet in Nottingham. Anna was overcome with jealousy. She beat me and threw me out in the clothes I stood up in – after more than ten years of humble service to the Church. She slammed the Priory door in my face and made me into a beggarwoman. Robin was the cause of my ruin. He caused me to be expelled from my home. I cannot believe that you would think I could love him.'

I was aware that my mouth was hanging open and I closed it hurriedly.

'When I had been expelled, I went to see Robin, in a rage, I don't know why – perhaps I hoped to kill him or hurt him in some way. But he sent his wife Marie-Anne to speak with me instead. She told me to throw myself on your mercy, that I would surely find a place in your household. She said you would never turn me away in my hour of need. She was right, and I will always bless you, my darling, for your kindness.'

Tilda reached out and took my other hand in hers. 'I love you, Sir Alan of Westbury, and no other, perhaps I have loved you since we were together in Normandy. I hated you, too, for a while, yes, that is true. But what is hate but the reverse of love? My love for you has never truly died. When Marie-Anne told me to seek your help, it made a kind of sense of all that I had suffered, all my life. It made sense of my expulsion. I discovered that deep inside my soul I wanted you. I knew you were good and kind. I knew you were brave and loyal and would never hurt me. You made my heart beat faster. I wanted to be close to you, even if I could not have you. I wanted to be at your side for ever.'

I could find no words but squeezed her small hands in mine.

'Then, when I was settled in your household, Robin came to me and told me that one day he would call on me for a special service and that the price of my continued residence in your home was obedience to that request. I had no choice. He told me if I did not do what he asked, he would see to it that I was expelled from your life. And what he asked was that I kill the King. I know I am damned for it but at least I shall have some happiness in my life with you, won't I, my love? Won't I?'

Her eyes were beginning to fill with tears.

I moved towards her and took her into my arms.

'You shall always have a place with me, if you so desire it,' I said, my throat constricting. 'Always.'

I went to see Robin that morning. When I found my lord seated with Robert at the long table in the guest hall on the other side of the courtyard, I saw that my son was smirking like an idiot and the cheery greetings and questions that I received about the state of my health, and the inquisitions about the quality of my sleep, were tantamount to outright mockery.

'Yes, I am quite well, thank you, Robert, and yes, it is a beautiful morning. But would you mind leaving us. I wish to have a few words with my lord alone.'

When the boy had gone, I took Robin to task. I accused him of manipulating me, of lying to me, of meddling in my affairs to an outrageous degree. I told him his behaviour towards Tilda had been despicable and that – as everyone seemed to know – now she was my lover, I would have no more of it. Enough was enough!

When I had finished saying my piece, Robin gave me a long

slow look. 'King John, our mortal enemy, the scourge of the people of England, is dead at my hand. You now have a mountain of silver in your counting house – more money than you could ever spend in this life. You also have a beautiful and, by the terrifying sounds we heard last night, extremely loving woman in your bed. What exactly are you complaining about?'

He was right. What *was* I complaining about? While I carefully considered my next sally, my lord poured me a cup of wine, shoved it across the table and said, 'Let us make a toast, my old friend – to new love!'

And so we drank.

'Now, Alan,' said my lord, 'if your wits have not been completely addled by too many womanly caresses, shall we consider the future? King John is dead – yet our country is still at war. The French have thrust northwards in strength and I do not think we may rest easy until we have driven them all from England. And there is the new King to consider. He is in urgent need of our help, I would say – wouldn't you?'

I swear that I had not even considered the succession. My mind filled with the image of a chubby boy in velvet and silk, sitting with his haughty mother and applauding with delight as three raggedy prisoners sang 'My Joy Summons Me' for him at Corfe Castle. I remembered him struggling to learn the fingering and bowing of a *canso* in his private chambers, watched by wolfish Flemings. I recalled his childish rages. Most of all I remembered his kindness, the generosity of his gifts when we were starving in the dungeon. Henry of Winchester. Or, as he must surely become, Henry, King of England, the third of that name.

I lifted my wine cup to Robin. 'The King is dead,' I said. 'God save the King!'

Chapter Twenty-nine

Although a blight had been lifted from our lives with the death of King John, there was still the matter of Robin's son Miles and Sir Thomas Blood's presence in the enemy camp to weigh down our souls. I had accused Robin of lying – or keeping information from me – and it occurred to me that I had been guilty of the same crime towards my lord. And so, as we rode south from Westbury a week later, heading for the coronation of young Henry at Gloucester, I decided that my duty to him and his family outweighed my oath to Thomas.

We had been summoned to Gloucester by William the Marshal, Earl of Pembroke. He, along with several other magnates, had been named in King John's will as governors of England, and it seemed the old soldier had deemed it vital Henry be crowned as soon as possible. St Paul's Cathedral in London was, of course, still in rebel hands, as was Westminster Abbey just outside the city, and who knew when, if ever, we might recapture the capital and be able to hold the ceremony in either of these venerable Houses of God. So Gloucester Cathedral it was to be – for this hallowed ground had the distinct advantage of being in a part of the land that had remained staunchly royalist.

I had spent a blissful week with Tilda, much of it in the half-privacy of our chamber at the end of the hall. But our bond was stronger than the mere shackles of lust and it was with a wrenching of my heart that I'd bade her farewell at the end of October and ridden out with Robin, Robert, Boot and a hundred men-at-arms to add our strength to the young King's forces.

Since that day at the feast in Lincoln, Robin had not asked me about Thomas. I was glad he had respected my vow, but it made it difficult to know how to approach the subject. I found the opportunity on the main road between Derby and Lichfield, when we all made camp for the night in the mostly intact hay barn of a burned-out manor.

The men had been well fed and were bedded down, and only Robin and I remained awake, sitting around the fire in a dry corner of the barn passing a mug of wine between us, a last drink before sleep.

Robin stretched and yawned and looked as if he were about to stand and seek his blanket roll, when I stopped him with these words: 'My lord, as you know I made a vow to remain silent on the subject of Thomas and his flight to the rebels.'

'I recall it very clearly,' said Robin, looking at me inquisitively.

'But it seems to me that I am doing both you and he a disservice by remaining silent.'

'Speak, then,' he said, settling down again and reaching out towards me, beckoning for the wine.

I passed it to him.

'Do you remember the day when Aymeric de St Maur came to Corfe Castle during our incarceration there and asked to speak to you?'

'I am not quite in my dotage yet, Alan, of course I can remember it.'

'Well, you told us the Master of the English Templars had ridden all the way from London only to give us some news of the war. Was that the truth?'

Robin just stared at me. 'Spit it out, Alan.'

I looked around the barn at the sleeping bodies of our men. There was no one to overhear us.

'Sir Thomas – and I for that matter – knew that it was not. You lied to us.'

'Alan, we have been over this,' Robin said quietly. Sometimes there are good reasons why I cannot tell you every tiny detail of my plans. Some things must remain secret. In the matter of the King, for example—'

'You should have explained that to Thomas. He took it into his head that you meant to betray him to the Templars for the killing of Brother Geoffrey, the Templar who . . . who . . . interfered with Robert at Pembroke Castle.'

'Why on earth would I do that? Thomas is one of mine. Or he was. Apart from the fact that I would never give up one of my own to an enemy, I thoroughly approved of his actions. No man deserved death more than that child-defiling turd-of-the-cloth. I would certainly have butchered him myself, if Thomas had not got there first. How could you even think I would betray him? Do you not know me at all, Alan?'

'It was the boon; the favour that you promised the Templars at Runnymede. You promised you would kill a man, even a friend, if they asked. After you changed sides in the war – something he deeply disapproved of, by the way – Thomas was convinced you would do anything, even hand him over to the Templars for their punishment, if it suited your interests. That I'm sorry to say is why he ran.'

Robin was quiet for a while. He passed me the mug of wine and stirred the fire into life with a stick. The leaping flames made his face look even more gaunt and angular against the darkness. I could see he was thinking hard.

'Thank you for telling me that, Alan. I know you take your oaths very seriously,' he said. 'And I concede you may be right. Sometimes my habits of secrecy are my undoing – even you and I have fallen out over my reticence in the past.'

We shared a wry smile of remembrance. And, in that moment, although a hundred sleeping men lay around us in that barn, it felt as if we were entirely alone.

'I will try to change my ways, Alan,' my lord said very quietly, 'and now I will tell you two secrets that I earnestly hope you will never reveal to anyone else. I give them to you as a sign of my faith and trust in you.'

Robin looked over his shoulder. I moved in closer towards him, setting down the mug of wine.

He leaned forward and said quietly: 'The first secret is that I too suffered – interference, as you put it – at the hands of a man of the Church when I was a boy. It was at my father's castle of Edwinstowe and I was a little younger than Robert is now. This man, this priest, was my tutor, placed in authority over me by my father to school me in Latin and mathematics, rhetoric and law. He beat me cruelly when I had not learned my lessons to his satisfaction, invoking the name of God as he wielded the rod. And, at night, he would come to my chamber, dress my bruises with goose fat . . . and his fingers would stray.'

Robin swallowed. It was clear that even decades later these memories were still extremely painful.

'He pleasured himself on my body,' he went on in a curiously dead voice, 'and told me that if I spoke about this to anyone he would beat me again. He told me it was my fault these things happened because I was a temptation to his lust. I tried to tell my father but I could not bring myself to explain in detail the foulness of these night-time visits. My father merely told me not to be a cry-baby and, when he discovered that I had spoken out, Father Walter beat me more harshly than ever before. With every stroke of his cane, this priest informed me that it was not he who was punishing me but God himself, for the sinfulness of my soul. He threatened me with the fires of Hell even as he fucked me. That experience put an end for ever to my faith in God and his son Jesus Christ. And, apart from dear old Father Tuck, I have never truly trusted a churchman since.'

Robin reached down for the wine mug and drained it.

'One day, after months of this treatment in my own home, I began to think about ending myself. I had had enough. I planned to throw myself from the battlements. I even stood there one night, with the wind whistling around my bare legs, summoning the courage to jump. I never found the necessary courage. Instead, I found another way. I made a sacred vow that I would never die at my own hand, never, rather I would fight – fight with all my strength against this foul tyranny, against all tyranny. And so I made my plans. And one night, while his back was turned, I knocked Father Walter unconscious with a billet of firewood, gagged him with his own robe and tied him to his bed. I brought the fires of Earth to play on every part of his body, a foretaste of the very fires of Hell that he had used to threaten me; I thrust his crucifix, the image of his false God, far up his fundament; finally, when he was half-mad from the pain, I cut his throat from ear to ear.

'I have never regretted what I did to that beast, never regretted a moment of his last torments. I would have done exactly the same to young Robert's molester, given the chance. And that is why I would never have betrayed Thomas for killing that fiend.'

I was stunned by Robin's tale, even though I had heard elements of it before from Little John, who had fled with Robin into Sherwood after that long-ago killing. My lord had never spoken to me of such an intimate and painful matter before – not once, not even when we were incarcerated together in Corfe. I recognised that night, too, how so much of Robin's character had been forged by his youthful torments in Edwinstowe: his bottomless courage, his implacable cruelty, his hatred of the Church and all her servants, the undying fires of rage hidden under his icy-cold exterior – I recalled that, long ago, Tuck had called him the cold-hot man for this very reason. His rebellious nature, I now grasped, came from the twin betrayals of his father, the representative of King who had failed to protect him as a child, and the predatory priest, the representative of Our Lord God Almighty who had used him so brutally and with such hypocrisy.

But Robin was not finished.

'The second secret I shall tell you, my friend, is what Aymeric de St Maur asked of me. He did indeed come to claim his boon – as Thomas rightly guessed. But can you guess what he really asked? I should have thought it obvious, Alan, even to you.'

'He asked you to kill the King,' I said, wondering that I had not seen this truth in all its blinding clarity before.

'Almost,' said Robin. 'This man of God, this high and mighty churchman, did not put it quite in such bald terms. He did not sully his tongue with talk of regicide. He merely asked me to do everything in my power to ensure that young Henry of Winchester was placed on the throne of England before the year was out. That was the boon he demanded. And that, my friend, I shall gladly do.'

On the twenty-eighth day of October in the year of Our Lord twelve hundred and sixteen, lauded by the choir and cheered by crowds of commoners, Henry was crowned King of England by Peter des Roches, Bishop of Winchester, in the soaring nave of Gloucester Cathedral. The nine-year-old boy had been knighted by William, Earl of Pembroke, now elected regent of England, and was then dressed in his ceremonial robes of red wool and black-and-white ermine, and acclaimed King by his loyal nobles: the Marshal and his nephew John; his half-uncle William, Earl of Salisbury; Ranulf, Earl of Chester; the Earl of Locksley; Aymeric de St Maur and many more. The ceremony was attended by dozens of knights, myself included, Savary de Mauléon and a few of the better mercenaries that the Marshal had persuaded to remain after John's demise.

Taking advantage of the truce at Dover, hawk-faced Hubert de Burgh had even brought himself right across the land to witness the happy occasion. I also glimpsed the scarred face and milky eye of my old enemy Philip Marc, the high sheriff of Nottinghamshire, among the throng. Most significant of all was the presence of the papal legate Guala Bicchieri, the Italian prelate I had last seen on the beach at Sandwich damning the French. The new pontiff, Pope Honorius III, had declared that Henry was indeed the lawful King of England and the upstart Prince Louis had been thoroughly excommunicated.

God was on our side.

The day after the coronation, I realised how little that meant. God Almighty might approve of our choice of King, but nearly two thirds of the barons of England did not – and the dire state of our situation was made clear at a meeting of King Henry's council in the great hall of Gloucester Castle. Robin was summoned with all the other nobles and I went with him.

King Henry, clad in crimson velvet, with his new crown, a thin circlet of gold, glinting on his brow, sat stiffly at the end of the hall in a huge black oak throne, a seat far too big for him and which made him seem even more of a little boy. He said nothing throughout the meeting and remained admirably still – except to give me a discreet smile, when I caught his eye. The Marshal whispered a few words in his ear, the boy nodded and then the grizzled veteran began: 'Gentlemen, to order, if you please.'

The Marshal was still an imposing figure for all his seventy years: wide-shouldered, grey-bearded, upright of carriage, and with a fierce eye – which he now ran over the assembled company.

'Yesterday was a day of great rejoicing,' he said. 'And rightly so. We have a new King and a new start, and I pray that all of our sorrows shall be forgotten in his new and no doubt glorious reign. But this is not the end of our troubles – it is the beginning. For now we must defend the King with all our might and return his rightful kingdom to him. And I suggest, gentlemen, that we now turn our minds to how this can be achieved. How can we rid this land of the enemy and return it to a state of lasting peace? My lord de Mauléon, I think you have the best grasp of it – tell us, if you will, how things stand.'

Savary de Mauléon stepped forward. 'First, if I may, I will tell you of my own plans. I am leaving England to return to Poitou, where I intend to take the cross and depart on a pilgrimage to the Holy Land. I served King John loyally for many years, but it must be admitted that I did many things at his word of which I am not proud. I obeyed my lord's orders and guided him to the right path where I could – I fulfilled my vow to him – but I am no longer a young man and I must look to my own soul. I wish the new sovereign all joy and success to his arms, but with his gracious permission, I must depart his lands and seek my own salvation.'

There was a slight pause and everyone looked at the boy in the enormous chair. King Henry inclined his head gravely in agreement but did not speak.

'As my final service to the crown,' said Mauléon, 'I shall tell you all how matters stand at present and I pray that by God's grace you may accomplish your aims.

'In the north, the French have taken castles and towns as far as Lincoln, which is once again besieged, but they are pushing on further every day, and there remains a good deal of northern support for Louis and the rebel cause. Alexander, King of the Scots, is ever their ally and he would be more welcomed than opposed if he were to come south again with his men.

'In the south-east, with the valiant exceptions of Dover and Windsor' – here Mauléon bowed to Hubert de Burgh – 'all of the

308

major castles are held by our enemies. Although this William of Cassingham has been leading them a merry dance. London remains in rebel hands, as we all know. In the middle of the country we hold Nottingham and Newark, and we are strong in the west, too. These are the castles we hold . . .'

The Poitevin lord began to read out a long list of strongholds but I confess my attention wandered. I was looking at the lean bearded face of Aymeric de St Maur and thinking of what he had asked Robin to do. I liked the man on the whole, but I was conscious of the sorrow he had caused Tilda, who despite our happiness believed herself eternally damned as a result of his plotting.

'To sum up,' said Savary de Mauléon, 'more than half of the country is against you. You have fewer men under arms and those are scattered in castles across the land, and you have no money to speak of to hire mercenaries. The loss of the royal baggage train and the priceless treasures it contained has weakened your cause considerably.'

He looked at Robin, who smiled blandly in return.

'Gentlemen, you have a hard fight on your hands and I wish you success in all your endeavours. But I will take no further part in it.'

'Thank you, Savary, most succinct,' said the Marshal. 'I now ask if anyone here wishes to speak. I beg you all to feel free to voice your concerns and offer suggestions.'

Robin stepped forward. I thought he was about to offer an excuse for the loss of the royal treasury: the treacherous quicksands, the untrustworthy guide, deep regret at not having been able to save it, and so on. But to my surprise he made no mention of it.

'The rebels went to war against the King in the name of a document. Their rallying cry was liberty and the great charter. I should know, for I fought against John for exactly that reason myself.'

There was a ripple of disapproving murmurs among the assem-

309

bled noblemen, who seemed to feel it in slightly poor taste to mention previous allegiances in this company. Many of them, too, had fought on the other side.

'So we can at one stroke,' said my lord, 'take the rebel's cause from him. With one move we can strip away whatever legitimacy they claim for their rebellion. We must reissue the great charter under King Henry's name.'

Now the murmurs turned to voices of argument. Some men approved of Robin's scheme, some were appalled at the implied curb to fragile royal power.

'The rebels say they fight for the great charter,' Robin continued. 'I say we also fight for it, but under the true English King. I guarantee you that – if we offer amnesty, mercy, forgiveness – we will deprive the rebels of at least half of their men, the better half will come over to us, swelling our ranks correspondingly.'

'What about the French?' someone shouted.

Robin scanned the room. By some alchemy, just with his eyes, he managed to quiet the whole of the great hall. Into the silence, he said: 'I say we slaughter the French. We kill every man jack of them until Louis renounces his false claim and takes his leave of these lands for ever.'

And so it went. Two scant weeks later, in mid-November, when the clerks had wrangled over the wording and one of the more contentious clauses had been removed, the great charter was once again drawn up, witnessed, sanded and affixed with the royal seal, and copies of the document were sent to the four corners of the Kingdom. As Robin had predicted, almost before the ink on the document was dry, rebels began coming in to do homage to Henry and swear to be his loyal vassals ever more. One of these was William Marshal the Younger, the Earl of Pembroke's eldest son, but he was only the first of many good men who came to our side.

* * *

Three days after the council meeting, I discovered Aymeric de St Maur at prayer before the altar in Gloucester Cathedral. As I waited for him to finish his devotions, I leaned against one of the huge round columns and stared up at the vaulting arches, filled with a yellowish light, the last of the short November day. Painted on the plaster were images of fantastic animals, demons and saints, in red and blue and black, scenes from the Bible, too – Adam being tempted by a half-naked Eve, who reminded me strongly of Tilda. I was longing to return to her and I am ashamed to say that even in that magnificent House of God, my thoughts turned to our lovemaking.

'The origin of all our sin,' said St Maur from my shoulder. I saw that he too was looking up at the first two people on Earth. I forced myself out of my reverie.

'How goes it with you, Sir Alan?' said the Templar. 'How do you like our gallant young King?'

'I like him a good deal better than the last one,' I said. 'But you must have guessed that. What do the Templars feel about our change of sovereign lord?'

'I cannot speak for all of us but personally I approve. I think he will do very well. Perhaps even be a great king when he is older. And, until then, if he is properly guided—' The Templar stopped. 'But it is not for me, a poor soldier of Christ to tell a puissant King of England what course to take. I'm sure our noble friend William the Marshal will always steer him in the right direction.'

'I heard a rumour the Earl of Pembroke has in fact joined your order.'

'He has. He wishes to be buried one day in the Temple Church in London. But he does not make our policy. No, sir. And we do not seek to control young Henry through him, I promise you. We merely hope the new King will honour his debts.'

I did not believe him. I knew the Templars would use any means at their disposal to further their cause. And having one of their own as regent of all England would hardly bode ill for the Order. But I merely said, 'King John did not pay them, I take it?'

'I do not wish to speak ill of the dead,' said St Maur, 'but you and I know very well, Alan, that John was an avaricious man who loved silver above anything else. He wrung every penny he could out of this land, from nobles and peasants alike. From the Church, too. He "borrowed" a good deal of money from the Temple – hundreds of thousands of marks – and when we politely asked for the promised repayment, we were threatened with the loss of our lands, expulsion of the Order from England, no less. I only hope the boy Henry will take a more reasonable line. All we ask is that our loans, offered to the crown in good faith, be repaid in due course.'

'Is that why you ordered King John's death?' I asked.

The Templar looked hard at me, seemingly very angry. I kept his gaze.

Finally, the man sighed and gave me a crooked smile.

'My, my, the Earl of Locksley is far less discreet than I'd hoped. He has a reputation as a man who can keep a secret but in this case he's been very loose-lipped.'

'I shall never speak of it to another soul,' I said. 'You have my solemn word on it. But in exchange for my vow of silence on this matter, I want something from you.'

St Maur looked wary. 'What do you want?'

'Absolution,' I said.

'Your confessor can surely give you that, Alan. But, very well, *In nomine Patris et Filii et Spiritus Sancti . . .*'

'It's not for me,' I said.

When I returned to Westbury a few days later, the sight of Tilda standing at the door of the hall filled my soul with a pure and shining joy. Once I had taken her into my solar and demonstrated

312

my love for her, I dressed again and went out to my saddlebags and brought her a large piece of folded parchment. The document was written in the Master of the English Templars' precise Latin. There was no mention of any specific sin – St Maur was far too canny to put down in written form what would have been tantamount to a confession of his guilt – but it named her and granted her absolution for all sins venal and mortal that she had committed up until this point in time.

Tilda wept as she read the document, her tears of joy falling on the vellum and smearing the black ink.

Chapter Thirty

I took part in no fighting that winter. A month-long Christmas truce was declared between the warring sides, and while there was some skirmishing in January and February, a second truce was declared soon afterwards that was supposed to last until Easter. The truth was the two sides were locked in stalemate. Over the cold months, more and more rebel English knights came over to King Henry's banner but the French remained strong in the areas they controlled and Prince Louis departed for France in February to bring back more men for his cause.

I occasionally inspected my small force of Westbury troops when the weather allowed it, recruiting a handful of farm lads from the local area to swell my numbers into a respectable-sized company, which I deemed to be twenty-four men-at-arms. I also exercised regularly to keep myself from going soft. And there was a serious danger of that happening. Baldwin had the manor well in hand. I had silver in my coffers and Robert had taken charge of the day-to-day running of the Westbury garrison, with two experienced men-at-arms Simon and Nicholas standing at his elbows to make sure he did nothing egregious. Therefore I had a prodigious quantity of leisure time to spend with Tilda. We rode together across the Westbury lands, even in the snows of January, when her nose grew red and her hands turned to blocks of ice inside the warm fur-lined gloves that I had had made for her. But the cold brought out her beauty: with her white skin and raven hair, deep red lips and little points of scarlet on her cheeks after a hard gallop, she looked like the Queen of Winter from some extravagant fairy tale.

There is no man more generous than one who is in love and who has ill-gotten silver to spend: I lavished affection on my Tilda, buying her furs and silks and jewels until she begged me to stop. 'I have been a servant in your household, Alan dear, and my bond with the other folk here has always been one of equals. How can I flaunt my new finery and not spark resentment among them?'

I moderated my spending at her request but how could anyone still consider my darling to be the equal of drab scullery maids?

We rode out almost daily and when the weather was too thick we curled up in my solar under the blankets with a brazier glowing cherry red in the corner of the room and found other amusements for ourselves.

We did occasionally have news of the outside world and of the war. William of Cassingham, it seemed, had paid no attention at all to the truce and he continued to harass the enemy on the Weald with remarkable success, killing hundreds of the enemy and making it impossible for the French to be secure even in the part of the country on which they had the strongest hold. He attacked the siege camp at Dover again, with his full strength, and burned all their engines of war; he very nearly trapped Louis himself at Lewes and the prince was only rescued from capture and probably a summary beheading by the arrival of a French fleet that bore him away.

Spring came like the arrival of an old friend and my joy was made all the greater by Tilda's shy announcement that she was with child.

I wept when she told me that Robert might soon be expecting a little brother or sister and I took her into my arms. 'Marry me, Tilda,' I said through my running tears. 'Marry me and make me the happiest man in England.'

We decided on a June wedding. But at the end of April, while Tilda and all the women were happily busying themselves with the planning of our nuptials, Robin came to Westbury with a hundred and fifty armed men and summoned me to my duty.

'The Earl of Chester has broken the truce,' said my lord, when he had congratulated me warmly on Tilda's condition and our forthcoming marriage. He told me that Ranulf of Chester, the most powerful of the royalist barons after William the Marshal, had taken it into his head to attack Mountsorrel Castle, some twenty miles south of Nottingham, which was now occupied by Saer de Quincy, Earl of Winchester, a stalwart of the rebel cause who had resisted all blandishment to return to the royal fold and who was a personal enemy of the Earl of Chester. The castle had once belonged to Ranulf's family and, telling nobody on our side, he had made a surprise attack with all his strength in an attempt to wrest it back from the rebels by force.

'Louis is back from France with a hundred and forty fresh knights and half a thousand men-at-arms,' said Robin. 'The Marshal is ready to fight, he says, and we are summoned to join him at Nottingham with all the men we can muster between us.'

I admit I was reluctant to leave the manor and the delights of Tilda's company, but when my lord called . . .

Two days later, I found myself in the great hall of Nottingham Castle in the presence of King Henry and his regent William the Marshal, Earl of Pembroke, and a dozen other magnates. The first person to greet me was the lord of Nottingham Castle, sheriff of Nottinghamshire, Derbyshire and the Royal Forests, my old enemy Philip Marc.

316

'My dear Sir Alan,' he said, smiling at me like a long-lost brother, 'I am so pleased that you could honour us with your presence. I was beginning to feel you were avoiding me. We are neighbours, you know, and I have been reliably informed that you have been in residence these past few months and yet never a friendly visit? A lesser man might be offended. Surely now we are on the same side we can put that little unpleasantness some years ago behind us.'

'You mean the little unpleasantness when you kidnapped my son Robert and held him in chains – that little unpleasantness?'

'Did I hurt the boy? Not one hair of his head. I'm sure it made a man of him. And here he is – the man himself. Robert, my dear fellow, how you have grown.'

My son looked at him the way one might regard a rearing snake about to strike.

'Or did you mean the little unpleasantness when your armed men broke into my home and pulled down my tower?' I asked.

'Pish-posh, my dear Sir Alan – all water under the bridge. At least I did not burn your hall to the ground. I gave my men strict instructions to harm nobody and to touch nothing but the tower. It was an illegal fortification, as you well know, and I had my orders from the King.'

He extended a hand towards me. 'Come now, let us forget the troublesome past and be friends. There is no need for us to be at daggers drawn over ancient history.'

And there wasn't. I found when I looked into my heart that I had no burning hatred for the man. I doubted we would ever be friends – but for the indignities that Robert had suffered, I had taken my revenge on Benedict Malet, spilling his guts in the courtyard of this very castle as he hanged by the neck – and there seemed no reason to nurture a powerful enemy such as the sheriff right on my doorstep. In those golden spring days, my love for Tilda made me want to see the good in all men.

I grasped his outstretched hand.

'Good man, I knew there would be no hard feelings. Now, have you met Ranulf, Earl of Chester,' he said, guiding me over to a short-legged but barrel-chested man with a vast red beard who looked utterly exhausted.

'My lord,' I bowed. 'I had understood you were investing Mountsorrel – you have abandoned the siege?'

'Had to, Sir Alan,' said the man in a deep voice. 'That swine Quincy persuaded Louis to come north in numbers. About half his total forces in England, or so I hear. So we had to retreat here for safety. But you mark my words, Sir Alan, I will recover Mountsorrel one day, even if it kills me to do so. And no man can stop me.'

'Sir Alan,' said a voice behind me and I turned to see a tall, very thin man with sparse but scrupulously clean white hair and a neatly cropped white beard. The skin seemed to hang off his bones as if it had previously belonged to another far larger man. And it took me half a dozen heartbeats before I recognised William d'Aubigny, our captain during the siege at Rochester and fellow captive at Corfe Castle.

'My lord,' I said, scrabbling to think of something to say, 'I am happy to see you have been released at last.'

'Very little gets past your eagle eye, Sir Alan,' said d'Aubigny, smiling. 'Yes, I paid the ransom and did homage to the boy' – he jerked his head at the far end of the hall where King Henry was sitting sipping a hot drink in an ornate X-shaped chair with the Marshal, in full mail and with a helmet under one arm, standing tall and glowering by his side – 'and I have been born anew, like our Saviour, but this time I am on the side of the angels.'

I was about to congratulate him and welcome him to our ranks, when the Marshal's booming voice echoed across the room.

'Gentlemen, gentlemen – time presses. Some of you have been here a day or two, some of you have just arrived. None of you should get too comfortable – we ride to Newark Castle tomorrow at dawn. The French, under the command of Thomas, Comte du Perche, and with a considerable force from London, have left Mountsorrel and are making north-west, heading for Lincoln. They are in the Soar Valley, ravaging the lands around Belvoir Castle.'

'Of course they are, the bastards,' said d'Aubigny beside me. 'That will be Fitzwalter's work. He always was a vengeful devil.' I remembered belatedly that these were d'Aubigny's lands and Belvoir his family's castle. I wondered if Fitzwalter were truly taking revenge on d'Aubigny's defection to the royalist cause, which seemed unduly petty, or if he was just laying waste to anything in his path.

'The enemy have made their move,' the Marshal was saying. 'They have divided their forces. Half remain in the south-east – and that is William of Cassingham's parish, and I have no doubt he will keep them busy down there. But the other half is heading for Lincoln to support Gilbert de Gant in his siege there. They mean to finally take Lincoln Castle. We mean to stop them. We muster at Newark – every man we can spare from other duties – and we shall attack from there with our entire strength. We shall trap them between the men of the castle they are besieging and our own forces, and crush them like . . .'

'A walnut between two stones,' said both d'Aubigny and I at exactly the same moment.

'Aye,' d'Aubigny said to me in an undertone, 'that's what we said at Rochester – and we both know how well that turned out!'

'This is it, Alan,' said Robin when the Marshal had finished and a royal priest had prayed over us for an interminably long time. I found I was staring at his chest, where someone had sewn a small white cross. 'Lincoln. This is where we will win the war.' He saw where I was looking and I could have sworn I saw him blush.

'Did you not know?' he said. 'The Pope has declared that those

319

of us who fight for the King are holy pilgrims. If we die in this cause we go straight to Heaven. It's just like that little jaunt we made to the Holy Land with King Richard all those years ago. Our bloodletting is sanctioned by God. You better get yourself one of these, too.' He tapped the cross with a finger. 'You don't want to miss out on a swift voyage from Lincolnshire to paradise, do you?'

I smiled at him. 'Do you think they will let *you* in to Heaven?'

'Of course they will. When I get to the gates, I'll just slip old Saint Peter a fat purse and that'll be that. Come to think of it, I'm sure he must owe me a favour or two, as I've sent him so many fine, holy clients over the years.'

I laughed, despite his appalling blasphemy.

'Seriously, Alan, I do need to talk to you about Lincoln. Were you paying attention when Pembroke spoke the name of the leader of the French?'

I had indeed marked the name: Thomas, Comte du Perche. The White Count.

'Du Perche is the Marshal's first cousin, did you know that? And Pembroke has let it be known privately that he would prefer him to be spared in the battle, if at all possible, and gently taken prisoner. I disagree. If we win, I do not think this young count should be allowed to live a long and happy life, do you hear me? Don't let him surrender. I won't have him ransomed and returning home to France a poorer but wiser man. I want him bleeding in the gutter. I want him screaming in agony. I want him to be raw, bloody meat. For Mastin. Yes?'

'What was that you said about revenge in Kent, my lord? Dig two graves? Or did I misunderstand you?'

Robin frowned. 'We are not taking revenge, Alan, that would be petty, irresponsible, childish even. What we are going to do is remove one of our lord King's worst enemies – an invader of our land who also happens to be the pale-arsed French bastard who thought he could get away with peeling my friend's skin from his living body. That is a completely different matter. Surely you understand.'

'Of course,' I said. 'It will absolutely be my pleasure – to kill an avowed enemy of my young King, I mean.'

'There is more, Alan, if you could stop sniggering for just one moment.'

I had not been sniggering, I had been expressing my mirth in a manly fashion. But I stopped and what he said next drove all thoughts of merriment from my head.

'I've just heard from Henry in London that Fitzwalter has taken his best knights with him up north. My cousin informs me that Miles will surely be at Lincoln among our enemies. He's taken to calling himself Lord Kirkton these days, by the way. Apparently, Louis has ennobled him. I suppose I should be grateful that he has not claimed the title of Earl of Locksley. And Sir Thomas Blood will be there, too.'

Chapter Thirty-one

We mustered at Newark Castle – a very decent force of some four hundred knights, thrice that number of ordinary men-at-arms, and a large contingent of two hundred and fifty crossbowmen under the bellicose Bishop of Winchester, Peter des Roches. Robin added his force of fifty bowmen to the good bishop's division, under the command of his son Hugh, and my lord and I led a little more than a hundred mounted men-at-arms under the Marshal's banner. We knew we would still probably be outnumbered but, if we could persuade the men inside Lincoln Castle to join the battle at an appropriate moment, I was confident we had a good chance of victory. The stone in our shoe was the presence of Thomas and Miles inside the enemy camp. I dreaded having to face either man in battle and Robin and I spent much time over the following nights discussing exactly how we might get a message to them to beg them to come over to our side.

William the Marshal had insisted we come at Lincoln from the north because, if we followed the direct road in from the south as we had last time, we would be attacking from the lower town, and trying to fight up the very steep hill inside the city and then through the wall that divided it, in order to reach the castle in the upper town. We must break in via the north gate, the Marshal decreed. So the royal army followed the banks of the River Trent north from Newark, with some of the heavy baggage being transported on barges, before swinging east when well north of Lincoln. In the afternoon of the nineteenth day of May, on the sixth day of Whitsun week, we camped outside Stow, about eight miles to the north-west of Lincoln, the army spilling over the fields and copses, cooking themselves hearty meals – perhaps for the last time – and punishing the ale vats and wine barrels to drown their fears.

I left Robin at Stow when the sun was still two hand-breadths above the western horizon, dressed in a brown, hooded monk's robe and without arms or armour, save for the misericorde strapped out of sight on my left wrist and a long oak staff. I was going into Lincoln incognito – and my bowels were gripped with the familiar icy fingers of impending mortal danger.

Robin had joked hilariously that due to my sparse locks, I barely needed a tonsure to complete my disguise as a mendicant. But though I might be thinning a little on top, Robin shaved an area on my crown clean anyway with a few swipes of the razor.

I did not plan to do any preaching, although I liked to think my Latin was good enough and I was sufficiently familiar with the Gospels to pass at a pinch. I only meant to use my disguise to get inside the walls of Lincoln. My biggest fear was that someone would recognise me as Sir Alan Dale, the valiant knight of Westbury – and with the White Count present in the town, I knew capture and exposure as a spy would mean the same awful fate that Mastin had faced. Having tied my horse to a bush in a stand of beech a mile outside the city, I smeared my face with dust and pulled my hood forward, then joined a stream of travellers hurrying along the northern road to get inside before nightfall.

The sun was a red ball just touching the treetops over my right shoulder as I approached the gate, and the weight of traffic took the edge off my fears – chapmen on foot with enormous packs holding their various wares, wagons laden with grain and wine, mules in long trains with towering bales of raw wool from the northern pasturelands strapped to their backs – for their numbers shielded me from the gaze of the French men-at-arms standing beside the open iron-bound doors.

I passed through without difficulty, keeping my hood well forward and only looking up discreetly to take note of the strength of that bastion and the number of men on its walls. It was a dispiriting sight: the gate was a powerful limestone box with three arched tunnels set into it, the middle one big enough to admit two wagons side by side, the two flanking entrances barely more than man-sized. I could see scores of men-at-arms lounging against the parapet atop the gatehouse, alert and looking out over the road to the north, some watching the passing throngs below, all in good mail and many armed with crossbows. Dozens more soldiers were on the town walls that stretched east and west either side. Inside the gate were barracks and stables, and stacked spears and piles of shields, and two taverns, one on either side of the main road, doing a roaring trade with the off-duty soldiery. It would be no easy task to take this grim portal by storm, I thought, and wondered if the Marshal had blundered in insisting that this was the place to force our entry. By my reckoning, the enemy could in a few short moments muster some two or three hundred men-at-arms for the north gate's defence.

But that was not my concern that day. My task was to avoid capture and an unthinkably horrible death and find my friends. I allowed the throng to sweep me into the upper town, noting that the high walls of the castle looked a little battered – but with the royal standard still flying proudly from the top of a round tower set into the north wall. Nicola de la Haye remained staunch in her defence, I saw with a spark of pride. Up ahead and to my left, over the tops of the houses, I could see the soaring, intricate stonework of the cathedral – its two small square towers, with corner spires, marking the entrance to the House of God, and behind them a larger square tower, where the transept crossed the nave. To my right, in the rubble of a once-grand house, I saw a gang of men-at-arms around a mangonel. A knight in a black surcoat barked an order in French: the men loosed the ropes, the mangonel arm swung up, thudding against the padded cross bar, and a huge boulder flew at the castle walls, soaring up in a long arc to crack against the round tower bearing the King's standard. Under the impact, a slice of yellow stone the size of my hall door slid from the walls and tumbled into the deep ditch below. And I saw just how crumbled and pitted the wall was in this northern section. The men-at-arms around the siege engine gave a cheer and started hauling on the ropes to bring the catapult bowl back to the ground for another shot.

A man in a dirty, torn gambeson, the wool stuffing leaking from the seams, and whose face was covered in ugly boils, stopped me and asked for a blessing, and I nervously muttered a few words in Latin while making the sign of the cross before his carbuncle-stricken face. I asked him in return where I might find a Lord Kirkton.

'English or French?' he asked and before I could answer he said, 'The Frenchies are mostly lodged over there beside the cathedral,' indicating the magnificent bulk of the House of God. 'English nobles are on this side of the road.' He pointed west beyond the mangonel team down a partly demolished side street at the end of which I could make out a row of large houses hard up against the western town wall, each with a standard plunged into the earth before the door to identify its inhabitant.

'We poor common men-at-arms are all down in the lower town with the rats and the filth and the whores. It's always the same, eh, brother?'

325

I thanked him and, pulling my hood even further forward, made my way in the direction he had pointed, slipping past the mangonel team and down the side street. I turned right at the end and walked up the line of houses, stopping before the smallest one, at the very end of the line, about halfway along the town wall. It was not much bigger than a cottage, straw-roofed and misshapen, seeming to sag drunkenly at one end. The walls were desperately in need of a fresh coat of whitewash. Outside the square flap of uncured leather that made up the entrance, next to a mound of household waste, animal bones, broken crockery, bits of decaying vegetables, a spear had been planted butt-first into the earth and a limp blue rag attached just below the spear-tip. I reached out a hand and unfurled the greasy standard. It was the fierce image of a snarling wolf crudely painted in yellow. He might have been granted the grand-sounding title of Baron Kirkton, I thought, but his new French lord had not been over-generous with his silver.

I summoned my courage. 'God's blessing upon this house,' I called out loudly and pulled back the leather flap and went inside. The stench was so strong it made me gag: stale sweat, wood smoke, sour wine, male feet and the musty, spicy tang of wet wool that had mouldered before it dried. It was the smell of poverty.

A figure was lounging on the cot over by the far wall, propped on a mound of old clothes and sipping from a large leather flask. To my left I saw the dark outline of an open doorway to another room.

'Go away, brother, I am resting. I am in no mood for another sermon about the terrible vice of drunkenness. I am not at all well today.'

I heard the heavy tramp of a man outside the doorway and stiffened. I had the terrible image in my head of me screaming from a gibbet while industrious torturers peeled the skin from my bones. But he passed by and I relaxed a little. I peered at the figure on the bed through the gloom. Lank blond hair slicked back with sweat over his high brow, he was glaring at me with pale blue, bloodshot eyes.

'I said, get out, you old fool. Do you want me to take my boot to you. Out!'

'Hello, Miles,' I said, pulling my hood down. 'If you are having a drink, d'you mind if I have one too? I could certainly use one.'

'God's blood, Alan Dale! What in the name of Hell are you doing here? And got up as a mystery-play monk, too.'

The young man swung his feet off the bed and stood up, a trifle unsteadily.

'Yes, have a drink, have a bucketful, there is plenty of good French wine at least in this godforsaken shit-hole.'

He seized a cup from the table by the hearth and after giving it a cursory wipe with the sleeve of his dirty chemise, he poured a dark liquid into it from the flask in his right hand and thrust it at me.

'Here's to your health, old man,' he said, throwing back his head and taking a giant gulping swig from the flask. I took a mouthful from my cup and felt the flow of warmth in my belly. I had never needed drink to bolster my courage before but I must admit I felt my fears beginning to recede as the wine did its work. I took another large swallow and put the cup back on the table.

'So what brings you to our fair city of Lincoln – have you come to take up arms on behalf of good King Louis?'

'Not exactly,' I said, dragging out a stool and sitting down.

Miles plonked himself back on the bed. 'No, that doesn't seem your style at all. That monk's habit suits you, by the way, you should think about hanging up your sword and retiring to a monastery.' There was an ugly tone to his voice, very close to a sneer.

'I've come on behalf of your father—'

'The turncoat sent you, did he? You always were his obedient lap-dog. He sent you to cajole and bribe me into abandoning my allegiance, just as he did. Is that it?'

327

'He wants you to stop all this foolishness and come home. He misses you and he says that you will always be his son. Many other men have returned to the King.'

'The true King is Louis of France, not that mewling child under William the Marshal's thumb. Louis knows my quality – I am Lord Kirkton now, don't you know? And when we are victorious I shall be made the Earl of Locksley, too, and the self-serving cut-throat who calls himself my father can beg my forgiveness then.'

'We can work everything out, Miles – your father loves you – even now. Come back to us. Please.'

'Come back to what? To a life lived for ever in his shadow? To being the second son, the spare to the heir. Even when the turn-coat dies, I shall not inherit – my sainted brother Hugh will be Earl after him. And he is not of true Odo blood. His claim is false. His father is Ralph Murdac, as everybody knows but is too afraid to say aloud. He's a bastard and yet he – he not me! – will lord it over our lands when Robin is rotting in his grave.'

'Hugh will treat you fairly, I'm sure of it. He's a good and honourable man.'

'He's a self-righteous prig. But that's your offer, is it? Come home like a good boy and all will be forgiven. No, thank you, Alan. I am somebody here, I am—'

The flap of the door swept open and a dark figure stepped into the house. I nearly jumped out of my skin, hand scrabbling for the hilt of the misericorde.

It was Sir Thomas Blood.

'I've brought you some soup, Miles, you can't live on wine alone; you've got to eat something—'

I stood up. Thomas stopped dead when he saw me. He gaped wordlessly. He took a step forward, dumped a huge, steaming tureen on the table and threw his arms around me, enfolding me in a bear hug.

'Alan, Alan,' he said. 'How good to see you.' He released me

328

but kept his hands on my shoulders. 'You look well – but, what? – have you taken holy orders?'

'Perhaps you two turtle doves would like to use the bed,' said Miles, getting to his feet.

I ignored him. 'It's just a disguise, Thomas,' I said. 'I've come to bring you and Miles home to Robin.' Thomas frowned but said nothing.

'I think I'll leave you two alone,' said Miles. 'I need air. This place stinks of hypocrisy.'

We watched as Miles pushed through the flap and disappeared. I saw that it was dusk. Thomas knelt and added a few sticks to the smouldering fire in the hearth, puffing it into flame with his breath.

'How is Mary, Thomas,' I asked, 'and your son? What is his name again?'

'We named him Alan,' Thomas said, smiling at me. 'After you. They are both well, thank you, safe in London. But I will not waste your time. I cannot go back with you to Robin. And you know perfectly well why.'

'It was a misunderstanding, Thomas. Nothing more. Robin would never have betrayed you. I know for sure he would not.'

'You were there with me at Corfe, Alan,' said the knight, suddenly angry. 'He spoke secretly to that damned Templar and then lied right to our faces. To our faces. Don't pretend you don't remember.'

'The Templar was not seeking you, Thomas, he wanted something else entirely.'

'What then?'

I shut my mouth. I had promised Robin that I would not speak of the murder of the King to any man and I had given the same vow to Aymeric de St Maur in Gloucester.

'Nothing to say?' said Thomas. 'Then nothing has really changed, has it?'

I looked at him in mute desperation. 'Come back with me,

329

Thomas, please. I ask for my sake as well as Robin's. Help me to bring Miles back, too. I cannot bear for us to be enemies any longer.'

'That is how the dice have fallen, my friend,' said Thomas. 'Lady Chance has spoken. That is just how this game has played out— Wait, did you hear something?'

He strode over to the door and lifted the flap, peering into the growing darkness.

'That treacherous little shit-weasel. You must go, Alan. At once. Miles is out there with a squad of men-at-arms. The Comte du Perche is with him. Trust me, my friend, you really do not want to be taken prisoner by that blood-drunk monster. Go! Go now.'

I was beside him at the doorway, my belly fluttering. God, it was true! Under the flap I could see Miles and the White Count in deep conversation. A score of men-at-arms in red and black stood behind the French nobleman – more men than I could ever hope to defeat. The White Count was resplendent in a cloak that seemed to shine like silver in the gloaming. Robin's son was pointing directly at the house, stabbing a finger towards us.

'Thomas, you must come with me,' I said, fighting a terrible urge to run, to run like a frightened hare.

'I cannot,' he said, 'but you must go, for God's sake, go!'

I thought, To Hell with vows, and to Hell with me for breaking them. 'Thomas, listen, now. He did lie to us. But the boon the Templar asked of Robin had nothing to do with you. St Maur asked Robin to kill the King. John was poisoned at Robin's command. That was the secret they discussed at Corfe. Please, come with me, now.'

'Sweet Jesu – is that the truth, do you swear it?'

Miles had evidently persuaded the Comte du Perche and he and his men were marching towards us.

'There isn't time. I'm a dead man if we do not go.'

Thomas looked at me hard. 'This way,' he said, and we went

back into the house and through the dark room off the side of the main chamber. I heard him fumbling with a wooden latch, I heard the sound of marching feet, the clank of metal. A square of grey opened before me. 'Out the window, Alan,' said Thomas, boosting me through the gap, handing me my staff. And then to my great joy, I saw his leg lifting over the sill and he was standing beside me in a narrow, filth-strewn alley behind the house, no more than two feet wide and stretching off into the dark, parallel to the town wall.

Just as Thomas was closing the shutter, I heard the voice of the White Count from the other room, saying in his silky Parisian French, 'There is no one here, Kirkton. If you're playing the fool with me, I will not be best pleased.'

'My lord, he was here just a moment ago . . .'

Then Thomas and I were sprinting along the alley, my terror giving wings to my feet, he in the lead, our shoulders brushing the wall. We stopped, panting, then scuttled along a gap between two houses, pressing our backs flat against somebody's wall and listening for sounds of pursuit. I could hear nothing. My heart was thumping like a tambour – just that brief glimpse of the White Count had unmanned me. I had my staff in both hands ready to strike. I would not be taken alive – I could not suffer that awful fate. Thomas, I saw, had a sword at his side. But was he with me – or against me?

'You swear that what you have told me is true, Alan, about Robin and the King's death?' Thomas whispered.

'I am finished with making oaths on this matter,' I whispered back. 'But as a friend I tell you, on my honour, that this is God's honest truth.'

Thomas said nothing.

A French man-at-arms in red and black walked round the corner of the house from the front side. I lunged at him with the staff, using the heavy oak pole as if it were a spear. The blunt end of it smacked into the astonished man's forehead with a crack. He dropped like a sack of turnips to the filth-covered earth between the two houses.

I whirled and looked at Thomas, my staff raised. He hadn't moved an inch while I'd knocked out the French man-at-arms – his comrade in arms.

'Thomas?' I said.

'I don't know, Alan. I just don't know. But I know that we must get you out of here now,' he said. 'Follow me.'

He led me further along the wall behind the houses until we were no more than fifty yards from the castle. There was no sound of pursuit. It was full dark by now and Lincoln seemed to be taking the curfew seriously for we heard little but the quick footsteps of men hurrying back to their homes before the watch caught them. Yet the castle was brightly lit, torches standing proud on the battered walls to ward against a night attack. They gave us just enough light to see by.

I saw the White Count then, no more than twenty paces away, marching along the line of houses with the company of men-at-arms at his back. There was no sign of Miles. I was frozen in terror, standing in clear view by the wall of the last house. I stared at the man who I knew would be my doom, unable to move, like a rabbit before a snake. I felt a pair of strong arms grip me round the middle, swiftly lift and hurl me back into the shadows behind the house. I collapsed into a heap among the filth, the staff clattering away, but I was aware of Thomas stepping into the dim light and walking straight over to the White Count. Inside my head, a voice was screaming: *He's not your friend – he's going to betray you. Just like Miles. He'll tell the White Count and then—*

'You there, Sir Thomas Blood, isn't it?' the Count said. Even his soft voice sent ripples of fear down my back. 'Your friend Kirkton tells me we have a spy in the town.'

'A spy, my lord?' said Thomas, the very image of innocence. I

332

eased myself further backwards, sliding on my belly through the refuse in the alley, out of the line of sight. But I heard the next exchange as clear as a bell.

'Are you deaf? Yes, a spy. Lord Kirkton says one of the pretender's lackeys sneaked into Lincoln to see him. He said he was in his house not a few moments ago.'

Thomas laughed. It sounded horribly false to my ear.

'Ah, my lord. One should not pay too much heed to my friend Miles. He enjoys his wine and sometimes he takes a little too much—'

'He's a disgusting sot. All men know it.'

'This is true, my lord, it is his curse. He has visions, he sees phantoms, my lord, when he has partaken too freely – and sometimes when he has not yet had enough.'

'You tell me that this is a figment of his imagination?'

'I am quartered there, too, my lord. I've seen no spy.'

There was a long, long silence. I grasped the handle of my misericorde. If they came for me, there would be no point in fighting. I would draw the blade, reverse it and thrust it double-handed into my heart. I would not be taken.

'You tell my drunken lord of Kirkton, that if he ever, ever troubles me again with this sort of nonsense, I will have the skin off his back for a saddle cloth. Tell him.'

And with a blessed relief, I heard the sound of the White Count and the company of men marching away.

A moment later, Thomas hauled me to my feet. I began to babble my thanks to him but he stopped me. 'You gave me no choice. And there can be no going back for me now.' He slapped me on the shoulder and I saw his smile in the dim light. 'But, damn it, Alan, yes, I do believe you.'

We waited a full hour behind the last house, squatting in the muck and listening out for any sounds. But the town was quiet. Then Sir Thomas led me stealthily along the town wall.

'Here, here it is,' he said. He was pointing to an arched doorway in the wall that was part bricked in and part filled with chunks of old masonry. Inexplicably, the smell of blooming roses filled the air.

'I noticed this the other day. This used to be the western gate to the town, I think,' said my friend. 'Built by the Romans but it fell into disrepair long ago and instead of fixing it, the doorway was filled up with stone and old bricks. It is not secure though; look, see here, the stones are quite loose.'

He reached over and pulled out a piece of masonry the size of my head.

In no time at all we had excavated a small hole in the archway, a foot or so wide, just enough to squeeze our bodies through. And then we were beyond the wall and running west into open countryside. I thought I heard the sound of a shout from the ramparts above the sawing of my own breath, but I did not waste time looking back. I ran for all I was worth.

With my friend Thomas Blood running at my shoulder.

Chapter Thirty-two

'Are you certain he betrayed you, Alan?' said Robin. 'Miles could not have been speaking to the Comte du Perche on some other matter?'

'There can be no doubting it, sir,' said Thomas. 'I am sorry to have tell you.'

Thomas and I had retrieved my horse and, riding double like Templars, we put several miles between Lincoln and us and then curled up to sleep under a hedge. Robin's scouts found us in the morning and brought us to my lord. The army had risen long before dawn and was bearing down on Lincoln from the north-west, aiming to be at its walls by sun-up. Our host was now no more than a mile away and would be clearly visible from the town walls and, we hoped, from the besieged castle inside it.

'That stupid boy,' said Robin. 'I do not know what to make of him; he seems to make the wrong decision every time, almost deliberately. Look out for him when we fight, both of you, and see if you can get him to surrender. I don't want Miles – Lord Kirkton, forsooth – to be hurt or wounded, if we can possibly prevent it.' Robin spurred his horse away to deal with other equally pressing matters.

My lord had greeted Sir Thomas's return with genuine joy – there had been no recriminations and, in a very brief ceremony in a muddy field with a dozen Kirkton men-at-arms as witnesses, Thomas had knelt before Robin, begged his forgiveness and sworn to be his loyal man once more. Robin had accepted his oath and confirmed him and his heirs and successors once more in the manor of Makeney.

In very short order we had both donned our war gear, found ourselves fresh horses and taken our places at the head of the ranks of the men of Kirkton in William the Marshal's battle. There were two other battles, as these divisions of the army were called, one under Ranulf, Earl of Chester, and the other under William Longsword, Earl of Salisbury, and each held about a hundred knights and between two and three hundred squires, sergeants and mounted men-at-arms. Bishop Peter's two hundred and fifty crossbowmen, and Robin's company of fifty archers under Hugh, were spread out in a loose cloud ahead of the three battles of our cavalry, as well as further down the slope, and we were arrayed for a full-pitched battle, for it seemed the enemy had decided to come and face us outside the town walls. Certainly, far to the south and below, I could see the bright colours of the knights' surcoats and the pennants and flags of the enemy as their horsemen spilled from the southern gate of the city, coming along the line of the river, metal spear points flashing in the rising sun.

I was greatly heartened by this because by coming out to face us in the pasturelands to the west of the city, the enemy was making a colossal blunder. This was a battle-losing mistake. Perhaps they had miscalculated the size of our force and thought they could scare us away with the thick ranks of their horsemen now gathering below us – but it was an error nonetheless. We wanted a pitched battle, we were honestly seeking it, and they would have to attack uphill to come at us or, if we attacked them, face the extra momentum that our downhill charge would deliver.

Furthermore, if we fought here, we would not have to assault the north gate and spill our men's blood on its formidable battlements.

We sat our horses and waited patiently while the enemy made his dispositions, the only combat being a desultory exchange of crossbow bolts from their skirmishers and ours in the green space between the two armies. Yet every man on that field knew this battle would not be resolved by bows and bolts, however deadly they might be, but by the thunder of a full-blooded cavalry charge.

It was inexpressibly good to have Sir Thomas at my side once more and I realised how much I had missed him in the previous months. He too seemed relieved to be back with his rightful lord, although we both shared a sense of guilt about the failure to bring poor Miles back into his proper place.

'His soul has changed, Alan,' said Thomas. 'He used to be such a merry lad – always getting into scrapes, of course, but with such joy, such natural good humour. I don't know what it was – perhaps the knowledge that he was betraying his family, or just the loneliness of being among strangers – but something inside him turned sour.'

I thought his constant consumption of strong wine might have had something to do with it – I knew from personal experience how easy it was to allow drink to take a grip on you – but I did not say this aloud. I did not wish to sound as if I were criticising Thomas for not keeping Robin's younger son under control.

'He became mean-spirited and cruel, sly even,' said Thomas, 'and very touchy. He killed a man-at-arms over a spilled cup of wine in a tavern last month. He is still strong and quick and deadly with a blade despite all those nights and days of debauchery. Well, he's young. But look, Alan, down there. Look!'

I looked down the hill at the bright ranks of the enemy knights – they were moving. Were they really going to attack us? Were they really going to make a full-blown uphill charge against a stronger enemy force?

The enemy crossbowmen who had been skirmishing with our bowmen were now streaming back between the *conrois* of French knights, leaving the field empty in front of their heavy horses.

Were they about to make their charge?

They were not. I saw that the troops in the rear ranks were turning their mounts and heading back into the city by the southern gate. *Conroi* after French *conroi* wheeled and put spurs to their horses' flanks and quit the field.

The men in our front ranks were shifting, moving forwards and back again, their horses neighing and pawing the earth. Clearly some felt this the moment to launch our charge into their departing ranks, turning an orderly retreat back through the southern gate into a full-fledged rout. But here was the Marshal himself, galloping along our front ranks, shouting: 'Stand, you eager rascals. Stand your ground. Curb your recklessness!'

The Earl of Pembroke was a dozen yards from me. 'Gentlemen, let them go!' he was shouting. 'You must let the enemy go! We must not enter Lincoln from the south. Our strength would be spent fighting up that damned hill and we would be done before we reached the upper town. There is our target. There!' He was pointing due east to the castle in the upper town. 'We go in from the north. By the north gate. The lower town is worthless to us.'

The Marshal's words steadied his men and, looking along the line of our front, I saw the other two battles had followed orders and remained where they were. Now the Marshal was beckoning to me, calling out: 'Sir Alan – over here – and you Sir Thomas. On me, if you please.'

I spurred out of the ranks to join the regent of England.

While the royal cavalry dismounted, stood down and began to unhook their ale flasks or dig out chunks of bread or pie, William the Marshal led Thomas and me to the rear of the army to a big red-and-white-striped pavilion, where we were served wine and swiftly joined by Robin and the other commanders: the earls of Chester and Salisbury and Bishop Peter of Winchester.

It was a windy day and the canvas of the tent slapped noisily against the many ropes and poles that held it upright. Lincolnshire rain pattered half-heartedly on the outside and then stopped as if embarrassed by its own impertinence. The Marshal gathered the six men present into a circle.

'It seems the Comte du Perche is not after all prepared to oblige us by attacking outside the walls,' he said. 'I'm not greatly surprised. He always was a bright boy – a bit odd in his tastes, I grant you – but bright as a button. So we are going to have to go in there and take the fight to him. This is the battle, gentlemen, this is the battle for England. Right here, at Lincoln. If we win here, half the French forces will be destroyed. If we win here, England is ours. Remember why we are doing this, gentlemen: we fight for England, for our King, and to drive these upstart Frenchmen from our lands for ever.'

To my surprise, he then addressed Sir Thomas Blood, perhaps the lowliest knight in that circle of powerful lords.

'I believe you know Lincoln well, young man,' said the Marshal.

'Yes, sir, I have been here some weeks,' said Thomas, looking embarrassed.

'Good, good – so tell us about the north gate. How may we unlock it?'

And Sir Thomas Blood began to speak.

Two hours later, about mid-morning, I found myself formed up with a reconstituted battle just out of bowshot of the town walls, opposite the castle. The battle contained fifty of Robin's bowmen, two hundred crossbowmen belonging to Bishop Peter, fifty mounted knights and men-at-arms including Robin who was in command, myself, Sir Thomas and Hugh. My boy Robert and his bodyguard Boot were with us too. I had argued that this was too risky a battle for Robert to blood himself on. But, surprisingly, Robin overruled me. He took me aside, out of earshot of my son and his guardian.

'If not this fight, then when?' Robin said. 'There is never going to be a completely safe battle, Alan. Hugh and Sir Thomas will watch out for him, and Boot, too, of course. We will not let him be killed. He desperately wants to prove himself – look at him!' I looked at my son; his young face was shining, he was fully armed and armoured, a steel helm on his head, a long lance gripped in his right fist. There was no sign of fear. He was all but bouncing with eagerness.

Robert had been especially pleased to have Sir Thomas Blood back in the fold. My son and the knight had met after the council with William the Marshal, had embraced each other warmly and then repaired to Robin's tent, where they spent a good hour in conversation about God knows what. I did not enquire. Sir Thomas had trained Robert in arms as he was growing, and had been a stern task master, but there was a great bond between them as a result, and I was glad such a skilled and experienced knight would be beside my boy in the coming storm of battle. God keep them both safe, I prayed.

There was another knight with us, too – a stranger. And once settled in our ranks, we all looked at him sideways, a little oddly, even suspiciously, as if he had just landed from the moon. He told us his name was Geoffrey de Serland. He did not come from the moon. He came from Lincoln. Not the town. He came from inside the castle.

I found out later how he came to be with us. John Marshal, the regent's nephew, had been reconnoitring the town walls early that morning. Riding up the western side, he had come face to face with Serland who had crept out of the castle hoping to make a link between Nicola de la Haye's forces inside the stronghold and our royal army outside the town. The castle's western wall, a hundred and fifty or so yards long, also served as the town boundary.

This wall had a broad gate set in it that led directly out to the fields beyond, where our army lay.

That gate was now due east of us, a mere two hundred yards in front of our horses' noses. All we were waiting for was the signal. I looked to my left, at the town wall stretching northwards, and tried to make out the hole in the blocked-up archway that Thomas and I had squeezed through. But shrubs, bushes and long grass obscured the bottom of the rampart along its length. As hard as I tried, I could not identify the crack from which we had made our escape.

A trumpet sounded, a long high note then three falling ones. It was coming from the castle walls ahead of us.

'My lord?' said Geoffrey de Serland diffidently. 'That is the signal.'

Robin nodded. 'Right. Let's go.'

We dug in our heels and surged forward – three hundred mounted men going from stock still to a trot, a canter and then a full gallop in the space of forty yards. We charged towards the castle walls as if we meant to punch through them with the weight of our horses alone.

As we thundered along, clods of turf flying from beneath our horses' hooves, I heard a shout of alarm from a French sentry on the wall. Out of the corner of my eye, I saw a crossbow bolt loosed, at maximum range, coming into the column behind my shoulder – but it either missed, fell short or was caught on someone's shield, for not a man was hurt, as far as I knew. As de Serland had promised, the big gate in the castle's western wall opened in front of us, swinging wide, pulled by unseen hands, and within a dozen heartbeats we were clattering up a cobbled slope and through the round arch to find ourselves in the open, familiar space of the bailey of Lincoln Castle.

It had not changed much in the months since we were last here. Even the washerwomen and their bubbling cauldrons of linen occupied the same spot near where I had made my bumbling thanks to Tilda. Yet now it was a good deal more crowded. Our three hundred blowing horses and their panting riders filled the space save for the great hall and a dozen other buildings. To my right was the keep, a tall round stone tower that overlooked the lower town on the far side. As Robin, Hugh, Robert and I dismounted, I saw a tall figure in mail and helm, with a long sword at the waist, come striding across the mud from the keep.

Underneath the helmet was a long lean face with shrewd bright blue eyes and a square chin. 'Well met, Locksley! I cannot tell you how glad I am to see you,' said this vision of martial glory in a low husky voice. It took me a moment to understand that Robin was being addressed by none other than the redoubtable Nicola de la Haye herself.

We made our bows, and as my lord and the lady castellan of Lincoln Castle exchanged pleasantries, I tried not to stare at this warrior woman. I had seen her only from a distance last time I was in Lincoln Castle, and then she had been adorned with flimsy silks and costly velvet. Now she looked as fearsome as any fighting man that I had encountered.

'Unless your men require anything, I'd like to get them up on the walls as soon as possible,' said Nicola de la Haye. 'We can certainly use their help. I've been expecting another French assault all morning.'

I looked up at the walls to the north and east, and saw that they had been much mauled by the French artillery. The battlements were cracked and chipped, with many of the crenellations blown away, leaving the fortifications looking like a mouth with several missing teeth. In several places on the north wall largish holes had been knocked in the walls as far down as the walkway. These had been crudely blocked with rocks, masonry, bricks, planks and barrels and large pieces of heavy furniture. Even as I looked on, a mangonel ball struck one of these patched sections of the

342

northern wall near the eastern end and the feeble makeshift barricade exploded, sending sharp splinters of wood and rock everywhere. I saw a man-at-arms struck in the chest by a shard of elm and knocked flying from the walkway to the bailey floor. He lay there, legs and arms convulsing while the blood gushed from his torso.

Nicola de la Haye looked on dispassionately as half a dozen men ran to aid the stricken man. The gap in the wall above him yawned even larger than before.

'That is where they'll come, when they come,' said the lady, nodding at the breach.

'We will stop them,' said Robin, 'and I think we might even manage to do better than that.' He turned and started issuing orders to the bowmen.

Less than an hour later, I found myself on the flat roof of a horse-shoe-shaped tower where the eastern and northern walls met, with a dozen archers, Nicola de la Haye and Robin. My lord had Mastin's seven-foot bow already strung and hooked over his left shoulder. On the three floors below us were the rest of the Kirkton archers, no doubt now peering out through the arrow slits at the enemy in the town, and about forty crossbowmen. The rest of Robin's command, with Hugh, Sir Thomas, Robert and Boot, was spread out along the eastern and northern walls – the only practical directions from which the French could attack us – with stern instructions to keep their heads well down and out of sight of the enemy. To my right, a mere two hundred yards away and on the other side of the main street that ran north-south through the whole of Lincoln, was the cathedral. To my front, northwards, I could see three mangonels all being busily served by eager teams of French engineers, and a mass of infantry, spearmen and a few crossbowmen in bright surcoats being marshalled into their attack positions about a hundred and fifty yards away between us and the northern gate that I had come through – was it only last night? – dressed as a mendicant friar.

'Surely those spearmen are in range of your long yew bows, if not the crossbows,' said Nicola. 'Why do you not loose and kill a few?'

'Your eagerness to spill French blood does you credit, my lady,' said Robin, 'but we have larger concerns than merely repulsing this attack. The Marshal has a strategy to take the town as well, and it dictates that we do our best to keep our presence here a secret for as long as possible. Have confidence in us. They'll not break through these walls.'

Just then a mangonel loosed and a ball arced high in the air and crashed plumb into the lower part of the tower, striking yards below our feet. I felt the tower shake and the air was filled with a choking white dust, and just for a moment I was rigid with terror. I remembered the terrible feeling of falling that I had experienced in Rochester as the tower collapsed beneath my feet. I clamped my teeth, all muscles tense, determined not to show weakness in front of the men.

'Well, I hope you know what you're doing,' said Nicola, casually wiping a veil of dust from her face. 'I must away and look to my people,' she said, turning, and then disappeared down the spiral stairs.

Robin came over to my side. He looked at my rigid face, slapped me hard on the shoulder and said jovially, 'On the other hand, perhaps we should put something of a crimp in those irritating machines, what do you say, Alan?'

I nodded mutely.

'Right, Simeon – over here,' said my lord. And the rangy black-haired man with a six-foot-long bow on his shoulder shambled over to Robin's side.

'No one else is to loose, hear me,' said Robin, looking round the circle of archers. 'Only Simeon. All right, see that fellow by the mangonel, there by the little church, the fellow in the yellow surcoat. Now listen, my friend Sir Alan here has just wagered a mark of silver with me that you, Simeon, cannot hit him in the eye from this distance.'

'What? A whole mark?' I was shocked.

Simeon said to me: 'Which eye? Left or right?'

I stared at the man. The fellow by the mangonel was more than two hundred yards away. 'Either,' I said.

Simeon drew his bow, hauling the cord to his ear and loosing in one smooth motion. The arrow sped away, rising, falling and thudding into the man's chest, knocking him spinning to the ground. The dark-haired archer beside me growled a filthy curse and begged Robin to be allowed another shot.

'No, you've had your turn, Simeon – and mucked it up. You've just cost me a sack of silver. Now I'll show you how it should be done. Alan, if you'd be so good as to choose another target. But from the big machine there, to the left of the main street.'

I looked out at the first mangonel team by the church. They were all gathered around the fallen man, some now looking fearfully up at the castle walls. Work on priming the siege engine had stopped. I switched my gaze to the bigger machine; they looked almost ready to release their missile.

'Fellow on the right, in the red gambeson, holding the taut rope. Left eye, same wager,' I said.

Robin nodded as if I had asked him to do the easiest task in the world. This mangonel was a good fifty yards further away than the first. He slipped Mastin's bow from his shoulder, selected an arrow from the bag at his waist, nocked it and drew the cord back, grunting softly with the effort it cost him. He held for a split moment and loosed. The arrow soared into the sky, descended and plunged straight into the eye of the man in the red gambeson. The right eye. He released the rope and fell to his knees. It was evidently a vital rope for, as he released it, it sped through his fingers in a blur. The mangonel arm swung up and slammed against the padded cross bar – but since the cup was empty, no missile hurtled towards us.

'You missed,' I said, grinning at him.

'I wasn't quite sure if you meant my left or his left,' said Robin.

'You missed, admit it. You owe me two marks.'

'All right. Two marks. Damn it,' said Robin. 'I must be getting old.'

At that moment, the French infantry began their charge.

Two hundred men in red-and-black surcoats, armed with shield and spear and sword, threw themselves at the breach in the northern wall to the left of our tower. They came at a full run, screaming their war cries, with those bearing ladders to the fore, and behind them came two score crossbowmen in yellow and blue.

Robin had our crossbowmen on their feet all along the line of the northern wall and they began to loose at will. His archers on the roof of the tower and the men on the floors below added our fury to the barrage, and I will always remember the sound – the creak of a hundred ill-fitting oak doors opening as the stiff yew was bent back, the swoosh of the arrow in flight, the excited cries from the men who had hit their targets, the far-off screams of those hit. The shafts and quarrels lanced into the oncoming French, lacerating them, shredding them, skewering limbs and torsos, faces and feet, punching them to the ground in gouts of bright blood. Our shafts lashed them like whips, and at every stroke another score of men fell, choking their lives away, clawing at blood-washed, shaft-sprouting chests and bellies punctured by cruel bolts, clasping their shattered limbs, ripped and flapping flesh. No more than half of them made it to the ditch at the bottom of the wall where, through sheer bloody determination, they planted their ladders and began to climb. I looked down and saw white faces, the glittering eyes of desperate men.

We shot them from the ladders, me wielding a crossbow and

346

Robin's men loosing arrow after arrow almost vertically, scouring them clear like a terrible broom. We took a few hits ourselves. Their crossbowmen, working in pairs, advanced behind the running infantry, one loading while the other sought out a target and loosed at us. A fellow named Gideon to my left was struck by a bolt in the throat, the black bar punching through his neck; he collapsed at my feet, coughing blood. But they were no match for us. Not a single man made it to the top of the breach and barely a score managed to run back untouched to the safety of a few half-demolished houses that gave them respite from our withering assault.

I heard trumpets calling – oddly distant, for I assumed it was the French recalling their men from the assault. But Robin gripped my arm and pointed over the heads of our fleeing attackers. Beyond the northern gate of the town, out on the green fields beyond, I could see massed horsemen and banners.

'It's the Earl of Chester,' said Robin. He looked up at the sky; the pale sun was high above us. It was noon. 'He's timely with his assault. Good – the Marshal's plan has not altered. That means we need to get ourselves ready, Alan.'

I nodded. 'Now the real work begins,' I said.

Chapter Thirty-three

We left all of Bishop Peter's crossbowmen and half the archers inside the castle to ward against further assaults and to harass unwary French troops inside the town. However, Nicola de la Haye, grimly mailed and armed, and ten of her best knights came with us – Robin, Hugh, Sir Thomas, Robert, Boot and me, along with fifty knights and men-at-arms, and twenty-five Kirkton archers, all of us mounted – as we hurtled out of the east gate and charged into a loose mass of French men-at-arms and knights gathered outside that castle entrance.

This was the sortie, an unexpected rush from inside a besieged castle, with luck taking the enemy completely unawares. It was one of the most dangerous manoeuvres in war, for once outside the safety of the castle walls the men of the sortie had sacrificed the advantage of their defences for the element of surprise. But it could be most effective.

We howled out of the gate in a tight formation, ninety-odd mounted men all in a compact wedge with Robin and me at its tip, and Hugh, Sir Thomas, Boot, Robert, Dame Nicola and the armoured knights and men-at-arms squeezed in behind. Then came the archers – each armed with sword and shield as well as his long yew bow and at least one quiver full of shafts.

In truth, many of the enemy were unhorsed and fled at the deafening clatter of our hooves on the stone cobbles. Directly ahead lay the cathedral and a few stalls selling vegetables and cheese in the forecourt of the House of God, and I remembered that it was a Saturday – market day. A makeshift barrier, a striped pole across two barrels, barred entrance to the cathedral yard. I rode down one man-at-arms who fled before me, disdaining to use my lance, merely trampling him under the churning legs of my steed. Beyond the market stalls, before the church façade, I saw groups of mailed men, several dozen, armed with swords at least, some hauling themselves into the saddle, some already mounted. I thought I caught a glimpse of a tall pale man dressed in a blinding, snowy cloak. But we did not leap the barrier to engage them. We stuck to the Marshal's plan.

'Left wheel, left wheel,' my lord was shouting and we turned, hooves sliding on the cobbles, spraying sparks from the iron horse-shoes, and rode north on the main street that led towards the gate, which even now was suffering the first onslaught of the Earl of Chester's valiant men.

It was a simple plan – the walnut between two stones – with the north gate of the town as the walnut, and the Earl of Chester's force outside and Robin's inside as the two crushing stones. If we could capture the gate and hold it, the rest of William the Marshal's army, which was massed to the north and west of the town walls, would surge through its gates and flood Lincoln with men. If we could take the north gate, the day was ours, the battle won.

If.

We surged up the main street, heading directly for the gate a couple of hundred yards away and sweeping all opposition out of our path. I glanced behind to check that Robert was all right and saw him crouched over the neck of his horse, still with his lance in his right fist, his young face screwed into a scowl of determination. I looked forward and saw smoke and flame leaping from the double doors that sealed the middle entrance on the old gate. Beyond one of the man-sized side gates I clearly saw a huge blond figure, wielding an axe, backlit by fire, chopping through the remnants of its oak planking. For an instant, my mind played tricks on me and I thought it was my old friend Little John carving his way through the enemy defences. But he was dead, God rest him, and the axe man soon joined him – a tiny French cross-bowman loosed from a yard away, piercing his huge chest, knocking him back from the doorway and out of view. A pair of axe men filled his place at once. There could be no doubting the courage of the Earl of Chester's men. Some of them seemed to have scaled the walls. Figures were battling atop them either side of the gate-house, a scrum of men in mail shoving, stabbing, falling to the cobbles, screaming, dying.

A company of dismounted men-at-arms, four score spearmen, perhaps more, was marching in good order down the road ahead of us; plainly they meant to reinforce the Frenchmen desperately holding the north gate. They heard our approach and turned about at an order from their officer, presenting their spears nervously, alarmed at being menaced from behind. We gave them no chance to form properly. I heard Robin yell, 'Charge! Charge!' and we smashed straight into them. A spearman poked at my face and I knocked the point aside with my shield and drove my own lance deep into the fellow in the rank behind him. Sheer momentum alone took us into the heart of their formation – I had Fidelity out by now and was lashing left and right like a madman, slicing faces, breaking shoulders, shattering limbs – and though they matched us in numbers, they were on foot and we scattered them like chickens before a pack of snarling dogs. I saw Nicola de la Haye crash her mace down on the helmet of a spearman with a most unladylike oath. Robert had his sword out and parried a spear thrust with ease. Boot was at his shoulder on an enormous carthorse. Then I saw my son kill for the first time. A man in red ran at him, yelling; Robert leaned back, allowing the spear to pass before his chest, and replied superbly with a cross-body overhand chop that split the fellow's helm and dropped him stone dead. An axe man on foot swung at Robert's back and my heart lurched, but Boot beat him to the blow, his long oak cudgel crunching into his chest before the axe could land. The man was hurled away and disappeared under the stamping hooves of a group of our archers.

The French company was running in all directions and the way to the north gate was clear but for a handful of men-at-arms at the gate itself looking fearfully at us over their shoulders. The enemy on its ramparts were now fully aware of our attack from the rear. I saw men throwing down their weapons and running. Chester's purple-and-gold standard appeared on the walls to the right of the gate.

The plan was working!

Then it all went horribly wrong.

I don't know how the White Count did it. Somehow he'd mustered a hundred mounted knights in full armour and brought them up from the cathedral on a street parallel to the main thoroughfare. When we were but twenty yards from the gate, twenty yards from victory, he sprang his ambush. Our men were disordered, out of formation, cutting down the remnants of the company of footmen, when he and his men charged out of a side street to our right and crashed into the mêlée. I saw a dozen of our men go down under the first onslaught, speared in their saddles by the galloping Frenchmen. The White Count was in the vanguard, a silver blade flashing in his hands as he hacked a poorly armoured archer across the torso, splitting his body with one vast blow. The assault shattered our ranks. I saw Robin desperately battling with two French knights, his face spattered with blood. A knight spurred at me, sword whirling – and missed. I took him with a low lunge to the groin, then hauled Fidelity free of his flesh in a spray of gore. I turned my horse. Mayhem all around. Blood and screams. The stench of shit from freshly opened bowels. Our men-at-arms and archers falling on every side. Our charge had been utterly halted; all cohesion gone. Our men were fatally entangled with the White Count's knights and the remnants of the company of infantry. All around was a sea of struggling men. Nicola de la Haye's face was a mask of blood but her mace was still swinging. Sir Thomas was ten yards from me, killing and killing again. Robert's horse had been pushed up against the side of a tavern; his right arm was bleeding, but Boot was before him sweeping enemy knights aside with giant loops of his cudgel. I tried to reach him but a pair of knights charged at me from either side. I blocked one blow on my shield and killed the other man, lancing my blade into his neck. Then both were gone, swept away in the mêlée like leaves in the mill race.

The second ambush hit us from the western side. A company of at least fifty men-at-arms charged howling into our other flank, long spears darting in and coming back bloody. Enemies were everywhere. I dodged a spear point, swatted at an enemy helmet. Robert had disappeared and my heart was scooped hollow with fear. I heard Robin shouting over the tumult: 'Back, back! Back to the castle!'

I slashed at a horse's head and the animal reared away, its knight cursing in French, but it cleared a path and a few moments later we were galloping away from the north gate, back down the main street. I glanced over my shoulder and saw a wall of charging French knights, and – thank God – Robert and Boot just spurring out of their reach.

I snatched a last glance up at the high wall and saw that Chester's standard had disappeared. French men-at-arms were once more thick on the ramparts, shooting down on the other side with crossbows. Hurling spears. I turned my horse's head south and kicked back with my spurs.

A hundred yards later, halfway to the castle, Robin halted us and we made a rough wall across the main street. Some of the archers dismounted, formed a line and started loosing sporadically at the French, who were gathered in a compact mass fifty yards away. Our remaining horsemen, their mounts lathered in sweat, eyes rolling, were miraculously in some sort of order behind the bowmen. Robert was there, and Boot, who was tying a bandage tightly around my son's wounded arm, and Sir Thomas. And there was Robin, Hugh and Nicola de la Haye. But of the ninety men who had thundered so confidently out of the castle a mere quarter of an hour earlier fewer than half that number remained alive.

The White Count had his knights well in hand. I saw him haranguing them from the front, ignoring the whistling shafts that sped past his shining cloak. The horsemen were readying for a charge once more, dressing their ranks, lifting shields and brandishing bloody swords. And flocks of spearmen were gathering on their flanks.

I looked over at Robin and saw to my surprise that he was shouting at my son Robert, with Sir Thomas standing beside him, looking shamefaced.

'We must retreat to the castle, Robert,' my lord was saying loudly, as if speaking to an idiot. 'Look at them there, we cannot hope to stand against them.'

'No, my lord. We can make a breach. I know we can do it. Sir Thomas agrees.' My son was pale as snow, with two pink marks on his prominent cheekbones as he argued with a man more than thirty years his senior. The wound on his arm seemed not to trouble him in the slightest. The embarrassed knight beside him was nodding slowly.

'It can be done, my lord,' Thomas said. 'I truly believe it can. It is certainly worth a throw of the dice.'

353

'We must get to the castle,' Robin repeated. 'It is only there that we will be safe.'

'And what then? A long siege?' said my son. 'Our grand plan, our attack, will have failed – will there ever be another? I think not. The war itself hangs in the balance. Lose here, lose it all. And we can win this. Please. My lord, we can still win. If only you will be bold. Please be bold.'

Robin caught my eye. I had no idea what was being discussed. I was still getting used to the idea that my stripling son was challenging the Earl of Locksley – the veteran of a hundred fights – on tactics of all things!

'I can't believe I am taking orders from a child,' Robin said. 'The price of a long life, I suppose. But never let it be said that I was too faint of heart to take the bold course.'

In a louder voice, his battle voice, Robin said: 'This way, men, this way – quickly now to the western wall.'

An instant later, we were cantering west off the main street, with Robert grinning like the schoolboy he had so recently been.

We charged down the street towards the town wall, forty or so knights, men-at-arms and archers, with Sir Thomas leading the way. We reached the row of houses and hauled back on the reins, coming to a confused and milling halt, and I could not help but look right to the untended hovel where I had encountered a wine-sodden Miles the night before. Our sudden change of direction of flight had clearly dumbfounded the French for we saw no sign of the massed ranks of their fearsome cavalry. But we would not be hard to find. And they could not be far behind.

'Where is it, Thomas?' Robin was asking the knight and he pointed south along the row of houses.

A few moments later, there it was – an arch of ancient stone in the west wall filled in a haphazard way with a tumble of rocks and crumbling bricks, old dry mortar and gravel. And, screened by an overgrown rose bush, a small hole through which Thomas and I had squeezed our way to freedom.

'Through you go, Thomas. Remember: as fast as you can,' said Robin. 'Every moment counts.'

The knight nodded briskly, squirmed into the tight hole and disappeared.

'Archers, form a perimeter on this line, now.' Robin indicated an arc around the ancient entrance and the dozen surviving bowmen dismounted, tied up their horses and shuffled into position. Not a moment too soon. Men in mail were boiling out of all the houses and side lanes in the vicinity and coming down the street behind us in a loose crowd. Spearmen in red and black were appearing, too. Sergeants were shouting in French, ordering the infantry forward. In the far distance I could see cavalry, the White Count's proud chevaliers trotting in perfect formation along the street, a little more than two hundred yards away. Sighting us, the French horsemen stopped, just out of bow range.

The White Count rode out alone towards us.

Hugh took command of the archers effortlessly. 'Pick your targets carefully, men,' he said, his voice steady as an oak. 'See if you can stick that fancy fellow out in front with the silver cloak. Ready now. Nock, draw and loose.'

'Everyone else – to work!' shouted Robin. As if to show us what he meant, he bent down and seized a tumbled block of yellow masonry from the ground under the arch and hurled it to one side.

'Wide as we can make it,' he said, bending once more and grasping another.

With every other man there, apart from the bowmen in their fragile perimeter, I rushed forward to the wall. I grasped a chunk of jutting masonry and heaved with all my strength, expecting it to come loose. Nothing happened. Perhaps it had been luck the night before when we had managed to make that small hole to escape through – perhaps someone had already loosened it. But the mortar holding the rest of the jumbled rock in place in the ancient archway was set solid. I stopped heaving, my arms and shoulders burning from the strain. I saw the other men were having as much trouble breaking the masonry from the wall. Some were using their swords as levers to wrest the stone free. Robin was hacking viciously with a dagger and I saw him loose only a single fist-sized piece of stone. We could not break through this archway – not unless we had a week of peace, a dozen crowbars and a battering ram to aid us in our labours.

I snatched a glance behind. The spearmen were creeping forward, shields held high, and, behind them, the White Count's cavalry were also coming on at a slow walk. Our archers were nocking, drawing and loosing with a swift and terrible rhythm and a handful of men fell at every second beat of my heart. But the enemy numbered many hundreds and more were appearing every moment. Very soon, the White Count would order the cavalry to charge and we would be crushed like beetles underfoot between the horses and the unbroken wall of the archway.

A crossbowman popped up and loosed from behind an abandoned cart fifty yards away. One of our archers fell with a strangled squeak, a quarrel embedded in his chest. Another quarrel clattered against the rubble to the side of the arch. I bent again to a big lump of rock jutting from the wall and heaved. I could feel my face turning purple, every muscle and sinew straining fit to snap. I released my grip and stood up. Another archer fell to a crossbow bolt. The hole Thomas and I had made was barely six inches wider – the work of one of the men-at-arms and his axe. I had to quell the urge to dive into it and wriggle my way through. Robin looked at me from the other side of the blocked-up entrance, one red half-brick in his hands. He threw it aside. I had evidently caught him in an unguarded moment and for just an instant he looked utterly appalled at the task ahead of us. The other knights and men-at arms were just standing by, beaten by the wall, hands bleeding, nails broken, heads sunk on their chests or staring bleakly at the enemy. Robert was sitting on a pile of rubble to one side, head hanging low, with Boot standing before him, his cudgel cocked, ready to defend his charge against all comers. There was no way through the archway. We were trapped. It was too late to seek sanctuary in the castle. The mass of French men-at-arms were just thirty yards away, the cavalry close behind them, and despite the archers' efforts they were coming closer all the time. Another bolt crashed into the wall beside my knee.

The White Count's cavalry had risen to the trot. I could feel the pounding of their hooves through my boot soles.

Robert was looking at me, smiling sadly. I took a step towards him. But the boy stood, grasped Boot's huge arm. 'I'll be fine. You must help Father now,' he said, pushing the giant towards me. Boot came lumbering over and I wordlessly showed him the block of masonry that I had so utterly failed to budge.

He bent his knees, seized the chunk of stonework. I took the other side and we heaved. The thick slabs of muscle either side of his spine bulged and knotted. My head felt as if it were about to explode. But then – by God – I felt the stone move. We heaved again and, with a great rumbling crash, and an explosion of old dust, we ripped it free and the heart was torn out of the blocked Roman gate. Between us Boot and I carried the enormous piece of stone to one side. As I stood panting with effort at one side, Boot returned and plucked a smaller block of masonry out of the gap. A gigantic cascade of rubble followed. There was now a hole as wide as two men underneath the arch and through it, as the dust cleared, I could see horsemen not fifty yards away, hundreds of them and in the first rank the dark face of Sir Thomas Blood, grinning like a demon under his helmet and waving the battle of William the Marshal, Regent of All England forward to the charge.

Robin's men set to work again with renewed vigour. Every man among us seized pieces of the walled-up entrance and hauled them out of the way. Like an army of ants, we swarmed over that ancient archway, the bowmen abandoning their perimeter and joining in with a desperate urgency, and I swear we had picked it clean of rubble in less time than it takes to say a Hail Mary – I do not jest! It was that swift. Boot was magnificent, ripping whole foot-wide sections from the gate. Even Dame Nicola deigned to seize a broken brick or two and toss them to one side. Just as the very last stone had been flicked aside, we all stepped back and William the Marshal, at the head of a hundred shining knights and twice that number of mounted men-at-arms, crashed through the arch to tear into the enemy that was now almost on us.

They smashed straight through them, tossing the White Count's men left and right with the surging power of their charge. And Robin's men were swiftly back in their saddles and following in their wake. The perfect ranks of the enemy horsemen disintegrated. There was no longer any sign of the Comte du Perche and his distinctive silvery cloak. The Marshal's men were laying about them with their swords, sending the footmen and cavalry reeling. The French were slipping away, some openly fleeing. I saw old William – at seventy years of age, mark you – shout a challenge to a knight in a yellow livery, charge him and send him running with a flurry of well-aimed blows.

I recovered my horse and called to Robert, aiming to follow the Marshal's men into the heart of the upper town, when I found Robin at my side.

'Wait, Alan, wait just a moment. I want you with me – Robert, too. We have to find Miles.'

With Boot's dust-covered form looming behind me, and my son and my lord on either side, I watched as the Marshal's cavalry swiftly dispersed the French. In truth, after a brief moment of resistance, the enemy mostly fled before them. Driven like sheep before a shepherd's dogs. Our horsemen halted at the junction with the high street and after a brief conference between the Marshal and his captains, a hundred mounted men surged up the street to attack the north gate once more. This time there could be no ambush, I knew; the White Count had shot his bolt. This time they would take the gate's defenders in the rear and destroy them – and it could not be too long before the Earl of Chester's brave men were inside the town.

'The battle is as good as won,' said Robin. 'The day is ours. The French are lost – even if they do not yet know it. So now it is vital we find Miles!'

I agreed with him. Through a gap in the houses I saw Hugh with a pack of our mounted archers and men-at-arms trotting down the street on the Marshal's heels, heading east towards the cathedral.

'I know where to look first,' I said.

We four made our way up the street that ran parallel with the town's western wall until we found ourselves at the tumbledown cottage right at the end. I dismounted and Robin and I pushed back the leather flap and entered the fetid interior. It was dim in there, though full daylight outside, and the stench if anything was worse than I remembered.

There was no one there.

'This is where he lives?' said Robin, appalled. 'These are the lodgings they allocated to Lord Kirkton? Sleeping in this place for even one night would have made me want to come home without the slightest encouragement at all.'

He poked with his boot at an empty wine flask on the jumble of dirty clothes and unwashed crockery on the floor.

'He's a very stubborn man,' I said.

'He's just a boy,' snapped Robin. 'He's got nothing to be stubborn about.'

I said nothing and Robin gave me a look of apology.

'His arms and armour are gone,' I said. 'Helm, too.'

359

Robin sighed. 'That's not good. Not good at all. Come on, Alan, we had better rejoin the war before it's too late.'

Gratefully, we pushed back out into the sunshine.

We followed the noise of battle, cutting east behind the mangonel, now merrily burning surrounded by a dozen corpses, and back on to the main street through Lincoln. Here and there we saw knights pursuing men on foot. I caught a glimpse of the Earl of Chester himself, resplendent in a purple-and-gold surcoat, battering at the door of a shuttered tavern, a pair of his knights hacking with axes at the window. A knight in a black cloak rode into the street ahead of us, took one look at our party and swiftly turned his horse and galloped away. As we approached the remains of the market, we saw that there was still plenty of fight in the French yet. They had retreated to the yard in front of the cathedral, perhaps sixty men, and had created a dense defensive formation known as the hedgehog, a half-ring of three ranks of spearmen, their shields locked, their long weapons pointing outwards like the spines of the animal. At the back of the half-ring, the doors of the cathedral were shut tight, barred no doubt from the inside. But no man of God would allow us to attack them from inside the House of the Lord. Behind the hedgehog, almost under the arch of the cathedral entrance itself, I saw Miles, grim-faced beneath a plain steel cap, sword drawn, standing to the right of a tall man in mail that had been so highly scoured it shone in the winter light. He wore a flat-topped tubular helmet, equally polished to a dazzling shine, that covered his whole head, with a broad horizontal slit about an inch wide to allow him to see. I caught a flash of his icy blue eyes. A long silver cloak hung from his shoulders. Three or four knights stood beside the White Count and one of them, I saw, was Lord Fitzwalter, captain-general of the Army of God, the last remnants of his grand holy army now surrounded on all sides and greatly outnumbered by his enemies.

'Surrender yourselves,' the Marshal was shouting in French.

'Give yourselves up to King Henry's mercy. There is no need for further bloodshed.'

'Never,' cried the White Count, his voice booming. 'I shall die like a man – and take a dozen of you English scum with me.'

'Cousin Thomas, be reasonable, for God's sake,' the Marshal was almost wheedling. 'You cannot escape. Lay down your arms, I beg you. For the sake of your family.'

The White Count shrugged. 'I choose death before dishonour.'

I saw that Miles was looking at us. He straightened his spine. He repeated the White Count's words, chanting them boldly, his face as grim as winter: 'Death before dishonour!'

'That skin-stripping ghoul is going to get our Miles killed,' said Robin in my ear. 'That cannot be allowed to happen. I'm going to take out that pale bastard myself and that will be the end of it.'

Robin stepped off his horse, turned away and I saw him speaking quietly with Simeon and half a dozen archers who had gathered around him. I dismounted too, grinned at Robert, and found Thomas Blood standing at my side: 'Alan, we have to get Miles out of there,' he said urgently. 'Any moment and the Marshal is going to crush them all without mercy and I cannot answer for the boy's safety.'

'I know,' I said. 'Robin is working on something—'

'Then be damned to you all,' shouted the Marshal. He made a signal with a fist clenched, pumped up and down.

A single crossbow cord twanged and then a dozen more. The deadly quarrels smashed into the packed ranks of the spearmen bravely defending their lords.

Robin whirled in surprise. 'There, there!' he shouted, pointing at a section of the hedgehog and I saw Simeon and six of his mates draw and loose, sending a compact cloud of arrows in an almost vertical line at the three ranks of spearmen, hammering into their shields but dropping one man and another and another one behind the last. The crossbow bolts of the Marshal's men were flying thickly, too, pelting the hedgehog with death.

'Again,' shouted Robin. And Simeon and his fellows loosed once more. 'One more time,' shouted Robin. I saw clearly what my lord was doing: he was using the shafts to cut a channel through the hedgehog. And it seemed that he had managed to make a gap. The men either side of the stricken spearmen, stuck with a dozen arrows, were slow to link up their shields with their comrades. There was a hole, only a foot or so wide, but it was a hole in their ranks nonetheless.

'Miles,' bellowed Robin, 'I'm coming, son!'

And he charged, alone, sword in one hand, shield in the other, straight into the bristling mass of his enemies.

Chapter Thirty-four

The spear is a fine weapon on the whole. Against cavalry it gives the foot soldier a long reach and evens the odds against the mailed knight high above on horseback. Packed ranks of spearmen, in a formation such as the hedgehog, can keep mounted men at bay almost indefinitely – horses will not willingly charge into a sharp hedge of steel. But there is a big drawback to using a spear in battle. A spearman can't strike sideways, as a swordsman can, nor can he tackle an enemy in front who is only a foot or two away from him. Once his enemy is past the point, the spear-wielder is a dead man.

Robin hurled himself into the hedgehog, past the outermost spear points, into the gap created by his bowmen, trampling over fallen bodies, living and dead. Shoving his way forward, he brought his sword to bear on the men in the second and third ranks, stabbing and hacking, hammering down on helmeted heads with his pommel.

I shared a quick glance with Thomas. No words were necessary. 'A Locksley,' I yelled. 'A Locksley for ever!' and with Sir Thomas screaming the same cry at my shoulder, steel drawn, we charged after my lord and plunged deep into the ranks of spearmen, following his line of attack.

I stabbed Fidelity into the face of a terrified spearman and he fell screaming; I jammed the sharp cross-guard on my sword into another man's neck and he flinched away. To my left, Thomas was doing terrible damage with short powerful strokes of his blade, piercing the ill-armoured bellies and chests of the helpless men. I flailed at the faces before me, snapping spear shafts, hacking shields apart, surging forward behind the point of my blade. With every stride forward, I was aware of the squelch of bodies beneath my feet. One man, under me, raked his knife at the chausses that protected my legs and I stamped hard on his head and felt his skull break beneath my mailed foot. I chopped into the leather-capped head of a cringing man and he dropped like a stone. Robin was through and Thomas and I were on his heels, batting men out of our way. The hedgehog disintegrated, with men hurling their weapons aside and running like hares from our blades, desperate to escape the death we offered them.

To be honest, it was not all our doing. William the Marshal's crossbowmen had decimated their ranks and that grizzled veteran had also decided the formation was ripe for annihilation, spurring his horse into the mêlée, urging his fellow knights to join the slaughter and slaying again and again with wide pounding chops of his long blood-slicked sword.

The surviving spearmen ran – not back into the cathedral but to their left, a flood of panicked men, a herd streaming across the shattered market and out through the main gate of the upper town, down the steep hill to the lower town. The crossbows clicked and twanged, swordsmen lashed at them as they passed and men fell from gaping wounds even as they scrambled to escape our wrath.

Yet not every man ran; the knot of knights by the cathedral door stood their ground. As Robin blundered through the last rank of the spearmen, the White Count stepped forward, his blade licked out towards my lord and Robin caught it only just in time, knocking the sword aside. But he was not giving his full attention to the man in mail before him. He was shouting, 'Miles! Miles!' and looking wildly around, even as the White Count struck again – a swingeing sideways blow at his head. Robin caught the blade on his cross-guard and thrust it away.

There was no sign of Miles at all. Robin, ignoring his opponent, turned to me, his guard lowered: 'Where is he, Alan?' His voice was despairing. 'Where has he gone?'

'Fight me, damn you,' said the Count in French, swinging his sword hard at Robin's shoulder. My lord stopped the blow with his shield, but he was unprepared, wrong-footed, and the force of the strike knocked him to his knees. The White Count leaped forward, smashing his sword down at Robin's head. By sheer chance, it caught the edge of Robin's shield, robbing it of some of its force. But it was enough to partially stun my lord and he sprawled to the floor in a loose tangle of limbs.

The White Count stepped in, drew back his arm for a lunge to the chest that would end Robin's life—

And I stepped over my old friend's feebly stirring body and swiped the blade aside.

'I'll fight you,' I said, moving forward, jabbing at his chest with Fidelity and forcing the White Count to take a swift pace backwards.

Behind me I was aware of Robert and Boot helping Robin to his feet. But I had not much time to think for the Count was on me like a tiger: a pounding smash at my helmet on the left side. I got my shield up just in time and felt the power of the younger man's strike shudder right down my whole arm.

Behind me I heard Robert say: 'Miles ran off with the others. I saw him. Down the hill. That way.'

'I've got this one,' I said to Robin without taking my eyes off the Count. 'Go after Miles, my lord – I'm going to deal with this bastard here then I'll be with you!'

The White Count stepped back, breathing hard.

'Are you going to fight, you English cowards, or just talk among yourselves?' His helmet muffled his voice but he seemed infuriated by our disregard.

'Thank you, Alan!' shouted Robin. I snatched a glance at him and saw him walking unsteadily across the market with Boot and Robert hovering protectively on either side.

I snapped my gaze back to the White Count, sword and shield raised, and as I did I heard Robin call out from a distance: 'Look at his hands, Alan. Take a good long look.'

I looked at the White Count's hands. They looked perfectly normal, clad in thick brown leather gauntlets to give some protection from sword cuts. Then I looked again. I realised with a creeping sense of horror that the gauntlets were covered in a mass of thick chestnut hairs, wiry yet too thin to be the fur of an animal.

'You like my gloves?' said the White Count. He lifted his right hand, gripping the blade. 'I had them made specially out of your archer's back. The hair makes them very warm, you know, and well-tanned human leather is much more supple than any other kind, don't you find?'

I was almost too shocked to move. The thought of him wearing Mastin's skin was so awful that for an instant I could not truly comprehend it.

I was aware that, to my left, Thomas was taking the surrender of a man in a blue-and-red surcoat. Another fellow, who looked vaguely familiar, was on his knees offering up his sword, his red-gold head bowed.

The White Count was alone.

The heat of battle had dissipated. The Marshal and his men were gone, chasing the mob of French men-at-arms down the hill.

Robin, Robert and Boot were gone, too. There were half a dozen archers with Thomas and I sensed rather than actually heard him warning them to leave us to conclude our fight.

'I'm going to kill you now,' I said to the man in silvery mail standing before me.

'I think not,' he said. 'I think I shall kill you. I think a greybeard like you has no place on the field. You should be tucked up in bed, old man, with a warm cup of milk.'

He sprang at me, a sweeping blow across his body that hacked down at my left shoulder, and I caught it on my shield, shrugged it aside and lunged at his belly in counter-attack. He danced back and came at me again, a sweep at my ankles – just a feint – and an upward lunge at my groin at the last instant. I twisted out of the path of his blade. He was fast, I will give him that, but he could not have been more than twenty-two. He was good, too. Well schooled. A cut at my right thigh nearly caught me – I got Fidelity down in time, but the blade banged painfully against my knee, thankfully well protected by my chausse.

I hopped back. 'I'm going to kill you now,' I said.

He snarled and slashed at my head. I blocked with my shield and stabbed at his chest. He jumped back. I stabbed at his right forearm, but he got it out of the line of my strike just in time. Then I bored into him, Fidelity cutting left, right, left, right, hard overhand blows that hammered at his defences and forced him back towards the cathedral. Using my weight and strength to weary him. He ducked under a heavy blow aimed at his head and circled away, keeping his distance. He was wary now, his confidence leaking away as he recognised my skill and experience. Greybeards who have survived more than a score of battlefields have often survived for a good reason.

'I'm going to kill you now,' I said.

'Stop saying that!' he shouted – and feinted at my belly, trying to turn the blow into a sweep at my knees – and I stabbed him in the top of his left shoulder, quick and hard above the shield, punching Fidelity through the mail, cloth, skin and muscle to draw a gout of red blood. The White Count stepped back, panting. His helmet was obviously restricting his breathing. Despite the burden of my years, with my conical, open-faced helm I did not have the same problem. He tugged at his right gauntlet with his left hand. I looked at his glove and felt the burning of pure anger in my belly.

'I'm going to kill you now,' I said.

I attacked his left side, his wounded side, and the instant I moved I saw he could not fully raise or lower his shield. He was a dead man. I stopped a hay-maker blow from his sword with my shield and in riposte cut hard at the back of his left knee. He could not get the shield down in time and my blade thwacked into the side of the joint. He stumbled, but kept his feet. There was blood on his leg, welling through the mail. I circled to the right, forcing him to move on the injured limb. Fidelity flicked out – a feint – and when he jumped back the left knee failed him and he tumbled to the floor. I leaped forward, my left foot landing hard on his right wrist, the gauntleted hand holding his sword. I heard the crunch of breaking bones. I kept my full weight on his broken wrist. He was making small mewling noises of pain as I stood over his prone form grinding my foot on the break. He could barely move his wounded shield arm; his chest pumped up and down desperately sucking in air, and from inside the mask of his helmet, his pale blue eyes looked up at me in terror.

He screamed: 'I yield, I yield to you, Sir Knight.'

'I'm going to kill you now,' I said.

He screamed again: 'Surrender, I surrender!'

'I only wish I could make this more painful,' I said, bouncing my weight on his shattered wrist. I placed Fidelity's tip in the eye slit of his helmet. 'But sadly I do not have the time to spare. This is for my friend Mastin,' I said, and thrust down hard with all my strength. I felt the blade go through his eye, encounter the resistance of bone and then punch into the brain.

'And for that poor kitten in London, too,' I added.

But I do not think he heard me.

Chapter Thirty-five

We left the prisoners under a guard of Kirkton archers – Lord Fitzwalter, captain-general of the Army of God, was one of them, having surrendered personally to Thomas without them exchanging a single blow – and my friend and I plunged down the hill in our lord's footsteps and in the wake of the fleeing French army. A few hundred yards into the lower town it became apparent that few of the enemy would escape. A huge mass of them had congregated at the bridge over the River Witham at the bottom of the hill, and such was the press of bodies that it was jammed solid. Only a handful were managing to make it across and out on to the southern road behind it.

Robin had cornered Miles, with a gang of French stragglers, outside a high stone wall fifty yards north of the bridge and the struggling mass of humanity. Miles had his sword drawn and the men with him looked desperate, some wounded and bloody, all wielding weapons of some kind or another. They were surrounded by a ring of thirty or so men-at-arms, crossbowmen and archers – and Robin.

'There is no escape, Miles. Be sensible, for God's sake. This foolishness has gone on for far too long,' my lord was saying as Thomas and I panted up behind him.

'Just lay down your sword and I can protect you. The alternative is . . . unthinkable.'

Some of our crossbowmen had their weapons spanned and all the archers had arrows on the string. It would have been the work of a moment to annihilate the Frenchmen pressed together by the wall. They lived only because Robin had stayed the archers' hands.

'Put down the sword, Miles. Just drop it. Look, whatever your grievance with me is, I am sure we can work it out as a family. See – I am sheathing my sword,' said my lord and he slid his blade back into its scabbard and stood two yards from his son, holding his empty hands up and spread wide as if in surrender.

'You always think it is about *you*,' said Miles. 'It can't always be about you.'

I took a step closer to Robin. Miles's face was a picture of misery, white and red, and none too clean, the marks of fresh tears clear against his grubby white skin.

'Miles,' said Robin, 'my dear boy, you must know that everything I have done has been for you and Hugh.'

Miles laughed then. An ugly sound.

'When I give the word, men,' he said in French. 'Be ready! Death before dishonour.'

The raggedy crew around my lord's son tightened their grips on their weapons.

'Miles, don't do this!' Robin was pleading. I'd never heard him speak like this. I'd never heard him beg.

Miles lifted his chin, took a breath, opened his mouth—

And Robin dropped his hand. The archers and crossbowmen loosed and in a whistling flash of white goose feathers and black streaking bolts every man on either side of Miles was struck by many shafts, almost simultaneously jerked this way and that by the punch of the arrows. They all fell, some quickly, some more

371

slowly. Only Miles was untouched. He looked about him, the only man standing, gave a shout of rage and plunged his sword deep into Robin's belly, thrusting hard with both hands.

My lord screamed: 'Miles!' and fell to his knees, and the boy tugged out the blade and raised its red length high over Robin's head for the coup de grâce.

I was already past my lord's kneeling form, Fidelity whirling, and with one savage blow I sliced through Miles's forearms, separating the raised sword and both his gripping hands from his body.

He fell backwards with a cry, crumpling to the cobbles, lying amid the feathered bodies of his dead and dying comrades, staring in amazement at the stumps of his arms, now pulsing out twin red jets in time with the beats of his heart.

I dropped Fidelity and knelt beside my lord, looking into his face. He stared at me blankly, both hands folded over the spreading stain on his surcoat. Inside my head I was shouting: *No, no, please God, no . . .* My vision was blurring; my belly felt cold as ice.

'I didn't think he would do it. I didn't think . . .' Then Robin closed his eyes, his shoulders slumped, and he gently slipped sideways to the cobbles.

Boot carried Robin up the street to the Jews' House, striding along at a brisk pace with me running alongside talking desperately, trying to get my lord to open his eyes. Like many of the richer denizens of Lincoln, the Jews had left the city when the French invaded, and we found their hall abandoned. But we made Robin a bed on the ground floor from our cloaks and pillowed his head on a rolled-up pair of hose.

We cut the mail hauberk from his body to get a sight of his stomach. It was bad, very bad. The sword had punctured the lower left side, just above the groin, and I knew it had entered the intestines and perhaps the bowel. The blood flowed thick and heavy, streaked with brown, and much as we tried to staunch it with rags they soon became sodden and useless. I got Robert to apply pressure on the wound with a wadded shirt and for the first time in an hour, Robin stirred. And screamed.

He opened his eyes and screamed again – the noise tore at my soul.

'Less pressure, Robert,' I said. 'Just keep it firmly in place.'

The first thing Robin said, in a weak, reedy voice was: 'Where is Miles?'

I confess this was the first time I had thought about Robin's son since my lord had been carried from the street.

'You hurt him,' said my lord. 'You cut him with Fidelity.' He said it in a wondering tone as if he did not quite believe it. The tears started to flow down his lean cheeks. I tried to give him watered wine to drink but he would not take it. He weakly shoved my hands away.

'Go and find Miles, Alan, go on. Make sure he is safe,' he whispered.

I got up from my knees and stumbled out into the street, my tears flowing too by now. As I headed down the street I ran head-first into Hugh coming up the hill. He was slathered in blood from thigh to neck, the iron mail on his arms thick with clotting gore.

'Miles?' I said.

'He's dead,' said Hugh, with a grimace.

'How did he die?'

'Badly,' he said. 'He started trying to walk down to the bridge, bleeding all the way, and collapsed in a gutter. No one offered to succour him. I found him half an hour ago, still living. I held him while he died.'

'Thank you,' I said.

'Don't thank me – I don't want your thanks. You're the one who killed him.'

'I'm sorry.'

373

Hugh looked at me. He seemed to be struggling to find any words to say to the man who had killed his brother.

'He always liked you, admired you. Did you know that? When we were children he used to say that you were the deadliest swordsman in the world. He boasted that one day he would be better even than you. He talked of you when he was dying. Said you were still pretty quick for a broken-down old man.'

I sighed. There seemed to be nothing useful to say.

'Me, of course, he abused with his last dying breaths. The little shit. Called me a bastard. A cuckoo. Called me Cain. Accused me of stealing his birthright.'

'What did you do with his body?' I asked.

'I left it there.'

'In the gutter? In God's name why?'

'They are excommunicate – all the rebels are. They cannot be buried in a churchyard. My father is not exactly going to give him a hero's burial at Kirkton. Let him be buried with the rest, with his comrades, in the mass graves. Serve him right.'

I stared at Hugh. How could he misunderstand his father so badly?

'Come on,' I said, 'we can carry the body up to Robin together.'

The pain grew worse over the course of that night. Despite Robin's efforts to hide his suffering, his face was taut with agony and from time to time he gave out a whimper. Outside the walls of the Jews' House, Lincoln suffered too. Victorious men-at-arms who had survived the bloody assault on the north gate took their revenge on the city in a brutal fashion. Boot kept the door for us, his bulk warding off even the most determined looters, but the rest of the town was subjected to one of the worst sackings I have ever seen. Gangs of drunken armed men lurched up and down the hill ransacking the houses of rich men and poor alike; women and children were raped, whole streets were set ablaze. Men-at-arms capered about draped in expensive lengths of dyed red and green wool stolen from the merchants' houses, quaffing from jugs of wine, joking, quarrelling and fighting with their fellows over the division of the spoils.

During all the chaos, I sat beside Robin and watched as he suffered, the sweat starting from his white face, his teeth grinding together. He grew weaker and weaker; the flow of blood slowed but never quite stopped, and I changed the sopping pad at his waist every hour or so. When the sun had gone down and the men were yawning, I sent them all upstairs to sleep, determined that I would keep my vigil with Robin alone. Hugh protested somewhat, but he had fought hard all day and eventually I persuaded him to retire on the promise that I would wake him in a few hours and rest myself. I had no intention of keeping that promise.

At around midnight, I awoke from a light doze to see Robin staring at me in the candlelight. His eyes seemed to shine with pain like silver mirrors but his voice when he spoke was serene.

'You killed my son,' he said. 'You took little Miles from me.'

'My lord, forgive me,' I said, fresh tears running down my cheeks. 'I would do anything to take back that blow. But I cannot. You must understand that I did not mean . . . I was trying to save . . .' I broke down into incoherent sobs.

'Shh, shh,' said Robin. 'Calm yourself, Alan. What is done is done and I will gladly forgive you, if you will do one small thing for me. One little service.'

'Anything, lord, just name it,' I said, cuffing away my tears.

'Do you still have your misericorde?'

The realisation hit me like a hammer blow.

'No, no – not that,' I said, flinching away from him.

'Alan, listen to me, we both know how this will end. Days of indescribable pain, hours of agony as I get weaker and weaker. Then, inevitably, death.'

I stared at him.

'You know that what I say is true,' he said.

I did know it – but what he was asking was too much.

'Please, Alan – a quick, painless end is all I ever wanted. It is all any warrior wants. Give it to me. We did it for Mastin. Your last service to your lord. I beg you. If Little John were here, he would do it, in an instant. Please, Alan.'

'My lord . . .'

'Alan, if you love me, you will do this,' he said and I saw that his mouth was trembling with pain as he spoke.

I got up and moved closer to him. I sat down and positioned his body so that his head and shoulders were resting across my lap. With my right hand, I pulled the slim blade from my left sleeve. The black metal seemed to glint evilly in the flickering light of the candles. I looked down at Robin; he was smiling, his lean face relaxed.

'Be quick,' he said, 'strike hard. And, if there is one, I shall greet you in the next life with my grateful thanks.'

I placed the tip of the blade in the hollow between his neck and his collarbone. One hard shove and the long blade would slide deep into his chest and pierce his heart, stopping it and killing him instantly.

'Ready?' I said.

'Do it,' he said.

'What in the name of God is going on here? Father, have you run mad? Put down that disgusting knife, this instant.'

Both Robin and I jumped at these words and I saw my son Robert, dressed only in his long flapping chemise, advancing on us with a candle in one hand and the righteous wrath of God written across his face.

'Were you seriously about to kill him? I cannot believe you sometimes!'

'Robert,' I said, trying to be stern, trying to ignore the blooming relief in my heart. 'This is not for you to see. This is a private matter. Go back to bed. Now.'

'And let you cut his throat? I don't think so.'

'It's all right, Robert,' said my lord feebly. 'I asked him—'

'You be quiet – you've caused quite enough trouble already!' said this skinny sixteen-year-old boy to the Earl of Locksley.

Robert fixed me with his iron glare: 'We don't have to kill him, Father. We can heal him. At least, I believe Tilda can heal him. She's done it before; she told me about it last year and it has only now come back to me. A knight had a deep stomach wound from a sword and after Tilda's ministrations, the fellow was walking again six months later. We have to get Robin to Westbury and as quick as possible. Come on, Father, look lively – help me wake the house.'

Chapter Thirty-six

It took us two nights and a day to get Robin to Westbury. Two nights and a day of jolting hell for my lord, who even carried in a donkey cart suffered all the torments of the damned as the vehicle bounced and bucked over the ruts in the roads. He took to stuffing a blanket into his mouth to muffle the sound of his screams, and I rode alongside him, my own guts burning with pity at his condition. At least twice I wondered if this journey were a terrible mistake, if we were piling agony upon agony on my lord and that the swift mercy of the misericorde might not have been the kinder option. But we were committed. My son Robert had committed us.

At Westbury, Tilda took one look at Robin, made him drink something powerful for the pain, and gave the rest of us a bare hour to wash and eat and saddle fresh horses before we set out on the road again heading north.

'I cannot possibly help him here, Alan,' she said. 'For a start I don't have the herbs, the salves, the *chirurgia*'s sharp blades and the cat-gut. I must put my hands inside his body to sew up the wound. I barely know what to do, even if I had all the right tools and medicines here. I have done this only once before, you know. I might easily kill him. There is only one person that I know who has the slightest chance of saving his life – and that is Anna, Prioress of Kirklees. And you know how things stand between us.'

'She will treat Robin if I tell her to, and she will use all her powers to heal him,' I said. 'If she gainsays me, if I get so much as a peep of protest out of her, I will cut her throat and burn her precious Priory down around her ears.'

And so we took the road again, this time with Robin mercifully asleep but as shadowy as a corpse. Hugh rode on ahead to Kirkton – he had the news of Miles's death to deliver to his mother, and the body of his brother, too, wrapped in a canvas shroud and bound to the back of a mule. In the moments when I was not consumed with fear for Robin, I writhed at the thought of what Marie-Anne would say to me about causing the death of her son.

Whatever she had to say to me, I would deserve.

Marie-Anne met us at Kirklees Priory, white-faced and seemingly much smaller in stature, shrunken by her grief. But she was all briskness when it came to Robin, supervising the Priory servants and our men-at-arms, having Robin carried into the infirmary on the ground floor and laying him on a long stone table, swathed in blankets. I tried to tell her how sorry I was about Robin – and about Miles. But she merely said: 'I cannot talk to you now, Alan. There will be a time for that later.'

The Prioress, a handsome, middle-aged woman with an aquiline nose and small, brightly burning black eyes, was the true master of the situation. She consulted with Tilda – their discourse was brief but perfectly amicable; workmanlike, you might say – then all the men were sent packing from the infirmary and Marie-Anne was recruited to tear up clean cloths, boil plenty of water and mop Robin's sweat-drenched brow.

I went and sat outside in the Priory gardens, next to their famous herbarium, with Thomas and Hugh, and we shared a glum jug of ale and a bite of bread and cheese while the three women laboured inside. Robert and Boot had been ordered to stay at Westbury, where they could attend to the gash in my son's arm, mercifully not a serious wound. It was late May and the sky was clear and blue. None of us felt much like speaking. Hugh, who had been a rock of dependability all through the journey from Lincoln to Westbury – organising and looking after his men, making sure the road ahead was scouted for enemies as well as rough patches that would cause Robin pain as his cart traversed them – seemed to have sagged, crumbled even, now he had no further responsibilities. He looked like a scared young man on the point of tears. His only brother was dead and his father lay dying a dozen yards away, and there was nothing he could do to save him.

'Do not fear, Hugh,' I said. 'I am sure the Prioress knows her trade. She has saved men from worse wounds than this one. All will be well, you'll see.'

Hugh looked at me. I could see he wanted to believe me and yet he knew my words were false. Inside him the grief-stricken son fought with the experienced man of the world. The man won.

'He has a deep stab wound to the lower belly; you and I both know what happens to a man with a wound like that. Have you, Sir Alan, personally, ever, even once, known a man to recover from such a wound?'

'He is strong,' I said, 'and the Prioress is skilful. He will make it. I'm sure of it.'

Hugh said nothing. He picked at a loose thread on the sleeve of his tunic.

I could not seem to stop myself talking – a condition produced by my own anxiety. 'You used to be a gambling man, Sir Thomas,' I said. 'What odds would you give our lord for a safe recovery? Evens, perhaps?'

Thomas looked at me as if I were an imbecile. I kicked his leg under the table and slid my eyes towards Hugh.

380

'Oh,' he said. 'I'd say better than evens on a full recovery. Yes, more like to get better than not, for sure.'

Hugh looked at the two of us, disgust plain in his eyes.

'I am going to pray for him – in the chapel yonder. Come and find me if there is any change in his state.'

The air was somehow easier to breathe without Hugh. Thomas and I sipped our ale and said nothing to each other while the sun shone on our backs.

Finally, just for something to say, I said: 'Do you trust the Prioress to do her best for Robin?'

Thomas tilted his head to one side. 'Yes, I do. I know she was unwilling at first but Marie-Anne spoke to her and after that conversation she agreed at least to try. She values her reputation as a healer – and the reputation of Kirklees itself as a place where healing miracles can be worked – so yes, I think she will do her best. That does not mean I think Robin will live. Hugh was quite right: have you ever known a man survive a wound like that?'

I had not. Once again I wondered if I were not merely prolonging his agony.

After a good three hours, I saw Tilda coming across the grass towards us. She was drying her hands on her apron, but there were flecks of blood on her neck and lower jaw, which made her look as if she had just come from a desperate battle. Which, in truth, she had.

'We have sewn him up, inside and out,' she said. 'And packed the wound with healing herbs, moss and spiderwebs and bound it tightly. He still lives but he has been in a deep slumber since we began. I cannot say if he will awaken or not.'

'Can we see him?' I said.

'There is nothing to see: he is asleep, he breathes. Anna is sitting with him. You had best not take the chance of disturbing him. But Marie-Anne sent me to tell you that she would like to speak with you, if you are at liberty.'

I found Marie-Anne behind the infirmary in the cloisters, a covered walkway around a square garden in which more of the herbs used for healing were grown. She was pacing slowly up one side of the space and I waited for her to reach me.

'Walk with me, Alan, please. I cannot bear to sit still.'

We paced the long walkway on all four sides, slowly but with a steady, measured step. I did not think it my place to begin our conversation and so I said nothing as we walked side after side, around and around.

'Tell me, Alan, of those final moments with Miles and Robin, tell me of the fight on the steep hill at Lincoln.'

So I did – at length, in detail, emphasising that Robin had sheathed his sword as a gesture of reconciliation; that he had not wanted to threaten Miles, even when his son stood before him with a drawn blade.

Marie-Anne wept as I told the tale. She said: 'He did not need his sword – he had you beside him. You have always been his sword. You are the swift sword that cut down my little boy.'

I did not know what to say. It was true. We walked on in silence.

'I am being unfair to you, Alan, I know,' she said at last. 'But grief is unfair – to me, to you, to everyone who feels it. In a few moments, in a foolish quarrel over nothing very much, I lost both my son and my husband. And here you stand, hale and whole, having failed to protect my man, your lord, and having killed my son.'

She stopped walking and looked up at me with her tear-stained face: 'I should hate you, Alan Dale – you have single-handedly destroyed my life. But . . . but I cannot.'

To my profound surprise, she reached out her arms and enfolded me in a tight hug. As I wrapped my arms around her, my own tears began to flow like a river.

From that moment onward Marie-Anne sat beside Robin day and night, holding his hand, occasionally spooning a little herb-infused water into his dry mouth and massaging his throat until he swallowed. Anna and Tilda changed his bandages twice a day, carrying away long folds of linen stained with blood and bright yellow pus. I put my head round the door every few hours asking Marie-Anne if there was any change.

On the third day after the operation, Robin opened his eyes, looked at Marie-Anne, smiled briefly, then fell back into a deep slumber.

On the fifth day, when we had all but given up hope, he opened his eyes again. Marie-Anne gave a shriek of happiness and I, who happened to be passing the door of the infirmary, shot inside, to see Lady Locksley fervently kissing the forehead of the patient and murmuring endearments, while Robin looked around, trying, I would say, to work out where he was.

His eye fell on me, standing halfway across the room, grinning at him like a mountebank. 'I'm alive,' he said. 'Unless we are all dead and this is your Christian Heaven.'

'You're alive, my love,' said Marie-Anne, kissing him. 'You are truly alive.'

'Can you give me some wine, my mouth is horribly dry,' said Robin.

'No wine, no ale, I am afraid, my love, just water boiled up with herbs,' said his wife. 'The Prioress's orders.'

'Herb water, then. I take it I'm at Kirklees?'

'Yes, lord, we brought you here after Lincoln,' I said.

Marie-Anne helped him sip from an earthenware cup. Robin looked over at me when he had taken his medicinal drink; he smiled warmly and then his expression clouded over. 'Miles is dead, isn't he?'

I nodded and saw my lord's face collapse in grief. His head sank back on the pillow and he closed his eyes.

'You need to rest, my love,' said Marie-Anne. 'Rest and grow strong again.'

*   *   *

They moved Robin up to one of the towers of the Priory for his convalescence, a small circular room overlooking the vast green parkland to the east. From the window, roe deer could be seen on occasion through the trees, and in the mornings the summer sun shone on the chair where Robin would sometimes sit for an hour or so. He grew stronger, week by week, the wound in his stomach drying and healing to a long pink scar. By early August he was able to walk a few steps – but he tired easily and often the hour a day I spent with him, playing chess or just talking quietly, seemed to utterly exhaust him.

We had news of the war in those long summer days. The victory at Lincoln had destroyed French power in the north of England. We had captured large numbers of enemy knights and killed a good deal more. Many of the fleeing troops had been ambushed by English peasants as they retreated south to London and few arrived at the capital alive. Young King Henry's cause was triumphant all across the north and the west; only London and the south-east were held by the French prince, and Louis's grip on them was tenuous. William the Marshal, we heard, was preparing to assault London and finally seize back the capital from the rebels who, since the capture of Lord Fitzwalter at Lincoln, had been lacking an effective leader.

Fitzwalter himself and many other rebel lords were being held in chains at Lincoln Castle. Many voices at court cried that he should be put to death for treason, but King Henry (or perhaps the Marshal) insisted on leniency for all former enemies to help to heal the wounds of the civil war. Thomas would receive a fat ransom for capturing Fitzwalter, when it could be arranged with the rebel lord's remaining family, and the erstwhile captain-general of the Army of God would then be released from prison on condition that he took the cross and vowed to depart for the Holy Land on a pilgrimage.

I saw little of Tilda in those days and weeks. I was busy running errands for Robin and Tilda had resumed her old position in the Priory and was dealing with the sick and ill from the whole district around Kirklees. When we did meet, there was nothing but tenderness between us. In this House of God, this nunnery, as unmarried folk we could not share a bed, yet we did allow ourselves to kiss and take walks together in the grounds. A public display of our love, I soon discovered, was not well received. One day, in the kitchens, I came across Tilda preparing some food for some of the local sick and took her into my arms, kissing her sweet lips. She was responding with enthusiasm, when we heard a loud crash behind us and broke the embrace to see the Prioress standing over the shards of an earthenware pot.

'Get your filthy hands off her, Alan Dale. This is a kitchen not a bawdy house,' Anna said, anger crackling in the air about her. 'And you, Tilda, should be ashamed of yourself: a pregnant nun carrying on like a scarlet whore in this house. Shame on you both!'

Tilda and I giggled about it afterwards, like naughty children caught stealing fruit.

Robin grew stronger and soon he was able to walk in the sunshine in the Priory grounds. And yet his diet was still restricted to boiled herb water and the plainest of grain pottages, by the order of the Prioress. However, he did persuade me to smuggle Mastin's huge bow and a full bag of arrows up to his room.

'I need to stretch my muscles, Alan,' he said, 'and pulling a bow cord is the best way for me to get back in trim. Besides, those deer out there are thicker than fleas on a blind beggar's dog. I don't think these lands have been hunted for a generation. When I am stronger I'm going to put a bit of venison on the Priory table – and then defy grumpy old Anna to stop me eating it!'

His words were as bold as ever, but in truth he was a shadow of his former self. He slept more than half the day and thrashed feverishly all night. He was still as thin as a spear shaft, and his cheeks and hair were as white as fresh snow, and though he tried manfully to draw the big bow, he could barely pull it back halfway.

In September, came the best news of all. Prince Louis had suffered a devastating defeat at sea near the port of Sandwich, in which ships bringing supplies to the beleaguered French forces in London were attacked and sunk by none other than Hubert de Burgh, the hawkish defender of Dover Castle. The French Prince, now abandoned by nearly all his English allies, agreed to a formal treaty in which he relinquished his claims to the throne of England and returned to his native land.

We had won. King Henry was the undisputed master of this land. The long bloody war between the barons and the crown was finally over. Soon, Robin and I could go back to our homes, to Kirkton and Westbury, and, I earnestly prayed, be allowed to live the rest of our lives in peace.

Robin and I were playing chess. And, for once, I had him. One move and my queen would swoop down and, protected by my knight, nestle up next to his king in the deadly embrace of checkmate. I looked at Robin across the board. Did he suspect? He seemed happily distracted by the glad tidings we had had from the south.

'This is news that deserves celebrating properly, Alan,' said Robin. 'Send down to the kitchens for wine and meat. Come on. It can't hurt just this once. We must toast the King and his splendid victory with proper victuals. I don't care what the Prioress has to say about it, if I never see another cup of herb water again it will be far too soon.'

'I'll go after this game,' I said.

'Come now, Alan. Would you refuse a sick old man a morsel to eat?'

I frowned. 'Do not touch this board, my lord. On your honour. I do not want there to be a so-called "accident" when I am gone.

A careless hand that slips and knocks the pieces to the four winds.'

'Why would I do that?' said Robin in an infuriatingly innocent tone. 'I'm about to thrash you soundly – you just do not know it yet.'

I went downstairs, thinking furiously, the positions of the pieces on the board clear in my mind. What had I missed? Was I making a blunder? Was he merely bluffing? It occurred to me once again that, even when you know for certain you are going to win the game, fickle chance can sometimes snatch victory from your grasp.

I had not planned to consult Anna about Robin's request, but as it happened I ran into her in the kitchens, and when she asked what I wanted, it seemed churlish to lie. 'The Earl wishes to celebrate our wonderful victory over the French with fine wine and good red meat – no more plain pottage and herb water, he says.'

The Prioress looked at me for a long moment, her black eyes bright. 'It seems to me that I have cured your master. Is that true, would you say? His wound is better now and I am the one who cured him.'

'Yes, yes, now about the food. Robin would prefer venison but—'

'Say it, say to me that I cured him and that I fulfilled my obligation.'

'Of course,' I said, 'you have cured him and we are all very grateful to you for your labours. I have no doubt my lord will reward you well—'

Again, she cut me off. 'If he wants wine and meat, I will send them to him.'

Half an hour later, up in Robin's room in the east tower, there came a knock on the door and Tilda entered carrying a heavy tray. Robin and I were on our second game. My cunning master had seen the trap with my queen and knight and had somehow slipped out of it. Then we had chased each other around the board until it became clear we had come to a stalemate. So we reset the pieces and began again: and now he had me in total disarray, my queen lost and two pawns, too.

'Are you sure this is wise, Alan?' said Tilda as she unloaded a jug of red wine and three cups on to the table. A platter with thickly sliced pork covered in rich gravy came next with a dish of turnips in butter and a basket of sliced bread.

'By God, that looks good,' said Robin, getting up from the chessboard, sitting down on a stool at the table and pouring out three cups of dark wine.

I was looking at Tilda. She had a strange expression on her lovely face, a sort of puzzled frown, her hand placed on her swollen belly.

'A toast,' said Robin, picking up his wine. I left the board and came over to the table, reaching for my cup.

'God save King Henry!' said Robin, downing his drink in one.

'Alan, come here,' said Tilda excitedly. 'I just felt the baby kick! Come, feel!'

I put down my wine, untasted, and went over to Tilda, placing a hand on her belly, which was now round and tight as a drum. I could feel nothing but the warmth of her skin beneath my hand.

I heard a loud groan behind me and turned to see Robin, grey-faced and clutching at his stomach. He was barely able to speak. 'The wine . . .' he said.

I looked aghast at the jug of wine on the table and the two untouched brimming cups. One evil word was fluttering around in my head like a moth: poison.

'You stopped me from drinking,' I said, staring wildly at Tilda. 'You stopped me drinking by pretending the baby was kicking!'

For a moment Tilda looked confused and then her blue-grey eyes flashed in fury. 'You think this wine is poisoned? You think I did it? Are you utterly insane?'

'You hate him, you told me so yourself. You said he brought about your ruin!'

'You stupid man. This wine is not poisoned. It is his belly wound, his lacerated guts are not ready for wine. I thought as much. Look, see this!' And before I could stop her, she seized one of the cups of wine and swallowed the contents in one long draught.

'See, Alan. I did not poison it. I cannot believe you think that I would. We will discuss your idiotic accusations later – you can be sure of that. For now just help me get him into bed.'

Between us, we easily managed to get Robin to his bed, but not before he had vomited hugely over my arms and chest. The spew smelled of wine and stomach juices but nothing else. I began to relax.

'Here, Robin, drink some water,' I said, holding out a cup of the herbal brew. But my lord gave a tiny shake of his head. I saw that his lips were pale blue. 'Can't feel my feet,' he said. 'They're gone. I think . . . I'm gone, too!'

I felt panic rising through my chest. I seized him by the shoulders, shook him: 'Can you vomit some more?'

'No, there is no time. Bring the bow and an arrow.'

I looked at him as if he were raving.

'Just obey me . . . without arguing . . . this one . . . last time . . . Alan . . . please,' he panted. And I did. I fetched Mastin's bow and a shaft from the corner of the room and, as I handed them to Robin, I saw that Tilda was sitting on the stool by the table, elbows on her knees, her face the colour of cold hearth ash.

'Now . . . listen to me . . . Alan . . . are you listening? Where this arrow lands . . . that is where . . . I wish you . . . to lay me to rest,' said my lord.

For an instant, by some trick played on me by my eyes, with that bow and an arrow in his hands, he looked exactly like the young and carefree Sherwood outlaw I had first met all those years ago. And then the illusion was gone. He was just a sick old man with an over-sized bow stave in his trembling hands.

I don't know how he did it but somehow, using the last of his strength, perhaps all the strength he had in his body, and lying nearly flat on the bed, Robin nocked the arrow, drew back the cord on that mighty bow to its full extent . . . and loosed. The shaft flew straight out of the window, soared high and disappeared into the vast blue heavens.

His body collapsed, the bow clattering to the floor, arms thumping down beside his torso, the air whistling out of his lungs in an alarmingly noisy rattle.

'Alan,' came a voice from behind me, 'Alan, my love.' I turned to see Tilda slide from the stool and crash ungainly to the floor. I rushed to her side, picked her up in my arms and held her tightly as she coughed up a thin black drool. Her lips, the red lips I'd kissed so many times before, were blue as a summer sky.

'It was not I, my beloved,' she whispered. 'I swear it. I would never hurt you. Never. I knew nothing of the poison. Truly I did not. I love you. But Anna . . . she hates . . .'

Then my lovely Tilda grew still. Her spirit left her body and the half-formed baby inside her – another fine son? A longed-for daughter? – perished with her.

I do not know how long I sat cradling my dead lover in my arms, stroking her round belly hoping for a miracle, hoping to feel the kick of life, perhaps. It could have been one hour or five. I was frozen with grief, unable to move or even think clearly. I was aware that I was making a high-pitched keening noise, a kind of singing, perhaps, or even whistling – although the sound may have existed only in my head. I looked over at the still body of Robin, his wide-open eyes staring at the ceiling as if pondering his next move on the chessboard. Surely, at any moment, he would leap up, laughing, and tell me I had been a fool to think him gone. He could not truly be dead; he could not be. But in my heart of hearts I knew my lord would never make another move again.

I was aroused from my long torpor by Marie-Anne. She came through the door humming something cheerful and when she saw Robin lying motionless on the bed, staring into eternity, she gave a wild cry, like the sound of a seagull, and threw herself on the body, mewling with grief. I put down Tilda's body as gently as I could and went over to console my lord's lady. When the first towering wave of her grief had crashed – it took the form of shrieking and weeping and beating with both small fists against my chest – I told her as best I could what had happened here this terrible day. I told her that Anna must have administered the poison in the wine.

When I had finished, I held her for a long, long time, feeling her quiver like a trapped bird against my chest, feeling her hot, damp cheek against mine. Finally she pushed me away, scrubbed her face with her hands.

'I want her dead, Alan Dale. I want her bloody and dead at my feet,' said Marie-Anne, her voice hissing with rage. 'At least you of all people can do that for me!'

I was stunned by her change of mood.

'You killed my son. You stood stupidly by while my husband was murdered. Go – do what it is that you do so well. I want her dead. Hack her head from her body!'

I stumbled from the room and down the stair with Marie-Anne's words ringing in my ears. Yes, I thought, yes. I touched Fidelity's hilt at my waist. Revenge. The Prioress must pay with her life for her crimes.

I found Anna quite easily. She was in the infirmary. But there was no need for me to take my vengeance. She lay lifeless on the slab on which she had saved Robin's life with her knowledge and skill, a half-drunk cup of dark wine beside her. On the stone beside her head, a shaky hand had written in chalk in good, clear Latin these words: 'If not together in life, my love . . .'

After the white-hot fury and an ocean of tears came a dull and awful calm. Marie-Anne and I were sitting in the garden a day later, holding hands, joined in grief. Neither of us had slept. An untouched plate of bread and cheese sat before us on the table. The silence was an echoing void between us, but as grey and heavy as lead.

'I cannot understand why Anna would do all this,' I said. 'Why would she first bring Robin back from the grave and then try to kill us all? She must have run mad. There can be no reason behind this.'

I did not really expect Marie-Anne to speak. And for a long, long while she did not.

'It is not madness – there is a twisted sense to it if you care to look out through her eyes,' she said finally.

I said nothing; merely stared at her.

'I made her swear that she would do everything she could to save Robin. I told her that if she refused, Hugh and I would use all our power to destroy her and her house, but that if she succeeded I would sing her praises across Christendom and endow the Priory with a fortune. She made an oath to me on her honour that she would heal Robin, if she could, of his wound. I forced her to. She kept that oath. But once she had done that . . .'

Fresh tears welled in Marie-Anne's eyes.

'She saw Tilda, Robin and me as the architects of her misery,' I said dully. 'How she must have hated us – all of us. Robin told her about Tilda and Benedict Malet. In her rage, Anna cast off the one person she had perhaps ever truly loved. Tilda. She blamed Robin for that loss. Yet, I believe, she must also have hoped one day to take Tilda back. Instead, Tilda came into my household. We came to love each other – and that was the coin that tipped the scales for Anna. When she saw that Tilda was truly mine, that she was happy and with child, that she would never return to her arms, our fate was sealed.'

'I pushed Tilda on to you,' said Marie-Anne. 'I sent her to Westbury to be your woman. In a way, God forgive me, this is all my own fault.'

'There is enough guilt for all of us to share,' I said.

The next day, Marie-Anne, Hugh, Sir Thomas and I buried Robin in the deer park of Kirklees Priory, under a spreading oak tree exactly where his last arrow had found its mark. Hugh made a long and rambling speech over his grave, praising his bravery and lauding his martial achievements, listing the engagements where he had fought, including the battle of Lincoln – which, to me, seemed a little crass. No mention was made of Miles or his death. Perhaps I ought to have made a stirring eulogy for my friend, for my comrade, for my lord, but I found at his graveside that I had nothing much to add to Hugh's testament. We had fought together, Robin and I, we had shared victory and defeat, joy and suffering, times of hunger and plenty – and now he was gone and I remained here on this foul earth. I found that I had said all I had to say to Robin in the long years that we were together, in the arguments, in the jests, in the moments when we were joyful or face to face with death. As I looked down into the square earthen pit that held his shroud-wrapped body, I merely said: 'Goodbye, my lord. Sleep well.'

We buried Tilda, and the unborn child inside her womb, in the churchyard surrounded by the sisters of the Order who had gone before her. She lay not far from Anna's grave – but I insisted they should not lie side by side. She belonged to me in the end. Not to her. I could find no tears that day – I was dry from a lifetime of weeping. But I covered her body with cut flowers and as the first shovelfuls of earth thumped down on her a wave of scent was released – a last memory of my love.

Thomas asked if I wanted him to burn the Priory to the ground to punish Anna's fellow nuns and make such a pyre that would be seen for miles around to mark the deaths of our loved ones. But I said no. Hugh would have been enraged. The new Earl of Locksley planned to endow the Priory with some of Robin's stolen silver, extend it, and perhaps even build a brother house for monks to serve God. Hugh wanted masses said for Robin's soul – that would have made my old friend laugh, although I devoutly hoped it might be enough to bring him to Heaven.

We rode away from Kirklees together, Hugh and Marie-Anne, Sir Thomas and me, and a handful of men-at-arms, but soon enough we all went our separate ways. Thomas, with many protestations of fidelity to the new Earl and of friendship to me, took the road south-west into Derbyshire and his manor of Makeney. Marie-Anne, still pink-eyed from weeping, with her straight-backed son Hugh and all the Locksley men-at-arms left me and took the road east to Kirkton. And, all alone, I rode south, to Westbury, where Robert and Boot and my own people awaited my return.

I say that I rode alone – but I am not sure if that is strictly true. I may have been dozing in the saddle, or my wits may just have been addled from too much grief and too little sleep. For all of a sudden, I found myself riding in a large company of folk. I could hear the creak of their saddles, the clop of horses' hooves, the low murmur of conversation, a chuckle or two. I looked to my right and there was Robin, a younger, more handsome Robin, laughing carelessly at some crude jest made by the big man beside him. For beyond him was Little John, massively alive, his fat blond plaits swinging by his ugly red face. I looked behind and there was Father Tuck, beaming at me with his round ruddy face, and my murderous old Bavarian friend Hanno, and there was Mastin, and Owain, and Claes, and Kit, and Will Scarlet, a mere stripling still sunburned from the Holy Land, and all of them, all of the good men I had ridden with down the long years. I looked to my left and there was my dead wife Goody, smiling at me from her perfect sunny face, and beyond her was Tilda, laughing at my confusion, and on the edge of the group even the hideous face of poor Nur, half-obscured under a black hood.

I looked back at Robin, who was looking over at me now grey-eyed and sombre.

'Why did you leave me, my lord?' I said.

'I didn't leave you,' he said. 'I will never leave you. None of us will.'

Epilogue

The King was weeping unashamedly as Brother Alan came to the end of his tale. As was I. He mopped at his streaming cheeks and said: 'It is strange, I know, that I should be so moved by the demise of a man who contrived my father's death and who robbed him of all his worldly wealth – and yet I cannot but feel diminished by his passing.'

'Robin did kill your father, Sire,' said Brother Alan, 'there can be no denying that – but he did it to ensure that you ascended the throne. If he had not done what he did, then who can say how the war might have ended? Prince Louis might well have triumphed had the crown not passed to you. England might even now be suffering the yoke of a French King, had Robin Hood not played his murderous part.'

The King looked thoughtful. 'You make a fine point, Brother,' he said. 'Nevertheless, I do not think that I wish for this tale of regicide to be broadcast to the world. I have seen you noting down this narrative, Prior Anthony – do I take it that you wish to make a romance, a bound book of these tales?'

'Yes, Sire,' I said.

'I cannot allow it,' the King said, getting to his feet. 'You will surrender to me all the parchments, all the notes, that you have made of this matter, and any others that pertain to Brother Alan's life. I shall hold them securely.'

'But, Sire,' I said miserably, 'this has been a long labour, the work of many, many hours – besides, it is Brother Alan's testament, a final record of his existence.'

'You will be compensated,' said the King. 'I will give you a pair of manors in Yorkshire to support this House and the good works of the monks here. Furthermore I give you my word that I shall not destroy these stories – I shall safeguard them and I shall leave it to my heirs to decide if they should ever be allowed to see the light of day. It may be that when I am dead – many years from now, God willing – these tales shall be told once more. But I cannot permit them to circulate while I rule this land.'

He turned to Brother Alan, who had just managed shakily to get to his feet when the King did. 'I thank you for your courage in my service, Brother. And I honour you for the eventful life you have lived but I must ask you not to speak again of these sad matters concerning the King, my father, to anyone else – on pain of death.'

Once again, I heard Brother Alan making that strange grunting noise. And I realised with horror that he was laughing in the King's face.

Finally, the old man calmed himself. 'I have told my tale, Sire,' he said, a little breathlessly. 'And I shall not tell it again. But not for fear of death – that holds no terrors for me now. I shall remain silent because my tale is told. I have no more stories to weave, no great deeds to relate. I have told the truth, all of it, and it has been set free from the cage of my mind and released into the world – and I know, too, that whatever great men, even noble kings, might desire, the truth cannot be locked away for ever. The truth finds a way of emerging, sooner or later, like a seedling blindly pushing up from beneath the soil and bursting joyously out into the sunlight.'

Brother Alan died the very day after the visit of King Henry, slipping away quietly in his sleep while I sat beside him and read to him by candlelight. He did not seem the slightest bit perturbed that the King's servants had collected and borne away a great mass of parchments that contained his stories – perhaps because he knew that I had ordered the monks of the scriptorium to make several copies of each chapter as he had been relating them to me. I have also had copies made, with his permission, of other wonderful tales penned by Brother Alan himself before he came to Newstead. I am confident that I have the chronicles of his whole life and all the adventures that he had with his lord of Locksley safely set down in ink on parchment. And while I know that it must be a sin to disobey the King, God's anointed ruler on Earth, I also know that I could not allow this extraordinary account to rot in the cellars of some dank royal stronghold. I will not allow the copies to be read – I do not wish to bring down the wrath of our sovereign – but I could not be at peace if I did not know that they were among the secret treasures of the Priory.

We buried Brother Alan in the churchyard of Newstead and sang a doleful mass for his soul. It was a miserable day, grey, with a thin, sour rain that fell without ceasing on the assembled monks. I had asked Brother Alan if he wished to be buried at Westbury, next to his son Robert, taken by God many years ago by the bloody flux. But he said no. He said he wished to be close to the copies of the parchments we had both laboured on for so long, the tale of his life and the truth of his service to his lord.

'My body will be dust and I pray that my soul will be with God,' he said, 'but in another fashion I may live on, with Robin, with my lord, in those written pages. My ghost will surely ward them until they see the light again.'

Then he laughed one final time before he slept.

When Brother Alan was finally in the earth, when the service had been sung and all our tears were dried away, I ordered another mass to be celebrated – a mass for a man long dead, for a thief and murderer, for a man who poisoned a King and made off with his treasury. A mass for the man who people once called Robin Hood.

The End

Historical Note

It is often claimed that England hasn't been invaded since 1066. I have heard it asserted, loudly and proudly, usually in pubs, up and down the country all my life. I think it was even taught to me in history at school. But it's not true; not even a little bit. During the Hundred Years War the French made dozens of successful raids on the Channel ports. Lambert Simnel, a pretender to the throne during the Wars of the Roses, landed with an army of Flemings and Irishmen in Lancashire in 1487. Then there was the Glorious Revolution of 1688, when a foreign but, crucially, Protestant ruler invaded England at the head of a Dutch army and deposed the ruling Catholic monarch James II. He was crowned William III and ruled for thirteen years.

As well as these incursions, there was the little-known French invasion of 1216, which I have described reasonably faithfully in this novel. Prince Louis, eldest son of King Philip of France, had a weak claim to the throne through his wife, Blanche of Castile, who was King John's niece. The Pope, who was in dispute with the English monarch, initially gave his blessing to the attempted coup against John and the takeover of England by France – but he changed his tune when John did homage for England to him in 1213, giving the Papacy ultimate lordship of the country. However, that did not halt Louis's ambitions and, with the tacit support of his royal father but now with opposition from the Pope, he began preparations for a full-scale invasion.

Louis assembled a large fleet and raised an army of knights, often the younger sons of French lords who were eager to claim new lands in England, and for a time he genuinely looked set to repeat the Conquest of 1066. However, John collected fighting ships from all the southern English ports, manned them, armed them and managed to keep Louis penned in the port of Calais for several weeks. As recounted in this book, a huge storm scattered the blockading ships and Louis was able to slip out and cross the Channel, landing on the Isle of Thanet on 21 May 1216. John did not contest his disembarkation and withdrew to Dover to seek reinforcements. Louis made his way to London, where he was proclaimed King of the English at St Paul's Cathedral, although he was never crowned at Westminster Abbey because no suitable English bishop could be found to undertake the ceremony. However, many rebellious English nobles and young Alexander of Scotland did homage to him for their lands.

By June, after the capture of Winchester, Louis and the English rebels controlled as much as half of England. John retreated to the west where support for him was strongest and did his best to avoid pitched battles with the French forces. However, the invasion *was* fiercely resisted in one region and by one extraordinary individual, who is known to history as William of Cassingham (now called Kensham) or Willikin of the Weald. We don't know much about William except that he was a young squire from Kent who raised a large guerrilla army of bowmen in the thickly forested Weald and savaged the French army of occupation, killing thousands of them and disrupting their supply lines. He successfully attacked the besieged castle of Dover and later trapped Prince

Louis at Lewes, nearly capturing him. William was renowned for his barbaric practice of cutting off the heads of his enemies. He survived the war, was handsomely rewarded by Henry III for his valour and lived to a ripe old age before dying in 1257. Some authors have even suggested that his exploits provided a model for the early Robin Hood stories.

One of Prince Louis's leading men was Thomas, Comte du Perche. He came over a couple of months after the initial invasion force, with the second wave of troops in the summer of 1216. He was at the siege of Dover and the next year he led an expedition north from London with Robert Fitzwalter, the English rebel leader, to relieve Mountsorrel Castle, which was being besieged by Ranulf, Earl of Chester. After chasing off Chester, both men and their retinues proceeded to Lincoln to try to subdue that castle, which was still being held by the doughty Nicola de la Haye.

It is unclear exactly how the battle of Lincoln unfolded, and some people doubt the existence of a rubble-blocked western gate in the medieval town walls, which I have Boot so heroically unblocking in this story. We do know that the royalist army, which comprised about four hundred knights, two hundred and fifty crossbowmen and many auxiliary troops, advanced from Stow, eight miles north-west of Lincoln, very early on the morning of 20 May 1217. The French and rebel forces came out to meet them in the fields to the west of the town but then, believing that they faced an army far superior in numbers (they didn't: they miscounted the standards of the English nobles), Louis's knights retreated back inside the town walls. The French plan was to hold the town's defences and try to take the castle before the royal army could overwhelm them. Accordingly, they intensified their assault on the castle walls.

However, a strong force of men-at-arms and crossbowmen under Falkes de Breauté, a mercenary captain, charged directly into the castle through a gate on the western side and, suddenly popping up on the walls and delivering a lethal barrage of crossbow bolts, they successfully managed to fight off a determined French attack. Meanwhile, the Earl of Chester's men were vigorously assaulting the north gate of the town. Having beaten off the French attack on the castle walls, Falkes de Breauté and his men then made a sortie into the town and caught the enemy between their surprise attack and the Earl of Chester's men, who had by now stormed through the north gate. That is how one version of the battle goes. Another version is that Falkes and his men (or possibly Peter des Roches) unblocked a disused western gate in the town walls, clearing away the broken masonry to allow William the Marshal to charge in to the town from that direction.

I have shamelessly stolen Falkes's valiant deeds and given them to Robin and his men, and I have also deliberately chosen to use the story about the unblocking of the western gate in the town, even though I think it unlikely to be a true version of events. When I visited Lincoln in the late summer of 2015, I spoke to several experts at the castle and no one could tell me where this blocked-up western town gate might have been. In fact, I suspect it may never have existed and has been confused by the chroniclers of the age with the western gate of the *castle*, which admitted Falkes de Breauté and his crossbowmen – but I believe my job is to make these stories as exciting as I possibly can and I wanted to add a little extra drama to the battle for Lincoln, so I hope I may be excused this blatant embroidering of the truth.

I did a little more embroidery when it came to Thomas, Comte du Perche. I don't really know much about his character and even less about his fashion sense: he was young (only twenty-two when he died) and apparently rather arrogant, but he has also been described as 'chivalrous'. I have absolutely no evidence to suggest that he dressed entirely in silver and white, nor that he did horrible things to kittens, nor even that he was the skin-stripping sadist I have described. I'm pretty sure he was a fairly normal young French nobleman of his time but for my own novelistic purposes I needed a really despicable villain, and I chose him. I offer my humble apologies to any of his living relatives who feel I have besmirched his good name.

The real Comte du Perche was, however, killed in the final stages of the battle of Lincoln by a dagger or sword thrust through the eye hole of his helmet just outside the entrance to the cathedral. He was surrounded and called upon to surrender by William the Marshal, his cousin, but bravely (or arrogantly) refused. He was then killed in combat by Sir Reginald Crocus, one of Falkes de Breauté's knights, who was himself killed later in the battle. It made sense to me, since Robin was stealing the glory that rightly belongs to Falkes, to have Alan Dale do the same to Sir Reginald. Again, apologies to any living relatives of either of these brave fighting men.

Many of the French knights and rebel English surrendered at Lincoln – Lord Fitzwalter among them – but large numbers tried to escape through the lower town across the bridge over the River Witham. In fact, so many tried to cross the bridge at once that it became jammed with men and wagons and the slaughter there when the royalist troops caught up with the fugitives was truly appalling. Worse still was the unrestrained sacking of the town by William the Marshal's victorious troops, a long drunken bloodbath that became known with mordant irony as Lincoln Fair.

King John's lost treasure

I remember my heart quickening when I first heard the story of King John's lost treasure as a child. The thought of all that gold, silver and jewels buried in the damp East Anglian earth made me want to rush out and start digging. And when I heard about a Lincolnshire legend that King John was poisoned by a monk named Brother Simon, who also stole his treasury and escaped to the continent with his loot, I knew that I had to have my Robin Hood do something very similar.

It is quite possible that the whole story about the lost treasure is a myth, which may stem either from some sort of ruse by King John to disguise his true wealth, or just be a fanciful tale tacked on to the story of John's demise to make it more romantic. And even if it is true that a good deal of royal treasure was lost in the Wash – a low, flat area of marshland between Norfolk and Lincolnshire where several rivers drain into the North Sea – no authority seems entirely certain of the sequence of events. However, it probably happened something like this:

The King was retreating from Lynn (now King's Lynn) under a threat from the rebels in the south and heading back to Newark Castle. When he left Lynn on 11 October 1217, he was already seriously ill with dysentery, which was probably caused by contaminated drinking water and exhaustion after a long campaign. (Some have maliciously suggested his illness was caused by gluttony.) He got as far as Walpole that day (or possible Wisbech) but the wagons that contained his baggage were slowing his progress for they could only travel at two and a half miles per hour. Ill as he was, he was keen to get to his destination as swiftly as possible and he ordered his baggage to cross the five-mile-wide estuary of the River Nene, while he took the longer, drier, more southerly road himself. This estuary crossing was a recognised route – between Walpole Cross Keys and Long Sutton – but a local guide was necessary and the timing of the crossing had to be just right. October is a bad month for the fens with the mists hanging low for some time after sunrise and it is likely that the wagons started out late on the sands and, with little time to get across before the tide came in, they fanned out to get over more quickly. Some of the wagons got bogged down and the incoming sea made it impossible to return and rescue them. Roger of Wendover, a chronicler of the time, wrote: 'The ground opened up in the midst of the waves and bottomless whirlpools sucked in everything'. John lost 'his carts, wagons and sumpter horses, his treasure, his precious plate and all that he valued most'. His portable chapel was also apparently lost to the quicksands.

It was a mortal blow for the King. By the time he reached Sleaford on 14 or 15 October, he was desperately sick. He had to be carried in a litter to Newark, where after making his confession, dictating a will and receiving Holy Communion, he died.

King John's death completely changed the war. It meant that nine-year-old Henry of Winchester was now King and English lords who had rebelled because of their hatred for his father had no cause to continue in their insurrection. A further blow to the rebel cause was the reissuing of the Charter of Liberties (minus a few of the more contentious clauses) on 11 November 1217. Rebels who had gone to war in the name of the great charter now had little reason to fight on. The victory at Lincoln was the turning point for Prince Louis's fortunes, too. And when his forces were defeated in a sea battle off the port of Sandwich on 24 August 1217, the game was up. He signed the Treaty of Lambeth on 11 September and accepted a nominal payment of ten thousand marks to renounce for ever his claim to the English throne.

So, with King John dead, young Henry III on the throne and the French sent packing, this seemed to me to be the perfect time to conclude the Outlaw Chronicles. It's been great fun for me and I hope you have enjoyed reading the books as much as I have enjoyed writing them, but like all good things the series has now come to an end. Robin Hood is in his grave, so too is elderly Brother Alan. But, like Alan's ghostly company of riders on the road from Kirklees to Westbury, I hope that a memory of them, of their comrades, their battles and their adventures, will remain with you.

Angus Donald
Tonbridge, February 2016

Acknowledgements

I would like to say a huge thank-you to my agent Ian Drury of Sheil Land Associates, who has been so supportive during the writing of the Outlaw Chronicles. I would also like to thank Ed Wood and Iain Hunt at Little, Brown for their gentle but expert editing and their enduring enthusiasm for the series. Finally, I owe a debt of gratitude to the authors of the history books that I have used as the basis for this particular novel: Sean McGlynn for the superb *Blood Cries Afar: The Forgotten Invasion of England 1216*; W. L. Warren for his magisterial *King John*; and David Crouch for his fascinating *William Marshal: Knighthood, War and Chivalry, 1147–1219*.

The Outlaw Chronicles

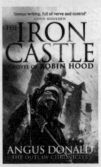

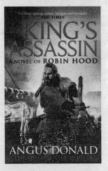